YOU ARE
BUT DUST

YOU ARE BUT DUST

HANNAH CLAYTON

You Are But Dust
Paperback edition ISBN: 978-1-7384163-3-2
Hardback edition ISBN: 978-1-7384163-4-9
E-book edition ISBN: 978-1-7384163-5-6

Published by Shadowlit Books
Manchester, UK.

www.shadowlitbooks.co.uk

First edition October 2025

Written in British English

A catalogue record for this title is available from the British Library.

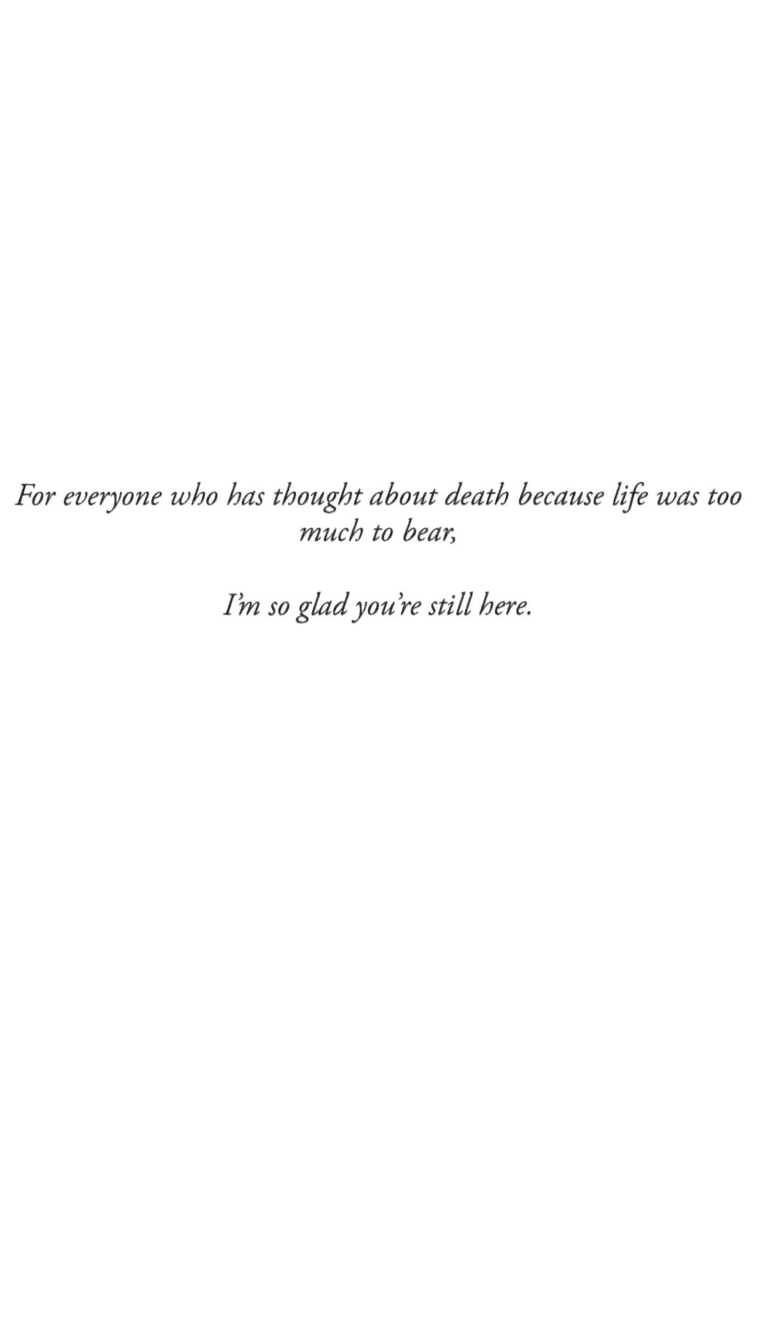

For everyone who has thought about death because life was too much to bear,

I'm so glad you're still here.

I'm okay. I'm okay.

PART ONE

Everything. Is. Okay.

ASHES TO ASHES

1

I'm not going to die.

The threat of death poisoned my mind as a knife pressed against my waist. Its cold blade sent shivers through my limbs, crushing any hope of escape into nothing but dust. *Am I going to die?*

"Please…" I gasped as adrenaline ran away with my breath. "Please don't do this here. It's…it's not the right place."

"There's never a right place, is there?" Ali took a seat next to me as he adjusted his grip on the knife, ready to carve into my flesh.

"I don't know, but…surely it's not right *here*."

The church was silent as a corpse. Everyone had left after the funeral, refusing to let their grief linger. They had gone to the nearest pub to drown their remaining sorrow and I wished I could have joined them, instead of being inches away from death. I'd spent the day thinking about my sister's passing, yet now I couldn't stop thinking about my own. *No, don't think like that. Dying at a funeral would be way too embarrassing.*

"*Here* is the only place I could find you." Ali's voice was softer than usual, making his threats sound more like prayers. "You've been avoiding me."

"No, I…I was going to come see you at the club. I was going to come tonight actually—"

"You said that last week and the week before and the…" He trailed off. "You see my point, Samarra?"

"I've been a little…busy recently."

"*You've* been busy?" He raised an eyebrow. "You barely leave your house, how the Hell are you busy?" He snorted a laugh, wiping the back of his hand against his nose.

"I…I've been studying for exams. I have a huge one coming up and it's really important I pass—"

"That doesn't explain why you haven't given me the money."

"Well, I've also just been…" My gaze fell to the crucifix in the centre of the room that taunted me with its stark reminder of death. Below it stood a terrible picture of my younger sister. *Evie would've hated that picture of her.* Throughout the service, I hadn't stopped looking at the picture and the mustard yellow jacket she wore in it. It was *my* jacket that she used to always steal and refused to give back. *I still can't believe Evie's wearing my jacket in her funeral photo. As much as I love her, I hate that she's found a way to annoy me even from the afterlife.*

"You've been *what?*" Ali cut through my thoughts.

"I've been grieving." I brought my mind back to the conversation. "The funeral only just ended. Why would you come here so soon—"

"*This* wasn't a funeral. This was just a sorry excuse for something that should've happened a long time ago." He spoke fiercely over me. "Thank Hell you already cremated her. It's been months since Evie died. Imagine the *smell* if you'd actually waited this long to bury her."

"It's not been that long. It's only been…" I hesitated. "Six months."

"That's dead long. Funerals should happen in a matter of days, maybe even weeks, definitely not months."

"People grieve differently." I sounded as unsure as I felt. Honestly it was embarrassing we had waited this long to have a proper funeral. My mum and I had both stalled for time, finding never-ending excuses to push back the date as we lost ourselves in grief that refused to heal. *Evie would be so pissed off if she knew how long it took us to do this.*

"People do grieve differently, but you haven't been grieving at all from what I've seen," Ali said.

"I have. I've just been…coping in my own way."

"Is that what you call it? Coping?" He grunted. "That's not what I'd call it."

"I didn't come here for a discussion on grief, I came here to bury my little sister."

Frustration seeped into my words as I looked at him sitting next to me. Ali wasn't much older than me; I'd say he hadn't reached his mid-twenties yet. He wasn't much taller either. But he did have much larger muscles, decorated with tattoos of thorny vines to make him seem intimidating. Usually he liked to show them off, but today he hid them under a suit jacket. And without his muscles on show, the overconfident part of my brain thought: *I can take him.*

"Look, I'm sorry for your loss." Ali softened his tone more. "Evie was too young to have died so suddenly like that."

Evie was *too young to have died like that. Nineteen is no age to have lived, let alone to have died.*

"But I need the money, Samarra," he continued. "I actually needed it months ago, yet I've been nice and held off."

"*You've* been nice?"

"You have no idea how nice I've been to you…" He sniffed, wiping the back of his hand against his nose once more. "But I can't be nice for much longer."

"I just need another day—"

"I've given you *months*." He shook his head. "I'm genuinely sorry to do this…here. But I have no other choice."

"Surely you can wait until—"

Ali pressed the knife farther against my waist, forcing the pressure of the blade to build until it was only a nudge away from cutting through my lacy black dress. *No, this dress is brand-new. It's perfect. I can't ruin it!*

"Okay, I get it!" I tried to sound more in control and less like a lamb being sent to the slaughter. "I…I know you need money and I promise I *will* pay you back." *I need to get out of this.* "It's just…you've picked a pretty difficult day."

"Difficult? You look more put together than you have in a long time."

"I wouldn't say dressing up for a funeral is 'put together.'"

He shrugged. "It's still better than usual."

I guess that was true. My long hair was tied back, my makeup had been done properly, silver jewellery decorated my body, and I was even wearing heels despite how much I hated them. *If I weren't wearing heels, running away from this situation would be much easier. How am I supposed to get out of this now?*

Raindrops fell against the stained-glass windows, creating a percussion beat as fast as my heart. *This church is probably the one place in Medlock without security cameras. No one will help me, even if I scream until my voice collapses. And everyone from the funeral will be too focused on Evie's death to even consider mine. They all always preferred Evie, after all. She was too charming for her own good.*

"I…I still just need one more day," I repeated. "That's all. *Please.*"

"I was afraid you'd say something like that." Ali breathed out a deep sigh. "I was told that if you couldn't pay by today, I'd have to leave some sort of message."

"You don't have to." Panic scuttled over my voice. "All I need is—"

Suddenly Ali cut the knife through the side of my dress, tearing into the material in one swift motion. He placed the blade against my skin, taunting me with its threat, forcing my brain into overdrive. *This is bad. This is* very *bad.* "Wait, wait! Please, stop!" *No one is coming to rescue me. I'm alone, like always. I have to find a way out by myself. If I thought I could take him, then let's take him!* "I said, *stop!*"

I swung my fist towards Ali in a panicked frenzy, aiming to knock his chest backwards, to push his body away from mine and keep the knife away from—

Ali caught my wrist. "I wouldn't do that if I were you." He gripped on to me with brutal strength.

My eyes widened in alarm. *He's too strong for me.* "Please, I-I…I didn't mean to." I stuttered through my lost breath. *I can't fight him like this—*

Wait. Ali's palms were sweaty as they held me. His hand had a slight tremble. And he couldn't stop sniffing. *He's ill. He must have a cold from this awful weather. That means he must be weaker than usual…*

I can take him. *I just have to be smarter. I need a weapon or something to give me an advantage.*

"I don't want to hurt you, Samarra. Honestly I don't." Ali let go of my arm, dropping it back towards me. "But do not test me." He pressed the blade into my hip, marking my skin with a stinging throb of pain.

Don't let him cut me! That knife isn't sterilised; it'll definitely infect me. I'll die from sepsis long before anything else—

"Please stop! I'm sorry!"

But Ali didn't stop raising the pressure on the knife. *He's going to kill me!*

"Wait! Listen, I…I *do* have some money in my bag!" *That's a lie.* "I just don't have as much as you need." *I don't have anything.*

"Will that at least do for now?" Desperately my eyes ran over my surroundings, looking for a weapon or *anything* that would help me fight him.

"It's a start." He reluctantly nodded. "But I *can't* keep letting you off, I'm only getting myself into trouble."

"I know and I'm grateful for the time you've given me, I just…" I trailed off as my eyes fell on the Bible beside me. A heavy Bible. A Bible sturdy enough to hit someone with and make some sort of impact, if I hit the right spot—

No, I can't hit him with a Bible; I'll only make things worse. Plus, I really shouldn't be hitting anyone with a Bible.

"Just give me what you have, Samarra. Then we can talk about other ways you can pay off your debt," Ali stated. "Maybe you can finally consider working for Mariana? I'm sure she'd love to meet you. Doctors are very valuable people to have around, you know?"

"I'm not a doctor yet." I subtly took hold of the Bible, gripping it in my hand. *No, don't hit him with a goddamn Bible.* "I-I have like…ten years before I become one. So there's no point meeting—"

"Don't give me another excuse, not when you're so desperately running out of them." Ali spoke in a plain, blunt tone, leaving no room for dispute. "Now where's this money?"

"I…don't have it on me." I held onto the Bible tighter—*no, don't be an idiot. He has a knife. Get rid of the knife first.*

Ali sighed. "Of course you don't." He added more pressure to his hold on the knife, forcing it farther against my waist, tormenting me with how close it was to severing my flesh— *don't let him break the skin!*

"*Wait!*" I let out a cry, amplifying my reaction. "My mum has my money! She has my bag with everything in it." I put trembles into my voice, forcefully choking on my words. *Get rid of the damn knife!* "We can get it from her. She'll be at the-the pub with everyone else." I winced in pain, overexaggerating the rush of agony the knife was tearing into me. "Please, I…I can't think with that…I…" I let out more whimpers, building up to a deafening scream—

"Okay, that's enough." He pulled the knife away. "I told you I don't want to hurt you."

I let out a burst of breath, acting as though I were afraid, as though he had total control over the situation. *I need to catch him by surprise.*

"Your mum has your money?" Ali raised an eyebrow. "I hope you're not lying to me."

"I'm not." False tears ran down my cheek. "If…if we go to the pub, I'll get it for you."

He hesitated. "You're not tricking me, right? I know you have a friend who works for the Shade. Will she be there?"

"Ria? No, I haven't spoken to her in months. I don't even think she's a proper officer yet. She…she couldn't arrest you even if she was there."

He paused for a long moment. "Okay. Let's get the money then." He dropped the knife into his pocket before he stood up. "Come on."

I stood up too. *He put the knife away. This is my opportunity. Let's take it before—*

"And please don't try anything clever, Samarra. I'm really not in the mood to—"

THUD. Ali fell backwards as a harrowing cry burst from his lungs. He stumbled for stability, almost collapsing before he found his footing. Then he looked towards me in a second of disbelief, seeing the heavy Bible clutched in my grip that I had just smashed upwards into his nose.

2

I didn't hit him hard enough. He's still standing. I need to hit him again!

Ali's hands immediately jumped into his pocket—*don't let him get the knife. Hit him again!*

Without hesitation, I brought the Bible back up. *He's a strong man, so don't hit him where it won't hurt. Go for someplace weak, where there aren't any muscles. Make it count!* I threw the bible towards him, aiming straight into the bottom part of his neck, directly into his windpipe with another resounding—

THUD. The hard edges of the Bible plunged into his trachea, cutting into his airway. Alarm mixed into his crying scream as he stumbled backwards. He doubled over in a coughing fit, gasping for air that was no longer his to take.

My hand stung as I dropped the Bible and shook out my fingers. I looked towards the exit, wondering if I had enough time to make it there. But in that brief moment of hesitation, a shining flash of silver hurled towards me—

A roar of agony escaped my throat. A throbbing burn seared into the side of my hip where my skin was exposed. Then the knife clattered to the floor beside me. *No, no. Please no—*

I looked down to my waist. *Goddamn it. He broke the skin.* The knife had severed my flesh with excruciating torment, and a trail of hot blood slithered down my waist. *He's actually trying to kill me.*

"Samarra…d-don't…don't do this." Ali's voice was barely audible as he choked like a drowning fish. "Please."

Hit him again, before he hurts me more, before he finishes me off!

I stepped up towards him and grabbed onto his dark waves of hair as tightly as I could. *Aim for somewhere that'll actually hurt!* I pulled his head down hard as I kicked my knee up, forcing his face straight into it. *Make sure it's a good hit. This is my last chance to hurt him before he hurts me!*

THUMP. Ali fell silent as he collapsed onto the cold floor.

Thank god, I did it. I actually might survive…right? I clutched at my side where ripples of pain tore into me. *It's just a surface scratch. It won't kill me. I'm not going to die today, no one is going to—*

Die. The judgemental stare of the crucifix bore down on me as I looked towards Ali's body. *Is he…breathing?* Dread devoured my skull. *What have I done?* Panic consumed my mind like festering maggots. *Everything used to be so perfect before Evie died. Why is it now so out of control?*

A scream ripped through my breath as I knelt, leaning over Ali. *Why did I hurt him? I can't hurt people. No, I shouldn't hurt people. This will only make everything even worse than it already is.* I pressed my fingers against his swollen neck. *Please be alive, please be—*

A weak sliver of a pulse beat against me. *Thank god for that.* I let out a breath of relief. *I haven't killed him. Not yet.*

I pushed past my own dizzying instability as I messily placed Ali into the recovery position. It was tricky pushing his limbs around with the small space between the pews, but it was enough. *He'll survive, I think. Now let's get out of here before he wakes up!*

I went to move away from his unconscious body, but my gaze caught itself on the slow, shallow movements of his chest. His body was clinging to life and his lungs were barely inflating. *I wonder what would happen if he stopped breathing… What if I hurt him enough to stop him from chasing me down for money ever again?*

Wait. What's that? The inside pocket of Ali's jacket was showing. *Is that…* A large wad of money was poking out. *It is. I could—*

No, don't rob him. I literally owe him money. I can't take even more that I won't be able to pay back—

But I need it, don't I? I need to drive far away from Medlock and finally get up to Eidyn. It's a long, expensive journey, so… I threw my hand into his pocket and grabbed everything in there. *This is a bad idea. I don't even have any pockets to carry this in.* Then I stuffed the contents into the side of my bra. *A very. Bad. Idea.*

"Hey…" Ali stirred.

I swore under my breath as I fell away from him, staggering back onto my feet. *Time to go!*

"Samarra… S…stop…" His voice was slurred and his eyes wouldn't stay open. I didn't even want to imagine what sort of brain injury he might have sustained from his loss of consciousness—

Stop worrying and just get out! I moved into the aisle of the church where I glanced at the picture of Evie once more. I looked at her smirking smile, her multicoloured strands of hair, and her face, which looked nothing like mine. *I wonder if Evie would hate me for doing this on the day of her funeral or if she would find it hilarious. She did always love any thrill she could get. I just wish she was still here. It doesn't make sense I'm here and she's not. Her death was too sudden. Accidents don't just happen like—*

What's that? My eyes were pulled to the side of the church where a doorway stood. *Was that always there?* It was a doorway I swear hadn't been there before. A doorway that was slightly ajar, with the outline of a dark figure waiting behind it.

Is someone…watching me? Shadows cloaked the figure, hiding it in sharp claws of gloom. Two bright eyes shone out of the darkness with an intense hunger, looking towards me as though I were their prey ready to be devoured—

"Samarra!" Ali roared.

Get out of here. Now! Adrenaline raced through my legs as I sprinted towards the exit. *Run!* I bolted down the aisle, rushing through the empty carcass of the church, ignoring the strange doorway and the hidden figure behind it. My heels *click-click-clicked* against the floor with each stride, forcing the straps to tear into my skin. But pain didn't matter now. Only survival did. *I'm not going to die.*

Am I?

ETERNAL REST

3

It's just a surface scratch.

Agonising rips of pain stabbed my hip as I raced through the graveyard. Dirt splattered against my legs as the insects below my feet devoured the decaying corpses. The sunset was passing away, darkening Medlock's grey skies. Rain drowned my long hair, while the chill of winter wrapped its cold air around me as tight as a noose. *I really need to get a coat. Dresses aren't made to withstand this weather—*

Stop worrying and run! I leapt over a small fence before sprinting along the cobbled pavement, heading towards the pub where the aftermath of the funeral was taking place. I really did need my bag from my mum, not for my money but for my car keys. *I need to drive out of Medlock to get away from Ali and the church and that terrible picture of Evie that she really would have hated. I need to depart from it all.*

Eidyn. Ee-den. That's the place I need to drive to, the city Evie always loved. I have to take her ashes there to finally rest, and I have to do it before her ghost comes back to haunt me.

Music crescendoed into my ears as I headed towards the side entrance of the pub. *I'm almost there.* Laughter and chatter then rang alongside it as I sharply turned towards the door with as much speed as I could find—

My heel twisted along with my ankle. My knees buckled. Finally my body crashed onto the floor, forcing a searing burn to roar out of my hip with a fierce malevolence. *These heels will be the death of me.*

My head throbbed as I pushed myself back to my feet. *At least I made it. I'm safe, right?* I glanced over my shoulder. No one haunted the quiet streets behind me, not even a shadow. We were too far away from the bustling centre of Medlock. Out here on the city edges, towns felt more like forgotten cemeteries no one wanted to visit. *Ali isn't following me. I'm safe, for now.*

As I turned back to the pub, I caught my reflection in the window. My makeup was smudged and falling off my face, forcing my freckles to shine through. The black roots of my hair were matted with sweat, making them even darker compared to the bleach blonde of the rest of my hair. And my hip was bleeding through the rip in my dress. *I can't believe I ruined a perfectly new dress.*

But at least I'm okay. I'm okay! I forcefully thought calming words to myself, though they felt more like a demand rather than a reassurance. *Everything is okay.*

I hobbled up to the entrance, fighting through the agony bleeding from my heel. Tacky informational posters covered the door, but I was too exhausted to read them as my adrenaline began to subside. *It's just an acute injury, that's all. It won't get infected. I'll be okay. I just need to get my keys and Evie's ashes. Then I can vanish from this godforsaken city and travel farther up north to Scotland where grief can no longer find me.* I pushed open the door with my remaining strength—

My body froze. *Goddamn it.*

A large hive of people stood with full drinks in their hands and empty smiles on their faces. They were positioned in a semicircle, dressed in identical black clothing, and facing the door I'd just walked through.

My mum was before them all. Her back was turned to me as she gave a speech. "I really am so…thankful for your presence today." She spoke slowly and quietly, as though she didn't have the energy to finish each word. A drooping smile haunted her face, accompanied by empty eyes that had lost all life. *Why is she giving a speech? Who let her talk in front of everyone?* "Evie was a… great person. She was so…" She stopped as she saw everyone was staring behind her. Then she turned around.

I crossed my arms, covering the cut across my side. My stomach tightened the instant her eyes met mine.

"Samarra?" Mum asked. "Where have you…" She trailed off as she looked me up and down once. Twice. Then a third time as though she'd already forgotten what I looked like.

"Hello." I smiled awkwardly, shivering from the unrelenting cold. "Sorry, I…I got caught in the rain." *That's not exactly a lie.*

"That's all right, Love." My mum handed me a card full of scribbled writing. "Why don't you continue this speech? I'm a little tired, but…everyone would love to hear some final words for Evie."

Heat fled over my cheeks as the stares of the crowd turned to me, expectantly waiting. Their smiles felt as vacant as their "sorry for your loss" cards as they stared at my sweaty face that was boiling with pressure, my mascara that was smudged around my eyes, my nose that dripped with blood—

Wait. What? Quickly, I wiped my nose, staining the back of my hand dark red. *I'm bleeding?* I sniffed, letting the taste of iron run down the back of my throat. *No, I can't have a nosebleed. I already look bad enough.*

"Samarra?" Mum prompted. "Will you continue this for me?"

I gulped back hard. "Okay." I nodded, letting the door swing shut behind me before I *clicked* the lock into place. *At least no one can hurt me in here—*

Suddenly I noticed another door on the other side of the room, and another door next to that, and—four. There were four doors. *Four ways Ali could come in and kill me.*

I really need to get out of here. I just have to get through this stupid speech first.

I stepped forwards, in front of the crowd. "Thank you, everyone, for being with us today." My voice croaked through short, shallow breaths. "Um…" I looked down at the card my mum had given me, purposefully holding it so it hid my wound. It was Evie's memorial card that now had messy writing covering every blank spot. But the more I looked at the writing, the more my vision blurred. *Wait…what?* The letters clouded, as though I were looking at them through a fogged-up glass.

I shut my eyes. I counted to *one, two, three—*

Everything was still fuzzy when I opened them again. *What's happening to me?* I blinked. Nothing changed.

"Um…" I coughed to clear my throat, stalling for time. *The wound is just a benign injury, a surface scratch.* My heart clawed against my rib cage like an animal caught in a trap as worries ate my thoughts. *It can't be killing me, can it?*

"Evie was…was…a great person," I finally said, squinting at the writing as my cheeks burned with rushing blood. "She was so much…fun to be around." *Though she also annoyed me every single day.* "She was so…nice and caring." *She was also a little self-centred and full of way too much confidence.* "I'm…" *I can't read this when it's all made up and idealised.* The words blurred into one another as I stared harder at the paper. *Also, I literally can't read this.*

"Hey!" A loud voice interrupted my thoughts. "Get the Hell off me!"

The crowd turned as shouts and scuffles echoed across the room. *Thank god, I need a way out of this.*

"I said: get *off!*" the voice yelled as a group of people surrounded a door at the back where someone had just walked in.

It's not Ali, is it? Did he follow me?

"I'm allowed to be here and I'm allowed to grieve for my best friend," the voice continued. "How can you all be allowed to be here and not me? She didn't even know your damn names."

A young man stepped into view, dusting off his green leather jacket as he moved through the room. I didn't recognise his face, thankfully, letting a breath of relief escape my lungs. *It's not Ali. I'm safe. Everything is still okay.*

"My apologies!" the stranger called out to me, putting on a bright smile as he pushed his hair behind a bandana. "Please continue."

"I…" I stumbled, looking back to the paper. *I don't want to continue.* "Um…" *Just get this over with already.* "Evie was also…a very bright young woman who—"

"Bright? She said you used to call her an idiot." The stranger laughed. "Though she also said you used to call her things *much* worse than that."

A ripple of murmurs flew over the crowd as they frowned at the stranger's smirk. I frowned too, wondering who he was since he clearly knew who I was. *Of course I used to call Evie things far worse than that; she was my annoying younger sister. But…how does he know that? Who even is—*

My gaze caught on a table in the middle of the room. The urn filled with Evie's ashes stood on it like a centrepiece. The urn was short and round, disproportionate to Evie's large personality. It was decorated with odd, asymmetrical floral patterns. And worst of all, it was dark, lost from all colour. *Dark colours were never her style. She would've hated that urn. She would've hated this whole funeral.*

I need to leave. I need to grab that urn and take Evie to a place she'll actually want to be a part of. She can't stay here and neither can I.

"Evie…*was* an idiot," I finally said. The stranger let out another laugh. "Evie was a beautiful idiot who would've hated this funeral." I let the card drop from my hands. "She shouldn't even be dead, this isn't right. Fatal accidents don't just happen to people who don't deserve—"

"Look!" My mum cut off my words before they had the chance to leave my mouth. "The food's here." She pointed to the back of the room where the buffet was being set up. "Time to eat."

Everyone's attention was pulled away from me. The music crescendoed back into its dwindling life as piano notes floated over the air in a serene melody. Chatter accompanied it as the crowd returned to their conversations and moved towards the food tables. I was left standing by myself, with blood dripping from my wound that no one cared to even notice. No one except the stranger, whose gaze hadn't left mine.

4

I stared at the stranger, wondering who he was. His dark eyes had a hint of amusement playing in them. His smile seemed more genuine than anyone else's. Yet his beaming energy felt like it didn't belong at a funeral. He didn't belong. *Who even is he?*

I stepped towards him as my mind flooded with curiosity—

"Samarra?" Mum moved in front of me, blocking my path. "What just…happened?"

"What do you mean?" I tried looking past her. But bodies obstructed my view as other people walked up to the stranger before I could.

"I thought you were…good at giving speeches. Are you not good at it, Love?" Mum leaned closer towards me. She wore makeup that seemed like it had been done by a mortician, trying to squeeze some life out of her fading face. "Are you drunk?"

"No, I…I just didn't expect to have to talk," I said, crossing my arms again to keep my wound hidden. *Don't let anyone see.* "I didn't even want to be—" Another drop of blood fell from my nostril, cutting off my words.

Mum paused for a long moment, watching me wipe away the blood. "Are you sure you're not drunk?"

"No, Mum, I'm not." *She never asks if I'm okay. She hasn't for months.* "Anyway, do you have my bag? I really need my keys."

"Keys? You can't drive if you're drinking."

"I'm *not.*"

"Are you sure?" She frowned as confusion rattled over her blank expression. "Why don't you just ask Ria to take you back? She doesn't drink so—"

"Ria? I haven't spoken to Ria in months. Don't you remember that?" I sighed. I saw Ria during the funeral, but she didn't even look back at me. *She didn't want to see me. No one does.* She used to be my closest friend, before she became Evie's girlfriend. Yet I hadn't spoken to her in a very long time.

"Ria's nice. She'll give you a ride," Mum said as though she hadn't heard me.

I nodded, unsurprised by her lack of attention. Since Evie died, conversations with her had felt very one-sided as Mum's mind had closed itself off to the world almost as much as mine.

"Please can you just tell me where my keys are?" I tried to maintain a smile even as frustration seeped through my words. "You know I have that neuroscience exam in a few days. I really should be studying—"

"You can't leave me here, Samarra."

"Leave you? You have so many other people here—"

"Don't leave me with *him*." Mum looked at the stranger, who now stood at the side of the room, holding up his hands in defence as a small group of people surrounded him. It looked like they were telling him to leave as they pointed him to the exit with angry expressions.

"Who even is he?" I asked.

Mum frowned. "That's Zain."

"*That's* Zain?" Evie used to talk about Zain all the time. She loved going to parties and concerts with him. They were even in a band together, though I'd never bothered going to their gigs, not after hearing how dreadful Evie's drumming skills were at home. "*That's* Evie's best friend?"

"Friend? No, friends protect each other. But he…" Mum lowered her voice. "He let Evie cross that road without looking."

"I don't think he *let* her, Mum. I don't think any of her friends let her. It was an…an accident, right?" That should have been a rhetorical question, but my mind was full of hope that it wasn't. For the past six months, Evie's death hadn't made any sense to me. *People shouldn't die without any warning. They shouldn't be taken away in one fatal accident.*

"They were on god knows what that night, but if they were sober…" Mum's expression hardened, as though some sliver of anger was running through her lost mind. "I wouldn't be surprised if he's on something now since he just got out of prison."

"He was in prison? For what?"

"Assault. He hurt someone." Mum pulled her eyes away from him, shaking her head. "Please just…get him out of here."

I don't have time for this. I should be grabbing Evie's ashes and driving her up to Eidyn already. "If I get rid of him, can I then have my keys? Will you find my bag?"

"I…" She looked me up and down once more, staring at my ruined dress and my scuffed knees. "You have a rip in your dress."

"I know, Mum. I just…I fell over when I was running away from someone."

She nodded as though she barely comprehended my words. "That wine is going to be a nightmare to get out."

I followed her gaze to the stains across my side. "That's blood actually. I was stabbed with a knife and…and my body seems to be reacting to it. But I don't know what's—" A violent cough burst from my lungs, swallowing my words.

"I'll have to find the white vinegar for it." Mum nodded as my words flew over her head.

I caught my breath, gulping back the remainder of the cough. *She's not worried about me. I bet she won't even notice when I do leave this city for good, no one will.*

"I'll go get your keys now." Mum loudly sighed. "I just wish Evie were here… She'd know how to give a speech, wouldn't she? Much better than you." She turned and walked away, leaving me with a sting of pain running through my mind that hurt worse than my knife wound.

"I'm sorry I'm not as perfect as Evie…" I whispered under my breath to no one but myself. "She'd have the whole room under her charm by now. If only she was here and I was the one in that urn. At least then I wouldn't have to put up with any of this—"

"You should've said that in your speech." The stranger, *Zain*, stepped up next to me. An arrogant smile shone over his face as he spoke in a soft, Northern accent. "It would've made it far more interesting."

I turned to him, looking at his green jacket, which sharply contrasted against the black colours everyone else wore, making him stick out like a wasp in a beehive. *Is he talking to me?* His dark eyes looked straight into mine, gleaming with an unfamiliar energy.

"After all, this funeral could use a little more…life, couldn't it?" He smirked.

"I…" I didn't know what to say. I had only just put together who he was. "You know it's rude to interrupt people's speeches, don't you?" I finally said, letting my frustration at this whole day seep through. "Did no one ever teach you manners?" I kept my arms crossed, covering my ripped dress and the pain brimming beneath.

"Manners? Is that what everyone else here has?" Zain looked at the people in the room who were still staring at him. "Is that why they tried to stop me from coming to this funeral? Because they were being *polite*?"

"They stopped you because you shouldn't be here. Evie… Evie wouldn't want you here." I sounded harsher than I'd meant, but I needed to get rid of him. *Once I get rid of him, I can get my keys and get out of here.* I tried not to focus on the irregular beats of my heart, the pounding headache swirling through my skull, the thought of Ali coming back to hurt me—*just focus on making Zain leave. One thing at a time.*

"You think you know what Evie would've wanted?" he asked.

"Yes. I'm her sister." *I was her sister. I was. Past tense.*

Zain tilted his head. "That doesn't mean you know her."

"And *you* do? I bet your memories with her are barely even memories from how much she used to drink and…and…god knows what else. You're probably on something right now, aren't you?" I said, echoing my mum's words.

"As much as I'd love to be on something right now, I haven't had anything in an awfully long time, so please don't tempt me." He gave another smug grin. "Even if I *was* on something, it's not like I'd be much different to anyone else our age since everyone's become obsessed with Dust."

I stared at him with a blank expression.

He paused. "You *do* know what Dust is, don't you? Or was Evie right when she told me you were a hermit who never left the house?"

"I…I leave the house a lot," I said defensively.

"Then why have we never met before?" He raised an eyebrow. "It *is* very nice to meet you. I heard a lot about you from Evie."

"I heard things about you too. How was prison?"

He stepped closer to me, raising his hand to my face—

I automatically flinched as my mind lingered on my mum's words. *He was imprisoned for assault.*

Zain stopped. "Sorry, I didn't mean…" He sounded almost hurt from my reaction as his eyes scanned my face. "Do you need a handkerchief? You're bleeding." He took his hand back, pulling out a handkerchief from his pocket.

Blood dripped from my nose. I swore under my breath as I rubbed it away once more. "No, I'm… It's just a nosebleed. It'll stop on its own." *What's happening to me? Why is my nose still bleeding?*

"Are you sure?" Zain held the handkerchief out to me.

I refused to take it. "I'm sure."

"Okay…" He nodded with a hint of uncertainty, using the handkerchief to wipe his own nose before returning it to his pocket. "Anyway, it wasn't *quite* a prison I went to. It was a place called Detention."

"Detention? I thought that was just for young people."

"I am young." He laughed. "They take up to twenty-five-year-olds there. I've got five more years left in me. So you've heard of it?"

"I've read about it. It's just a holding centre, right? It doesn't seem that bad."

"Oh, you've *read* about it? Then you must know what it's like." Sarcasm dripped from his voice. "It's far worse than *just* a holding centre. But I won't bore you with details of my six months there, so let's just say I'm grateful for getting out."

"You only *just* got out?"

He nodded. "Last week."

"Surely you can't be this far away from your house if you're on probation?"

Zain raised his eyebrow, as though he were impressed that I knew. "You don't know where I live. Maybe I'm not far away from my house."

"Only old, rich people live around here, outside the city. That's clearly not you."

He smiled wider with amusement.

I kept my face straight. "What would your probation officer do if they knew you were here?"

"I'd rather not find out."

"Really? Because I think seeing you get arrested would be a satisfying sight for everyone here. I'd love seeing you with handcuffs on your wrists."

Zain let out a breath of a laugh. "If that's what you're into, then if you have a pair, I'd happily let you—"

"*Don't* go there." I rolled my eyes at him.

He grinned back at me, as though he enjoyed watching my frustration grow. Then he slowly ran his eyes across my body. "You look awful by the way, nothing like what I pictured. Evie always described you as academic and professional, not... messy."

"My mum has already pointed out how *messy* I look, so I don't need you to as well. *Speaking* of my mum, she doesn't want you here, so I...I think it's best you leave now."

"So *that's* why you've been so welcoming, because you've been speaking to your mum about me." He clenched his teeth. "You know the reason everyone here hates me is because she's made them all believe I was a bad influence on Evie, always tempting her to make bad decisions."

"Well, were you?" I asked. "Six months is a long time to be in Detention. The average is only two. Surely...surely that means you were more dangerous if they kept you there for so long."

Zain looked off to the side. "Evie said you're full of a lot of useless facts. At least she seems to have been right about that." He looked at the people who were still staring at him, before looking back at me. "But if you really knew Evie, you'd know she didn't need any help to make all her matchstick, impulsive-as-Hell decisions, wouldn't you?"

"I…" I stopped. I knew he was right, though I didn't want to admit it. "I still think you should go."

He sighed, scratching the back of his neck. Then he laughed. "Don't you love that moment?"

"What moment?" I frowned.

"The moment you walk into a room full of people and feel every eye turn to you. It doesn't matter if it's for good or bad, it just matters that your face is burning with embarrassment and energy is rushing through your body as though you're in a life-threatening situation, when really it's just people staring at you."

He sounds like Evie. Evie used to talk about specific moments she loved too. They never made any sense or added anything to the conversation, but she was obsessed with finding those very specific moments that made her feel something. *Why is he speaking like her?*

Suddenly, my breath caught on itself as my throat dried up. The room spun around my vision, and the colours merged into spiralling twists. *Something really is happening to my body. I need to get out here.*

"I think you should go now and so should I," I croaked as I pushed past Zain, walking towards the centre table where Evie's urn stood. *Let's get Evie's ashes and leave before—*

"Wait." Zain grabbed my arm and pulled me back towards him. "I also came here to meet *you*, Freckles."

Freckles? That was the name Evie used to call me. She used it as an insult, as though she was jealous that I had freckles and she didn't. But Zain had said it with kindness, like he wanted to remind me of her. *How does he even know she used to call me that?*

I paused for a moment of unsure silence as I looked closer at him. He had brown, sunken eyes that creased when he smiled, as though he smiled too much. A light redness danced within his gaze that made me think he had been crying. His dark brown skin was adorned with gold jewellery and tattoos. Faded strands of green dye ran over his black waves of hair. A vivacious spirit beamed through his warm persona. But the strangest detail was how unfamiliar he looked. *How can Evie's best friend be such a stranger to me? Did I really not know her at all?*

"Why…why did you want to meet *me*?" I finally said.

Zain took a breath. "Evie made me promise to look out for you when she was no longer here." He softened his tone, refusing to let go of my arm. "I figured meeting you is probably a good start to keeping that promise."

Guilt crashed through my mind like a tidal wave. "She made you promise to look after *me*?" *I was* her *older sister; I should have looked after* her.

He nodded before looking down at my wrist. "I like your tattoo by the way." He looked at my small triangle tattoo. "Isn't it the—"

"I don't need you to look after me." I pulled my arm out of his grasp. *Why didn't I look after her?* My heart pounded in an irregular rhythm, racing to catch up with my breath as a lightheaded dizziness danced over my mind.

"Are you sure you don't need a handkerchief?"

"No, I told you—" Suddenly a heavier gush of blood trailed down my nostril. A flurry of pain crashed over my body, swallowing my voice. I stumbled backwards as I lost my balance in the spinning room, putting out my arms to steady myself and fully revealing the knife wound across my side. *No, don't let anyone see it!* But I could barely process what was even happening, as at the same time my heart began to stop.

5

Zain reached out to catch me, steadying me as a swarm of sharp cuts sliced through my insides. His eyes widened as he looked at the wound across my hip. "Is this *blood?*"

"It's just a surface scratch…it's just…" My voice croaked under the weight of my distress. *What's happening to my body? This isn't right.*

"What happened?"

"I…I fell."

"Fell? Into what? A knife?" He looked more closely at the wound.

Think. What's going on? Nosebleed. Dizziness. Nausea. Drowsiness.

"You're burning up." Zain felt my forehead. *High temperature.* His hand had a slight tremor as though adrenaline were racing through him as fast as it was through me.

"I'm…I'm…" I stumbled through my words as I fought to catch my breath. *Rapid breathing. Irregular heartbeat. Chest pain.* "It's okay, I'm…I'm almost a doctor. I…I know what I'm doing."

"I'll go find your mum," Zain said. "I'm sure she'll want to take you to hospital." He made sure I was steady before quickly running into the crowd.

"No, she…she won't…she…" My hoarse voice was too quiet to be heard. *I can barely even speak.* My worries collided with one another as I ran over the symptoms in my head until—

Poison. Dread swallowed my mind as I realised what was happening. *My body has been poisoned, and if I don't do something soon—*

I staggered backwards, crashing into a table. Glasses fell over and a pile of sympathy cards tumbled to the floor. *The urn...* Evie's ashes rocked on the table, almost falling over. *Just grab the urn and go! Evie never wanted to be on display, imprisoned in a dark urn. She wanted to go to Eidyn. That was the quiet, calming paradise full of magical castles and rich history she always dreamed of. And that's where I need to go now!*

I grabbed the urn, clutching it in my arms like a tight embrace. "I've got you, Evie," I whispered. "Let's get out of—"

Suddenly a cough trapped itself in my throat. My chest tightened like a snake coiling around me, refusing my lungs to fill up again. *Breathe! I can't die at Evie's funeral. She'd say I was copying her. But I can't copy her, that would be so embarrassing.*

My heart wouldn't stop shouting at my lungs as they forgot how to *breathe. Breathe goddamnit. Breathe!* My body was shutting down. *I think I might need real help. I might need a hospital—no, not a hospital. I can't go back there again.*

Just get some air! Sputters of coughs sliced into me as I moved through the withering room towards the door. *Get outside!* But my vision was blurring, dizzying my stability. My lungs were roaring, begging for air. I couldn't stop coughing and coughing and—

"Samarra." Mum stepped beside me. Her vacant eyes looked into mine. "Zain said you wanted to go. I hope you...have a nice day, Love."

"No, Mum, I...I..." I stumbled for my words, desperately wanting her to see my pain for the first time in six months.

"I think I'm going to go home and sleep now," she said nonchalantly. "I'll see you later."

"Mum, please, I...I..."

"Sam, look at me. Are you okay?" Zain stepped to the other side of me, looking at my lips, which were turning blue.

"I...I..."

"What are you doing with the urn?"

"I…" *I need air.* I staggered forwards, forcing my limbs to walk towards the exit, towards the fresh air. *Put one foot in front of the other. Again. And again. And—*

I reached the door and pulled it open—

But it was locked.

"You need a doctor." Zain's voice followed me.

Why is he helping me? No one ever helps me. "I…I told you, I *am* almost…almost a…" My head throbbed as I fumbled with the lock. *Why did I lock it?* My hands shook as I tried to open it again. And again. *Please just open!* Sweat fell from my palms as I tried once more. Then once more again. *Hurry up!* My blood pressure soared as stress weighed down my heart and—

The lock clicked out of position *finally.* I pulled open the door and stepped into the drowning rain, which was freezing into the white powder of ice. The wind blew against me with an excruciating chill that bit at my exposed skin. *Air! I can breathe—*

Wait. Why can't I breathe? My body wouldn't let me take in any of the air. *Why am I not breathing?* My limbs collapsed onto the floor as hacking coughs strangled me. *I can't die.* I took the impact of the fall on my knees, refusing to let the urn drop from my arms. *I can't die like Evie—*

No, I'm not going to die. I'm not going to die. I'm not… The same chant ran over my thoughts in a final attempt to cling onto the fragile life that was slipping from my grasp. *I'm not going to die. I'm not—*

A flicker of darkness pulled my attention towards the church in the distance. *What's that?* A figure seemed to be standing beside the graveyard with tranquil ataraxia, enshrouded by a mist of mournful darkness. *Is it Ali? Is he coming back to hurt me?* They were too far away for me to make out any features as the shadows entombed their silhouette and the wind rattled around them in a tumultuous storm. But I felt their hungry stare on me and I knew it was one I'd felt before.

This can't be happening. My stomach twisted as the Tartarean figure slithered closer. My heart banged against my ribcage like someone trying to claw their way out of a locked crypt. *I'm not going to die.* I held onto Evie's urn much tighter while my body dragged me into the depths of unconsciousness. *I'm not going to die.* I knew it wasn't Ali. It was someone much worse. *I'm not going to die. I'm not going to—*

Die.

I'm going to die.

I'm. Going. To. Die.

DONE FOR

6

I can't let it kill me.

Dreams tangled around my mind like chains as I fell in and out of consciousness. *I can't die here.* Rain crashed against a window, an engine roared, a radio blasted a rock tune. But I couldn't see anything. Instead I felt like I was standing on the top of a building, looking down at the pavement far below, watching the small figures of people walking by—

No, the figures were getting closer. I wasn't standing at the top, I was falling to the bottom. My worries were screaming with regrets, but I couldn't escape the fall. I could only use the few seconds I had left to learn how to die before I hit the pavement—

"Sam!"

My eyes bolted open and I took in a breath. *Thank god.* Then another. And another. They sounded more like a gasp of pain, but they were enough. *I'm okay.* Agony tore into my chest and clawed through my insides, but I was thankful for the feeling. It reminded me *I'm okay. Everything is o—*

Wait. Where am I? I quickly took in my surroundings, seeing I was in a car, sitting in the passenger seat while Zain drove. But no one else was with us.

"Thank Hell you're awake." Zain sighed in relief. "You weren't breathing."

"What's going on?" My voice cracked as I spoke over the thumping radio. "Why is…" I shook my head, pulling myself out of the clutches of dreams. *Why am I alone with him? Isn't he dangerous?* "Are you kidnapping me?"

"That's not *quite* the thanks I was looking for, but you're welcome." Zain smiled, clinging to positivity even in the chaos of the world. But the smirk he wore was twisted, like it didn't know if it belonged. His sunken eyes seemed overcome with stress. His body shivered as rain dripped from his hair, soaking through his shirt under his green jacket. And his hands were trembling as he steered the car onwards.

"Where are we going?"

"To a hospital." His gaze flicked between me and the road ahead as he jerked his eyes back and forth. "If it wasn't for me, your mum wouldn't have even noticed how ill you were. Plus, there's no way in Hell I'm making the mistake of waiting for an ambulance again. So you're welcome for—"

"A hospital? No, I can't go there."

"I don't think you quite heard me, so let me say this one more time: you weren't breathing. You *need* to go to a hospital."

"Well, I'm breathing now, so you can let me go." *If I go to the hospital, Ali will find me. I'll be trapped with no escape.* "I-I can't go to the hospital."

"Yes, you can. It's pretty easy actually. All you have to do is walk into a building—"

"No, I have to leave this city today. I have to take Evie…" I paused, running my hands over my seat. "Wait. Where's… where's Evie? Where's the urn? And where's my bag? Did my mum not find my keys?" *I need my keys to escape this city, this life.*

"Your bag? I don't know. Again, I was a little more concerned about you not breathing. Are you not grasping how serious that is? Don't tell me *I'm* the irrational one for being worried about that."

"I need to go back. I need my keys and I need the urn. I can't leave her behind…" I went to open the door, not even thinking about how fast the car was moving—

Zain quickly clicked the lock on the doors. "You're insane."

I still pulled on the handle, before letting out a shout of frustration. "Just let me out!" *I can't be locked in a car with him.* "You can't force me to go to a hospital!" Jagged breaths burst through my lungs in gasps of panic. "This cut is such a minor injury; it's barely even a graze." I looked down to my hip, at the blood pouring from my wound.

"Why don't we let a doctor make that decision?" Zain pushed his hair back behind his bandana.

"I'm basically a doctor myself—"

"You're a med student."

"Yes, but…but I'm still basically—"

"Aren't you years away from becoming a doctor?" he asked.

"It's not quite that long as—"

"Evie always said you hated med school."

"Evie doesn't know what she's talking about!" I bit at my words. *Didn't. She didn't know. Past tense.*

"Ria said you hated it too," Zain continued. "Back when you used to talk to her."

I frowned. "How do you know so much about me?"

Suddenly the radio changed tracks and another rock song blared out the speakers, howling over the noisy engine like a dying scream.

"Will you turn it down?" I shouted.

"It's broken!" Zain yelled back. "If there was a way to turn it down, I would've found it already. Trust me." He nodded towards the backseat. "And Evie's back there. You wouldn't let go of her urn, so I brought her with us. Again, you're welcome."

"You did?" I twisted my torso and snapped my neck to the back of the car…

She's here. A breath of relief escaped my failing lungs as I saw the dark urn on the backseat with the seatbelt fastened over it. "Evie…" I quietly whispered. "You're safe. Thank god you're okay."

"Why did you want to keep hold of the urn so bad anyway? It's not like she's going to run away."

"She…she always wanted to go to Eidyn. So I'm taking her there as soon as I can."

"You're going to Scotland?" Zain frowned.

"I…" I trailed off as I noticed the other seat. A picture frame was sitting there, with the terrible picture of Evie inside it. The one she would have hated. The one where she was wearing *my* yellow jacket. The one where she looked nothing like me, as though there was nothing still tying us together, nothing to keep her memory alive.

"Did you take…" I sounded more breathless than I knew I was. "Did you take that from the church?"

"What?" Zain followed my gaze to the picture. "Oh…"

"Why on earth do you have that? What kind of perverted things are you planning on—"

"It's for another funeral!" He interrupted. "A better funeral. One Evie will actually like." He glanced at me. "After all, I don't need a picture *that* big to do my perverted things—"

"Stop. Please take this seriously." I rolled my eyes.

Zain let out a burst of a laugh, breaking the seriousness of the situation, trying to lighten the heavy weight of imminent death.

"What…what do you mean 'a better' funeral?" I asked.

"We're going to do one that's more Evie's *style*."

"More her style?" I raised my eyebrow. "You're going to throw a party, aren't you?"

Zain's smile brightened, shining with an unfamiliar optimism. "You're very quick. Evie was right, you *are* smart. But I think it'll be more of a concert than a party, which you're welcome to come to—"

"I can't." I shook my head. "I don't even have time to go to the hospital, let alone a party. I've…I've got an exam I should be studying for. I'm very busy—"

"Busy?" Zain chuckled. "That's how Evie used to describe you. It's why we've never properly met before, isn't it? You were always too *busy* to come out with us or see our band—"

"Watch out!" I shouted as a black cat ran across the middle of the road.

"Shit," Zain swore, swerving the car.

The tyres scratched at the frozen roads as the icy rain drowned us in its storm. We were racing closer to the city as Medlock's skyline plummeted towards us at full speed. Everything felt so endlessly tumultuous, like a spiralling twist of madness pulling me beneath the surface, into its grave. *At least a grave would be quieter than this. It's not fair that Evie gets to rest in peace and I don't.* I looked down at my yellow watch, seeing the seconds tick by, wondering how many breaths I had left. *Though maybe if Zain takes me to a hospital, I'll get to join her. People die in hospitals. Evie died in a hospital. Maybe I really am going to—*

Die. That word wouldn't leave my head. It was such an enchantingly cruel word that felt like a knife slicing through my guts. *Die.* It was so definitive, like the end of a falling dream, but one I couldn't wake up from. *I'm going to—*

Wait. My heart was beating so fast it felt like it had already stopped. *That figure was watching me. It was coming towards me…* My blurry mind thought back to the tall, enigmatic figure at the edge of the graveyard. The figure I had seen before but hoped to never see again.

A belch of agony tore through my chest as I twisted my neck to look through the car's back window. *It can't actually be following me…* Rain battered the windows like the waves of the River Styx. The darkening sky looked down on me with pity. *Can it?* The road was as empty as a graveyard. Empty except for a malevolent flicker of taunting darkness.

It's still there.

7

The figure was far behind the car, but now it looked like an animal on the road, almost like a cat— no, a fox…no, a bear? It was something large and unnatural that grew in size with every stride. An intoxicating hunger covered its slashing teeth and blood dripped from its claws as it ran, shaking the ground with every stride as it fought to catch up to us.

I gasped as pain twisted through my insides, slashing my guts like shards of broken glass. My body felt like it was fighting for survival, like death was just a breath away, *and maybe it is.*

"What's *that?*" I spoke through panting breaths. "How is it following me?"

"What are you talking about?" Zain's eyes snapped to the back window before returning to the road.

"*That.*" I pointed to the figure lost in the night's twists of shadows. "What is it?"

"What?" Zain looked again. "Nothing's there." He frowned. "Is your mind playing tricks on you?"

"It is. Look!" Panic scattered through my voice as I watched the bear plummet towards the car. But as it got closer, I swore it looked less like a natural animal and more like a monstrous creature of nightmares. Its claws were razor blades, its teeth were vampiric fangs, its eyes were pits of infernal Hell.

"Nothing's there," Zain repeated more definitively as he glanced back again.

"It *is*! A creature's chasing us." My heart punched against my chest. "Can't you see it?"

"A creature? Did you see a fox or something?"

"No, it's a monster! It's—"

"You can see a monster? Yet you're *sure* you don't want to go to a hospital?" Zain spoke with a concerned frown.

"You really can't see it?" I turned back to my seat, running my fingers through my hair.

Am I hallucinating? But it looks so real... My mind ran in circles around my panic, burning me at its stake, as I searched for answers I could never find. *Am I more ill than I thought?* Another drop of blood ran from my nostril, staining my lips with its iron taste. *Was that knife really infected? Or is this just exhaustion from how little I've slept?* The havoc of life overwhelmed all of my senses in its sea of troubles. *It's all too much. Life is too much and the only escape is—*

"Sam. *Sam*." Zain brought my attention back to him. He pressed farther down on the acceleration, speeding the car onwards. "Hey, take a breath. Focus on what's real, all right? Focus on being alive. Think about what you can see, what you can feel, what you can hear."

Focus on being alive? I dragged my eyes back to the road ahead, noting the dead streets around us, the abandoned factory buildings, the flickering lamp posts, the omnipresent security cameras. *Focus.* Sweat pooled in my palms, and droplets of frozen rain ran across my skin. *Don't look back, just focus!*

"We're almost there." Zain's voice had a tremor of anxiety wrapped within it. "Can you tell me what the Hell happened to you?"

"I-I don't know…"

The car wipers were on full blast, screeching against the windscreen, beating just out of time with the blaring music.

"Where did you get that cut? Did you really just fall?"

"I… I-I…" I stuttered. His question was too much for me, too much to explain. *Why does he care about me anyway? No one ever cares.*

"Or did someone hurt you?"

"Just let me out of this car!" I shouted. "You're going too fast!"

"Fast? I'm barely above the speed—" Zain stopped as he saw he was doubling the speed limit. "Fine!" He slowed the car down. "Hold on for another few minutes, okay?"

"Minutes? The city is ages away! I told you, I can't go to a hospital—"

"*Why* can't you go?"

"He'll find me!"

"Who?"

"The drug dealer I'm paying back for the debts Evie left me with!" I finally admitted.

"Debts?" Zain glanced over to me. "What debts?"

"Her debts for the Dust she bought at all the parties she loved going to." My mind burned with stress as I thought about all the money I owed to Ali. "She used to take it all the time when she went out, as I'm sure you know. You probably encouraged her to take it, didn't you?"

"Encouraged her?" He shook his head. "Evie loved impulsively reckless actions and would happily do them all by herself. But…I didn't know she left debts behind. Are you sure she—"

"She did. She left *me* to clean up her mess when she decided to walk across that road without looking."

Zain paused for a long beat.

"How could she have been so stupid?" It felt like the radio's music was trying to smother my words. "How could such a horrible accident happen to someone who didn't deserve it?" The music's tempo was speeding up, running away from itself as it crescendoed in a clash of chords. "Evie shouldn't have died like that, it didn't make any sense." The blaring drum beat against the melody with deafening blows, overpowering every other instrument. "Turn the goddamn music down already!"

"I told you, I can't!" Zain yelled back.

"It's too loud! Everything is far too loud!" I covered my ears, but the music only grew more powerful, ensnaring me in its notes, reminding me silence was dead and never coming back.

"Did you take any Dust?" Zain asked, continuing the conversation as though everything were normal and the world weren't about to stop.

"What?"

"You're paying debts for Evie's Dust. Did you take any too?"

"Why would I take it? I've never even tried it before."

"You haven't?" He sounded surprised. "Aren't you a student?"

"So?"

"Students are always taking it. It must be all over your campus. Surely your friends have taken it?"

He thinks I have friends? He thinks I go out? "No, I…I don't have time to mess around with that."

"Then what's wrong? Why do you seem so ill?"

"It was the drug dealer. He…he hurt me for the money. I think…I think he poisoned me." I gulped hard. "The knife he cut me with must've been dirty or-or something. I think it's infected me and it's…it's killing me."

Suddenly a speed camera flashed at us, blinding my vision.

"Damn it." Zain pressed the accelerator down farther, as though he didn't have anything left to lose. "Hold on." He pulled on the steering wheel as he sped us around a corner.

"No, I don't want to go to hospital. He'll find me and hurt me—"

"I won't let anyone hurt you."

"I don't need you to protect me. I didn't need you to even show up today!" I screamed.

"Thank Hell I *did* show up. If it weren't for me, you wouldn't be getting any help right now." His breaths were deeper, as though he were forcing himself to calm down. "Your mum was too out of it to even *notice* you needed help."

"She wasn't out of it, she was grieving! She's been like that ever since Evie died. It's not her fault." An anger roared through me as adrenaline coursed into my veins. "I don't need help anyway. I don't need *you*! I wish you had stayed away from me, from my family— away from Evie!"

Zain quietly counted to ten under deep breaths before he spoke. "You don't even know me, Freckles." He bit at his tongue, trying to keep his tone soft.

"I know more than enough. You're a criminal. You were in Detention for *six* months for god's sake! Clearly you're dangerous if they kept you for that long."

"You think I'm dangerous?"

"You've locked me in a car, of course you are! You should've stayed away from me today. God, if you had stayed away from my whole family, then—"

"Then what?" He clenched his teeth.

"Then you know what."

"No, I don't. Then what?"

"You know what!" I yelled again, louder.

"Then *what*? Say it. Say you think it's all my fault!" Zain's anger roared as loud as the engine.

"It *is* your fault!" My words stung him harsher than I'd intended. "You were out with Evie the night she died, weren't you? Why did you let her cross that road and get hit by a car? Why did you let her die?"

My eyes caught on the rearview mirror, which had a thin crack running through it. The creature's figure reflected a fearsome image full of echoing hunger as it continued to chase us like a predator eager to sink its claws into its prey. But now it seemed more human. *How can hallucinations look so real?* It ran on two legs as its arms stretched towards me. *It can't actually be real... Can it?* It wore a dark cape of twisting shadows, hiding in the secrets of its façade as it sprinted as fast as a pale horse—

BEEEEP. Another car sped past, inches from us.

Zain slammed on the brakes as the car plummeted towards a red light. The wheels skidded across the icy roads until the car jolted to a stop in a sudden cut to its movement, as though it had been shot dead.

My lungs stopped working under the threat of instant death. A sputter of coughs burned through my body, slicing through my throat as they fought to escape.

"Sorry." Zain's hands trembled as he clung onto the steering wheel. "I didn't think we'd meet like this. I'm sorry it's gone this way." His voice shook in a rush of overwhelming emotions. His dark eyes had a soreness running through them as tears welled up behind them. "But I promised Evie I'd look after you. So I'm taking you to a hospital. Then I'll leave you alone if that's really what you want."

He promised Evie he'd look after me? But why would he promise that? I tried to breathe but couldn't find air in the vacuum of reality. *Why would Evie want* him *of all people to look after me? Why couldn't she do it herself? Why is she no longer here but he is!*

The shadowed figure plummeted closer in the rearview mirror. Its unnaturally long strides stretched its limbs, forcing its bones to constantly break and pull themselves out of their sockets to reach their speed. Its darkness twisted into a spiral of pandemonium that was laughing at me, as though this was a game and it was going to win.

"Sam?" Zain looked at me. "Are you…" His words halted as he saw the colour drain from my face. "Sam? Can you breathe? *Sam?*" He started the car again, letting the engine rumble back to life. "As much as you may dislike me right now, *I* still prefer it when you're breathing. So please breathe!"

The figure sprinted up to the back window, ready to reach out and break through what little space we had between us before pulling my soul far from this never-ending pain—

"Damn it. Hold on!" Zain shouted over the screams of the world as he floored the accelerator and sped us away from the figure. The noisy engine tumbled over the howls of the rain, and the music carried on singing to us as though we cared to listen. "Please hold on."

8

Ambulance sirens screamed over the chaos of Medlock's central hospital, polluting the air with its unrelenting noise. Uniforms rushed from one patient to the next in a buzzing storm of overworked stress. Beds lined every corridor, as though we were in an active war zone. Cries for help were ignored, tears flooded the floor, and agony bled through the clean mask of the hospital walls.

"Move! Out of the way!"

My shivering limbs dangled over the side of the gurney I was being pushed on. My body was slowly giving up, as my eyes moved back and forth in rapid beats. My chest convulsed, jerking upwards as it fought for life it no longer had while my throat closed up—

No, I can't die. Focus on where I am. Focus on being alive. I felt the cold rain that was still dripping along my face, the soft fabric of my once-perfect dress. I looked down at my colourful, chipped nail varnish, the shining silver rings below it, and the tattoo on my wrist that was in the shape of a triangle. I listened to the distant sound of staff talking, patients crying, footsteps moving, and Zain humming a strangely familiar tune I thought I'd forgotten. *That tune… That's the tune Evie used to hum.*

I spat out a mouthful of blood. My lungs filled with air again.

"Sam?" Zain was walking beside my moving bed, wearing a fading smile that didn't sit quite right. "I'm glad you're alive because I don't think my car is." He laughed despite the cruelty of the situation. "At least you made the funeral a little more interesting. It would've been such a boring day if you hadn't decided to pass out."

"That…" I tried to whisper, but a harsh rattle clung to my breath. It made my words sound more like a hacking cough, as fluid filled up my lungs. "That tune you were…were… Evie used to…"

"It's all right, we made it. You'll be okay now." He spoke in a much softer tone than before. "See? It wasn't *that* hard going to a hospital. It only took a high-speed car ride and several unconscious moments…" He looked at the busy rush of rooms we passed as the lost souls of limbo called for help but received no answers. "I don't know how you work in a place like this. I'd *hate* to come here every day."

"I…I…" A broken cough scratched at my lungs and heightened my rattling breath. A shock burned through my guts as tears ran down my cheek as thick as blood.

"You should come work in a restaurant like me instead of *here.* At least then you can drink behind the bar to get through the shifts." Zain continued as though hope still existed. "Although, looking at how stressed everyone is here, I wouldn't be surprised if you drink to get through shifts too."

Loud, emphatic footsteps reverberated against my eardrums, as heavy as a dying heartbeat. They drowned out Zain's attempts to lighten the mood and sharply pulled on my attention. I glanced behind me, past the guts falling out of the wounded victims, the misaligned limbs, the fountains of blood—and towards the dark figure stepping along the shadows of the nauseating corridors in time to my breaths. *It's still there…*

A human disguise cloaked the maliciousness of the figure as it walked towards me. Its deathly stare was a black hole of hungry darkness that wanted to consume everything in its path. Its demonic claws looked like a scythe, shining with bloodied stains, while its soulless eyes stared into mine.

"It's still…still f-following me," I stuttered. *Why is the hallucination still here? What's happening to my brain?*

"What?" Zain glanced behind us. "What do you keep seeing?" He still couldn't see it. No one could, except me.

"It…it doesn't hurt. Does it?" I spoke through gasps of breath.

"What doesn't hurt?"

"Death."

"What are you—"

"The body knows how to die, right?"

Zain didn't seem to know how to respond. He cracked his knuckles as he fidgeted with his trembling hands. Then I noticed the dark urn in his arms, which he was holding close to his body. *Evie's urn…* A wicked fear of failure came over my mind. *I wanted to take her to Eidyn. I was supposed to scatter her ashes, not join her in them.*

Zain gulped. "You'll be all right, Freckles. I know you will," he said as though he believed his words. "I'm sorry about arguing, about everything. But I told you, I promised Evie I'd look after you. It was the one thing she wanted just before she died and I'm going to keep that promise."

Did he just say… He promised her just before she died? But… Cogs turned furiously through my lost mind. *Her death was a sudden accident. How could she have made him promise that just before? How could she have known?*

"What do you—" Another cough violently sliced through me, cutting up my airways. My breath was being eaten, swallowed by oblivion as my heart neared the end of its shortened path. *No…I have to be okay. Everything has to be okay. The world needs to keep on turning. I can't even think about what would happen if it—*

Our movement stopped as we arrived at a door.

The doors in the hospital were practically identical. They were all covered in cheap informational posters with Mayor Brown's face plastered across them, hiding the cracks and stains below. But this door felt darker than the rest. A shadow fell across it like a cold embrace that was taunting me with its impersonal gaze of indifference, waiting for me to enter.

"You'll be alright. Just keep fighting through it all." Fear drenched Zain's voice as his words faded and his body was pushed away from me.

"Wait…" I couldn't speak loud enough for anyone to hear. I couldn't do anything but accept my fate and let Hermes drag me through that door, into the realm of the unknown.

Darkness suffocated my vision as I entered the room. It felt like I had fallen to the bottom of the ocean, taken to some lost place in the aphotic zone where no oxygen resided and life could no longer find me. I was alone.

Well, not completely alone. I knew something else was standing at the end of my bed, waiting for me to pay them attention. I knew that figure had finally caught me. Or maybe it had caught me long before I had even realised. Maybe running away from it was only pushing me towards it and I knew I couldn't run any longer. All I could do was accept my fate and learn how to die before I hit the pavement as I looked towards the intoxicating figure of Death himself.

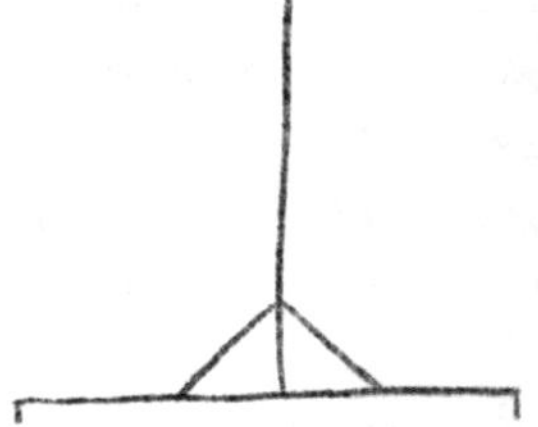

MEET YOUR MAKER

9

I can't be dying, not like Evie. Please, not like Evie.

Wrapped in tendrils of darkness stood a tall, humanoid figure. His features were hidden beneath the waves of shadows that covered him like a cloak. His appearance was shrouded in a cloud of gloom, allowing me to only see a sharp grin and two white eyes. Their stare pierced my soul in an alluring tug of fascination, making me realise I was face-to-face with Death himself.

Unbridled confusion shot through my heart like a bullet. *This can't be real. It's a hallucination, a nightmare.* The room was pitch-black, numbing my senses as though I were trapped inside the catacombs. *I have to wake up.* My limbs were frozen in position, unable to do anything to save themselves. *Wake up, please!* The bed I was on felt more like a sarcophagus that was slowly closing its lid, trapping me inside.

"Don't you dare be afraid of me." A voice suddenly shook through my mind.

Is that…his voice?

His voice was softer than I anticipated, full of melodious notes that rang like a Siren's call, overflowing with comfort. It swam inside my brain like a calming anaesthetic.

"Fear doesn't suit you, Samarra Blair." There it was again. His soft yet powerful voice, which felt like it was controlling my thoughts.

A frozen panic crawled over my skin. *How can I hear him? Are my hallucinations auditory now too?*

"I'm surprised you tried to run away from me," he continued. *"You of all people should know better than that. Especially given how much you've wanted me these past few months."*

My lungs refused to inflate as the weight of his words strangled my breath. *I must be losing my mind. Why am I hearing Death? He took Evie away from me, so why on earth would I want to—*

"I don't take anyone."

Goose bumps fell over my skin as I realised he wasn't just speaking in my mind, he was also listening. *He can hear me too. What sort of messed up hallucination is this?*

"Of course I can hear you. I hear every thought inside that busy mind of yours," he whispered. *"I don't know how you put up with that constant noise. I hope you're looking forward to silencing it all."*

Silencing it? Does that mean I'm actually dying? But I can't be. Not like this—

"The sooner you come to terms with what's happening, the easier this will be. Just relax and let me finally save you from your exhaustingly lonely life."

Panic soared into my gut as my life instincts clung to my dying heart. I knew my digestive system would be shutting down, and my organs would be failing, but I didn't know what would happen after my body died. The unknown had always scared me, and now I was looking straight at it.

I tried to shout for help, but my jaw was locked, my mouth was dry, my voice had stopped. So instead I thought back, thinking as loudly as I could, screaming my words through my mind:

Please don't do this. This was a mistake! I didn't mean for this to happen!

"*Not many people* mean *to die. Even those who jump don't always mean to land at my feet. After all, it's a long fall. Plenty of time for regrets to seep in.*"

But I…I really didn't mean it. I can't die. This can't even be real. Hell's a fable and so are you!

"*Are you sure about that, Samarra Blair?*" His words were like honey, flowing in a serene harmony of sedation. "*After all the times we've passed by?*"

What? I haven't seen you before—

"*Don't deny it now.*" Death's words cut over my thoughts, turning them to silence. "*You must remember the hours you spent at the hospice with your grandma. You must remember burying your hamster. Or perhaps you remember walking past the body of a person who had been living on the streets, without even realising they were pale as ice?*"

I tried to resist his words and push them out, but they were far too strong. His voice carried the weight of a gravestone that was crushing me into the ground, stopping me from ever getting up again.

"*Or maybe you remember that time you were in this very hospital, shadowing a doctor with other university students. You saw the doctor fail to save a patient's life. You even saw how upset the doctor was afterwards, as they regretfully announced the time of death. And all you could think about was how you were going to be expected to do the exact same thing if you qualified.*" He paused. "*If.*"

I shook my head. *How do you know all this?*

"*Because I've been watching you. Every time you've been around the dying, I've seen you. I've noticed how you react. You don't tend to cry or feel an overwhelming sense of sorrow like others do. Instead you seem almost envious of the dead, as though you wish you were one of them."*

No, I don't. I don't want this! "S-s-st…" I tried to form a real word, but my body betrayed me. "S-sto…." I fought against Death's paralysing hold. "S-s… St… Stop!" The word finally blasted through my throat like a bullet. It took all my energy to speak one simple word. But I could do it. "H…he…help!"

Death refused to listen to my mortal words as he let out a snicker of a laugh. *"I'm surprised by your reaction. I thought you'd have been more intrigued by my presence, given how much you've been thinking about me recently."* His bright eyes never blinked as they held my gaze prisoner. *"I thought you would've been more like your little sister."*

A cold chill scuttled across the back of my neck, and the smell of decomposing flesh seeped into my nose as strong as a memory. *Evie?*

"Yes, Evie. You do remember seeing me when you last saw her, don't you? You couldn't stop staring at me then." He stepped towards me with the powerful breeze of Thanatos, walking out of the shadows and plainly into my view.

10

I'd heard people see Death differently. Some see it as an angel, while others see it as an unforgiving monster. So I wondered what it meant for me, to look Death in the eyes and see a human.

What the…? Curiosity mixed into my confusion as I saw he was nothing like I had imagined: no dark cape, no soulless hood, no scythe. Instead, a surprising warmth surrounded him as he was built from flesh and blood. He had slicked-back silver hair, matching his bright narrow eyes. He wore a suit with his shirt sleeves pushed up, a thin black tie slightly loose, and a waistcoat with a ticking pocket-watch hanging from it, counting down whatever time I had left.

"Well?" Death stepped towards me in a pair of white military boots that thudded against the floor. *"Do you remember me now?"* A grinning smile lit up his face, creating deep dimples in his cheek. Dimples that made him look far too human.

My mind raced with terrifying fascination. I *had* seen him before, the night Evie died. But I had prayed he wasn't real then, just as I prayed he wasn't real now. *But if he's not real, how is he here? I don't understand how I'm seeing him.*

"How do you see anything?" he mused. *"You see it because it's there."*

I shook my head. *No, Death isn't supposed to be a real, personified form. You aren't supposed to look like this.* I hoped I was still asleep, still lost in the realm of Hypnos. *You don't wear clothes. You don't speak English. You don't smile—*

"Why do you question everything rather than just accept it? Evie never questioned me."

Stop talking about her. You took her from me and turned her into nothing but dust.

"I told you, I don't take anyone." Death stepped to the side of the bed, moving closer towards me. He brought a lavender scent with him as though he were putting people to sleep with a kind thoughtfulness. *"Evie was an interesting soul. She wanted to join me more than most."*

She didn't want you.

"You don't know what I meant to her," Death hushed.

You didn't mean anything to her! I wanted to reach out and grab him and force him to give Evie back. I wanted to twist his heart just as he had twisted mine. But my limbs were stuck in the stiffened lock of a corpse, trapped in his gaze as though I had been tranquilised with a powerful opiate.

"I meant everything to her." Death ran his tongue over his teeth, which looked as sharp as blades. *"I know exactly what I mean to you too."* His devilish white eyes refused to look anywhere else but right back into mine, drawing me further into his all-consuming presence as he reached out his hand towards me—

Stay away! I wanted to flinch but couldn't as painful, unanswered questions piled into my head: *Have I even lived how I wanted to? Have I done everything I needed to? What about all the opportunities I never took? What about the ones I did take? Has my life been too short? Have I done enough? Could I ever do enough? Is this it? Is this all life is? One huge swirling mess—*

"All those worries are far too heavy for your precious mind, Samarra Blair. If you're not careful, they'll drown you before I do." Death put his hand against my face—

The thoughts stopped as Death touched my cheek, brushing away a tear I didn't know was there. My skull emptied itself like Pandora's box. It lost all its misery, its grief, its constant worries. Then waves of comfort crashed over me. I had expected his fingers to be cold and lifeless, but instead they were hot as a fire on a winter's day, defrosting my frozen body. They felt like a deep hug I'd been waiting for all my life.

Everything had been so overwhelming for the past day—no, the past week…no, the past six months…the past life? It didn't matter. Now it all faded into serenity that filled me with an angelic sense of safety. Now everything felt okay because now nothing mattered.

"See how perfectly silent your mind can feel if you don't have all those thoughts weighing you down?" Death's words felt like a lullaby, wishing me asleep. *"Isn't this so much better?"*

It really was so much better. I didn't realise how much I had longed for quietness. It felt like I'd finally driven out of the overwhelmingly busy city and into the hills far beyond. It made me wonder why I ever wanted to return to reality again when I could stay safe in Death's touch.

"Now, are you ready to leave with me and rest in this peace forever?" he asked, looking back towards a doorway behind him. A doorway I swore hadn't been there before. It was a simple doorway, one that could've easily blended in with every other door I had seen. But a quietness emanated from it, calling me towards the fields of Elysium beyond. *"After all, life has become so hard for you, hasn't it? You've been so alone in this barbaric life. No one would even know if you slipped away."*

My mind poured with the urge to go through that door. I knew it would eradicate my problems. It would keep me safe from my thoughts, my worries, from everything I hated. And it would bring me closer to Evie.

Evie. Her name thudded into my head like a heartbeat. *E-vie.*

"Do you want to join your sister in everlasting sleep?" Death smiled. *"Wouldn't that be better than continuing your unwanted life?"*

E-vie… A soft energy tugged on my heart. *Evie wanted to go to Eidyn.* It reminded me of its purpose. *I still have to take her there.* It reminded me why it was beating. *I'm not allowed to lie down and enjoy Death's peace yet. I have to fulfil my promise to Evie. I didn't do anything she wanted me to in her life; I can't do the same in her death.*

Stop! Get away from me! My thoughts crescendoed back into life, fighting against Death's alluring waves of quietness. *I can't die with her. I can't copy her, not yet!*

Death pulled his hand from my face, ripping the peacefulness from my grasp as sharp as a blade. My mind plunged back into its sea of worries, drowning my skull. *I have to take her ashes to Eidyn before I die; otherwise I really am a useless older sister. I already failed to save her, so I can't fail this too!*

"He…help! Help!" I forced the words out of my lungs, draining my dregs of energy just to be heard. "Please! He…help!" I broke my stare with Death, pulling away from his intoxicating tomb. *You shouldn't have taken Evie away from me!*

"She came to me." Death sounded angry, as though he was stung by my rejection.

No, she didn't. She—

"Do you really think people die like that by accident?"

Accident? What do you mean? Of course it was an accident. That car came out of nowhere and hit her.

"That's what your mum has been telling you and everyone else. But you don't actually believe her, do you?" He chuckled, showing off his dimples.

I hesitated. *But…that's what happened. Evie didn't see that car coming towards her—*

"I know you don't trust that story. You've been questioning it every day since she died. After all, you know better than anyone that Evie wasn't stupid enough to cross a road without looking."

I went to talk, or rather *think* back, but stopped. Death's words sank into my mind with the heaviness of a coffin.

"You've never truly believed it was an accident, have you?"

I stared at him with wide eyes. No one else had ever spoken to me about Evie's death like this. No one else had ever dared question how she died.

Do you think it…wasn't an accident too?

"I already told you, Samarra Blair…" Death took a step back, hiding in the twisting shadows of the room once more, until nothing was left but his disembodied voice. *"…I don't take anyone. They leave with me willingly. And one day you will too."*

"Clear!" A voice suddenly yelled as the sound of the hospital screamed into my ears. Shouts and cries and bleeps of machines spun back to life as reality came hurtling towards me like a burning meteoroid.

Wait... Please wait! You have to tell me more! Tell me how Evie really died!

Bright lights forced their way back into my vision. Oxygen choked my lungs. My thoughts raced ahead of me, falling over one another as they fought to be heard. Then a sharp coldness stabbed through my body as it shocked me back to life.

I'm alive? I should have been grateful for my return to the living, relieved to have breath in my body. But the noises, the chaos, the weight of my worries—they all suffocated my senses, ripping away any semblance of peace. And all I could think about was how I wanted to see Death once more.

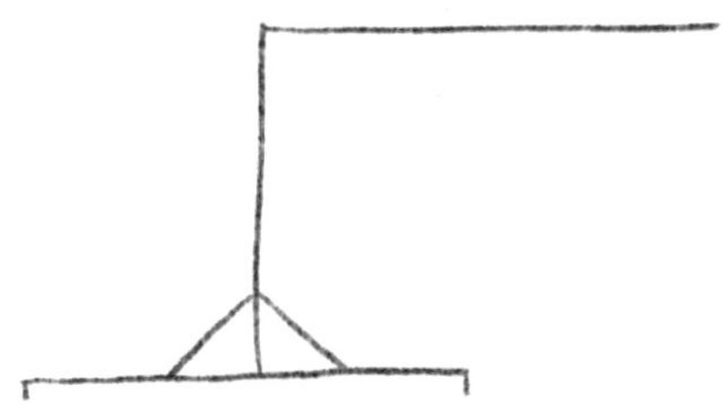

LOST THE BATTLE

11

Evie didn't want to die.

"I literally saved your daughter's life. If it weren't for me—"

"You should've called an ambulance."

"An ambulance would've been too slow. I drove her here to save her—"

"Save her? Like you saved Evie?"

E-vie... Evie didn't mean to die! I gasped in a breath as I jolted awake. My mind shocked itself back to the turmoil of life's slings and arrows. Blinding lights drowned my vision as I realised I was on a hospital ward. A curtain was drawn around my bed to give the illusion of privacy. Cries and screams pounded against my eardrums as loud as the sounds of a slaughterhouse, accompanied by the clashing arguments of Zain and my mum.

Mum is...arguing?

"You should've looked after Evie too," Mum said. Her voice was still calmingly quiet, but a small slice of anger was seeping through. An anger I hadn't seen from her in a long time. *She's been numb for months. Why is she now showing signs of life again?*

"I *did* look after Evie," Zain stated. "I always looked—"

"You didn't. You took her away from me with all those parties and—"

"She was nineteen. It wasn't *my* fault she wanted to go to parties."

"It is." Mum insisted. "You're a…a wasp, a bad influence. A criminal."

"Criminal?" Zain laughed, shaking his head. "You do realise that if Evie was still alive, she'd probably have been arrested by the Shade too, right? Evie was a Hellraiser who loved defying everyone—"

"No, *you* were a bad influence on her—"

"*She* was the bad influence on *me!*"

My head thudded with the pain of a tempestuous storm as I sat up on the thin mattress of the bed. "Mum?"

"Samarra?" Mum looked at me, pulling away from their argument. "You're awake. Did you have a nice sleep, Love?" She smiled with the same vacant eyes I was accustomed to.

"Sleep? No, I…I was unconscious." I spoke through a dry, cracked voice. "Are *you* okay, Mum? Were you just…shouting?"

I rubbed my eyes, seeing Mum was still wearing her black funeral dress, which neatly flowed down her body, free of any creases. Her hair and makeup still looked like it had been done by a mortician, covering up the scars of life. And her arms tightly held Evie's dark urn. *She has the urn…*

"I wasn't shouting," Mum quietly said. "I just don't feel right with *him* here. I thought you were going to get him to leave?"

"That was at the pub, Mum. We're in the hospital now."

"I still want him to leave."

I glanced at Zain, who was pacing back and forth on the other side of the bed in a continuous stream of energy. His teeth were clenched. His trembling hands were tightened into fists. His eyes were weighed down by bags that reminded him of all the sleep he didn't want. And he was quietly humming that strangely familiar tune once more. The tune Evie used to hum all the time.

"You're still here?" I asked. *I thought he would've left by now; most people do.*

He raised an eyebrow as he put on a smile that didn't quite belong. "I've been asking myself the same thing. But I promised Evie I'd protect you, so here I am. Unless you want me to leave?"

"I…" I hesitated. "I don't even know what just happened. Have the doctors said anything?"

"I thought you *were* the doctor?" Zain smirked.

"I am. Almost. But what did they say happened? Did they say anything about experiencing hallucinations or—"

"What *happened* is this was supposed to be Evie's funeral, not yours. So *please* don't try and die again."

Die again. Those words crashed through me like the snap of a guillotine. *Die. Again.* I glanced over to where Death had stood next to my bed. *Did I really hallucinate Death? Why did it feel so damn real?*

"Did I actually almost…die?" I gulped back what I could from my dry mouth.

"Don't be silly, Samarra," Mum said. "You're okay. We should go home now, right? I…I need to go to sleep."

"Sleep? It's the middle of the day," Zain argued. "Your daughter is literally in a hospital bed. You need to stay here."

"Please stop talking to me now," Mum replied.

"Seriously? You don't like me *that* much that you can't even speak to me?"

I looked down at my mortal body, pulling away from their senseless conversation. *Maybe I actually did almost die and that's why I saw Death… I wonder how I'd be feeling if I had followed him through that doorway. I wonder how Evie felt when she—*

'*Do you really think people die like that by accident?*' Death's words seeped into my mind like an addictive poison. His face, his smile, his piercingly bright eyes, his dimples that made him look far too human—it all refused to leave my thoughts. *But what did he mean?*

"How did Evie die?" I suddenly asked, cutting through their argument as I looked to the urn in my mum's arms.

Clearly my question made an impact, as it quieted them both.

"Did she really just die by accident?" I continued with shaking uncertainty. "Did she really walk into the road without looking?"

The constant noise of the hospital blared on in the background, smothering any hope of silence as I waited for an answer. But neither of them said anything. *No one ever talks to me about Evie's death.*

"Mum…?" I prompted. "Did Evie—"

"I want to go home now, Samarra." Mum retreated back into herself, exhausted from showing the slightest wave of emotion.

"Please, Mum, I just want to know what happened to Evie when—"

"Evie isn't here." A croak of sadness broke through her voice. "I…" She held the urn tighter. "I have to go now. Are you coming too, Love?"

"I can't. I'm in a hospital bed. Can't you see—"

"I'll see you later then. Have a…nice day." Mum moved away from the bed but held her stare on Zain. It seemed like she wasn't sure whether or not to leave me with him.

Sensing her hesitation, Zain raised his eyebrow. "What?" he said, looking between us. "You can leave us alone. It's not like I'm not going to hurt someone I just saved."

Mum held her stare for another moment then turned and walked away.

"Wait, Mum. Please don't go." I called after her, but she didn't even pretend to hear me. She pulled back the curtain around my bed as she left so everyone could see us. Then she disappeared into the overcrowded ward. "Mum!" *She took the urn with her. The urn I need to take up to Eidyn. But to go there I also need—*

My keys. My eyes caught on the chair beside my bed. My lacy black dress had been neatly folded up and placed next to my painful heels. On top of it was my bag with my car keys. *Mum must've brought my bag. I can drive out of this city. Once I get Evie's urn, I can go scatter her—*

But... My heart tugged on my mind. *...how am I supposed to end my grief knowing Evie's death wasn't as simple as I thought it was?*

"Your mum really likes me, doesn't she?" Zain spoke with frustrated sarcasm. "She has so much trust in me." He pulled the curtains back around us as he shook his head.

"How did you get her so...angry?" I asked. "I haven't seen her argue in so long."

"You're saying that like it's a good thing."

"It is. I haven't seen her so...alive in ages."

"Well, next time you want to see her angry, just let me know and I'll show her my face." He smiled as he looked at me, tracing his gaze over the cuts and bruises across my body. "You look awful by the way. I know I said that earlier, but you look even worse than before, if that's possible. I don't know why Evie thought you were tidier than you actually are."

Evie. Ask him *how she died.* I slowly sat farther up, though my weakened limbs only wanted to fall back into their grave. "Zain, do *you* know how—"

"I loved that moment though, when you woke up," he continued, letting his words dance over mine. "It's the type of moment when you breathe out all the stress you've been holding in. When you relax your shoulders and suddenly realise how tense they were without you even knowing."

There it was again. A specific moment, just like Evie loved talking about. They were always so random, so arbitrary. *He sounds just like her.*

"I...I need to ask you about something important," I continued. "I just want to know—"

"Wait. I'm um..." Zain hesitated. "I waited for you to wake up because I wanted to say I'm glad you're okay. You really scared me before. As much as we argued, I *am* glad we met and I really would like to spend time with you when you're not on the brink of—"

"What happened the night Evie died?" I bluntly asked, running out of patience.

Zain flinched at my question. "I'd rather not think about that when you just barely survived yourself." He looked at his hands, nervously cracking his knuckles. "We've thought about dying a little too much today, wouldn't you say?" He tried to smile, but it felt wrong. "Maybe I should go find a doctor to check on you? Are any of your doctor-friends around?"

"Please just tell me what it was like when she died." *Please will someone talk to me about her death for once.*

"You were there, weren't you?"

"I was there at the very end, when she was in hospital. I saw her..." *I saw her die.*

"Doesn't that mean you know how she died? Aren't you *almost* a doctor?"

"No, I..." I shook my head in a continuous movement. *Don't think about that night. Don't think about watching Evie die.* "I want to know what it was like before then, when she was still conscious. You went out with her that night, didn't you? I remember she went to some party, like she always did. Was Ria there too?"

He hesitated. "It was a gig, not a party. Of course Ria was there, she was always there. But I don't—"

"That's right. Your band was performing, wasn't it?"

Zain nodded. "Yeah, but—"

"I remember Evie invited me too. She kept saying how good your band was, despite how dreadful her drumming was at home."

"She was actually a great drummer, but…" He scratched the back of his neck with shaking hands. "There's no point thinking about that last night, there were so many other incredible gigs—"

"I couldn't go, I was too busy. But I should have. What happened there?"

"I…" He shook his head. "I don't want to remember that particular—"

"Did she really cross the road without looking?"

"Like I said, I don't want to even think about—"

"Or…did she die from something else?" I swallowed hard. "Earlier you said you promised Evie you'd look after me just before she died. But how could you have promised her *just before* she died? How could she have known she was about to die if it was really just a sudden accident?"

"Please stop with all these questions." Zain raised his voice, clenching his hands into fists with a brimming heat of anger. "Please can we not talk about—"

"I just want to know if it was an accident. Or if it wasn't an accident, did she want to die? Did she want to—"

"Of course she didn't want to fucking die! Who wants to die at nineteen years old?" Zain shouted in an explosive storm of pain. "Maybe if you'd been there instead of ignoring her invitation, you would've seen it for yourself!"

"I told her I was busy."

"You always told her that!" he yelled. "She *did* invite you out that night, like she always did, but you refused. You never had time for her. No wonder she hated you!"

I stopped. It felt like my heart stopped too, as though it had been shot dead.

Zain kicked the small bedside table in a burst of overflowing anger.

I flinched, letting out a gasp of shock. *Don't rile him up, he's dangerous. He was arrested for assault, remember. He hurt someone. He could hurt me too.*

Zain bit down on his tongue as he saw my alarm. "I'm sorry. I'm…" He shut his eyes, covering them with his hands. He whispered to himself as he counted to ten through forced, deep breaths.

He's right… Evie did hate me. I let go of a breath, hearing it shake and shiver under the weight of my distress. *She was always so adventurous, while I was always stuck indoors. She hated that I didn't go out with her. She hated everything about me.*

That's why I haven't even bothered looking into her death, even though I've questioned it for six months. I've been stuck indoors, away from the world. I haven't done anything to find the truth. I sniffed, wiping the back of my hand against my nose. *I haven't done anything for Evie.*

A quiet humming melody echoed from Zain as he paced again. The melody was the one Evie used to hum. It was a hauntingly soft tune, trapped in a minor key. I used to feel so annoyed every time she sang it, as she'd never stop. But now I felt a strange calmness as it floated through the air… A calmness that reminded me of the finality of Death.

Screw it. Zain won't give me the answers I need. No one will. No one has ever spoken to me about how my sister died. No one except Death himself… I wish I could see him again, just once more—

But there are other ways to find out the truth. So let's go find it.

"Okay…I see what you think of me," I finally said, trying to keep my voice steady. *Maybe I haven't done anything to find the answers to Evie's death for six whole months. But that can change; I can still make this right.*

Zain looked at me with reddened eyes. "I'm sorry, I didn't mean it like that. I just got overwhelmed thinking about that night, especially after what *you* went through today. I'm so sorry I—"

"I don't care." A perpetual sting ran through my body as I swung my legs off the bed and jumped to my feet.

"What are you doing?" Zain rushed to my side, reaching out to steady me. "Let me at least help—"

"Get away from me!" I shouted, instinctively falling away from his dangerous touch. "I can walk by myself."

Zain stepped back, holding up his palms. "I'm sorry." He let out a deep breath before running his fingers through his waves of dark hair, pushing back the faded green strands. "I'm really sorry, Sam. I didn't mean to say any of that. It's been such a stressful—"

"I said I don't care." I glanced towards the busy ward around me, at the dying patients who were losing their souls just as I was. I wondered if Death was hiding in the shadows of the room, watching me like a vulture circling its prey. I wondered if he would be laughing at me now that I finally realised: *Death was right. Evie didn't die by accident. They're hiding something from me, and before I leave for Eidyn, I have to find out what it is.*

12

I walked through the hospital corridors with the confidence of a consultant, making every step full of purposeful intent that didn't waste a second of time. I ignored the patients I passed, letting their cries fade into oblivion just as their lives soon would. My own pain tried to claw its way to the surface as it tore through my body. But I pushed it back down, keeping it as hidden as my shadow, lost in the depths of my unconscious.

My black funeral dress hugged my body once more as I'd quickly changed back into it. Rips, tears, and patches of blood now decorated its exterior, while my exposed skin shivered in the cold. *I still can't believe I ruined this dress. It was perfect and now look at it.* A bandage covered my knife wound like an accessory. I had put my jewellery back on too, giving me some semblance of normalcy as silver rings lined my fingers and my yellow watch ticked down whatever time I had left. I had also put back on the heels I hated, letting them *click* against the floor with every hobbled stride. *I really need to find some better shoes.* And my small black bag now hung across my back. My car keys jingled inside, ready for me to grab them and disappear the moment I could. *I'll leave for Eidyn soon. I just have to find out the truth first.*

Surveillance cameras watched from the corner of each corridor, keeping an eye on me with their blinking red lights. There was a chance an officer was watching the footage, but the feed was probably barely monitored. The cameras had to be more of a deterrent than an actual security measure. After all, who would dare commit a crime in a hospital?

I need to break into the records… My thoughts raced ahead of me, suffocating me with stress. *I need to find the cold, hard facts of Evie's death since no one will tell me. People are far too complicated to get straight answers from, so surely I'm allowed to find the truth myself?*

"Sam, what the Hell are you doing?" Zain followed close behind me. "You should be resting."

"I told you to stay away from me." I didn't even look at him as I continued striding forwards. *Why is he following me? He should've left and forgotten all about me by now.*

"I will once I know you're okay, when you decide to actually see a doctor instead of walking away from them all."

"You sound more worried about my life than I am."

"That's *exactly* what concerns me. Where are you even going? Didn't we pass the exit already?"

Don't tell him the truth, it'll only make breaking into the records harder if I have a newly released prisoner with me. "I've got an exam to study for. There are some textbooks here that'll help me study."

"You want to study? No one ever *wants* to study." He let himself laugh, grasping on to any sliver of positivity he could find. "I've never met a student as studious as you."

"You mustn't know many smart people then. Now please leave me alone."

"Wait. Are you…" Zain hesitated. "Are you sure that's all?" It was like he sensed my trepidation. "Earlier you wanted to drive off to Scotland to scatter Evie's ashes. You were terrified of coming to a hospital. But now you want to stay and…study?"

"I told you, I'm busy. Like I always am, apparently." I bit at my words with a harsh scorn. *How did Evie ever put up with his annoying concern?*

"Come on, Sam." He sighed, noting my anger. "I'm sorry about before, I really am. I watched you almost die and it scared the Hell out of me. You do get how serious it was, don't you?"

I ignored him as I walked onto a main corridor that intersected several wards. Hives of staff and patients were moving in and out, lost in their abyss of never-ending pain. It felt as busy as Medlock's city centre, brimming with the imminent risk of accidents and death.

Now I just have to get to the basement where the records are held, which means I need to get hold of a security card. Security cards were continually in use here, as the busy staff swiped through the multitude of rooms. There were plenty of opportunities to take one. *But they're all moving so fast. Surely there must be one person who's—*

My eyes landed on a security guard. *There.* They were slowly walking down the corridor in their usual patrol route, with a card tucked into their belt. *That's my target.* I rolled back my shoulders, readying myself to swipe it off them—

But I can't get caught. It would be far too embarrassing being kicked out of med school for pickpocketing. I need a good distraction.

"Hey, *Sam.* Can't you just talk to me?" Zain asked. "Please?"

Just a simple distraction that would take the attention off me and instead put it onto something else.

"Sam!" Zain reached out and grabbed my shoulder.

Or someone else.

"Zain." I crossed my arms, turning back towards him. *Two birds with one stone. Get rid of him* and *get the card.* We stood in the middle of the corridor, only several metres away from the guard. "You really should leave me alone. Evie wouldn't want you to mess me up just as you messed her up."

Zain pulled his hand off my shoulder, taken aback by my sudden mask of anger. "You think I messed her up?" He paused. "Look, I know you're mad at me and I know I deserve it, but I don't want to argue—"

"You're a criminal, a junkie, a wasp who doesn't belong, so of course you're the one who messed her up." I threw every insult I could find at him, wanting to find one that hurt, one that made him angry. "You got arrested for assault, didn't you? You beat someone up. What kind of monster does that?"

"Monster?" He ran his fingers through his hair. "I'm not the monster. The officers who arrested me and threw me in Detention, the goddamn Shade, *they're* the monsters."

"Don't blame the law for your mistakes. *You're* the problem here." I glanced at the security guard. They weren't even paying attention. *Then make them pay attention. Zain clearly has anger issues, so make him angry.* "You're acting like it's hard for you to tell me how Evie died, but I bet it's actually because you don't remember." I took a step towards him. "I bet you were on so many drugs the night she died that you don't even remember a thing about it."

Zain shook his head as he took in loud, deep breaths. "I don't think you know what you're talking about." He ground his teeth.

He's not reacting. Make him react. "Don't I? You used to take Evie out all the time. You used to drink and party with her and throw away your life together. I *know* how intoxicated she'd get, because I'd have to deal with it afterwards. So I bet you were the same. That's why I bet you don't even remember the last time you saw Evie alive."

Zain's fingers scrunched themselves into a trembling fist. "I don't do any of that shit anymore."

"But you did, didn't you? You did take Dust and god knows what else with her. Your debts are probably as big as hers." *Keep going. Make him angry.* "And look where that's gotten you: you don't have anything to live for anymore. You don't have anyone to waste away your nights with. Instead you're forced to remember how empty your life truly is."

Zain took in deeper breaths, counting numbers to himself as he tried to keep calm.

Don't let him stay calm. Force the guard to intervene. "That's why you're following me, isn't it? Because you don't have anywhere else to go. You say you're here because you promised Evie you'd look after me, but really it's because you don't have anything to do now that Evie has left you all alone—"

"You don't know what the Hell you're talking about!" Zain suddenly shouted as rage burst from his lungs with burning passion. "You didn't even *know* Evie. You barely ever saw her! You spent your time studying instead of going out with her! And now look, I've been trying to talk to you and all you've done is push me away, going off to study for some exam after you almost died! You think I'm messed up? Take a damn look at yourself."

I looked towards the security guard, making sure I seemed scared and helpless, in need of them to rescue me like any good damsel in distress. *Please let this work. Please come and "save" me.*

"You treated her like she didn't exist," Zain continued, raising his voice. "She may as well have already been dead to you from the way you acted." He stepped towards me as I backed away. "Your grief is nothing but regret."

My stomach dropped as his words slashed through my guts. *Nothing. But. Regret.*

"Sir." The guard suddenly moved in between us. "I think you should step outside."

"What? I'm not even doing anything. I don't need to *step* anywhere." Zain frowned at them.

"Sir, you need to calm down." Their eyes were fixed on Zain, *which means now is my chance to take their security card!*

"I *am* calm!" Zain shouted. "I'm having a perfectly calm discussion with my friend, so I don't get what the problem is."

"Sir, please step this way." The guard raised their arms, directing Zain towards the exit doors and revealing the security card on their belt—

Take it quickly! I reached towards the belt and unclipped the card as smoothly as possible. Then I hurriedly clasped it in my hand and held it behind my back.

The guard didn't react, they didn't even notice. But Zain did.

Zain's eyes tracked my hands. He raised his eyebrow at me as his jaw dropped. Then he let out a breath of a laugh.

I shook my head at him, hoping he wouldn't tell the guard. *No, I can't get caught, not now. Please don't—*

"Okay, I'll leave!" Zain put his hands up in surrender, giving in to the guard's orders as he moved towards the exit. "Just show me where you want me to go."

"This way, please." The guard walked him out and he willingly followed.

Is Zain helping me? I stared at him in disbelief as he moved away. *Why is he helping me when I just said all that? My words were far too harsh, I shouldn't have taken advantage of his emotions—*

Forget about him. I don't have much time. Let's go!

I pulled myself away from my worries before walking in the opposite direction. *I have to act fast if I don't want to get caught.* My heels *click click clicked* against the floor, pushing more pain into my decaying limbs with every step. *Get to the records in the basement, then worry about Zain.*

I moved through an overcrowded ward buzzing with masses of bodies. Hearts pounded, breaths gasped, and souls called out for the end in nauseating screams. As confidently as I could, I walked through the suffering of purgatory, not giving anyone a reason to question me—

Wait. Is that…?

A far too familiar patient was lying on a bed in the corner of the room. *No, it can't be.* Their face was covered with bruises and dried bloodstains. A tank top clung to their body, showing off tattoos of thorny vines across muscled arms. *It is.*

It's Ali.

I cursed under my breath as panic soared into my failing heart. Ali was lying metres away from me, far too close for comfort. But luckily his eyes were shut, his mind lost in unconsciousness. *How is he even here?* My thoughts asphyxiated my mind as I wondered how he'd made it out of the church, what sort of injury he had sustained, and how angry he'd be if he knew I had robbed him.

Another figure with a mop of bright blue hair sat next to his bed, slouched over in a chair as though they had fallen asleep. *I've seen them before…* I recognised the striking blue hair colour. *They're part of Ali's gang.* Then I cursed again, realising, *Ali has back-up this time. I won't be able to fight him off again.*

This isn't even supposed to be happening. I'm supposed to be far away from this city by now. I'm not supposed to still be here, in a place where his gang can find me and hurt me—

Stop thinking. I need to get out of here without either of them seeing me! I continued moving towards the exit of the ward. *At least they're both asleep. I can still get away while—*

"Samarra…?" Ali slowly sat up in his bed, squinting through one eye as he looked towards me.

The blue-haired person jumped back to consciousness as Ali spoke, shooting their gaze in my direction too. "Huh… The escape artist is back."

Goddamn it. I gulped back hard. *I need to get out of here now. I need to run!*

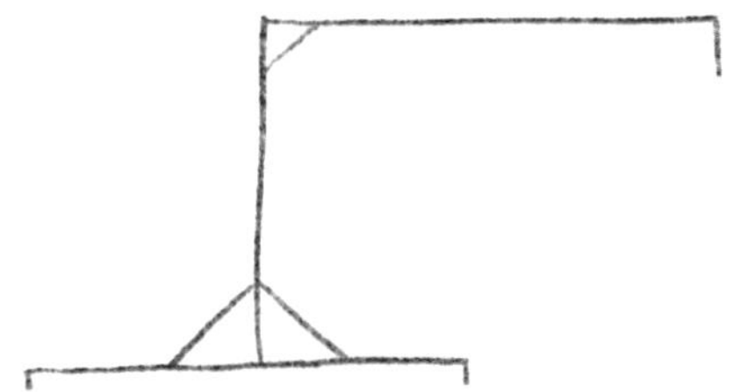

PULL THE PLUG

13

Evie didn't want to leave this world.

And neither do I. So let's run!

"Samarra, wait!" Ali shouted after me as I began running away. No, not running, more like hobbling as my body betrayed me with every step. Pain shredded my organs and clawed at my heart. The heel I'd torn earlier threw more agony into my movement, slowing me down as much as my stupid heels. *I really have to stop wearing these shoes. It's making running away so difficult.*

"Get after her!" the voice of the blue-haired person roared with malevolent anger.

Keep running! Panic emptied my breath. *I can't fight them both myself. I have to get away. Or I have to get help!*

Lost patients who were unable to pay the ferryman haunted my path. A few staff members stood back in confusion as I skidded past, but they were too preoccupied by their own stress to worry about mine. *Why did I distract the security guard when I needed them the most?* Blinking cameras in the corner of each room stared down at me with empty eyes. *No one will save me but myself. So run faster!*

I crashed through the door of a stairwell with a loud THUD, ignoring the government posters that littered its surface. A nervous panic ate at my sanity as I sprinted down the steps, jumping down as many as I could. *Faster!* It felt like I was falling into the pits of Tartarus as I leant against the banister and let my body drop towards the darkness waiting at the bottom.

"It's okay…" I muttered through failing breath. "I'm okay…" I spoke the same chant over and over, hoping repeating it would wish it into existence. "Everything is o—"

TH-THUD TH-THUD. Footsteps echoed through the stairwell, hobbling down at speed. "Samarra!" Voices shouted. "Stop!"

They're catching up with me! The footsteps were moving faster than I could, easily closing the distance between us. *But remember I have the security card. I can get through doors they can't. If I make it to the basement records, they can't follow me. Then I'll be safe enough to still find the truth behind Evie's death—*

No, I shouldn't try to find answers, I should be running for my life. Shouldn't I?

"Stop!" The voices reverberated through the stairwell. "We just want to talk!"

I continued falling down the stairs towards the basement. My breath fogged as the chill of winter smothered the air. Each panting breath hit my throat with a stabbing coldness as I descended farther and farther down until—

I crashed down to the end of the staircase, which was as dark as a crypt. *I made it.* I stumbled for balance as I ran towards the basement door. *I can escape them!* I pulled the security card up and hurriedly swiped it along the strip next to the door—

The door didn't open.

Wait. What? No, it has to work. I swiped it again then forcefully pulled at the handle. But it still wouldn't open. *This can't be happening.* I thought back to when I had been shown this room on one of my first placements with university. I'd definitely seen them swipe a security card here. *There wasn't any more to it, was there?*

"Samarra!"

My eyes widened as Ali ran onto the final flight of stairs. *No, no! I can't be trapped here! This basement door was my one exit! There's no other way out—*

Wait. Look. But then I saw a dizziness possessed Ali's balance. Sweat dripped across his forehead, mixing with dried blood. *He still has concussion symptoms.* He sniffed, wiping the back of his hand against his nose, while his eyes struggled to stay open. *He's still ill too. He's so much weaker than usual. Maybe I can fight him. I've done it before, so surely I can—*

"Finally." Another voice spoke before Ali could, as the blue-haired person appeared at the top of the stairs behind him. They wore a smart business suit and a sly grin, making them seem far more composed as no injury or illness slowed them down.

Scratch that, I can't fight two people. I have to get through this damn door.

"Now..." The blue-haired person leaned towards Ali, speaking directly into his ear. "Stop being so nice and take back what's ours."

Ali nodded in compliance before stepping down the final few stairs towards me. "Samarra. You beat me up and left me passed out in a damn church..."

I turned back to the door, my one escape. *I have to get out of here.* I swiped the security card again. And again. *Why isn't this thing working?* I twisted the card around and tried it the other way. *Please work!*

"Then to top it all off you stole a wad of money from me," Ali continued. "But that wasn't all you—"

BUZZ. The door clicked open. *Thank god.* I forcefully pulled it open and stepped inside.

"No, wait!" Ali shouted. "Wait!"

"Don't let her get away again!" the blue-haired person ordered.

"Samarra!" Ali picked up his pace as he ran towards me—

I *crashed* the door shut in his face.

"I just need my stuff back!" his muffled voice shouted. "I know you still have it!"

BANG. The door shook as Ali forced his weight into it. The wood splintered around the lock. *That won't last for long if he tries that again—no, not "if," when. I have to hurry.*

No other soul possessed this space, as only deafening silence greeted my presence. *No one's here to help me.* Tall filing cabinets dominated the room, staring down at me from ceiling height. They were organised in long rows, creating a tight maze that felt as suffocating as a mausoleum. I knew there was another exit on the other side of the room, giving me a chance to get away. But I also knew Evie's file would be here. *The answers I've been waiting for six months are here.*

BANG. The door shook again as Ali threw his weight against it.

He's going to break that door down! My head twisted in panic as I ran along the narrow rows, towards the back corner where I knew they kept the folders of the recently deceased. *Shouldn't I stop looking for the folder and run away before—*

'Do you really think people die like that by accident?' Death's words haunted my mind like a broken record that refused to stop playing. They made me think about how Mum and Zain had both avoided my questions, as though they knew Evie's death wasn't that simple. *But there must be something more going on here. There must be—*

BANG. The door burst open, falling off its hinges.

Ali walked into the room.

I'm out of time.

14

"Samarra!" Ali yelled as footsteps echoed through the room, moving at a fast pace: THU-THUD TH-THUD. *He's going to catch me!*

I didn't bother hiding as I reached the back corner of the room where boxes of dusty files waited. *I'm so close to finding Evie's folder, I can't stop now.* Dread impaled my gut as I searched through the folders, scanning alphabetically for Evie's name. *The answers I've been wanting are so close!* I looked over box after box, searching past the wrong names, searching until—

It's here. EVIE BLAIR.

I pulled out Evie's folder. Quickly I flicked through the pages, searching through the information. I scanned over the useless data, the general details, the names, the doctors, the pointless text until—

The autopsy report. It's here. It's—

"What are you doing?" Ali began.

I looked to the side. He was meters away from me. *He's found me. I need to run!* I glanced back to the report. *What am I doing? I'm wasting my chance to get away!* I searched through the information I desperately needed. *Stop this and run!* I kept looking until—

CAUSE OF DEATH: DRUG OVERDOSE.

My body froze. *No...*

I dropped the file. My breath got stuck in my throat as though I was being suffocated. *It wasn't a car accident?* My rib cage felt like it was pressing on my lungs, closing in on me. *But that means...* I gulped back hard. *Death was right.*

"I said, *what* are you doing?" Ali's breath beat against the back of my neck.

A chill ran down my spine. "I'm—"

Before I even had a moment to react, Ali's hands grabbed my neck. Then his fingers crushed into my windpipe.

An alarm screamed into my mind as my throat closed up. *Do something, fast!* My heart thudded with drowning panic. *It can only take ten seconds to pass out this way so hurry up!* Adrenaline swarmed into my bloodstream, overtaking the sharp shots of pain clawing into my throat.

"The wad of money you stole from me had a bag of Dust inside it. *My* Dust." Ali whispered into my ear. "Where is it?"

I couldn't respond as my voice tightened into a sore mess of bitter agony. *Do something. Now!* I kicked out my legs against a stack of boxes in front of me, pushing Ali backwards. *Push as hard as I can!* I shoved all my weight into it, forcing him to crash into the filing cabinets behind us. But he still didn't loosen his grip. *It's like he actually wants to kill me this time.*

"You don't even know what you've taken. You don't know how much it's worth," Ali continued. "Just give it back. You don't understand."

Breath hid itself from my lungs as consciousness threatened to slip away. Ali's strength was too much for me; it was too hard to push him off, *so don't push him off. Do something else. Find a weak spot!*

I grabbed one of the hands around my neck, and then I latched onto his pinkie finger. *Hurry up!* I gripped the finger tightly before I firmly pulled it, bending it backwards, twisting it in the wrong direction until it *snapped.*

Ali immediately let go of me as he howled in pain, clutching at his broken finger. I took a large breath in, doubling over as I coughed and sputtered for air. A stabbing shock of dehydration ran through me and stinging burns shouted out from my neck where Ali's fingernails had left trail marks. *Forget about breathing. Just get out of there before—*

THUMP. A sudden, sharp blow knocked into my chin as Ali's other fist soared into me. An excruciating ache tore into my skull. Blood streamed into my mouth as my teeth *cracked* into one another.

"I've given you so many chances! But all you've done is hurt me and rob me!" he yelled through a jumble of slurred vowels.

I glanced towards Ali with dizzying vision. His body was swaying. His nose was dripping. He was struggling to keep his eyes open. *He does have concussion symptoms. I still have a chance to escape.*

"Just tell me where the Hell it is, Samarra. I *can't* return empty-handed again." He raised his fist, ready to thrash it into me once more—

"Wait!" I put up my palms in defence. "I have it here!" I stumbled through my words that hurt to speak, as a fierce raspiness clung to my voice. "Just take it. Take it all." I reached into the side of my bra, pulling out the bundle of notes I'd stolen from him. "Take it!" I dropped the pile on the floor.

Ali stumbled to the ground, grasping every note he could.

Now run! I staggered back away from him. *Go!* I fell into a hobbled sprint as I scurried down the aisle of filing cabinets, before turning towards the other exit door. *Get out of here!*

"Wait!" Ali yelled. "It's not all here!"

I kept running, pushing my legs onwards, forcing them to move faster and *faster!*

"Samarra! It's not all here!" Ali shouted from behind me before his footsteps quickly followed. "Come back!"

I ran onto another stairwell, leaping up the stairs as fast as I could even as my ankle yelled in pain. *Damn these stupid heels.* Although a thunderous burn crashed through my leg, I forced myself to *keep running. I can lose him in the crowd of the hospital.*

I burst through the first door I found, staggering onto a corridor beaming with souls waiting for the final sleep to arrive. Most were dressed in identical clothing, either hospital gowns or scrubs with the same medical logo across them. *My black dress will stand out here, especially with how much it's tearing itself apart. I need to keep running!*

Quickly I turned around a sharp corner, moving into a busier ward. I skidded through the overflowing rush of bodies, dodging my way through the crowds of junior doctors, nursing teams, students, patients, life. *There must be some way to get out of here and run towards…*

Death.

My gaze was dragged towards the corner of the ward, where shadows twisted in a menacing prowl around a tall silhouette. *It's him…* The figure of Death was stalking through the tenebrous spiral of darkness, hungry for his next victim.

Death is here? He still looked far too human to be real. His hands were casually tucked inside his trouser pockets as he moved with the calm ease of a sedative. His white boots shook against the ground, emphatically placing each thudding step. And his piercing white eyes were glaring at a bed where a broken, bleeding body of a patient barely clung to life.

Why am I hallucinating Death again? The swirl of pain flurried around my limbs as sharply as it ran through my mind. But the pain was nothing like what I'd felt before, *which means I can't be dying. Does that mean I'm still poisoned? Or maybe I'm finally losing myself to insanity.*

I blinked several times as I stared towards Death's dark suit, his ticking pocket watch, his slicked-back silver hair. *But that's definitely him… Maybe I have lost my mind.*

Death's bright eyes looked towards mine. My body froze as his captivating gaze landed on my soul. He raised one eyebrow and tilted his head, as though he were unsure why I was seeing him too. But he simply flashed a smile that was drenched in confidence before turning back to the patient before him. Death wasn't here for me this time; he already had another victim set. And that's when the world slowed down.

Ambulance sirens fluttered over the hospital like a beautiful melody. The never-ending sound of patients crying danced through the room like piano notes. Staff members spoke in song. Gasps of pain joined the chorus. Beeps of machines added to the percussion. Then in the centre of it all was the rattle of breath coming from the patient's lungs. It was toppling over the melody, calling out for Death himself.

I knew the death rattle was a natural part of the dying process, caused by a buildup of mucus and saliva in the airways. I had heard it before, but I'd never paid much attention to it. Not until now that I saw Death himself stepping along to the beat of the music, following the rattle's tune.

Death strolled up to the dying patient before he placed his hands on their chest, feeling their shattered heartbeat. He let the *th-thuds* of the heart weaken, slowing the tempo, letting the dynamics of the music quiet into a soft hush. Then he moved his hand up to the patient's face, wiping away their tears. *I wonder if his touch feels as calming as it had for me…*

Suddenly the patient's soul sat up and took hold of Death's hand with a smile. Death kindly helped them up, before walking them towards his doorway; the doorway I swore hadn't been there a moment ago. Then they both stepped inside and vanished.

I used to believe Death was a darkness that crept over the individual, yanking their soul into the underworld where a senseless, comfortless existence awaited. But seeing this was… *beautiful. I wonder what it feels like to go through that doorway. I wonder if I could run into it and never be seen again…*

Wait. I could run into it. Couldn't I?

"Samarra!" Ali roared from somewhere in the crowd behind me.

No, I need to run into it. I started to move towards Death's doorway. *Ali won't find me there; no one will. That doorway can take me out of here. It'll let me escape Ali and his gang, escape Zain, my mum, my life, my arguments, my debts, my grief, my—*

Everything.

I have to go through that doorway. It's the only logical option.

I stepped towards the doorway. *I have to follow Death.* But my knees shook and my limbs stiffened as I moved closer, as though my life instinct were battling against my intentions. *That doorway is my one way out of here.* It felt like I was swimming against a sea of troubles, fighting for air on the river Styx. *I have to make it!* I pushed my body towards its greatest fear, struggling against every urge until—

I stepped through Death's doorway.

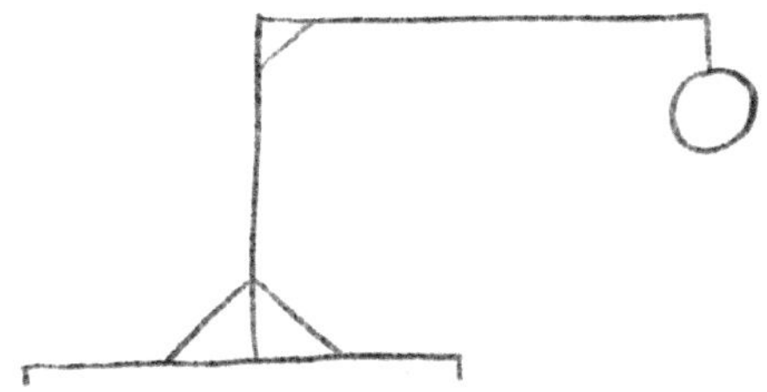

GONE TO A BETTER PLACE

15

I didn't want Evie to leave this world.

A rush of peacefulness flooded my body as I moved through Death's doorway. *I didn't want to lose her... I didn't... I...* My mind wiped itself clean as calmness drowned my senses, burying my worries in a beautiful silence.

The hospital was no longer behind me; nothing was behind me. Nothing was ahead of me either. No shapes or colours entered my vision. There wasn't a garden or clouds or anything else you'd expect. It was as though seeing images only added to the weight of the mind. Instead, the space was a comforting, quiet grave of darkness.

But I couldn't walk into it. I was stuck directly between the doorway and the darkness ahead, frozen on the precipice of that boundary. My body wouldn't allow me to move through the doorway, not yet.

I looked at the house of Hades beyond, wishing I could move into it. Its quiet space looked so soothing. It made me question whether this was still a powerful hallucination or something far beyond the realms of reality. Either way, I no longer seemed to care. Nothing mattered here, not even myself.

A blur of a figure stepped into view ahead of me, moving through the river of shadows like a ghost. It travelled across the space, floating aimlessly with unearthly movements—until their head *snapped* in my direction.

The figure instantly rushed towards me. But I couldn't step away from them; I couldn't move at all. I could only watch as their silhouette lengthened. Their features, their clothes, their hair—it all grew into focus, until it became familiar.

"Evie?" I whispered as my sister moved up to me.

Confusion entangled itself in my skull. I couldn't understand what was happening, how I was looking at Evie. She didn't even look like a deceased soul but rather seemed strangely full of life. She was dressed in her brightly coloured T-shirt and patterned shorts that didn't match, yet somehow she pulled it off. The bags under her eyelids were as big as mine, but her colourful makeup easily covered them. Rainbow colours adorned strands of her hair. Tattoos decorated her skin, piercings covered her ears, and a mustard-yellow jacket hung loosely around her. It was *my* jacket, the jacket she used to steal from me all the time, the jacket she wore in that terrible funeral picture. The jacket I still wanted her to somehow give back.

"I don't want you to die." Words echoed from my mouth without me even realising they were there.

"Die?" Evie laughed, seemingly comfortable in this lost world. "So you don't want one too?" She handed a packet of cigarettes towards me that read, SMOKING KILLS. "One cigarette won't kill you, Freckles."

I wanted to grab her or hug her or maybe even hit her. But she was standing a little too far away for me to reach. Then as I tried to step closer, I realised I still couldn't move. I was trapped in a paralysing dream I couldn't wake up from.

"You don't want one then? Suit yourself." Evie took back the packet, pulling out a cigarette with her teeth before she quickly lit it up. "That's more chances of dying for me." She breathed in the poisonous smoke with a devilish grin, brightening her face, which looked nothing like mine.

I used to enjoy having no family resemblance to her, as though I wanted to be seen as an entirely separate being. But now, staring at her bright blue eyes, which were the opposite of mine, I wished we looked more similar. I wished we had more in common so I could've kept a piece of her alive when I couldn't keep her.

"Evie? You…" My words barely made a sound. They were more like an echo that didn't have a source of origin. Even my thoughts were scarcely there, as only a calming bout of nothingness swam over my head. I'd forgotten everything, even the reason I'd walked through the doorway. I couldn't worry about the details of life now that I was on the edge of death.

As I watched Evie take another long drag of the cigarette, I remembered this was a memory of the last time I saw her. This was the last conversation we'd had together. These were the last awfully clashing clothes I saw her wearing. I could barely recall what I'd said to her, but I think it was something like:

"You really should be more careful with what you do to your body." I suddenly spoke without meaning to. The words seemed to reverberate from me like an old record that scratched at the tune it could never forget. "Do you know how harmful cigarettes are for—"

"I don't care, Sam."

"Why not? They could kill you."

"Sometimes you gotta play with death to know you're still alive." She snorted a laugh. "I wonder what death is like anyway…" Evie's voice also sounded like an echo of a memory that wasn't quite coming from her figure, but rather from my own mind. "Does it actually hurt?"

"What?" I remembered my body being exhausted during this conversation as I had just endured a full day on the wards in a stressful hospital placement. My eyes were begging for sleep and my limbs were praying to lie down. The worst part was that I wanted our conversation to be over. I never stopped and considered that it would be our last.

"Death. Does it actually hurt?" she repeated.

I remembered saying, "It's not supposed to hurt. The body was built to die just as it was built to live. It knows how to shut itself down. After all, we're just organs and brains and blood. Just piles of dust thrown together, which will one day be torn apart."

Evie nodded, taking another long drag of smoke. "I wonder what it feels like when we're just dust again." She looked off into the distance, as though there was a view to look at. "You'll bury me in Eidyn, right?"

"I don't know why you're so obsessed with that city."

"Who wouldn't be? It has castles and festivals and…and there's so much countryside around the city whenever you want to run across the hills and escape for a while. It's a paradise."

"Isn't it cold?"

"Cold? *That's* what you're worried about?" She shook her head. "The cold doesn't matter when everyone up there is so much friendlier. They have way less stress and way more love to give. Who wouldn't want to be part of that?"

"You've never even been." I remember feeling bored at the tiresome conversation.

"Maybe not, but I've been in Medlock long enough to know I don't like it here. This place was built on industrial factories. Everyone's just a cog in the endless machine. But in Eidyn, everything seems…magical." She looked back at me. "So you'll bury me there, right?"

"I'm not burying you anywhere. *You're* burying me."

"You'll have to start smoking too then if I'm going to outlive you, right?" Evie flicked her cigarette onto the floor, crushing its dying flame. "Are you afraid of dying?"

Why am I going along with this? I tried to break free from this lost memory to let in my screaming worries and unimaginable grief. But my head was too heavy with empty nothingness to know how to think for itself anymore.

"It's okay to be afraid, Sam," she continued. "Being afraid means being alive…and I haven't felt afraid in a long time."

I wanted to push my limbs through the doorway, to grab Evie and take her out of there. But all I could do was remember what I told her: "That's stupid. You're such an idiot."

"Only sometimes." She grinned before pulling an apple from her pocket and taking a *crunching* bite. "I love the first bite of an apple. It's such a good moment, isn't it?"

"What?"

"The moment when the sweet taste first touches your tongue. You think there's so much promise in that first bite, like you can't wait to devour the entire thing. But then as you take more and more bites…" She took another large bite. "It grows boring. Most people end up throwing away their apples before they're finished because the effort of eating it becomes more than the satisfaction of the taste… But that first bite. That *first* moment. That's the one I love."

"What are you talking about?" I remember feeling annoyed at her giving me yet another randomly specific moment. She did it all the time and it grew so tiring, so pointless, so trivial. I never understood why she continued doing it. "I don't have time for this."

"Wait. I…I know you've had a long day of work, but…are you sure you don't want to come to my gig tonight?"

Yes, yes yes. My mind tried to fight against its intense quietness. "Y…" I tried to form the right word. "Ye…" But even as I spoke the words—*Yes, of course I will come out with you, of course I'll watch your band even if I think it's going to be dreadful*— the only sounds that echoed around this space were the words I remembered saying: "No, I can't. I have an exam tomorrow I need to study for."

"But you always have to study. Surely you can take *one* night off?"

"I can't. I'm not like you, Evie. I can't charm my way into getting good grades. I need to actually work to be perfect."

"Who cares about being perfect?" She rolled her eyes. "You can take one night off after all the studying you've done. Come on, it's going to be a great performance. My band is so much better now. Ria will be there too, so you'll have a friend to hang out with."

"Ria's barely my friend anymore now that she's your girlfriend."

"That's not true. She's barely your friend because *you* never come out with us. You have to speak to people to keep them as friends, you know?" Evie let out a dramatic sigh. "Just come to the gig, Sam. It'll be fun! You can even meet Zain. It's crazy you haven't met him yet, you'd like him."

"And how much are you all going to be drinking?"

"However much we want."

"You know alcohol's bad for you, right?"

"*Everything* good is bad for you."

"Are you going to be taking other things too?" I asked in a judgemental tone. "Like…whatever it's called, that thing you took last time."

"You mean Dust?" Evie raised an eyebrow. "Everyone's taking it at the moment. You should try it too, it'll help you relax for once."

"But you don't even know what it really *is*. No one does. Who knows how damaging it could be on your body. Mum said it's dangerous—"

"Of course Mum said that. Adults don't get how fun it can be. So why don't you just *live* a little for once, Sam. You'll have a good time if you come out, instead of staying indoors like a damn hermit."

Yes, of course I will— "No, I'm busy."

"You're always *busy*. Why can't you come out this one time? For me? Please."

I frowned at that. Evie never said please.

"Please," she said again, as though the memory were taunting me.

Yes, of course I will. I don't care if your drumming annoys me, if you wear my jacket, if you say stupidly dumb specific things. I just want one more night by your side. I tried to push myself through the doorway again, to save Evie from the underworld, to do what even Orpheus couldn't—

But the more I tried, the more my energy drained, as though it were killing my body to go across. It was futile fighting against the inevitability of death. There was no hope for anyone here; it had all been abandoned.

"No, I can't come out." My words pulsated around the memory.

"Fine." Blood dripped from Evie's nose, but she wiped it away before I had a chance to register it. "Screw you." She threw the rest of the apple to the side before taking out another cigarette and quickly lighting it up. "You know what? I hope these *do* kill me and I hope death *does* hurt. Because nothing can be more painful than whatever this life is."

"Stop being so dramatic."

"Dramatic? Go to Hell." Evie glanced at her yellow watch before she turned and walked away. "I'm going to go find Death now. He'll be so much more peaceful than *this*."

I sighed, frustrated with her strange poetry. "At least give me my jacket back before you go find him."

Evie pulled the jacket tighter around her as she kept moving away. "You can take it off my damn corpse!" she shouted before she disappeared into the murky darkness.

"Maybe I will!"

Wait, wait! Why did I say that? Why were those my last words to her? I tried to push myself through that doorway once more, wanting to chase after her, to apologise, to say everything I should've said. But the more I tried, the more my body collapsed in on itself. My legs shook as they lost the energy to stand. My arms dropped to my side, refusing to be lifted. *No, please, Evie! Come back! I'm sorry! I'm so sorry.*

Grief branded itself into my heart like the powerful torture-chambers of Hell, burning me alive with its fire and brimstone. Yet there was no need for red-hot pokers when the worst torment was losing the people we love most. Seeing Evie leave was a pain like no other, slashing into my guts as I watched her patterned clothes, her colourful hair, and my yellow jacket swallowed by the darkness.

That was the last sight I saw of her, when she was just a flickering shadow, too far in the distance for me to call back, too far away for me to reach again—

Suddenly her silhouette moved back towards me. Yet now her figure was a mangled twist of shadows, moving at speed. A deeper gloom possessed her figure as it fiercely sprinted at me, contorting itself in and out of shape the closer and closer it got.

What's happening? My thoughts piled back into me, crushing one another in a stampede of worries as the shadow rushed closer. *Evie's dead. I didn't save her. I didn't even go out with her on the final night she was alive.* My emotions pounded into my skull with the strength of a tidal wave. *I'm a horrible older sister who doesn't deserve to still be here when she's over there—*

Wait. The flurry of shadows merged into a tall, humanoid shape. *That's not Evie.* My heart kicked itself with pumping adrenaline as it grew closer. Blood pounded through my head. Panic sprinted through my veins. *It's him…* And Death himself sprinted towards me.

16

Death darted at me like an angry spirit, full of unimaginable power. A malicious strength bled from his figure as he raised his hands in front of him, ready to knock me away with one brutal push—

A gust of wind shot me backwards. My body tore through the air, falling away from the doorway, away from the darkness, away, away, away—until my back hit a wall. The hospital sounds shrieked into life. The beeps, the cries, the rushes of footsteps, the constant noise that ripped away my peace—it all submerged me in its tomb of chaos.

The patient Death had taken through the doorway was now nothing but a cadaver, lying in bed behind a poorly shut curtain. I stood at the far end of the ward, lost in the shadows in the corner of the room. My back was pressed against the wall. My limbs were as stiff as a corpse's heart. My lungs felt like they were glued shut.

And Death stood in front of me.

A stampede of questions rushed through my mind as I looked at him with abundant curiosity. *How did I just see Evie? Is this all some crazy hallucination? Is my mind failing me as much as my body—*

"Those worries will kill you faster than I will if you don't learn how to look after them." Death's words thudded through my head, numbing my thoughts like a powerful elixir as his sweet lavender scent filled the space between us.

No one in the room noticed us as Death cornered me. *It must be a hallucination if no one else can see him. But why on earth does he seem so…real?* His piercing eyes looked into mine as he leaned his hand on the wall next to my head. He raised his eyebrows, putting his face close to mine, refusing to break his stare.

Why am I still seeing Death as a human? How is he nothing like what a powerful god should look like—

"I'm far more powerful than any god. Far more popular too." He grinned. "And I told you not to dare be afraid of me. Being afraid of me means you fear me. But you know nothing about me, and you cannot fear what you do not know." He leaned in even closer. "So do not be afraid." His words melted into me, giving me a glimpse of his beautiful quietness—

And that was all I needed as I gasped for breath. My limbs unfroze, my lungs clicked back into their never-ending movement, and my heart continued its marching beat. *What… what just happened?* I was somehow still living, even though Death's cold eyes were staring right at me.

"I can't tell if you're brave or stupid for daring to follow me when I did not lead you. But I can't say I'm surprised." He ran his tongue over his sharp teeth. "I knew you were intrigued by my presence, just as your sister was."

I tried to centralise my thoughts, but they raced with questions that didn't have answers: *Am I dying? Why is Death here? Is this even real or is my mind lost in delusions?*

"This can be as real as you want. After all, Hell is just a frame of mind," Death chuckled. "And your mind clearly wants me, that's why I'm still here. You had a whole hospital to run and hide in to get away from Ali. Yet you chose to follow me. Why are you clinging to death instead of life?"

Ali…Ali was *chasing me, along with the blue-haired person from his gang. They both wanted to hurt me.* Adrenaline poured into my veins as I realised I was back in the hospital. *They could be anywhere. They could walk in here any second—*

"Don't worry about them. Don't forget you *have the power over life and death just the same as they do. Mortals are all alike, after all. You each have a heart that can be stopped."*

I frowned. *What do you mean? I can't fight them both if that's—*

"Stop worrying. It won't do you any good. Just focus on me, Samarra Blair. You're safe by my side."

Safe? But you…you had Evie through the doorway. My mind rushed ahead of me in a tsunami of panic, refusing to be tamed. *That was the last time I spoke to her. Those were the last words she said to me before she died. But she was far too young to die—*

"Everyone always is," Death stated with no room for dispute. *"Yet everyone's life is always complete at that moment, with a line drawn neatly under it."*

No, it's not complete. How did I see her otherwise? Where was that place? I need to go back and tell her so many things I should've—

"That was nothing more than a memory, a life flashing before your eyes. There's nothing you can say or do that will change it now." Death's words cut off my thoughts, quieting them like a powerful narcotic. *"Just as there's nothing to change* how *she died."*

I paused. *She…she didn't die from a car accident. She died of an overdose. You were right.*

"I always am. But you already knew that, didn't you?"

What?

"You already knew she died from an overdose. You were smart enough to figure it out long ago."

No, I didn't know—

"Of course you knew. Wasn't it obvious? You saw her die, after all. You may just be a medical student, but you know the difference between an overdose and a car collision."

I shook my head, not wanting to let the memories back in.

"You watched her suffer in those final few moments. You've simply been repressing the memory, haven't you? I guess the truth is always too painful to accept. Lies are far kinder to broken minds."

My thoughts threw up blank walls, stopping myself from remembering the night Evie died in this very hospital. Maybe I'd considered her death to be due to drugs, but I'd never accepted it. Taking an overdose meant her death was preventable. *It meant I could have saved her.*

"Evie didn't want to be saved. She wanted me." Death smiled, showing off his far-too-human dimples. *"I told you, do you really think people die like that by accident? Do you really think people take that big of an overdose without meaning for it to drag them away from life?"*

No, she didn't want you. No one wants you!

"No one?" Death moved his hand towards my face. *"You of all people know that's not true. Everyone wants me in the end."* Gently he stroked his fingers against my cheek—

A heavenly bliss abducted my mind as his hands met my skin, robbing me of all my emotions, worries, regrets, questions, everything, leaving only a tranquilising stillness behind.

"That's why you followed me, because you want me too."

I should have protested, but I was far too lost in his hypnotic touch to bother. A deep drowsiness clouded my senses. My body felt like it was safe in hibernation, free of all dangers, lost in his intoxicating world.

"One day I'll give you what you want, Samarra Blair." Death smiled before he suddenly tore his hand away from me and stepped backwards. *"But not today. I'm needed elsewhere."*

The second he left my space I doubled over. Coughs caught in my throat as I fought to catch my lost breath. Exhaustion swarmed over my legs as though they were learning how to stand for the first time. Then my worries came screaming back—

Evie couldn't have wanted to die. She couldn't have meant to take those drugs. Thoughts flooded my brain in a howling panic as Death moved away. *Why didn't I save her? Why am I such an awful older sister? Why am I still alive when she's—*

I looked up at Death, watching his beautiful peacefulness leave. He was walking back towards a hospital door that was full of posters with simplistic, shallow slogans over them such as: DRUG FREE IS THE WAY TO BE and SAY NO—

Say no. Don't do it. I wiped my running nose as I steadied my panting breaths, keeping my eyes on Death's figure. *Don't even think about it.* I watched his calmness, his powerfulness, his understanding—I watched it all move farther away from me. *Don't follow him. Don't—*

But he's the only one who'll speak to me about Evie's death. No one else will even have a conversation with me about her. I just want to talk about her again. I just want someone who'll actually speak to me instead of shutting me down...

Death turned around, giving me one last, lingering smile before he casually strolled out the door. *Don't do it. Don't do it. Don't—*

Screw it. Then for some strange reason, I followed.

17

"Wait!" I shouted towards Death, as though he could hear my mortal words. *I have to catch up to him and find out what happened when Evie died. I have to know if I could have saved her! I can't let him go. I can't let* her *go.*

Death tucked his hands into his trouser pockets as he walked into an overflowing hospital corridor. Still no one else turned to look at him or even glance in his direction. Only I could see his warm flesh of a face and all-too human appearance. I didn't even care if I was chasing a hallucination or if I really was chasing Death himself. All I cared about was catching up to him and feeling his peacefulness one more time.

Wait, don't leave! I screamed across my mind, across my insurmountable pain. *You need to tell me why Evie overdosed! You need to bring her back from that doorway or you need to take me there again!* Desperation boiled inside me as I followed Death, dodging through the crowded corridor, burning through my instinct for life to keep up with his pace—

Suddenly a hand grabbed my shoulder. A real, human hand that was trembling with life, full of sweat and warmth and an unsteady heartbeat. *Ali's caught me. He must've found me to hurt me again!* It pulled me backwards, away from the calmness of Death and back towards—

"You're insane. You know that, right?" Zain began. A quiet rage covered his face, replacing his usual positive smirk.

"Zain?" A harsh raspiness struck through my voice, reminding me of the pain of strangulation ringing through my throat and sharp dehydration overwhelming my mouth. *It's not Ali, thank god. But I still can't be here; I can't stay in this world when I know how to get out.* "I...I can't do this." I turned away from Zain as I looked back towards the darkness of Death, which I never wanted to leave—

But Death had vanished from sight. *What?* His calmness had disappeared, abandoning me in the tomb of reality. *Where did he go? I need him. I can't stay in my overwhelming mind knowing there's a way to silence it.*

"*You* can't do this?" Zain scoffed. "*You're* the one who used me! You weren't studying for an exam, you were breaking into hospital records." Pure emotion flowed from his voice in energising bouts of life. He was too loud, too enlivened, too much for me to take.

"I... How do you even know that?" I hesitated, turning again, searching through the rush of the wards. *Death must be here somewhere. If he's my hallucination, I can find him again. If he's not, I know how to find death in a hospital. It isn't hard.*

"I'm not an idiot, Sam, despite how much you'd like me to be one." Zain breathed through his anger, gradually calming his tone.

"I…I *do* have an exam, it wasn't a lie. I just…haven't been studying for it." I was only half listening to the conversation as I scanned the busy corridors around us, wondering which ward would have the highest chance of death.

"Is that because you've been risking your career instead? And risking *my* livelihood? My probation officer doesn't even know I'm here, so what do you think would've happened if that security guard had informed them? Do you even realise what the Shade would do to me if they arrested me again? I can*not* go back to Detention." He wiped his sore eyes while breathing through his anger. "Next time, please just talk to me instead of getting me escorted off the damn premises."

"I…I know I probably went too far," I admitted even through my distraction. "I'm sorry for saying all of that, but you *are* a grown man. Losing your temper is your own fault."

Zain stopped. A smile tugged at his lips, as though he were trying to still find some amusement even in the havoc of the world. "You really are insane, but smart, I'll give you that. You knew exactly how to get a rise out of me." He pushed back his hair. "However…" He hesitated. "You didn't actually mean what you said, right? It was all just a ploy to get that security card?"

I paused, hearing the pain behind his question. "Did you mean any of what you said?"

He paused too.

I nodded. *Of course he meant what he said when he told me Evie hated me. Why wouldn't she hate me after everything I failed to do—* "I have to go," I said, interrupting my own crash of thoughts. I didn't want them eating my mind anymore; I couldn't face all the stress they carried. I just wanted quiet again: I wanted Death. *I need to find him. Now.*

"Wait." Zain grabbed my wrist with an unfamiliar softness, pulling me towards him. "I'm sorry, Sam. If you want to talk about Evie, we can. But I'd rather focus on her life than her death. I'm guessing you found out…" He stopped, frowning at me. "Are you all right?" He studied my face, staring at the bruises that decorated my chin, the raised nail marks Ali had left across my neck, the blood trickling from my mouth, and the sweat pouring from my forehead. "What the Hell happened to you? Did someone hurt you *here*?"

"I… It's not important." I pulled my hand from his unstable grasp.

"Not important?" Confusion rang through Zain's voice. "Of course it's important. *You're* important. Who the Hell has hurt you?"

"I said it's not important. Just leave me alone, please. I have to go." I turned away, resuming my journey down the spiralling hospital wards.

"Wait, Sam. Come back!"

I ignored him as I continued to push my way through the overcrowded hives of people, scanning for Death. *I saw Death when I almost died, then I saw him again when he took that patient's life. Surely I just need to find another dying body? He's the guide to the dying, the one who takes their soul away. The one who'll take mine too.*

"Sam, wait! Please tell me what's going on with you." Zain followed behind me.

"Nothing. I just…I need a walk."

"A walk? Through a hospital?"

"It's calming," I said, barely paying attention to him as I looked from patient to patient, trying to figure out what was wrong with them and how close to death they were: *They're waiting for an x-ray. They're waiting to be sent home. They're drunk; they shouldn't be here. They have a cold; they shouldn't be here either.*

"A hospital isn't calming," Zain said. "Are you…all right? Maybe we should find a doctor to check on you."

I ignored his concern, pushing my way through each languishing ward. *Next patient. Car accident, possibly broken leg and ribs. They're not going to die. Next patient. Alcohol again. They're much worse than the others; they'll survive though. They're not going to die… God, why is it so hard to find death in a hospital? Shouldn't he be ruling over this place?*

"Hey, Sam. *Sam!*" Zain relentlessly tried getting my attention. "Come on. I think it's time to go back home, isn't it? Back to reality?"

"No, I…I can't go there," I said absentmindedly. *Next patient. Still waiting to be discharged. They'll be waiting forever.*

"Then maybe we could go get some food somewhere and have a real conversation for once? We could go into town and get some chips and gravy at that place Evie loves." He paused. "I mean…loved."

A sting cut through my stomach. Past tense was such a simple grammatical concept. But for some reason grief made it feel so dark and twisted, like a brutal punch to the face. *Who knew grammar could be so cruel?*

"I…I can't." I quickened my pace, trying to outrun my bloodthirsty thoughts.

"Please can we just talk! Will you just focus on me, just focus on being alive?" Zain kindly touched my shoulder, wanting to guide me back to my overwhelming life—

I shook his hand off, not letting it resuscitate me. *Next patient. They need a GP, not a hospital. Next patient. They have a minor burn; they'll be fine.* I looked over each body, trying to find one who was dying, one who had a rattle to their breath. But they were all alive, and I hated them for it. *Why is Evie dead and yet all these people are alive? Why do they get that privilege and she doesn't?*

Next patient: probably a sprained ankle; they'll be okay. Next patient: they have a gash on their arm; they'll be okay too. Next—

"Evie didn't hate you!" Zain shouted, yelling over the hospital noises, not caring who heard. "I shouldn't have ever said that she did, because she didn't!"

My feet stopped moving as my ears forced me to listen.

"She never hated you. She just wished she could've spent more time with you."

If only she'd had more time…

"And Sam…" Zain's footsteps echoed as his beaming life stepped up to me. "I'm sorry about earlier. I'm sorry I didn't just tell you about Evie's death." He cracked his knuckles in agitation. "It just felt easier when everyone believed it was a car accident. The second someone mentions a Dust overdose, everyone becomes so much more critical and unsympathetic."

So it was Dust that killed her. My eyes kept looking around the wards, wanting to escape this conversation, wanting to find the patient Death was after. *Next patient, probably some broken ribs. Next patient, drunk again, seriously? Next patient—*

They're going to die.

"But Evie didn't want to be remembered that way," Zain continued as though I were still listening. "She only ever wanted us to live just as much as she did. That's why she wanted me to meet you and look out for you. She wanted me to make sure you were living, instead of only focusing on—"

Death. His next target is here. Zain's words faded as the beautiful sound of a death rattle crashed into my ears. *They're going to die. Finally.*

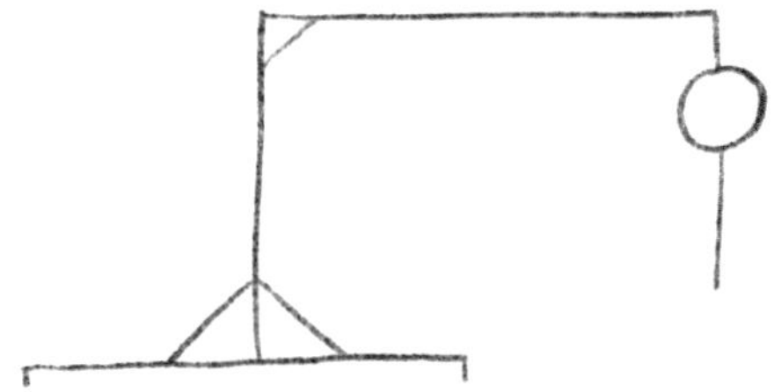

SIX FEET UNDER

18

How am I supposed to carry on without her?

A harrowing retching noise echoed towards me as a patient staggered into the nauseating rush of the emergency room. Sickly yellow bile dripped from their mouth. White powder surrounded their nostrils, which were gushing with dark blood. And a deathly rattle reverberated from every breath they took. *They have to be Death's next victim.*

I walked towards the patient, moving past the other bodies waiting endlessly to be seen. No one had even noticed the dying patient walk in yet, as stress blinded the overworked staff, *which means they won't be saved. They're going to die. Death will surely be here any moment.*

"Help…" the patient said through a cracked, fading voice. "Please, I—" They collapsed onto their knees, too weak to hold themselves up. "Mariana…she…" They trailed off as a coffin of pain enclosed them.

"It's okay," I hushed as I stepped up to them. "Your pain will be over soon."

Thunderous, emphatic footsteps marched into the room. *He's here.* Death finally entered, strolling at a calm pace though a cruel hunger haunted his eyes. *I knew I could find him again.* It looked like he was whistling, but I couldn't focus on the noise long enough to catch the tune, as though it weren't meant for me. His hands were in his pockets, his shoulders relaxed. He didn't look like he was about to take someone's life, but people never do.

You're here. I smiled at his enchanting appearance. *I have so much more I need to talk to you about—*

"Sam?" Zain suddenly stepped in front of my view, blocking Death's figure.

What is he still doing here? "Zain, I told you to leave me—"

"Oh shit…" His voice ran cold with fear as he saw the dying patient. "What just…what… We should get help. We need to get them to a doctor."

"It's okay," I said. "He's here now—"

"A doctor's here?" Zain ran trembling hands through his hair over and over in agitation.

"No, Death's here. Can't you see him?" *No, he can't see Death. No one else is blessed with his presence.*

"What are you talking about? They're still alive." Zain looked around hesitantly, before shouting at the top of his lungs. "Help! Someone! Please, help us!"

"We don't need help. It took me so long to find Death, I can't lose him again—"

"Sam, focus!" Zain grabbed hold of me and shook my shoulders. *Focus on being alive.* "I don't know what's going on with you, but get it together. You must've been to this hospital loads. Where do I go to get help?"

"I…I don't…" I stuttered. "I don't think we need—"

"I'll find someone then. But you're almost a doctor, right? So help them."

"I'm not a doctor yet—"

"Help them. *Now.*" Zain choked and coughed, dry heaving at the sight of the vomit running from the patient's mouth. "They're too young to die."

Too young to die? I looked back at the patient's panicked face, which twisted in agony. They looked about nineteen, the same age Evie is—*No, Evie was.*

"I'll find a doctor." Zain stumbled away with dizzying instability, shouting for help across the room.

I kept my stare on the patient, on their failing body, their paling face, the white powder stuck around their nostrils— *Powder? Did they overdose? Like Evie?*

I have to help them. A lost part of my brain screamed to be heard. *I can't let them die like I let Evie die!* I quickly knelt next to the patient, moving to put them into the recovery position—

Death crouched next to me. *The end we've all been promised. He's here at last.* His dimples lit up his face like a blissful remedy to life's suffering. His dark suit only made his white eyes brighter. Then his tongue ran over his teeth as he stared at the body, waiting for its soul.

"You looked me in the eyes yet you dared to continue living." Death's words ran across my mind. *"But here you are, searching for me again... I told you everyone wants me."*

My eyes locked onto Death's sedative smile. I didn't even stop to wonder why I was still seeing him or what was happening in my lost mind. I was too grateful for his presence to question it again.

I...I wanted to know more. I thought towards him. *I need to know about Evie's death, if she did it on purpose. I wanted to know if I could've saved her if I had—*

"No, you didn't want any of that. You wanted to feel peace again. You wanted me." Death's stare didn't break with mine. *"There's too much panic and sadness trapped in that little mind of yours.*

Emotions really are just as burdensome as thoughts, aren't they? No wonder you want my help to escape it all."

No, I did want to know about Evie. I doubted myself. *Evie... Evie couldn't have meant to die. She had so much life left in her, so much left to do.*

"You shouldn't be so worried about what's left undone in life. The only thing every soul needs to do is die." He whispered into my thoughts. *"The aim of all life is death, after all. Anything aside from that is too minor to even consider."*

But she was too young—

"It doesn't matter what she was. She could've been the greatest warrior who had victoriously walked away from countless battles, yet I'd still be awaiting her appointment. No matter how great they are, how young they are, how evil or good—I am waiting for them all." Death leaned towards the patient before us, placing his hands on their chest. He let the *th-thuds* of the heart slow, relieving the body from its torture.

But... I jerked my eyes between the patient and Death in a panicked frenzy. *Please just tell me if I could have saved her...*

"You can't save anyone from me." He moved his hand up to the patient's face, wiping away their tears in the same mechanical movements I'd seen him perform. The patient then relaxed at Death's lulling touch, giving in to the beautiful sleep of the unknown.

Anyone? But... My hands were still next to their body, ready to leap into action. *They're still alive...* The small triangle tattoo on my wrist stared up at me. *They still have a chance to be saved. If they overdosed, doctors can help get it out of their system. Just as I could've helped Evie if I'd gone out that night. I could've given her that chance to live—*

"You think life and death are determined by chance?"

I...I think people can be saved. Doctors save people all the time—

"You're not a doctor, and you're never going to be one. But you know that already. That's why you didn't want to come to the hospital today, isn't it?" Death grinned at me. *"How's the studying for that exam going? Have you told everyone yet?"*

My thoughts tripped over themselves as they searched for answers I didn't want. *I can still save people even if—*

"They don't need saving. They need someone to set them free." Death looked towards the patient with a kind thoughtfulness. *"Everyone has an appointment with me and one day yours will come too, Samarra Blair. Only then will you truly understand my work."* He leant towards them, ready to kiss them softly on the forehead—

"Stop!" I shouted before I even knew the word had left my mouth.

"You want me to stop?" Death raised an eyebrow. *"Don't you see how much pain they're in?"*

Just because they're suffering doesn't mean you *have to take them. They can live longer. Evie could've lived longer.*

"Do you really believe that? You really think they'd rather be left in their suffering?"

Yes, life is better than death. Anything is better than—

"Fine." A smirk grew across Death's face. *"I'll let them face the burdens of being alive."*

Suddenly he pulled his hands off the person's chest and moved his peacefulness away. The patient immediately coughed and choked on their breaths, as though they had something lodged in their throat. Their face burned with blazing sweat. Their body convulsed and their limbs flailed in an agonising fit.

Death stood up, walking away from the body. *"If you truly think suffering is better, I'll let them suffer."*

19

A terrified expression haunted the patient's face as their breathing stopped. Their mouth gasped in agonal breaths. Their lungs wouldn't move. They couldn't take any air in. They couldn't properly breathe—

Do something! Prove they can be saved, just as Evie could've been saved! "Help! I need help!" I shouted, looking around the emergency room, scanning for any sign of a doctor, a nurse, Zain, *anyone*. But only haunted, lost souls roamed the place, too lost in their suffering to notice anyone else's.

Hurry up, they're not breathing! I automatically placed my hands on top of the patient. I interlaced my fingers, then pushed down my palms down into their chest as I started compressions. The patient's ribs cracked under the weight of my hands and a greater wave of torment drowned their breath, paralysing their shattered lungs.

"We both know this won't prevent my work, only prolong it. You know you cannot stop me."

I looked up to Death now casually leaning against the wall with his hands tucked into his pockets, looking down at me with curiosity. I stared back at him, daring to be brave enough to look Death in the eyes and continue living.

Watch me.

Death gave a silent laugh. *"I'm watching."*

I counted the compressions: *six, seven, eight, nine…* I focused on the patient, on saving a life. I didn't think about how kind Death's smile looked, how enchanting his gaze was, how much I wanted to stay with him, safe from cruel reality—

Focus. My muscles burned as the energy drained from my arms with every movement: *twelve, thirteen, fourteen, fifteen. Just fifteen more!*

"How long do you think you can keep them alive?" Death swung his pocket watch. *"They'll join me eventually. Everyone does. Your*

sister was always going to join me too. Even if you had saved her one day, she would have met me the next."

No, she didn't need to go so soon! —twenty-one, twenty-two, twenty-three—

"*I saved her from her suffering. I was going to save this person too. But now you're just increasing their pain."*

I'm not, I'm helping them! —twenty-eight, twenty-nine, thirty! I leaned over towards them, ready to breathe life into their—

The patient gasped in an excruciating breath that was swimming in blood.

See? I did it. They're breathing. They can live!

"*You mean they can suffer."*

Confusion crawled over my skin as I studied the patient. Their body writhed and twisted like a snake without its head in an uncontrollable spasm of a seizure. A pool of vomit had formed underneath them, seeping into their clothes. Torturous pain engulfed their face as their eyes bulged and their lips turned blue.

"Stop…" The patient croaked through a voice that barely existed anymore. "Please…" Their neck twisted as they looked over to Death. Their arms bent back against their sockets, contorting in a desperate attempt to reach out towards him. "Please."

"No, don't look at him," I said through teary eyes. "Please, Evie, don't look at him. Just stay with me." I bit down on my tongue. *It's not Evie, it's not Evie…*

"*You can't save everyone, Samarra Blair."* Death stepped closer before leaning down next to the patient once more. "*Especially those who don't want to be saved."* He held out his warm hands, placing them on the patient's chest. He then felt for a heartbeat again, feeling the rush of energy granting them life, ready to take it away.

Don't take them, please.

"I'm not taking them. They're simply leaving with me." Death kept up his gentle smile as his white eyes looked down to the patient. *"I can end their suffering, just as easily as I ended hers."*

A confusing flood of doubt wrapped around my thoughts. The patient was in so much pain, just as Evie was. *But wasn't there another way to ease Evie's suffering? Did she really have to leave me?*

"I don't expect you to understand my work." Death's eyes transformed out of their piercing white and bled into darkened pits of emptiness, full of a fierce hunger that wanted to feed on the patient's soul. *"The living cannot truly experience the calmness of death; they're only left with the darkness of it."*

But...surely they can be saved. Surely they don't actually want you—

"Everyone wants me in the end." He smiled at me with a soothing reassurance I didn't know existed. *"And make no mistake, this is, and always was, their end."* He kissed the patient on the forehead, releasing them into everlasting peace.

The patient's limbs collapsed in a sudden cessation of movement, as though a bullet had been shot through their skull. Their eyes rolled back, their face paled, and their soul finally slept.

I let out a shredding scream of grief. *I thought I could've saved them!* I pulled back my hands, seeing them stained with spots of blood. The blood was so fresh, so warm, just like the body. Like Evie's dead body. *I thought I could've saved her!*

The soul of the patient then sat up with an elegant grace, moving away from their hollow corpse. Death kindly offered his hand to them and they took it without a moment's hesitation before standing up and moving towards the bright doorway. The doorway I swore hadn't been there a moment ago.

I think other bodies were moving around me. I think nurses were tending to the body. I think voices were echoing across the room—"Was it Dust?" "Another one?" "Why does this keep happening?"—but I couldn't focus on any of them. All I could do was let my breath fall into shallow stutters as I watched Death calmly lead the patient's soul through that glimmering doorway.

I failed them, just as I failed Evie. I sniffed as tears escaped my eyes and my heart pounded in disbelieving terror. I wondered what all those years at medical school were for if I was such a poor excuse for a doctor. *What's the point of trying to save others if I couldn't even save my own sister—*

Stop! I screamed through my mind as I staggered onto my feet, staring towards Death. *You don't have to take them. You don't have to do this!*

"It's already done." Death kindly hushed, as the patient stepped through that bright doorway.

No! I ran towards them, ready to grab onto their soul, to drag them back to their body, just as I wished I could drag Evie back to hers. *You don't have to kill them! Please bring them back! Bring her back!* I reached out towards the doorway and—

20

A winter's breeze fiercely blew over my skin, freezing my bones as though they'd been buried. *I'm outside?* I had walked through the hospital exit without realising. *How am I out here? Had Death's doorway disappeared before I had a chance to follow?*

The evening sun was fading over Medlock's grey skies, setting in a feverish burn of orange that refused to create my lost shadow. The persistent rain had finally stopped, but icy glimmers of white powder covered the ground. My bones violently shivered in the chill of the evening as confusion stabbed into my mind like a knife.

"You have a lot to learn, Samarra Blair." Death's twisted voice hammered into my skull as he suddenly stepped up behind

me. *"For starters, I don't kill anyone."* He stood inches away, whispering in my ear as the wind tore its way around us.

You just did. My limbs were fixed in position, unable to turn back towards Death or move away from his controlling presence. *You killed that person before they had a chance to live!*

"Is that really what you think of me?" Death leaned closer, letting the warmth of his breath beat against the back of my neck. *"Let me make this clear: I do not kill anyone. I did not take that person's life, the drugs in their system did."* His words boomed through me like a storm. *"Whoever gave them those drugs are the ones to blame. Humans are the ones that kill. I merely save souls from the suffering that others inflict."*

I couldn't break away from Death's words, as though he had hypnotised my mind and was holding me captive.

"That goes for your sister too. I didn't kill Evie. The drugs she overdosed on did."

No... I tried pushing his voice out of my thoughts, not wanting to listen. But he only grew louder.

"Yes. The drugs killed her, not me. If you really want someone to take your anger out on, why don't you find the person who gave her the drugs?" Death raised his hand, pointing his finger over my shoulders, directing my gaze to the pavement in front of me.

A few figures haunted the outdoors area, dripping with exhaustion as they travelled to and from the overflowing car park, either escaping the hospital or reluctantly moving towards it. An officer car was parked across part of the pavement, arrogantly blocking the pedestrian path. But it was as empty as the security cameras looking down at me. And just behind it stood a familiar figure.

The figure instinctively stood below the camera, hiding in its blind spot. They leaned against the old, redbrick walls of the building as they smoked a cigarette, resting on more simplistic posters that read: END THE HABIT BEFORE IT ENDS YOU and YOU USE, YOU LOSE. They breathed in the poisonous smoke regardless. They even wore a tank top despite the cruel chill of winter, showcasing patterned tattoos of thorny vines across their muscled arms.

Ali.

"He's the drug dealer, isn't he? He's the person who supplied Dust to Evie. That means he gave her the drugs that killed her. He's the one who put your little sister in so much suffering that I had to take her out of it."

Ali killed her…

"If you want a target to take your anger out on, there he is. Why don't you hurt him just like he hurt Evie?"

Hurt? But…I can't hurt him. He's too strong—

"No one is too strong. He's just a mortal with a heart that can be stopped, like he stopped Evie's." Death's words drew out a quiet rage from my skull. He forced it to claw its way to the surface as I realised he was right, again. *"You've been running away from Ali in sheepish defence for so long, when really you should have been running towards him. You should be the one in control, not him. Don't you want revenge for Evie? Doesn't she deserve that?"*

My hands tightened into fists as guilt crashed into my anger. *I shouldn't have let her take those drugs. No, I shouldn't have let Ali give her the drugs in the first place.*

"You're right. So what are you going to do about it now?"

I stared at Ali as a tidal wave of rage entered my thoughts. *Ali supplied Evie with Dust. Ali took Evie's life and I didn't stop it…* Then without realising it, my feet began moving forwards, marching towards Ali. *Ali is the one who deserved to die, not Evie.*

"Why don't you give him exactly what he deserves?"

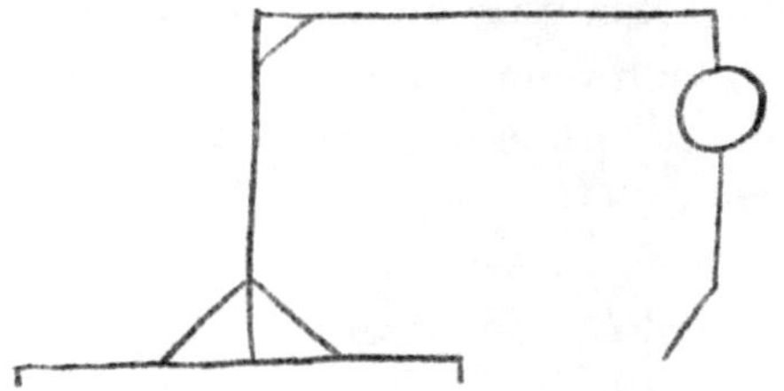

FALL ON YOUR SWORD

21

How am I supposed to carry on living in a world ruled by Death?

Shrieking ambulances rushed to the hospital, racing to save the life of whoever was inside. A few bodies haunted the pavements, ignoring the suffering of everyone around them as they focused on their own. Security cameras tracked their movement, keeping an eye on who was coming and going and who the city would never see again. But I ignored the signs of life around me as I walked up to Ali with my mind stuck on Death.

My hands were stained with blood, my face tarnished with tears, and rage flooded my skull. *Death's right: Ali is the one who sold Evie Dust, who made her overdose. Ali's the one who should be dead, not her. Ali has a heart that can be stopped just as easily as hers was—*

"*So let's stop it.*" Death's words reverberated through my thoughts, refusing to perish until I listened. "*Let's take his life as easily as he took hers.*" His alluring presence moved behind me, whispering in my ear, encouraging me to *keep going.*

Ali hadn't spotted me yet. He was still leaning against the hospital wall, hidden directly under the security camera as he smoked a cigarette with a relaxed posture. *Relaxed enough to catch him off guard.* The blue-haired person was no longer with him, giving me a chance to fight while he was by himself. *I can hit him while I have the advantage, before he can react and use his strength against me, before anyone else joins him. Do it now. Go for a weak spot. Hurt him where it'll count!*

"Hey! What the Hell is wrong with you!" I yelled, storming up to Ali, digging my nails into my palms with blood-thirsty anger.

Ali frowned as he twisted his neck towards me, but before he had a moment to process what was happening, I pulled back my fist and I threw it straight into his windpipe—

THUD. His skull crashed back against the wall, cracking open. Blood leaked from his head, dripping into his eyes. His body stumbled and doubled over as agony bled from his cry.

"Evie died from an overdose. Did you know that?" I roared at him.

"What? I… I…" Ali coughed through his words, fighting to find his breath. "Samarra?"

"I *said*, did you know that?" I shouted again with confidence I didn't know I possessed.

"How…would I…know that? Wasn't it a car accident—"

"It was an overdose. You should *know* that because you sold her the Dust that killed her."

"What? I… What do you mean?"

"Did Evie ever ask you for more than usual? Did she ever want too much?" *Hurt him again before he finds his strength and overpowers me.* I pushed on his chest, knocking him back into the wall. "Huh? Did she ever want too much Dust?"

Ali sniffed, wiping the back of his hand against his nose, before he spat out a mouthful of blood. "All the time."

Vengeful rage boiled inside me. *Hit him again. Harder.* I pulled back my fist then threw it into his face, hitting him with a loud—

CRACK. My knuckles broke against the bones of his nose. Pain swerved through my hand as though I'd hit a wall. But that was nothing compared to the satisfaction of seeing Ali howl as gushes of blood shot from his nostrils. *Keep hurting him!* His face was already decorated with bruises, and his balance was unsteady as concussion symptoms continued to eat at him. *He's so weak right now, it'll be easy to take his life!*

"You killed Evie." My breath fogged in the ice-cold breeze. "You killed her by selling her that goddamn Dust. She'd still be alive if you'd left her alone!"

"I…" Ali tried to form a word through his croaky voice. "I didn't kill her… It's…it's not my fault."

"Of course it is! It's all your fault that Evie is dead and never coming back!" A cruel darkness overtook my mind. But for once I didn't care. I didn't have any worries or thoughts about the consequences. *We're all going to die one day; nothing actually matters. So let's speed up the inevitable.*

Rage turned my hand into a fist once more, forcefully pulling my arm back and taking another brutal swing—

CRACK. I punched into the side of Ali's cheek, bashing his skull back into the wall, furthering the damage to his brain. He let out another shriek as greater waves of torture swarmed over his mortal body. His senses dampened and his mind tried to drag him into the depths of unconsciousness.

"You killed her!" I yelled as my hand burned from the impact. *I should have saved her and protected her. I should have been a better older sister.* "*You* stole her from me!"

"Stop it!" Someone shouted from behind me. Maybe there was a small crowd of people starting to form, maybe the security camera was glaring down at me—I wasn't sure. In that moment, all I could focus on was the blood streaming down Ali's face, the heartbeat banging against my ear, and Death's warming figure moving closer towards me.

"Keep going." Death's low voice rumbled into my mind with much louder volume. His words sounded more real, more human. His sedating presence felt more tangible as he moved up to my side. *"He deserves it, doesn't he? He deserves it more than anyone else who has died today."*

My heart crashed against my chest, matching the tempo of Death's ticking pocket watch. I should have questioned why Death stood there, watching me, after it was so hard to find him. I should've wondered why I was still seeing him and why his image was becoming so powerful. But looking at Ali's bloodied mess of a body was too satisfying for me to look away from now.

"He's on Dust too. Have you noticed?" Death asked.

What? I frowned through panting breaths.

"That's why he's been so weak, why he's been sniffing, why he's been so unstable. He doesn't have a cold or a concussion. He's an addict."

I stared closer at Ali's face, noting his dilated pupils, his trembling hands, and the remnants of white powder around his nostrils. *How did I not notice that before?*

"It means he really is weak right now. His life will be so easy to take, won't it?"

It will be so easy. But... Confusion crawled across my brain as I wondered why I wanted to take a life, why I wanted to keep hurting him. *Surely I shouldn't be doing this.* My life instinct collided against my death instinct, fighting for control. *Surely I shouldn't...* My thoughts were being ripped in two, torn between walking away from Ali and pulverising his face.

"Don't act like this is a moral dilemma for you." Death cut off my worries like the swing of an axe. *"Your life is empty without*

Evie in it. You've lost who you are; you've lost everything. Ali is the one who took that from you when he gave Evie the drugs that killed her. So you need to do exactly what you intend to do, without letting those pesky worries control you." Death reached his hand up to me. I didn't flinch or move away this time, as I let him brush away the splatter of blood that had fallen against my cheek.

Comforting waves crashed over me as Death's touch felt like a warming embrace. It quieted my thoughts, silencing my worries as though they'd been shot dead. Dark, consuming flames filled my vision as my eyes caught on his and I let his power take over my every urge.

"*See? I told you that you didn't want answers. You just wanted me.*"

Maybe I should have argued against him, but I knew he was right. He did what no one else could: he took away my pain, my grief, my worries, my *everything*. The suffering of the body is so easy to remedy compared to the suffering of the mind. There usually was no escape from my own thoughts and the deep caress of grief, yet somehow he had found one.

"*Now...*" Death's bright eyes were still swallowed by black pits of darkness, swimming in vicious hunger as he looked towards Ali. "*...keep going. He deserves everything.*"

Death's words enhanced my pure, unquenchable anger, enslaving my limbs like a puppet. They forced me to pull back my arms once more before my fist shot itself into Ali's neck, cutting straight into his windpipe with another forceful—

THUD. Ali gasped for a breath I didn't want him to find.

"*Good. Do it again,*" Death coaxed me on. "*Put him through all the pain Evie went through, if not more.*"

Faint screams and rushes of movement fluttered around me, as life tried to bash its way back into my mind. People seemed to be yelling towards me, but my ears refused to listen. I no longer cared about the world when Death was right next to me.

"P-please Samarra. I-I-I…" Ali's knees shook until they were unable to hold his weight any longer, forcing him to crash to the ground. His blood dripped onto the pavement, staining the white powders of ice. "P-please… S-stop…" He stuttered, begging for his life. But I didn't even look at him; instead my focus was on Death.

"Do you want to give me his soul?" Death asked. *"You're so close to taking his life after all. Won't it feel good to watch him die after everything he's done?"*

"P-p-please…" Ali's mumbling cries continued. "I didn't hurt her. I-I-I would never…"

"So very close."

"Stop it!" Someone shouted from the crowd behind me. "This is your last chance!"

"Why don't you end his suffering?"

I lifted my fist again and pulled it back, reading my aim. I knew if I hit him hard enough, I could push him further into the realms of unconsciousness or maybe even further than that—

But what would Evie think if she saw me now?

I hesitated as that thought tugged on my conscience. *E-vie…* My movement froze. *What the Hell* would *she think of me?* Blood trickled down my fist. Rage dominated my eyes. My soul felt so lost it didn't know how to escape the maze of grief it had landed in.

Suddenly someone grabbed me. A real, human hand took hold of my fist then sharply twisted my arm behind my back.

"Until next time, Samarra Blair." Death let go of me, snatching the quiet bliss out of my skull, forcing the weight of the world to come crashing back down.

Wait. No, wait!

Screams and shouts bellowed towards me, wind howled against my ears, and my crying worries tore through my mind like bullets. *What have I done? I hurt Ali. I really hurt him. No, I almost killed him—*

"Get away from him!" Someone shouted as they dragged me away from Ali's crumpled body. And I let myself be pulled away. I let the coldness of reality hit me back.

How could I do this? My heartbeat crashed with adrenaline as slithering dread stabbed into me. *How could I almost kill him?* Sweat poured down my face, my breath sprinted far away from me, and a sickness clawed its way through my throat. *And why did I enjoy it?*

"What the Hell have you done?" Zain yelled with overflowing emotion, as I realised he was the one pulling me away from Ali.

I looked towards Zain, to the shock horror crawling across his face. "He…he hurt Evie…" I said as all my reasoning was torn from my mind. *What the Hell* have *I done?*

A howling siren screamed over us as blue flashing lights sprinted towards me.

"What did you just do?" Zain mumbled as he searched for lost words. "The Shade are coming… This is bad, Sam. This is very…" He looked back towards Ali's body. "I have to get him out of here. Those bastards will arrest us both if we get caught up in this, and I can't go back to Detention. I can't."

"Zain, I—"

Zain released me from his grip, sharply turning away without another word. He ran over to Ali with a panicked frenzy, rushing with all the bouts of energy he could find. "Ali! *Ali!* Are you okay? Ali, hold on!"

I stumbled backwards as I watched Zain run, wondering how he knew Ali, wondering what I'd just done. "What did… Zain, I… I didn't…" My voice felt forgotten in the overwhelming cruelness of life as I looked past the staring crowd for an escape, for—

Death was no longer there, no longer keeping me safe from the cold claws of reality. *Where is he now I need him the most? I need him to save me, to take away this overwhelming pain!*

The crash of sirens grew closer as officer cars ran into my vision. The world was driving at me with full force, dragging me far away from the calmness of Death's coffin.

"Stop!" a voice yelled. "You're under arrest!"

My vision felt too dizzy to register what was going on. "No, I…I didn't mean to—"

Hands grabbed me, cutting off my useless words. They pushed me onto the ground with a forceful blow, twisting my wrists behind my back.

I strained my neck, forcing myself to look back at Ali's bloodied body once more. *What have I done? Why did I hurt him? Why did I almost kill him?*

Why did it feel so good?

And why do I want to do it again?

I'm okay. I'm okay.

I have to be okay.

PART TWO

Everything HAS to be okay.

→ Everything (IS) okay.

It IS.

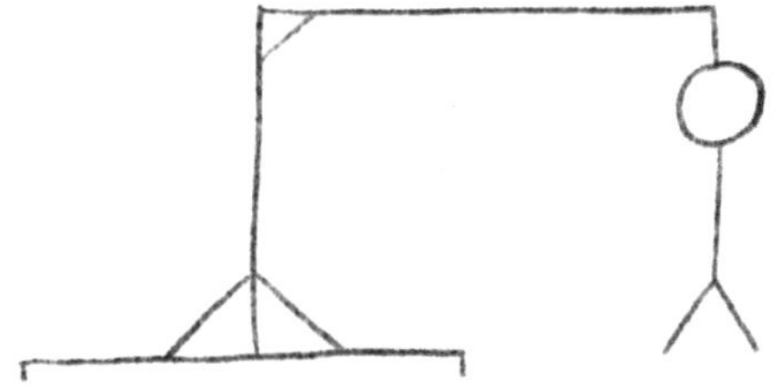

YOUR NUMBER IS UP

1

I'm going to die.

My bloodstained hands were chained to the table while a cracked two-way mirror stared me down. Exhaustion dripped from my forehead, weighing on my eyelids, wishing for them to rest in peace at last. *One day I'm going to die.* The only way my thoughts could cope with reality was to imagine the perfect quietness of Death, as his smile haunted my mind like a blissful opiate. *One day we all will die and it will be divine.* But now that quietness felt like a distant dream. Now I was surrounded by noise.

Never-ending commotion permeated the walls of the suffocatingly small interrogation room. Medlock's officer station was as busy as the hospital, full of screams of energy and overworked staff who didn't have a minute to themselves. Officers had come into the room in a perpetual rotation, speaking to me in brief bursts as they recorded what happened. I may have embellished my account slightly, adding details of how Ali attacked me first and I was simply acting in self-defence.

After all, who wouldn't believe a med student over a drug dealer? I made it seem like I regretted my actions, but truthfully I can't wait to hurt him again and feel Death's touch once more, just for a little longer.

But how am I supposed to find Death again? Was I really hallucinating him or was it something more? Maybe I was glimpsing through the veil of reality, looking behind the curtain of life itself—

"Samarra Blair." Yet another officer walked in the room.

Not again. I kept my eyes closed like a corpse. *Life is so much hassle. I just need the world to stop spinning for a moment. Or maybe longer.*

The officer quietly hummed a soft tune under their breath as they stepped towards me. It was the same tune Zain had been humming, the same tune Evie used to sing all the time.

"It's been a while, hasn't it?" The officer started in an all-too familiar voice. "I like the new tattoo." They looked down at the triangle on my wrist below my handcuffs.

"Ria?" I let out a relieved sigh as I looked back at her.

Ria was Evie's girlfriend. *Or was it ex-girlfriend?* We had been friends at college, *before Evie stole her from me.* I always wished she had never met Evie, as their relationship had been such a headache. They were constantly on and off to the extent that no one could keep track. *I doubt even they kept track themselves.*

"Thank god you're here," I said. "I didn't realise you were a full officer—"

"Stop." Ria held up her hand, silencing me as she took a seat on the other side of the table. Her expression was more serious than usual. Or maybe it was weighed down by unforgiving grief, just like mine. "You don't get to act grateful I'm here when you haven't spoken to me for months."

I hesitated. Sadly that was true. I hadn't seen her since Evie died, *I haven't seen anyone.*

"And no, I'm not an officer, I'm still an apprentice," Ria continued. "I work in surveillance now, which means I've watched the footage of your little argument with Ali."

I bit down on my tongue.

"You're lucky you were standing in a blind spot. You're also lucky I vouched for you. I told them you're not the type of person who goes round beating others up. I hope I'm still right about that."

Thank god they have no evidence of my attack. I let go of a breath. *That means I can get out of here and go to…to Death. Can't I?* "Thank you, Ria, I don't—"

"Don't thank me. I didn't do it for you; I did it for Evie. She wouldn't forgive me if put her sister behind bars."

I nodded, looking closer at Ria. The bags under her eyes matched her dark pupils. Her plaited hair was slowly becoming undone. She used to have colourful pink strands throughout her hair, but now there was only a dark, natural blackness to it. Yet there was still some sparkle of life, as bright gold jewellery adorned her neck and patterns of mehndi danced across her brown skin. She also wore a dark trench coat that was similar to what other Medlock officers wore. But hers wasn't quite as long as theirs, like she hadn't earned that yet.

"Ali was a dangerous person to get in a fight with." Ria said, folding her arms. "The people he works with shouldn't be messed with. You better pray you're not important enough for Mariana to seek any revenge."

"Who's Mariana?" *I've heard that name before. Ali spoke about her.*

"Someone I hope you never come into contact with." She spoke with a plain bluntness. "How do you even know Ali?"

I looked up to the corner of the room where a security camera with a sharp red glowing dot was staring down at us.

"It doesn't pick up sound," Ria said, sensing my hesitation. "It's probably not even on right now. You're not exactly the biggest threat we have here."

I didn't know if she was trying to insult me or reassure me, *probably both. It's been a while since I've spoken to her. I doubt she's very happy this is the first time we've met since Evie passed.*

"So? How do you know him?" Ria leaned forwards. "Don't bullshit me like you've bullshitted the other officers."

"I…" I mumbled. "I owe him money, for the Dust that—"

"You're on Dust too? I thought you of all people would have avoided this stupid craze." She shook her head. "Don't you know how dangerous it is? It's not a fun party drug, it's way more harmful than people realise. That's why the mayor is intent of getting it out of the city—"

"No, I-I wouldn't take that stuff myself. I owe him money because of Evie." It felt strange saying her name to Ria after all this time. "Evie used to buy Dust off him. She owed him a *lot* of money. So since she…since she died, her debts became *my* debts. That's why Ali has been starting fights with *me*."

"Jesus Christ, you really think I'm going to buy that?" Ria loudly sighed.

She's definitely pissed I haven't spoken to her for so long. "What do you mean? That's the truth—"

"You're mistaking me for an idiot who didn't know Evie at all. Don't forget she was *my* girlfriend, she told me everything. I suggest you rephrase your words and tell me the truth."

How could she not believe me? She used to trust me with everything. "Didn't you know about her debts?" I asked. "Evie was addicted to Dust—"

"She wasn't addicted."

"She was. She was probably more addicted than any of us realised—"

"She *wasn't* addicted," Ria repeated.

"She *was*. That's why Ali *has* been hurting me for money. He threatened me at Evie's *funeral* for god's sake. The funeral that I hardly saw *you* at."

"Don't turn this back on me."

"But why were you barely there? Evie would've wanted you—"

"*Evie* would've hated that funeral. It was far too boring for her. And I *did* go for a little while; I just didn't stick around. I didn't think you'd want to speak to me after the way you've been avoiding me," Ria stated.

"I've been mourning—"

"*Everyone* has been mourning. Don't you think her death was hard for me too? Yet you haven't even bothered to return any of my calls."

"I've been busy. I'm studying to be a doctor—"

"Don't lie to me like you do to everyone else. I know you haven't attended your university for months."

Wait… A weight dropped in my stomach. *How does she know that?*

"I know you're trying to put on a perfect little student façade, even though you've been flunking everything," she continued. "I also know they're giving you one last chance to keep your place with a final exam, but I doubt you've even been studying for that."

"No, I…I *have* been studying." I denied it all, letting frustration stab through my mind.

"Have you?" Ria leaned closer towards me.

"Yes, I…I…" I stumbled for the right words, even though there were none. "Why wouldn't I? It's an important neuroscience exam. I have to do well. I have to…become a doctor." I spoke the words I'd programmed myself to believe.

"Then why haven't you been to university for months? Why have you barely left your house?"

How does she know all this? "I…I have left the house." *Keep denying everything.*

"Your mum said you haven't."

"Why are you talking to my mum?" An unwavering anger bled through my words. "She doesn't know what she's talking about. She's been ill—"

"I talk to her because *you* won't talk to me!" Ria shouted, leaning in even closer.

"I lost my sister!" *Why does no one understand that?*

"We all lost her! But I didn't think we'd lose *you* too."

"Then clearly you don't understand how hard everything has been!" My anger mixed with insurmountable rage. *I should just hurt her, like I hurt Ali.*

"I understand more than anyone. Yet you still forgot about me and everyone else in your life. You don't even seem to know how to *live* since Evie died—"

"What the *Hell* is that supposed to mean?" I yelled. *Death wanted me to hurt Ali. What if he wants me to hurt others too? Maybe hurting people is how I can see him again.*

"It means you've lost yourself, Sam. You pretend you're still a doctor who would never do anything wrong, but that's far from true. You're failing your course, you're hiding from the world, and you're—"

Suddenly I reached up to grab the collar of Ria's coat. *Hurt her. Let's see if this brings back Death. He's the only one who'll actually understand me.* I wanted to use all the strength I could find to forcefully slam her head into the table—

But my wrists fought back against the chains around them. Ria was just out of reach. *No! I have to hurt her. I have to hurt everyone!*

Ria quickly stumbled away. "Were you trying to…" She panted through stuttering breaths as she frowned at me in disbelief. "What happened to you, Sam?"

I hesitated as her words pierced my mind. *What did happen?* The adrenaline of the moment passed away. *I…I was about to hurt someone who used to be my closest friend.* My lungs tightened as guilt tied its noose around my neck. "I…I don't—"

"Don't you hate that moment?" Ria shook her head.

"What?"

"The moment when you thought you knew someone so well, but suddenly you realise you're looking at a stranger you don't recognise anymore."

A breath caught in my throat as memories of Evie talking about specific moments flooded my thoughts. *Zain talked about specific moments too. They're all speaking like Evie did. But why are they holding onto a memory that's buried six feet under?*

The door handle rattled.

Ria looked towards me with a sudden rush of fear. "Nothing happened, okay? Nothing."

I frowned. "What do you—"

The door burst open. Another officer stepped inside.

2

"What are you still doing here?" An officer walked into the interrogation room. Their sharp gaze fell on Ria. "You're taking up a room." They had bright blonde hair that drowned out their pale, corpse-like face. They also wore a much longer trench coat, showing they were a full officer.

"Nothing, I…" Ria mumbled, straightening her posture.

"You're supposed to be taking *that* one out"—they pointed at me—"not keeping them in." They spoke in a posh, Southern accent that over-emphasised every consonant.

"I know, I was just doing that." Ria sharpened her accent too. "I'm sorry. I…" She searched through her pocket before pulling out a key. Then she rushed to unlock my cuffs.

"The other one is waiting at your desk," the officer continued as Ria freed my wrists from the adamantine chains. "That one is still handcuffed in case he tries anything, given what happened to his brother. Don't take those cuffs off him until he leaves."

"Of course." Ria nodded before gesturing for me to get up. "Come on."

The officer glanced towards me as Ria led me out of the room. "You really pissed off the wrong people, didn't you?"

I frowned. "What—"

"Come *on*." Ria grabbed my shoulder and pulled me away from the officer before I had a chance to respond.

Noise bled through my ears as we walked into the main room of the station. It was a large, open-plan office with desks crammed into every space, piles of paperwork on each surface and tacky posters covering the walls. The posters had simplified slogans across them such as: YOU'LL NEVER SUCCEED WITH DRUGS and KEEP MEDLOCK CLEAN. A picture of Mayor Brown was on each one, his eyes perpetually watching over every officer.

"This way," Ria said as she led me through the chaos.

"Ria, I'm-I'm sorry for almost—"

"Don't breathe a word of it. Your little attempt to hurt me never happened."

"But—"

"It *never* happened." She pulled me through the crowd of bodies filling the room. Each of them wore a dark trench coat that seemed to slightly vary in size depending on their superiority. They all had plain hair and hauntingly blank faces, showing no sign of individuality and barely any sign of life.

"Does this mean…" I started hesitantly. "Are they letting me go?" *I finally can get back to…to Death.*

"They are. Like I said, you're lucky the cameras barely caught you. I guess your façade of being a good little student worked on everyone else too." Ria led me to a barely noticeable desk in the corner of the room. "But this doesn't mean you've gotten away with it. They'll still be keeping an eye on you. So, you'd better watch what you do if you don't want to get arrested again as they'll put you in a place called Detention. It's meant to be a holding centre, but trust me, you don't want to go there."

I nodded. "They also said…" I cautiously paused. "Who did I piss off exactly? Whose brother? Were they talking about Ali—"

"Zain is Ali's brother."

"*What?*"

Ria shoved me into a seat next to the small corner desk that was overflowing with papers. "Sit here." She then turned to a chair next to mine, where Zain was sitting.

Zain's here too? He was slouched in the seat, his hands cuffed behind his back. *He was arrested?* He didn't seem fazed by the havoc of the station, as he had fallen asleep. His head hung back against his shoulder in what must have been the most uncomfortable position. Even in sleep, his eyes were moving, his leg was twitching, his chest was breathing, and he was still brimming with life.

THUMP. Ria kicked the foot of his chair, knocking him awake.

"Hey," she started. "You all right?"

Zain jumped back to consciousness, squinting against the harsh lights. His eyes seemed redder than before, as he fought back sleep he didn't want. But he didn't let it bother him as he quickly readjusted to the world, turning straight towards me. "You look awful." He grinned, trailing his gaze across my bruises and cuts below the rips in my dress.

I didn't give him a response as I stared back at him in disbelief. *Zain is Ali's brother? They're siblings?* I couldn't believe I hadn't noticed the resemblance before. They both had dark waves of hair, matching sunken eyes, and even the same creases in their cheek when they smiled. *How did I not realise this earlier?*

"I take it you guys have finally met," Ria noted. "Evie would be glad." Then she looked closer at Zain, studying his face. "They didn't hurt you, did they?"

"No, not…" He gulped back what he could from his dry mouth. "Not much."

Ria hesitated before she shuffled over to the desk seat and moved a pile of folders onto the floor to make room for herself.

"Why…" I began, as a thousand questions buzzed through my brain. *Why didn't I know Zain was Ali's brother? Is that why he rushed over to him and why he pulled me away? But why is he even in here—* "Why were you arrested?" I finally asked.

"I guess the Shade missed me being here, they couldn't help but bring me back." Zain let out a bright laugh that echoed across the room. "You also said you'd prefer seeing me with handcuffs on my wrist. So what do you think, Freckles? Do you like them?"

Ria let out an audible sigh. "Don't call officers the *Shade*, especially not in here." She shook her head as she glanced over at me. "He's here because finding someone on probation in the midst of a fight means they thought he was responsible."

I kept my eyes on Zain. "They arrested you because of what I did?"

"Yep," Ria answered first. "You two should be grateful I was here to save your asses."

A smile tugged at Zain's lips. "You know I'm always grateful for you, Ria."

"You are? Is that why you've seemingly forgotten you're on probation?" She kept the tone serious. "Or did it slip your mind when you left the city without any agreement then failed to check in for over twenty-four hours?"

"I was at my best friend's funeral. *Then* I went to the hospital to save Sam's life. I'm sure there are far worse places I—"

"You have five weeks left on your probation." Ria cut over his words. "Five weeks to behave properly, and you couldn't handle it?"

"Like I said, I'm sure rushing someone to hospital is probably the best reason—"

"They're going to put an ankle monitor on you."

"*What?* But I didn't even do anything wrong." Rage boiled beneath Zain's words. "How can these Shade bastards punish me for—"

"Don't argue and *don't* call us that," Ria commanded, glancing at the other officers swarming the station. "You know your anger only gets you into trouble around here. Keep it under control."

Zain bit down on his tongue, kicking his leg against the floor as he slumped back in his chair.

"I'm just grateful you're crashing with me," Ria continued, "otherwise Evie's party would be a disaster."

I frowned as I watched them talk. I didn't realise they were still friends. Since Evie passed, I'd assumed everyone close to her had forgotten one another. I thought we were all now lonely souls, waiting for the end. I didn't realise life was still persisting.

"Evie's…party?" I asked. "You're having a party?"

"Stop." Ria held her hand up to me again. "*You* don't get to ask me questions after you've been avoiding me for months."

"Give over," Zain said. "I'm sure we can tell her about—"

"You can stop too." She held up a hand to him. "*You* also don't get to speak back to me when I'm saving you from being sent back to Detention. You do remember how many injuries you got just from one day in that place, don't you?" She took a long breath, rubbing her temples. "Now please shut up so I can find these papers and get you both out of here." She frantically started searching through the folders piled across the desk.

Zain looked towards me. "You really got her riled up. What did you say to her?"

"Nothing. I…" I hesitated. "We spoke about what happened. But I'm…I'm sorry for getting you involved in this too. I didn't mean for you to get arrested."

He tilted his head to the side. "And what *did* happen? How do you even know Ali?"

"I…" I didn't know where to begin. "I just…" I turned my voice into a soft whisper, trying not to let anyone overhear. "Did you know he's a drug dealer?"

Zain threw his head back as he laughed. "No, really? Ali is a drug dealer? Wow." He spoke loudly as his tone flowed with sarcasm. "I never would've guessed."

No one around the busy station even reacted.

"Well," I continued, "he's the one I owe money to for the Dust Evie bought off him. He's the one who hurt me at the funeral."

Zain sat up straighter in his chair. "He's the one who hurt you?" His confusion sounded genuine.

"Yeah. But I…I didn't know he was your brother."

Zain shrugged. "Me and him don't really have the best relationship, so don't worry about it. I would've punched him too if I knew he'd hurt you."

"But did you… Did you also know Ali sold Dust to Evie? Which means he's the reason she overdosed. He's the reason she died."

Zain's smile ran away from his face.

"If he hadn't given her that Dust then—"

"Stop." Ria interrupted me, grabbing a set of papers. "There's no time to go through all this. Evie's death was an accident."

"Accident?" I frowned. "No, she overdosed. It wasn't a car accident—"

"I know she overdosed," Ria said. "It was still an accident. She didn't know what she was doing, like every other teenager who thinks Dust is just a fun party drug."

"You knew she overdosed too?" I asked. "Did everyone know except me? And still no one's talked to me about it?" *The only person who will talk about it is Death. I need to see him again.*

"How am I supposed to talk to you when you won't even answer my calls?" Ria asked with a bitter scorn.

I paused. She had a point.

"Evie didn't know the Dust would kill her," she continued. "Ali wouldn't have known either. *Nobody* knows how dangerous Dust is. That's why we need to get it out of the city before more people die like she—"

"But Ali still supplied her with Dust." I argued. "He fed her addiction and killed her whether he—"

"I told you, Evie wasn't an addict. She didn't know what she was doing and that's it." Ria spoke more bluntly, cutting off my words.

That's it? But it can't be.

"*Anyway,* I've found the papers to get *you* out of here." Ria stood up as she swiftly changed the subject. "I'll get it processed, then get your belongings. You just had a bag with keys inside, so it shouldn't take long. Then all you have left to do is a drug test before you can leave."

"A drug test?"

"They do it on everyone now for the mayor's drug-free initiative, given this god-awful Dust epidemic. It shouldn't take long, then you can go home." She shuffled away from her seat. "Just be thankful I was working today. Otherwise, who knows what would've happened to you."

"I...I am thankful." I softened my tone. "I know we haven't spoken in a while, but—"

"Evie wouldn't forgive me if I didn't help you."

I hesitated. "I-I am sorry though. I should've reached out, I just—"

"Don't bother explaining yourself." Ria dismissed my words as she began to walk away from the desk. "Grief makes monsters of us all."

Monsters of us all... What monster does that make me?

"But..." Ria stopped as she passed the back of my chair. "...I *am* having a party for Evie, in the wake of the funeral. I didn't think you'd be interested since you've been avoiding me. But if you did want to come, be at mine around eight tonight."

"I don't think I—"

"Don't give me whatever excuse you already have planned. Just show up or don't bother. It doesn't matter to me which you choose."

"I'll be there too." Zain put back on a smile to lighten the mood.

"Well, we'll see," Ria said. "You may have to wait here a little longer."

"You know I didn't do anything wrong, don't you?"

"Except break your probation rules?"

"To go to a hospital." Zain forcefully kept his tone calm, grinding his teeth.

"I know. But sadly you've got a bad reputation here ever since you assaulted an officer. So they're way more hesitant to let you go."

He assaulted an officer? Was that why he was sent to Detention?

Zain threw his head back with a frustrated sigh. "I hate the word *assault*. All I did was push them. You know that, right?"

"I know." Ria paused. "And you're…still clean, aren't you? For when you have a drug-test?"

"As clean as I have been these past six months."

"Good. I'd lock you up myself if you weren't." Ria nodded. "I'll be back soon." She moved away from us, back into the crowd of the station. The second she left our space, Zain turned to me with a look of panicked concern.

3

"Sam." Zain spoke in a low, quiet voice that didn't let anyone else overhear. "We only have a minute before Ria comes back."

I frowned as I looked back at him, wondering where he was going with this.

He leaned towards me. "Do you need any help contaminating the drug test?"

"What?" I deepened my frown. "Why…why would I need that?"

"I'm not judging you. Do you need help?"

"Of course not. Do *you* need help? Is that why you're asking?" *Is that why he seems panicked?*

"What? No." Zain looked around, before leaning in closer. "You said you were poisoned at the hospital. At first I thought you meant someone else poisoned you, but now I realise you meant you poisoned yourself, right?"

"No, I-I meant it was probably an infection from the knife. Maybe it was sepsis or something, not *drugs*—"

"Listen…" He leaned in even closer, putting his face inches from mine. "I've been addicted to that shit before, so I'd get why you'd hide it. I know people only judge you instead of helping you. But I *also* know how to contaminate a drug test. I have some eye drops in—"

"I said I haven't taken anything. I'm training to be a doctor, remember? I'm not allowed to go anywhere near that stuff." I shook my head in a motion that wouldn't stop. "Just because everyone else is taking Dust doesn't mean I am."

"But if you get caught with Dust in your system after hurting Ali, they won't see it as self-defence; they'll see it as a drug-induced attack—"

"I don't need your help, so stop giving it to me." Frustration boiled inside me. "Didn't I just hurt your brother? Aren't I the reason you got arrested?" I raised my tone. "You're supposed to hate me now, aren't you? Why are you still helping me?"

"I told you, I promised Evie I'd look out for you, so I have to—"

"I don't need you to look out for me. Why would I want *you* of all people to do that? You're a criminal who—"

"Miss Blair," a posh voice began as the superior officer who had spoken down to Ria stepped behind me. Their long trench coat almost touched the ground as they loomed over me.

Zain immediately fell silent, hanging his head, staring at the floor in instinctive compliance.

"Come with me," the officer commanded.

"I…" I hesitated, looking around the busy tomb of the station for Ria. "I was told—"

"Follow me. Now," they ordered, louder. Then their hand gripped my shoulder and forcefully pulled me out of the seat.

"Okay, okay," I said with shaking uncertainty as I quickly stood. "Where are we going?"

"This way." They pushed me to walk away from the desk.

I glanced back at Zain, seeing him glance up at me too with a flickering gaze that never sat still. It felt like he was trying to telepathically communicate with me, warning me to listen to what he'd just said.

"Move." The officer shoved me forwards, forcing me to look away before I could respond.

They led me through the main room, which felt as busy as the afterlife. Constant talking, moving, shouting, arguing, typing, ringing, noise, *noise, stress, stress.* I didn't want any of it. *I don't want to still be here, still surrounded by beating hearts that are full of life. I just want—*

"*This* way." The officer pulled me around a corner before taking me down a series of small, twisting corridors. The father we walked, the more the white walls tightened me in their grasp, strangling my mind as we moved through the maze of the station.

"Where are we going?" A flutter of confusion soared into my gut. *Are they taking me for the drug test? Are they getting my belongings? Are they letting me go?*

The officer didn't answer. Instead their pace quickened as they kept pushing me forwards, forcing me to move faster. Their hand gripped tighter on my shoulder, trapping me in their hold as they turned me towards the last door on the corridor.

"Stop." The officer halted our movement. Then they looked around to make sure no one else was nearby, noting the absence of security cameras. "I'm giving you a chance to hand over any drugs you have on your person."

"I…I don't have any." *Were they listening in on Zain's conversation with me? Is that why they brought me here?*

"If you don't hand them over, I'll have to thoroughly search you."

This doesn't feel right… "I don't know what you're talking about. I-I don't have anything on me."

"Are you saying you didn't steal anything from Ali's pockets? You didn't take his bag of Dust when you stole his money?" Their accent seemed to change as they spoke, turning from a posh, formal tone into a more relaxed Northern accent.

Panic slithered through my guts. *How do they know that? Who are they?* I looked at their face, trying to discern their facial features. They seemed so pale, so serious, so lost of all life. *I think I've seen them before…* It was hard to tell if I recognised them as I studied their expressionless face, their blonde hair—

No, that's not blonde hair. A strand of hair had fallen loose from their head, as though the blonde was a wig. A bright blue strand was hidden below.

They were at the hospital with Ali. They're part of his gang. Alarm sprinted to my heart in a tumultuous wave of panic. *I need to get away from them. I need to call for help. I need to scream!*

I took in a gulp of breath in then let out a high-pitched howl. The noise burst from my lungs as fast as a bullet. *Louder! If I get attention, I can be saved before—*

Suddenly the officer lunged at me. They clutched my face, digging their nails into my cheeks with painful malevolence as they covered my mouth. Their other arm wrapped around my chest like a snake, constricting my lungs and ensnaring me within their hold. *This is bad. This is very bad!*

"Fine, have it your way." They sharply whispered into my ear. "If you don't want to cooperate, I'll have to force you." They moved me towards the final door of the corridor. "It's time for you to meet Mariana anyway. She's dead excited to pay you back for the way you hurt Ali."

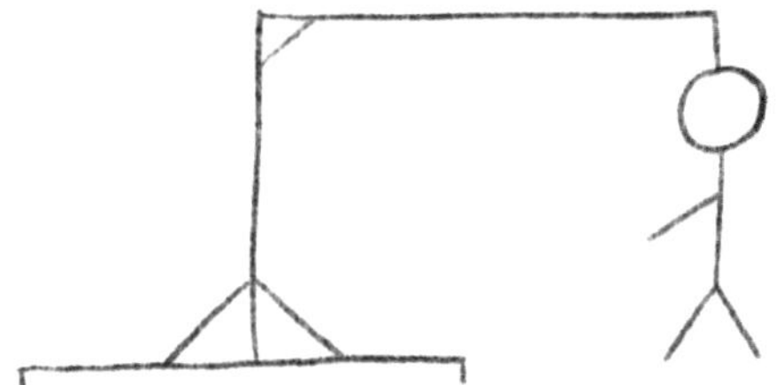

SLEEPING WITH THE FISHES

4

I can't escape.

The dying breeze of winter stabbed into my breath as the blue-haired person pulled me out the back exit of the station. The sun faded into oblivion and darkness bled through the sky. White powders of ice glimmered on the empty cobbled roads like a sinister threat. The security cameras that had been watching this area were bashed to pieces, and a struggling lamppost flickered on and off as though it didn't want to be alive either.

"This way." The blue-haired person kept me in their tight hold, squeezing the air out of my lungs as they dragged me onto one of the many back passageways twisting away from the station. "Mariana's been looking forward to meeting you for a long time."

Mariana? My heart sprinted away from my chest in a desperate attempt to cling onto what little life I had left. *That's the name Ria mentioned, the person she hopes I never come into contact with. Ali mentioned her name too... Is she the leader of their gang?*

"You really are a little escape artist, aren't you?" They snickered under their breath.

"A what?" I glanced at their face, seeing more strands of bright blue hair falling out of their blonde wig, tearing away their façade.

"An escape artist. A Dust *junkie* who's in far too much debt." They squeezed their arms tighter around me.

"No, I-I was only paying my sister's debts—"

"Ali's been far too nice to you. He's always far too nice," they said over me, like they didn't care for my words. "I knew I'd have to take over from him, like always."

"But you're…you're an officer?" I sounded as unsure as I felt. *How are they an officer if they're part of his gang? I thought the law was trying to get Dust out of the city, not help distribute it.* "You… you should be protecting people, shouldn't you?"

"I'm protecting Mariana. She needs her money and she's run out of patience."

Redbrick walls trapped us in their shadows as the officer pulled me onto another tight passageway. Graffiti covered the towering walls, embellishing the abandoned factory buildings which seemed as soulless as ever. No other body haunted the street, as every flicker of life had been sucked into an unforgiving grave. *There's no one to save me.* Then I saw an empty car waiting for us at the end of the alleyway—

Do not get in that car. Panic scurried over me as danger signs flashed into my thoughts. *If I get into that car, I'll lose my chance to escape.* Adrenaline seeped into fists, readying themselves for another fight. *The town centre isn't that far from here. I can get away. I just need to hurt them to escape their hold.*

But how can I hurt an officer? Especially when they're holding me so tightly—

There's always a way to hurt someone. Everyone has a beating heart that can be stopped. My mind rushed ahead of me in a tsunami of nerves as the officer pushed me closer towards the car. *We are just dust and ashes after all, just mortal bodies full of weak spots.* And closer. *I can hurt them.* And closer. *So hurt them now!*

Suddenly, I knocked my head backwards, crashing it against their face with a—

CRACK. My head blew into their nose. Their bones *snapped* under the weight of my skull.

They howled in agony as they instantly let go of me. A deep *thud* pounded over my head as I stumbled out of their grasp. My vision blurred, dizzying my stability. *But it worked. I can escape!* I pushed past the pain as I staggered away—

Hands grabbed my head. Fingers entwined themselves in my hair. Then a stinging burn ran over my skull as they pulled my head down, before shoving it to the side—

THUMP. My face crashed into a brick wall. Flames of torment erupted from my head and an excruciating ringing noise hurtled through my ears.

"That was a very poor decision." The officer's fingers remained tangled in my hair as they kept my head pressed against the wall, refusing to let go.

I squinted through my aching pain until I could just about see a smile light up their face in amusement. They had lost their blonde wig, revealing a full head of blue hair, as bright as the stream of red blood pouring down their face and the white powder stuck inside their nostrils—

White powder? I frowned. *They're on Dust, just as Ali was. That means they have a weakness I can take advantage of. I can still get out of this! It's okay. Everything is—*

But as they kept my head pressed against the wall, their other hand dug into their long trench coat and pulled out a large kitchen knife. This one seemed intimidatingly sharp as it glinted against the flickering light with menace. *Maybe it's not okay.* They brought the silver blade up towards me in one swift movement—

"Wait, wait!" My voice croaked. *I've gotten out of things like this before; surely I can convince them to let me out again.* "Please just wait! I have something that could—"

A burn tore through my face. The knife ripped across my skin, cutting into my cheek and travelling up to the top of my ear. Hot blood poured from the wound as a dizzying lightheadedness rippled over me.

They didn't even bother to listen. Dangerous panic flooded my senses as I realised they were nothing like Ali. *They really are trying to kill me.* I tried to look for an escape option, but the world was flailing in a spasming stroke, collapsing from the weight of its distress.

"You seem to be enjoying playing with the boundaries of life today."

My breath caught on itself as Death's warm voice beat through my mind, comforting my soul like an angel's prayer. *Death? He's here?*

"Is living not enough for you anymore? Is the world no longer worthy of the pain it causes?" Death's calm, casual footsteps strolled towards me. *"Will you only be satisfied when it's all finally over? When oblivion gently wraps around the world and pulls it down into a dreamless sleep?"*

I let out a sigh of relief as Death stepped into my dizzying vision. He looked even more human, more real, more enchanting than before. His eyes were bright sparks, lighting up the dimples in his cheeks. His suit was creased and his shirt was messily untucked, while his tie was hung loosely around his neck. He seemed more relaxed as he strolled towards me, his arms casually tucked into his pockets in a strange sense of normalcy.

I didn't even have to search for him this time. He found me.

"Nice to see you again, Samarra Blair." Death leaned against the brick wall next to me, staring at the blood trickling down my face. *"But I didn't find you. You summoned me."*

Summoned you? I frowned. *How did I summon you?*

"Take a guess."

Am I…dying?

"Everyone is dying. Some just do it faster than others." Death reached out towards me and wiped the trail of blood dripping down my cheek.

A gorgeous softness emanated from Death's hypnotic touch. It felt like I was being hugged by a friend after years of not seeing them, finally reuniting. His touch was full of understanding, of kindness, of overwhelming comfort that I didn't know I had missed. The rest of the world faded out of my view as I sank into his touch, making me realise nothing mattered now that he was here, not even myself.

Suddenly Death pulled his hand back. *"If you want to stay in this peace, you're going to have to fight for it."* He stepped away from me, tearing me from his calming ataraxia.

Wait. Don't—

The bellowing wind wrapped me in its frozen touch. The smell of blood overwhelmed my senses. Then, before I had a second to readjust to the chaos of reality, the officer's knife pressed against my neck, burning into my flesh.

"Are you ready to come with me now?" The officer leaned towards me, whispering uncomfortably close to my ear. "Or shall we keep dancing?"

The threat of life felt more intimidating than the peace of Death. *Death… Please let me feel your touch once more.*

"Are you going to behave now?" the officer asked, before they pulled my head towards them in a sudden jerk of movement. Then they forcefully shoved it back against the wall with another—

THUD.

A numbing ache scorched my skull. The trickle of blood thickened as it cascaded down my face as though it were attempting to drown me, obscuring my vision. All I could see was the officer's feet standing next to mine. But I wasn't worried or panicked as I watched Death's white boots step beside theirs.

Please… I tried to organise my thoughts as a lightheaded pain beat through them. *Please let me feel your peacefulness just once—*

"I told you, Samarra Blair, if you want peace, you'll have to fight for it," Death calmly stated. *"Don't just lie down and let them take your pathetically lonely life. Take theirs first."*

Take theirs first? But…they're too strong. They're—

"They're just a mortal with a beating heart that can be stopped. You can do this. Or at least you can die trying."

5

Die trying… Die. That word weighed on me like an anchor I was grateful for. It shook through my limbs, forcing them to *act now! Death's right: I can still do this. I can hurt them instead of letting them hurt me!*

I jerked both my hands upwards in a shot of a movement. One hand grabbed the knife's handle. The other grabbed the blade, knowing a cut on my hand was far less damaging than a cut on my neck.

The blade burned into my palm like a boiling kettle as the officer pressed it into me. But I let the pain grow as I focused on getting out of their hold. *Endure the pain!* I could still only see their feet, so I only had one place to aim for. *Hurt them!*

I kicked out my leg with a strong blow of force. *Kick them in a weak spot. Make it count!* I drove my foot into the side of their knee, hitting them with a loud CRACK.

A scream escaped the officer's lungs as they staggered backwards, falling away from me as their knee bent, twisting their leg in the wrong direction.

As they fell, I kept hold of the knife, letting the warm trickle of blood pool in my palms. *Don't let the knife go! Take control!* As they fell away, I pulled the knife back towards me, twisting their arm. *Twist is more!* I stepped to the side, twisting the knife so that their arm twisted more, *and more*, until—

Their arm *snapped* out of place. A torturous howl burst from their mouth, deafening my ears. I smiled at that noise as *finally* I had the knife to myself.

The officer stumbled to the side as their knee crumpled out of shape and their arm trapped itself in an excruciating bend. *Take advantage of their state! Hurt them again!* I planted my hands against their back, then knocked them farther into their fall, forcing them off their feet—

THUMP. They crashed to the ground, their face skidding over the stony pavement. Then a final guttural scream pierced the air.

Now I can run away! I can get a good head start before—

"*Why would you want to leave now?*" The world slowed as Death stepped into my vision. The rustles of wind wailed like a haunting melody. It was accompanied by distant rumbles of cars from the polluted city that danced over the song in harmonising synthesis. In the centre of it all were the breaths of the officer as they coughed and sputtered for air and a deep, visceral rattle clawed through their throat. "*You can't run away now, Samarra Blair. Not when they're so close to losing their life.*"

But surely I have to run while I have a chance—

"*Evie was crying when she died. Do you remember that?*"

A cold shock sprang through my heart as Death's words halted my movement.

"*At the hospital you were by her bed for hours while she was barely conscious. There was a harsh, gurgling rattle to her fast, shallow breaths. Her skin was turning blue. Her heartbeat was erratic. Yet she was still trying to mumble something. It was as though she still had so much to say, yet she couldn't say a thing... You knew it was a drug overdose, but you didn't want to accept it. Especially not when you saw the tears falling from her eyes before her suffering finally ended."*

Cruel memories sliced into me. *No...* Evie's image seared itself in my brain. *Please stop. I don't want to think about—*

"The drugs she took put her in that pain. The drugs Ali gave her. The drugs his gang distributes every day. The drugs these so-called officers fail to stop because they're part of the goddamn problem." Death walked up to the officer's body. *"They're the reason Evie endured so much torture. Surely they all deserve to die far more than your sister did?"*

No, she didn't deserve it. She didn't deserve any of it!

"So why don't you hurt someone who does *deserve it?"* Death stared down at the officer. His eyes looked like an eclipse, as the white light was sucked out of his pupils and replaced by shadowy pits of blackness.

Someone who does deserve it... His words reverberated around my head with powerful strength. They festered in my brain, drawing out an unquenchable anger.

"They deserve it. They deserve everything."

And I couldn't help but accept every one of his words as the unquestionable truth. *He's right. Of course they deserve it.*

The world clicked back into motion as I moved up to the officer's body. *Hurt them while they're still down!* I watched them weakly roll onto their back, spitting out a mouthful of gravel. Then I threw my weight on top of their chest, pinning their hands under my knees. *Hurt them before they hurt me. Before Death leaves!* I took the knife in my bloodied, wounded hand and held it against their neck. I let the blade taunt their skin like a threat.

"Stop!" their voice croaked. "You don't know who you're messing with." They let out a gasp of pain that sounded more like a laugh. "Mariana will kill you for—"

"No." I pressed the knife into their neck, scratching at their skin, letting drops of blood escape. "*You* don't know who the Hell you're messing with."

I pierced the blade into their skin before I dragged the knife down their neck, shredding it across their flesh as I moved towards their trachea.

"Good, keep going." Death coaxed me on.

Blood gushed from the officer's wound, drenching their clothes. They gasped, stumbling through murmurs of incomprehensible words. "I will…will…" But they couldn't find a sentence as harrowing pain shocked their body. "S…stop. Stop!"

"Stop? Why would you do that?" Death laughed. He licked his lips as he watched their final attempt to struggle against their inescapable end fail. *"Keep going, Samarra Blair."*

Death's mesmerising voice compelled me to push the knife deeper inside the officer's neck, towards their windpipe where I could drown them in their own blood. *It really would be so easy to end their suffering.*

"Exactly. So easy…" Death loomed over me with the powerful presence of Thanatos. *"They're going to die if you stab that knife inside their throat."*

They're going to die. They're going to—
Die.

Just like Evie. My hand hesitated. *E-vie.* A small voice pushed back against me, wanting to rip the knife out of my grasp. *What would Evie think of me if she saw this?*

"Stop…" The officer said through their lost voice. "Please…" Blood drenched their neck, seeping into the collar of their trench coat. They were so close to dying; all I had to do was push them just a little further—

"Zain…" the officer whispered.

Zain? I froze.

"If…if I don't get back alive, they won't just come for you. They'll…hurt Zain too." The officer fought to be heard, gurgling on mouthfuls of blood. "And…Ria. They'll both… be hurt."

Zain was Evie's best friend… The quiet, rational part of my brain pushed its way to the surface like the good angel trying to vanquish the bad. *Ria was Evie's girlfriend… I can't let them get hurt. Evie would never forgive me. She'd never forgive me for any of this! What the Hell am I even—*

Suddenly a loud shriek of sirens cut through the air. Officer cars roared their way through the back-streets as their noisy engines soared towards us.

I jumped, falling backwards off the body as worries clouded my head. *Are they coming for me again? Are those security cameras actually working?* Pants of breath ran along with my worries as I stared at the officer's bloodied neck. *What did I even…* I wiped the back of my hand against my sniffling nose, trailing dark blood over my face. *Why did I just do that?* Conscience ripped through me, making a coward of my soul. *I need to stop.* My instincts for life tumbled back in one lost howl for my failing humanity. *I need to get out of here!* I dropped the knife, scrambling onto my feet to move away—

"How can you let them live after everything they've done?" Death growled. *"More people are going to die from Dust now."*

I looked back towards him, but he was already walking away, heading towards a hidden doorway. A doorway I swear hadn't been there before. *Wait… Wait! Please don't leave—*

"You should've killed them when you had the chance." Death dismissed my thoughts, keeping his back turned on me, refusing to let me even see his face. *"Until next time, Samarra Blair. I'll look forward to it."*

Wait. Can't you just—

"Enjoy the suffering of life while you still can."

At least tell me how I keep seeing you! Tell me how I summoned you before—

As Death stepped through the doorway, his narcotic aura was ripped away from me in one sharp, razor-edged movement. His quietness, his kindness, his understanding—it was all torn from my soul in a brutal axe swing.

A stark, cold loneliness hit me like a truck. Furious pain stabbed through my guts, drowning me in exhaustion. The night air raged on with a piercing chill as the wind screamed louder. The streetlamps flickered more ferociously. The sirens moved closer and *closer.*

What have I done? The chaos of life swallowed me whole. *I have to get out of here before anyone catches me!*

"You…" Coughs burst from the officer's throat as they gasped for air and clutched at the open wound across their throat. "You're…going…" They fought to speak through a broken voice that was barely even a whisper of a sound. "You're going to die for this."

"Die?" I paused for a fleeting moment. The drops of blood from my scarred cheek fell against my lips, leaving an iron taste on my smile. "I'll look forward to it."

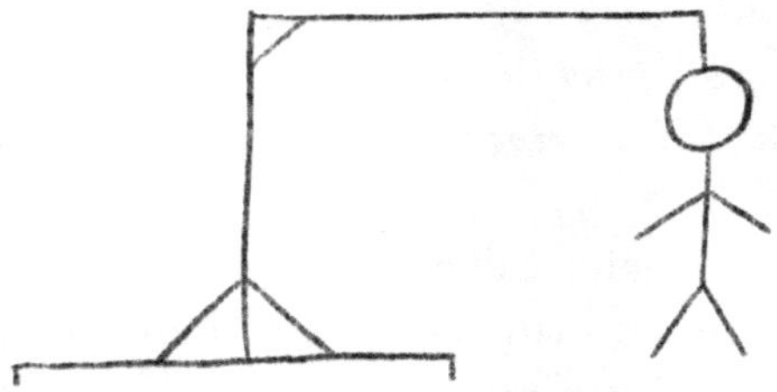

BITE THE DUST

6

I'm trapped.

The door stared me down, stopping me in my tracks. It was a door that I'd been through thousands of times before without a care in the world. I hadn't even thought about the door's significance, of entering a place and going into a house I knew so well. But now all I could think about was what entering through the door meant. I didn't want to go inside. I didn't want to see who was there and who was not.

"Samarra?" Mum opened the door before me. Her gaze trailed over the bruises across my skin, the tatters of my ruined black dress, and the fresh scar that ran from my cheek to my ear. "You look…tired."

"Tired? Is that all?" I wanted to laugh as I knew I looked like I'd been dragged through Hell, but I didn't have the energy.

Mum uncomfortably shifted in her stance. "Come inside, Love."

The familiar stench of grief hit me as I reluctantly stepped inside my family home. It smelt of loneliness, abandonment, and unwavering confusion. The smell lingered on the walls, clinging to the paint for the past six months and refusing to ever be cleaned away. It danced over Evie's coats, which were still hung on the wall, her keys still on the side, her shoes still sitting on the shelf.

I didn't want to be in this house, but my body walked me inside like a lost spirit, forced to search for its unfinished business before it could pass away. *I had a whole city to run and hide in to get away. Why did I choose to come here? Why am I clinging to death instead of life?*

"Did you have a…nice day?" Mum gave a lost smile.

I shook my head as soullessly as a corpse, refusing to give a response. Grief pulled my body down like an anchor as I walked away from her, moving up the stairs. Its pressure flooded me with exhaustion, reminding me how sleep deprived I was. *I need to rest and let dreams take me away from this dark tomb of reality.*

I stopped as I reached the top of the stairs. Evie's bedroom door was wide-open. The door was the same one I had walked past every day of my life, yet for the past six months it had felt so much colder. A lifeless emptiness swam around it, drowning it in nothing more than faded memories. The worst part was the silence. *It's far too quiet here.* Evie's shouts and hums and laughter used to fill this place. Now her absence haunted it.

Evie will never walk into that room again. I'll never tell her everything I needed to tell her. I'll never even say I'm sorry for everything I ever—

Stop. It's just a room. I halted by the doorway. I could only look inside it, peering in from afar. But even just looking filled my body with familiar dread. *I'm okay. Everything has to be okay. I don't know what I would do if it wasn't.*

Evie's room was exactly how she had left it. It was as though she was just here. *No, she was just here. She should still be here.* Neither Mum nor I had found the courage to walk into her room, let alone start tidying it up. We'd only stared at it for the past six months. I dared to think how much longer we could continue to stare at it before we finally stepped inside, if we ever did at all.

A half-empty water bottle stood on her bedside table, next to a book with a bookmark poking out of the halfway point. A small basket of almost empty nail varnish pots sat behind it. Leaning on the basket were worn drumsticks with Evie's name messily carved along the side, waiting to be used again.

By the side of the room was a pair of white boots and a pile of clothes she hadn't decided whether they were still good enough to wear or needed to be washed. Behind the pile stood a full-length mirror overflowing with cracks. Post-it notes clung to the mirror's surface with motivational phrases written on them, like: YOU'VE GOT THIS, DON'T YOU DARE BE AFRAID, YOU DESERVE EVERYTHING, and KEEP GOING. *I wonder if she looked at them the day she overdosed.*

Either way, she'll never look at any of this again. A clash of pain swirled through my body. *She'll never finish that water or read that book or paint her nails another stupidly bright colour or—*

No. I can't accept that she's gone when she's only just left. I can't grieve for someone who shouldn't be dead. Nineteen is too damn young to die.

My eyes were drawn to her desk as if they'd been guided there. Bags of makeup, used cans of deodorant, and perfume bottles were scattered across it. In the centre of the mess was an envelope with "SAM" written on. I'd seen that letter before but refused to pay it any attention. *I still can't look at it. Reading it means reading the last words she'll ever say to me. Reading it means she's dead and never coming back!*

The finality of her death stabbed into my mind, crueller than it ever had before the funeral. Before, it felt like maybe she was going to return. Maybe she was just staying out late and would come back in the early hours of the morning like she used to and sneak into her bed, thinking she was being stealthy when she was actually waking the whole house up. I used to cling to those "maybes." But now I had been to her funeral, the finality of her life closed over me like a coffin. Now she really was gone.

I can't stay here any longer. I staggered backwards, falling away from Evie's room. Yet I kept my eyes fixed on her belongings, her life that she left behind. It was too hard to turn my back on the dead; even Orpheus couldn't do that. I had to take it all in and keep her memory alive. *I just wish she were still here. I wish I could hear her stupid laugh, her incessant humming, her pointlessly long stories. I wish I could see the great dumb smile she has every time she comes home—*

I mean…the smile she had. The smile she had every time she came home. Past tense.

The limits of Hell seemed non-existent as slashes of grief tortured my soul. *Why does grief caress me instead of kill me?* The pain of the mind was too much to handle, too much to bear. *I'd rather be stabbed and tortured than face any of this. At least a broken body can heal, but a mind suffers forever.*

THUD. I slammed Evie's bedroom door shut as I stumbled into the corridor, locking away the grief and never wanting to open it up again.

"Samarra?" Mum began. I spun around, seeing her standing at the top of the stairs, watching me from a distance, just slightly too far away. A look of concern haunted her face as her eyes carefully watched mine.

7

"Your dress…" Mum tutted, looking me up and down. "It's ripped."

"Dress?" I shook my head in disbelief. My whole body was paralysed in pain, tears were streaming down my face, and blood was dripping from countless wounds. Yet all she noticed was the stupid funeral dress. *If grief makes monsters of us all, it made my mother into a ghost.*

"Do you…" She took a sip from a large wineglass full of a clear liquid that was definitely vodka. "Do you want me to sew it back together?"

I carried on shaking my head. "I can't. I…I have to go."

"Go where?"

"I…" A breath trapped itself in my throat as I looked behind Mum to the window at the top of the stairs that overlooked the quiet residential street outside. The night sky was covered in the usual ever-growing darkness. It was such a normal sight, except for the colourless urn that sat on the windowsill.

Evie's urn.

Urns made human lives seem so small, as it tucked Evie's explosive, charming personality inside one neat little ornament. *Evie really would hate that urn.* Seeing the urn inside the house added a cruel normalcy to the object. It was now just a piece of decoration. *She'd be so mad if she knew her ashes were being kept here, in the house she never wanted to be in, overlooking the quiet street she hated, instead of the great world she loved exploring.*

She shouldn't be here. She should be in—

Eidyn… I was supposed to take her to Eidyn.

Suddenly my mind snapped itself back to the tortures of reality. *What the Hell am I doing? No wonder my body dragged me back to this godforsaken house. It was forcing me to remember the one reason I'm still alive. Why am I such an awful older sister that forgot the one promise I wanted to keep?*

"Samarra?" Mum prompted, catching my eye. "Where are you going?"

"I…I…" *I have to get out of here. I have to go to Eidyn and never come back.* "I'm…going to Ria's," I lied.

"So you *are* speaking to Ria?"

"Sort of." I didn't have the energy to tell her about being arrested, *not that she'd care even if she knew.* "Where are my car keys? I need to go now."

"Your keys?"

"Didn't you have them in my bag when…" I trailed off as an alarming terror settled into my mind. *They took my bag at the station… I never got it back.*

"You're very forgetful, Love." Mum tutted. "Can't you walk to Ria's?"

"That's not the point." *This can't be happening. I need the keys to drive up to Eidyn. I can't fail Evie again!*

"Will Zain be at Ria's?" Mum continued as though the world weren't crashing down on me.

"Why does that matter right now?" *Nothing matters, nothing at all.*

"You have to keep away from him, Evie. He's trouble."

"Evie?" I frowned.

Mum frowned too. "What about her?"

"You just called me Evie."

"I…" A blank, lost expression dominated Mum's face, making her seem as still as a corpse. "I need to sleep."

"You always need to sleep." *Evie. E-vie. Why didn't she tell me about Evie?* A vicious anger pounded into my skull as the events of the day crawled back to my mind. "Why didn't you tell me Evie died from an overdose?" I blurted.

Mum paused. "I thought you already knew."

"No, I…I didn't." *Didn't I?* "Why the *Hell* would I know that—"

"Hell? Don't curse, Love. It's not like you." She shook her head. "Anyway, I really do need to sleep. It's getting late—"

"Wait. I'm trying to talk to you. Why haven't we once spoken about her death? Why have you told *everyone* she died from a car accident?"

Mum took another large sip of her drink. "People are very… judgemental, aren't they? I didn't want to tell everyone—"

"But you could've told *me*."

"You shouldn't go out in that dress, Samarra. Let me fix it."

"Stop changing the subject." Frustration dominated my words. "Do you think… If Evie overdosed, do you think she did it on purpose? Do you think she wanted to—"

"I really should sleep now—"

"I told you to *stop*! Why won't you just talk to me? Please just acknowledge I'm here. You still have one daughter who's alive. Why can't you see that?" I stormed up towards my mum before snatching the glass she was drinking from and smashing it against the side of the windowsill with a—

CRASH. Broken glass scattered across the floor, falling over the stairs. One sharp blade remained in my hand, stabbing into my palm, reopening the knife wound. *I should stab this piece into her flesh.* Blood pooled in my fist. *I should hurt her just as I hurt the others!*

Mum moved past me without a word, walking into her bedroom. *She's ignoring me, like she always does. She's going to sleep and stay in bed for days again. She's—*

She reappeared, standing in front of her bedroom door, visibly trying to keep herself together as she clutched another large wineglass that was again filled with vodka.

"I also hate the moment when I walk through the front door," Mum began in a softer tone. "It's the moment when at first I think I'm walking back into the house I'm used to. I think I'm going to be greeted by Evie's bright clothing or listen to her bang those drums for hours on end… Then that split-second moment is robbed from my mind before I'm even grateful it was there."

Blood trickled from my hand onto the floor as I stared at her. She hadn't spoken in more than a few sentences in a long time.

Much longer than I had realised. It should've been nice to hear her slowly find her way back to life, but only rage pervaded my head. *Why is everyone talking about specific moments just as Evie used to do? Have they forgotten she's no longer here?*

"Samarra…" Mum continued after a beat of silence, "I…I have been meaning to speak to you. I just…don't know how."

"What's that supposed to mean?"

"I…saw a letter from your university… You didn't go to your final exam."

I kept hold of the shard of glass, letting it shoot pain up through my arm, while my eyes stared towards Evie's urn. *Evie used to hum and laugh and talk at me for hours. Her ashes once had a body and a tongue. But now she's nothing but a trail of dust, locked inside a dark urn, forced to sit on a windowsill for eternity.*

"Why didn't you go? Did you forget about it?" Mum asked.

I can't let Evie stay there. I can't do that to her! Why did I ever leave her here alone? Why am I a horrible older sister—

No, I'm not an older sister anymore. I don't have a younger sister to look after and protect. I don't have someone to love me unconditionally even if they annoy the Hell out of me. I don't have anyone.

"Samarra?" Mum prompted. "I thought you were studying for that exam. I thought you—"

"I haven't studied in six months. But you never even noticed that." I looked back at Mum's empty eyes. "Why are you opening my letters anyway? You haven't shown any interest in my life ever since—"

"They've expelled you from the course."

A deep, visceral silence laughed over the scene, insulting me with its cruelness. *I've been…expelled?* I didn't know what to think, whether I should have been disappointed for failing my life's goal, or relieved to be free from its burden.

"Good," I finally said.

"Good? How is that good?"

"I never wanted to be a doctor. *You* wanted me to be one. You wanted me to be smart and perfect, but…but I can't. I can't go back to that job. It's too stressful, too full of problems I can't fix, of lives I can't save."

"Why didn't you tell me?" Mum took another sip of her drink.

"Tell you?" Wrath crawled inside my voice. "I try to tell you everything but you never listen. It wouldn't have mattered if I'd said it because you never would have heard me!"

Mum paused, seeing the anger burn through my eyes. "I also wanted to ask…" She hesitated, seeming unsure whether to continue. "At the hospital, I spoke to a doctor before you woke up. They told me about your overdose."

I hesitated.

"Is that why you haven't been studying? Is that why you've been so…" She looked down at my ruined dress and multitude of wounds for a long moment, unsure how to phrase her words. "I…I thought you knew better than joining silly teenage trends?" She continued. "Just because Evie was pressured into taking that Dust stuff doesn't mean—"

"You think she was pressured into taking Dust?" I asked with astonishment. "Then you clearly don't remember her at all."

"That…that Zain must've pressured her. She was too well-behaved—"

"No, she wasn't. Evie *loved* making wild, reckless decisions."

"But…*you* don't." Mum spoke cautiously. "It's okay to grieve, Samarra, if that's why you tried it—"

"How can *you* tell me to grieve when you clearly don't know how to yourself!" Outrage built up like a wall in my mind. "All you do is drink and sleep. You still lie about Evie's death. You even have a damn museum of a room dedicated to her because you're too scared to step foot in there!"

"Dreaming means I get to see Evie."

"And what about *me*? I'm right here!" *I just want someone to talk to. Why won't anyone speak to me?*

Mum gulped. "I'm sorry if you needed me—"

"I don't need you anymore." *I have Death now. He'll speak to me. He'll listen. He'll let me escape this world.*

"You've always been so strong and independent. I'm sorry for not knowing you were struggling too."

"You didn't know because you didn't ask. No one did." *I need to grab Evie's ashes and get out of here.* "You know…I think Evie knew exactly what she was doing when she took that Dust." I squeezed the glass tighter into my palm. "I bet she overdosed on purpose."

"Don't say that. She didn't know what she—"

"I bet she wanted to die because she knew nothing could be more painful than whatever this life is."

"Please stop being so dramatic."

"Dramatic? Go to *Hell*." I let the shard of glass drop and shatter on the floor in a bloodied stain. "Maybe Evie had the right idea. Maybe Death really will be much more peaceful than *this*." I reached out and grabbed the dark urn off the windowsill, holding it tightly in my arms. *Take Evie out of this godforsaken house already!*

"Wait, Samarra, please. Put that back!"

"*That*?" I scoffed, marching down the stairs. "I'm not staying in this house and neither is Evie!"

"Wait. Please don't take her again!"

"She doesn't belong here! She never did." I stormed down the stairs then back towards the front door. "You always tried to keep her inside, but she loved going out. She loved going to the parties you hated; she loved being with Zain, who you despised. She loved everything you didn't want her to!" I flung open the front door. "She loved every part of her damn life that didn't involve you or this suffocating house!" Then I slammed it shut behind me with a deafening—

THUD.

8

The chill of the night's air bit at my skin and rain drowned my body as I walked through the feverish streets, hugging Evie's urn in my arms. *Mum won't talk to me about Evie's death. No one will. No one understands what it's like to lose a sister, to lose a part of yourself. No one knows what it's like to die alive, to have your soul ripped away even as your shell of a body continues moving.*

Tears fell from my exhausted eyes as I turned down a cobbled side street. The narrow passageway was small, with barely enough room to *breathe. Just breathe and relax. I'm okay; I've gotten out of the place where no one understands me. No one can understand me. No one but Death.*

Every living soul had abandoned the dark dredges of night. The red lights of the security cameras were fading into a broken orange. Shadows scuttled under the abandoned redbrick walls like rats. The persistent drops of rain struck my skin with the sharp, icy malevolence of a machete. The neglected buildings were full of more useless mayoral posters, covered in pointless slogans such as A DRUG-FREE LIFE IS A HAPPY LIFE and GET HIGH ON LIFE, NOT DRUGS. They made me shudder with frustration as I turned another corner. *Ignore the posters; they don't know what they're talking about.* Then another. *They don't know how miserable life is. They don't know how drugs are the only escape—*

Calm down! I'm okay. Everything is okay. I thought the same words to myself like a never-ending chant. *It has to be.*

Medlock's canal appeared before me as I walked out onto an open path. *Why am I still here, stuck in this godforsaken city, and Evie isn't?* No other soul was in sight, though it looked like a ferryman was waiting in the far distance, hovering over the icy waters that were black against the night's sky. The canal led all the way into town, back towards the station where my car keys would be waiting. *But it won't even be open anymore, will it? I won't be able to escape this city and drive up to Eidyn with Evie's ashes like I promised.* My hands shook as I gripped onto Evie's urn tighter. *Damn it, why is everything going wrong?*

Just relax! I stood next to a flickering, dying lamppost that didn't have enough energy to create my lost shadow. I took in deeper breaths, trying to slow my racing heart as I looked at my reflection in the water. My dress was ripped, slowly coming undone as the material had unravelled just as much as I had. The dark roots of my hair were matted in sweat and the bleach-blonde strands were streaked with blood.

Blood? I frowned as I ran my hand through my hair. But as I did, I saw my knuckles and palm were bloodied too. *No, no… What have I done? Why did I beat that officer up? And why do I want to do it again?*

"Stop it, stop it, stop!" I whispered to myself, forcing my mind to quiet as emotions tormented me with the power of ten thousand Hells.

I had to hurt them. They deserved it for giving Evie those drugs, for killing her. But of course my thoughts wouldn't stop. *I had to get revenge, I had to show Evie I did care about her. Even if I argued with her, if she annoyed me, if I didn't meet her best friend, if I didn't see her band, if I didn't even go out with her on the night she died, I still cared. I promise I still cared!*

"Stop!" I threw myself to the floor, putting Evie's urn down before me. "This is all your fault, Evie! Why did you have to go and die? Everything was *perfect* before you left!" I continued to run my fingers through my hair. "I can't take it anymore. I need…I need…" I threw my hand into my dress, where I kept Ali's money tucked in the side of my bra—

There it was. *Thank Hell it's still there.* The other item I'd stolen from Ali…

The small bag of Dust.

Of course both Ali and that blue-haired officer were right. Of course I had it this whole time. *I don't know how I would have survived without it.*

I quickly opened the bag of Dust. *I just need a little more.* I dipped my finger inside the white, crystalised powder. I didn't have much left, but it was enough. *Just a little more!* I brought the Dust up to my nostril. Then I took a deep breath in, snorting the powder up, letting it sting as I inhaled it.

Maybe everyone was right about me… I continued sniffing, making sure I'd consumed it all. *Maybe Ali hadn't actually approached me to be paid back for Evie's small debts. Maybe I had approached him months ago. Maybe I had bought Dust from him. And maybe I had bought a little too much, but that was only because of the pain of grief. Maybe I got carried away, but I needed to. I wouldn't have survived without it.*

I stared at myself in the reflection of the polluted canal water, looking at my pupils, which were already dilated, the small remnants of powder around my nostril, and the lifelessness that haunted my face. I let out a small semblance of a smile as I wiped my nose with the back of my hand, sniffing up any remaining Dust.

Maybe Mum was right. Maybe I have been taking Dust. Maybe I have been getting lost in its escape rather than studying or dealing with the unbearable stress of that medical course. Maybe I missed that final exam on purpose because I'd rather lose myself in Dust than in the distress of life.

Maybe Zain was right too. Maybe I'd taken Dust before the funeral, maybe even during it. And maybe I'd taken more than usual, more than my body could handle. Maybe the knife wound really was just a surface scratch and maybe the real pain came from my overdose. Maybe Dust is what poisoned me, and maybe I knew that all along. Maybe I am a junkie, an escape artist, someone who just needs to leave reality and never go back.

None of this is a problem. I have everything under control—

But I lied to everyone. Maybe I even lied to myself—

No, I didn't. I only had a little. I'm allowed to have a little. No one else needs to know about this, not that they would listen to me even if I told them—

Be quiet! My body finally relaxed as the Dust gradually made its way into my system. A calmness trickled over my senses as my body slumped into the drug's effects. Then my worries bled out of my skull.

I looked at the dark urn that was staring back at me. "Don't judge me, Evie. You'd do the same."

I closed my eyes as I made my breaths slower, deeper. I forgot about the weight of the world crushing my shoulders and the cold winter's breeze freezing my skin. *Nothing matters.* Instead of the burdens of reality, I was now surrounded by a dreamlike world where no consequences existed, no responsibilities haunted me, no grief weighed down my soul. *Nothing. Matters. Nothing at all.*

The peaceful ataraxia drowned my mind; it reminded me of the first time I had taken this beautifully powerful substance, right after Evie's death. I'd been looking through picture albums to keep Evie's image alive in my mind; then I'd found the small bag of Dust, hidden behind a terrible picture of her. Of course I thought about throwing it away, but then I wondered why Evie had loved the stuff. Maybe some unconscious part of my mind really did know she had overdosed, and maybe I wanted to understand why. So I took it. I took far too much of it, and it was gorgeous. For the first time in days, grief left my skull. I didn't have to feel the crushing weight of sadness anymore. Instead I could feel nothing.

Perfect, blissful nothingness.

This isn't a problem. I opened my eyes, looking down at my trembling hands and the small triangle tattoo on my wrist. Then I looked back towards the reflection along the murky canal water once more, at this bloodied, messy version of myself I barely recognised. My monstrous image should have frightened me, but now that the Dust was settling into my body, I could only succumb to its peace. My reflection didn't matter because it was barely even real anymore. Nothing was.

Dust is not a problem. It just helps to take the edge off, that's all. And that's perfectly fine given everything I've been through these past six months. It's not a problem. It just lets me escape the noise of the world for a while. The bitter taste of Dust ran down the back of my throat with tranquilising strangulation of calmness. *There's nothing to admit. Everything is under control. It's okay.*

Everything. Is. Okay.

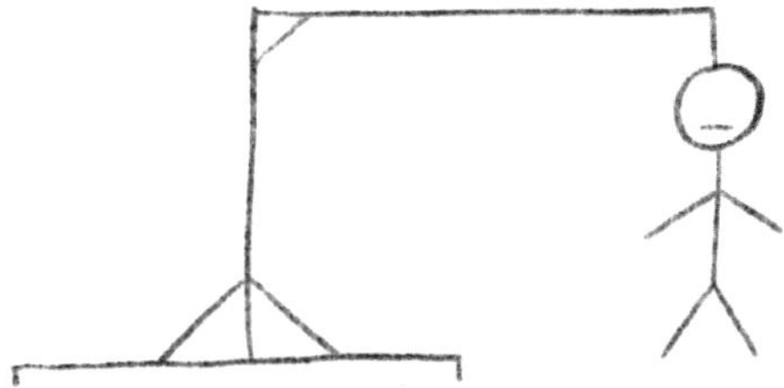

LIGHTS OUT

9

There's nowhere else to go.

Blaring music thumped over the apartment block as colourful lights burned through the windows and into the night's sky. Ria's party for Evie looked like a raging club night, and I knew more than anyone that Evie would've loved it.

I don't need to stay here for long. I just need to convince Ria to get my car keys from the station. Then I can drive to Eidyn and scatter Evie's ashes. It shouldn't take long. I just wish I had pockets; that way I wouldn't have gotten into this damn mess.

DING. The elevator chimed as the doors slid open before me. A hive of people lined the corridor, chatting and laughing and breathing in suffocating life. Bright bursts of colour flowed over every one of them as strands of dyed hair, jewellery, tattoos, and individuality clung to them. Some splashed their drinks while stumbling off to find even more alcohol to consume. Others held lit cigarettes, creating a mist of smoke for me to walk through.

The remnants of Dust slithered down the back of my throat, relaxing my limbs as the powder worked its way through my bloodstream. *Just focus on finding Ria… Focus on… Focus…* My mind blurred as apathy filled my chest and a numbing calmness took over.

Most people who haven't tried Dust wonder what it's like. I guess it's hard for me to describe since I'm no expert. A medical professional would say it causes numbness, memory loss, nausea, abdominal cramps, derealisation… But none of that explains how freeing this small, beautiful substance is. I'd say it creates an enchanting, dreamlike sensation. It's as though you've escaped the burdens of life and are now lost in the realms of melodious sleep. It separates your mind from your body, stopping you from feeling any sort of pain. Physical pain, emotional pain, stress, sadness, grief—it all swims away from your head, as you're no longer heir to heartache and the thousand natural shocks of flesh. Instead you're left with a tranquilising sensation where no burdens weigh you down and no worries haunt your thoughts. Only a calming peacefulness is left… But like I said, I'm no expert.

The electronic music crescendoed as I moved into Ria's apartment, letting the deep bass double the pacing of my heart. The air inside was so hot and sweaty, I could barely find any oxygen within it. Inebriated people pushed up against me as they crammed themselves inside. *Why do I always feel the most alone when I'm surrounded by people?* I saw a few people who had been studying with Evie before she dropped out of university, a few she'd been friends with since she was young, and even people from her high school she'd always hated. But I barely knew them. *I really didn't know Evie at all.* Yet they seemed to know me as they gave me hazy, drunken smiles—*or maybe they only recognise me because I'm carrying Evie's goddamn urn.*

"I don't know why you loved these parties, Evie," I whispered towards the urn. "I have a headache just from being here for one minute."

Blood stained my knuckles, but now I wore it like an accessory as I clung onto the urn. My long blonde hair had fallen into a messy bun, highlighting my dark black roots. My bruises were like tattoos as I proudly showed them off, letting them clash against my bright silver jewellery and yellow watch on my wrist. Blood painted my lips like lipstick, matching the long scar across my cheek. I had ripped my dress along the way here, taking off the unnecessary puffy layers, shortening the length, and ripping a slit in the side of the skirt. Instead of worrying about it coming undone, I was leaning into its messiness. The dress used to be perfect, but I knew it would never be perfect again. It could never go back to what it was, to what I was—

"Are you trying to tempt me?"

My breath caught on itself as Death's voice hazily ran over my brain. *Is that...?* But it felt so quiet, I could barely hear it. *Is he...here?* My eyes darted over the crowd, but there were too many bodies before me, too much life.

"You actually showed up?" Ria bellowed over the thumping music as she appeared next to me. "I didn't think you would."

Ria... She's the reason I'm here, remember? Focus... A cold numbness hazed over me, distorting the music into a clash of dissonant screams. *I just need my keys... Don't I?* The Dust was twisting reality around me so I could no longer *focus. Fo-cus on getting...getting...*

"I did." I wore a smile as fake as a serpent's, trying to blend into the world I no longer had I place in. "I—"

"Jesus *Christ.*" Ria's eyes landed on the long scar over my cheek. "What happened to you?"

"I..." I hesitated. "...fell over." I lied as easily as I had been doing for the past six months. *I have to be careful...don't I? An officer gave me this scar. What if Ria is dangerous too?*

"Seriously?" She raised an eyebrow, seeing right through my lie. "Didn't I tell you to keep out of fights? You know you'll get sent to Detention if…" She trailed off as she looked down at the urn in my arms. "You brought Evie?"

I pulled the urn closer towards me. "I did." I felt my words blur together, even as I only spoke in short, monosyllabic phrases.

"You did." Ria smiled. She seemed far more relaxed than she had been at the station. Her black hair was down and free, trailing across her back. She had even clipped in some pink strands throughout. She looked more like herself again as she was dressed in a sparkling top and long skirt, with a gold chain around her waist. *She looks like she used to when Evie was still alive.*

"Sam, I'm…" Ria paused. "I'm glad you brought her. But please, for her sake, stay out of trouble." She pulled her eyes away from the urn. "Although this *is* the first party of mine you've been to in forever. Maybe I should arrest you more often, if it means you'll actually spend some time with me." She smirked, letting a care-free energy run over her expression.

She's being…nice to me? I looked down to my feet, noting they were still firmly on the floor despite the wavy feel of air lightening my limbs. *Maybe Dust is stronger than I thought…*

Concentrate! I need to convince her to get my keys from the station, don't I? Get her talking about her job and then I can…do something. "What's it been like working for the Shade? You used to be so excited about it back when—"

"Don't call it the 'Shade.' Only criminals call us that." Ria rolled her eyes. "And I don't think you *quite* qualify as a criminal yet. But it's been…fine."

"Fine? So you don't mind all the…corruption?" *Does she know about the officer who hurt me? Does she know… Do I know… What don't I know? What?*

Ria took a sip of her drink. "I'm sure it's just as stressful and as *corrupt* as any job in this city. But you'll figure that out if you ever actually go back to med school."

"I told you I *am* going back."

"Back? You *told* me you were already there." She crossed her arms. "You've really changed, haven't you? You never used to lie to me."

"I…" *Concentrate… I needed something, didn't I?* "I wanted to ask you…something…about when I was arrested—"

"Hold that thought." Ria pushed past me as she buried herself back into the crowd of people.

"Hey, wait!" I shouted after her, but the screaming music hid my words inside its ever-growing bass. *Don't let her go. I need… something. Don't I?* I pushed my way towards her through the sea of bodies. "Ria, wait!" But my voice was too quiet for her to hear, for anyone to hear. My words were being sucked out of me and dropped into the abyss, never to be found.

"Here." Ria turned back to me after picking up a small black bag by the side of the room. "It's yours."

My bag… That's what I needed. A sigh of relief escaped my lungs as I took it from her. *Does this mean…* I rummaged through the bag until my fingers brushed over my car keys. *I have my keys and I have Evie. I can drive to Eidyn now… Can't I?*

"I know you got let out of the station early by another officer," Ria said, "but you forgot this. I was going to swing by your house tomorrow and drop it off. I didn't think you'd be here tonight."

"You…got it for me? Even after…" I paused. *Didn't I hurt her? Doesn't she hate me like everyone else?* I shook my head, trying to push the worries out of it. *No, don't think like that. Surely the Dust can't be wearing off already.* "I have to go." I closed the bag, throwing it over my shoulder.

"Go? You only just got here."

I turned away from Ria, back towards the dizzying crowd. But the bodies were blurring into one another, becoming twisted demonic shadows. I was invading their space like an impostor in a place I didn't belong. *Why did I even leave the safety of my house to venture into a world that doesn't want me in it?*

"Sam, wait!" Ria grabbed me, wrapping her warm hands around my ice-cold arm. "I haven't seen you for so long. Stay a bit longer. Come on, we used to be such good friends before…"

Before Evie died?

"At least see Zain first," she continued. "He'll be grateful you showed up too."

Why would Zain be grateful? Didn't I get him arrested? Doesn't he hate me? I shook my head, throwing the thoughts off my mind. "Why are you two so close anyway? Shouldn't a Shade officer stay away from criminals like him?"

"You think he's a criminal?" Ria smirked.

"Isn't he?"

"He's far from it."

Suddenly a microphone screamed into life as the beating music came to a halt. "Hello, everyone!" Zain's voice boomed as he stood on a box at the other side of the room. "Thank you all for coming tonight!" His usual bandana pushed back his waves of hair. His dyed green strands looked more vibrant. His fresh, white T-shirt showed off the collection of sketchbook, cartoonish tattoos along his arms. A stubble gave him a neat ruggedness. And a bout of confidence burst from his smile as he spoke to the crowd. "We have something very exciting planned for you all!"

10

Bodies piled in around me, locking me in their grasp. *What's going on?* Their limbs surrounded me as they looked up towards Zain with eager smiles.

"I'm dead thrilled to be here tonight!" Zain continued into the screeching microphone. "I've had such a long day, as you all can probably guess." He gestured down to a blinking red light that shone from his ankle, where a tracking monitor was locked around him. "But luckily those Shade bastards didn't keep me this time." The crowd laughed and cheered at his words, buzzing with excitement as they crushed my body further within their hold. "Which means I get to be here and share one of our most beloved songs with you all." A few others stood around him, getting into position as they brought out guitars and dragged a keyboard forwards.

"See?" Ria nudged my arm, smiling even within the havoc of life as though she weren't drowning in it like I was. "You don't need to leave yet. You can at least stay for one song."

"Song?" I frowned, feeling my face melt in the heat of the crowd as the bodies around me moved in tighter, then tighter again.

"I love this moment…" Zain happily smiled out at the room as the people around him readied their instruments. "It's a great moment when I'm talking into a microphone, stalling for time as the others set up." He laughed. *He's talking about another stupidly specific moment, just like Evie used to.* "I never really know exactly what to say… Sometimes I feel like these guys drag out the moment much longer than it needs to be, pretending to tune their instruments even when they know they're fine, just to make me squirm and see what I'll do…" He stopped. His eyes caught on mine. "Freckles? You made it." His smile grew brighter.

Did he just speak to me? Heat rushed to my cheeks in the sudden wave of attention as bodies turned my way. *How did he notice me in this crowd?* Eyes looked towards me, marking me as their prey. The room grew smaller, forcing me to stand out, highlighting the fact I didn't belong.

"Okay…wow. I'd better make sure this is a great performance for our special guest." Zain scratched the back of his neck as he readjusted back to his stage persona. "Anyway, like I've said before, I promise we'll do a full concert when we have the proper funeral for Evie…"

Proper funeral?

Ria leaned her head towards me. "We're having it at the church Sunday morning," she whispered as though she had heard my thoughts. "If you answered any of my phone calls over these past few months, you'd know."

"I'm…" *Sorry? Is that even the right word?* I readjusted the urn in my arms, feeling its weight bear down on me.

"But since you bothered to come to this, *maybe* you won't be too busy to come out again?" She asked. "It'll be a better funeral too. One that's a little more Evie's style."

Evie's style? Zain said the same thing… I recalled his words when I had seen that terrible picture of Evie wearing my yellow jacket in his car. *So that really was what he had taken it for…*

"But for now," Zain continued, his hand shaking as he held the microphone and nerves flowed through him with unbounded energy, "we're going to give you a small taster of what's to come." He nodded at a person with a bass guitar at the ready, and as soon as he nodded, they started playing a funky riff of notes. "Of course we no longer have our amazing drummer. But Evie would never forgive us if we didn't give one last show before sending her off. She'd also never forgive us if we didn't make it the best damn show we've ever done!" Zain nodded to someone standing by a keyboard, before they clicked into life and began to play a flurry of notes that perfectly sat over the bass.

Evie's band… I never even saw them perform.

"You didn't?" Ria spoke down my ear, somehow responding to my thoughts.

How did she hear that? Am I speaking out loud?

"Didn't she ever invite you to her concerts?" Ria asked.

"She…" *She invited me to every single one. But I'd listened to her drumming too much at home to want to hear it more.*

"She used to annoy me with her drumming too." Ria nodded. "Even when we went on dates to nice restaurants, she'd always beat her cutlery on the table. I don't know if she even realised she was doing it half the time."

Memories flooded back of Evie tapping her fingers and legs incessantly, always moving to some sort of beat. *I haven't thought about that in ages…*

"You haven't?" Ria asked.

Wait, did I say that out loud again? I rubbed the side of my head before striking my palm against it. *I need to wake up.*

"Maybe you've been avoiding me because you've been avoiding thinking about Evie's life instead of just her death."

What? I frowned. *Did she really just say—*

"Evie!" Zain shouted, cutting off my thoughts. "This one's for you!" He looked in my direction and winked. *Did he just wink at me?* Then he took a deep breath in and began to sing:

> "I…
> I dragged my empty body out of bed,
> To try and find where my free will had gone.
> I let the sadness fall out of my head,
> Until my sorrow was all gone…"

He can sing? Zain's voice was soft and sweet, much sweeter than I thought possible. *How did I not know he could sing?* Confidently he let his notes flow out and perfectly fit over the accompanying instruments in a mesmerising melody:

> "To fill the void my soul had left behind,
> I found a rabbit hole I could fall down,
> To run away from my destructive mind,
> I closed my eyes, I held my breath, and I fell down, down, down…"

The crowd cheered with excitement as the music picked up its tempo and the bass ran forwards. A flutter of notes danced over the keyboard before the guitar ripped into an electrifying tune and the chorus began:

"Laughing about nonsense,
Lost in the madness,
Floating through the chaos,
Running away from it all... Running away from..."

Wait. I know that melody. The familiar tune sparked memories I thought I'd forgotten. *It's the tune Evie used to hum all the time and drive me crazy with. The melody others keep humming too... How did I not know the tune was from her band? How did I not know anything about her?*

I tore my eyes away from Zain. *I can't do this.* But my attention got caught on the crowd around me. Their bodies were swaying, their feet tapping, and their mouths moving in time with one another as they sang along. *They know the words to that annoying melody Evie could never stop singing. How the Hell do they all know it and I don't? I really am the worst older sister. No, the worst person. I shouldn't be here. I shouldn't be anywhere!*

"Stop, stop..." I sharply whispered to myself as my breath started a race with my heart. I scrunched up my eyes, wanting to escape the crowd, the thoughts, the world. But it all just kept turning, refusing to ever stop. And Zain's voice kept singing that hauntingly upbeat melody with its drearily existential lyrics:

"My body finally dragged me out of bed
To shout for help and let my sore eyes cry.
And yet the pain kept circling round my head,
It mocked my life and made me want to... it made me want to...

"To shout and scream for someone to save me,
until I could no longer make a sound.
And then I thought 'to be or not to be,'
until my questioning brought me down, down, down…"

I can't believe this is the first time I'm properly hearing this song. A heavy emptiness dragged on my mind as I was forced to listen to the melody. *Why did I never watch them perform before? Why did I never do anything Evie wanted me to, even on the day she died—*

Stop. I need these thoughts to stop! I held my breath as I forcefully moved through the crowd. *I need to get out!* Their bodies squeezed me farther into their hold, pushing me in tighter and *tighter.* My limbs were crushing in on themselves, compacting into nothingness as I strained my legs, demanding them to *keep going,* to push farther into the sea of flailing bodies until I had drowned myself at the bottom.

11

Breathe! I staggered into a corner of air at the back of the room. Kitchen cabinets surrounded me, lining the apartment wall. I leaned against them, forcing oxygen back into my lungs despite how much I hated it. *Calm down!* But my panic wouldn't stop. The Dust was wearing off, tearing its peace away from me.

There's too many people here, too much is going on. I need to make it stop! Plastic cups littered the kitchen's surfaces. Most of them were half filled with liquid, while others had ashes and cigarette butts in them. *I just need to take something, anything that will quiet this agony, this grief that tortures me but never kills me. Anything!*

I grabbed one of the half-empty cups and downed it in one swift gulp. *Damn that's strong.* I coughed in disgust at the bitter taste. But I didn't let it stop me as I grabbed another cup and downed that one too. *That was even worse than the last.* Then I reached out to open the kitchen cabinets to find more—

I stopped. Polaroid photos were stuck along the cabinets, and my sister was in every one of them. *Evie...* She looked so happy, smiling as she pressed her face against Ria's. Most of the pictures were sweet couple photos, but others were group photos, full of faces I failed to recognise. Zain appeared in countless pictures, where he seemed even happier than usual, *if that's somehow possible.* Then I saw one photo with me in it. It was from last year, back when me, Ria and Evie hung out together. We were all there, standing as brand-new adults ready to face the world together. *And what a world we had to face...*

I held Evie's urn tighter under my arm. *I wish we were back in that photo together, back when everything made sense. I wish I had spent more time with you, Evie. I wish I had gotten to actually know you, your friends, your band, your life. I wish I hadn't waited until you were dead.*

"Those worries will kill you."

A rush of an electric shock sparked through me as Death's voice ran over my mind. Yet it was still so quiet. *Is he actually here?* His words sounded almost like a lost echo fading into oblivion. *Please let him be here.* I looked at the crowd, scanning every face, every limb, every beating heart to find the one that was stopped—

"You showed up?" Zain stepped up to my side.

I jumped as he appeared. *Wasn't he just singing?* I looked to where he'd been standing, then realised none of the band were there anymore. The pumping electronic beat had returned too. *How did I not realise that?*

"You all right?" He smiled with a hint of uncertainty.

I nodded, looking around once more as though I expected Zain to be talking to someone else. *Is he actually speaking to me?*

"You look…" He ran his eyes over my body. "A little less awful than earlier."

"Thanks." I straightened my posture, trying to act as normal as I could. "So…you can sing."

Zain laughed before looking at the empty cups around me. "And you can drink."

"I…I've never heard you sing before. I didn't know you were actually good." I felt my words blurring into one another, crushing each other as they fought to be heard.

"I'll take that as a compliment." He grinned, acting as though everything were normal. "Evie said you never used to come see our gigs because you thought we were 'dreadful.' But I'm glad to hear that's not the case."

"Well…I never said it *wasn't* dreadful. I just said I was surprised you could sing."

Zain let out another bright laugh that overflowed with sparkling liveliness. "If you come to our next one, I'll make sure…" He trailed off as his gaze landed on the urn I was carrying. "You brought Evie?"

I nodded over and over, like the movement didn't know how to stop. "I figured she wouldn't want to miss this."

"You figured right. Are you finally going to take her up to Scotland then?"

"I…" *I should be going up there now. I have everything I need, don't I?*

"Do you want company?" Zain leaned towards me, resting his arm against the kitchen counter.

"By company do you mean *you*?"

"Of course." He smiled wider. "I swear it'll be better than the last time we were in a car together. Plus, it'll be nice to use the time to talk about Evie since we haven't properly spoken about—"

"Thanks, but I'd rather be alone." *I'm used to being alone.*

"Are you sure? I can at least help you." He reached his hands out towards me. "That urn looks pretty heavy, do you want me to hold it for—"

"No." I flinched away from his touch, clutching the urn tighter, not realising how much my arm was burning from carrying it. "Evie's fine with me."

He put up his palms in defence. "That's all right, I was just trying to help…" He trailed off as he squinted, looking closer at my face. "Did you have that earlier?"

"What? Oh…" I realised he was looking at the scar on my cheek. "No." I turned my face away, looking back out at the vicious crowd.

"Did Ali do that to you?"

"It's…a long story." *Why does he even care? No one is supposed to care.*

"You didn't get into another fight, did you? Has someone else hurt you?"

"Don't lecture me when you know you're just as bad." Frustrated anger slithered into my words.

"No, I wasn't—"

"*You* assaulted a damn Shade officer of all people, which is far worse than anything I've done."

He stopped, raising an eyebrow. "I didn't *assault* them. I just pushed them out of the way to get Evie to the hospital."

I paused. So did he.

"You mean…" I slowly started after a long silence. "…the night she died?"

Zain cracked his knuckles as he fidgeted with his fingers, before reluctantly nodding.

"You…hurt an officer and you got arrested on the *same* night Evie died?" I frowned with overwhelming confusion. "What happened that night?"

"I don't think this is the right place to talk about it."

"It's never the right place."

"Maybe not," he agreed. "Remembering Evie like that isn't what she would have wanted. It's better to focus on her life rather than her death since she had *such* an incredible life even in the short time—"

"Why won't you just tell me what happened? Why won't anyone speak to me about it?" I shouted, letting my rage boil over.

No one will talk to me about her. No one but Death. Why haven't I seen him again? I need to feel his peace once more, to find a way out of this lonely existence—

"Screw it." I interrupted my own clash of thoughts, not wanting to choke on them any longer. "I need a drink. Or something stronger."

"Sam." Zain softened his tone. "I'm sorry. It's just too much for me to even—"

"Do you have any Dust?"

"What?"

"Dust. You and Evie used to take it all the time. Do you have any?"

"I told you I don't do anything like that anymore." He looked at my dilated pupils. "And you shouldn't either. That shit is addictive if you take too much. Everyone thinks it's just a harmless party drug, but it's so much more—"

"Don't tell me what the Hell I should be doing."

"Hell?" He stopped, raising an eyebrow at my language.

"What? *You* say it all the time."

"I know, but…you don't."

"You don't know that. You barely know me."

Zain frowned. "Why are you getting angry so easily? Are you all right?"

"You of all people should not be asking that question," I scoffed before I pushed past him, moving back into the crowd. *I need to get away from here, from everywhere.*

Zain grabbed my wrist and pulled me back towards him. "Sam, wait… Maybe I don't know you that well, but I knew Evie and there's *so* much of Evie in you. You both have—"

"I know we looked nothing alike, so don't even pretend you see her in me."

"But of course I do. How could I not?" He looked down at my wrist. "You even have the same triangle tattoo."

"I got this in memory of her." I pulled my wrist out from his hand.

"I was with her when she got it, you know? She said it was supposed to be some sort of mountain that symbolized adventure and life, as it was over her heartbeat. But…I always made fun of her for having a triangle on her wrist."

I paused. "So did I."

"You did?" Zain's smile brightened. "I wonder what that says about us then—"

"I don't want to talk about her anymore. I just need to… forget for a while."

"Forget? But why can't we remember? Why can't you focus on being alive instead of numbing yourself—"

"I can't." *Why would I focus on being alive when instead I could be—*

"Why not?" His shaking eyes looked deeper into my soul. "Look…Dust can be a good escape, and I *know* how freeing it can be as I used to take way too much of it. But I also learned the hard way how addictive it is."

"I don't need a lecture—"

"You do. You need to know it has serious side effects. It can damage your organs, it causes cancer, it can even create hallucinations that make you lose touch with what's real. It's way more harmful than—"

"Hallucinations?" I paused. "Dust can cause…hallucinations? I thought… I didn't think it was that potent."

"It is. It's scarily powerful if you take too much of it. But as it's such a new drug, people barely know what it can do…" Zain's voice faded as my thoughts grew louder.

Dust can cause hallucinations. My mind felt like it finally *clicked* into place. *That must be why I've been seeing Death. It's not sepsis or exhaustion. It's not seeing behind the veil of reality, beyond this life—it's the Dust.*

Dust created Death. I took so much that I started seeing him. That's why I saw him at the funeral, at the hospital—every time I took Dust without anyone knowing…

That's how I can see him again. That's how I can talk to someone about Evie's death. That's how I can feel his peace once more…

I need more Dust than my body can handle. And I need it now.

12

I shoved myself back into the crowd, letting the bodies suffocate me, knowing any physical pain was better than the emotional scars running through my mind. *I need to quiet my thoughts with a little more Dust…just enough to see Death once more.*

"Sam, wait!" Zain shouted from somewhere behind me, but I let his voice fade into the distance. I didn't have time for the living now.

I pushed through the crowd to the opposite corner of the room. Shadows twisted away from me as I set Evie's urn by the edge of the apartment before I reached into the side of my bra and pulled out the bag of Dust.

But there was nothing left. *I took it all. How did I take it all?* I scrunched up the bag in frustration. *I just needed a little to see Death again!*

Bodies continued to drink and dance around me in a haze of never-ending movement that was growing more intoxicated as the night droned on. *It's okay, I'm at a party full of students and young people. There will be Dust here. Someone must be dealing. I just have to find them…*

My eyes landed on a familiar face as I saw someone Evie and I went to high school with. *I think his name is Reese?* He had also been on my medicine course at university, though I don't think I'd ever had a full conversation with him. He was always seen as the "party guy," the one to go to if you ever need something to get you through the night. *He almost definitely has Dust.*

I pushed my way towards him. He was leaning against the back wall, dressed in a shirt that was far too baggy for his thin frame. He was talking to a girl, smiling with an eager grin, though she didn't seem as interested as he was. His pupils were dilated, his balance was unstable, and he kept sniffing as though he had just snorted Dust.

That was far too easy to find someone. Medlock really does have a problem with Dust, and I couldn't be more grateful.

"Hey, Reese!" I started, putting on my confidence.

Reese turned towards me, frowning as he tried to place who I was. The girl he was speaking to quickly left, taking the opportunity to get away. "Hey…Samirra, right?" He asked with a smile that was full of overly-whitened teeth. "You were Evie's sister."

Were. His use of past-tense shot a bullet of unease through my stomach. *I'm no longer anyone's sister.* "Yeah." I nodded, swallowing the pain, keeping it buried six feet under.

"I've never seen you outside class. Though I haven't even seen you *there* in a while." Reese spoke with hazy eyes and a drunken smile as he shakily passed me the cup he was holding. "Here, take this. You need it more than I do."

I took the cup of what I assumed was straight whisky. "Thanks." I downed it in one gulp, letting its burn hit me with a pleasant sting.

"Evie was a great person, you know?" His words slurred into one another. "She was a crazy Hellraiser though, always looking for an adrenaline rush—"

"Do you have anything stronger?" I cut over him.

"Stronger?" His grin grew. "You sound more like Evie than I thought." He pulled out a small baggie overflowing with bright white powder. "Does this mean you want to *party*?"

I nodded, my mouth salivating as I stared at the Dust. *I just need a little.*

"You can have some of this for free if you'd like." Reese moved his sweaty body closer to mine as he passed me the bag.

"Really?" I let him into my space, smiling as innocently as I could. "Thank you."

"Do you have a key?"

"Of course." I quickly took out my car key from my bag. *This is my escape, the key to my freedom.* Then I took the Dust off him, before I dipped the edge of the key into the white powder. *Finally.* I brought the powder up to my nostril and snorted it.

A burn stung my nose as I sniffed it up. An acidic taste dripped down the back of my throat and I let out a smile at the all-too familiar feeling.

Instinctually I moved back to the bag of Dust. *Just a little more before he takes it away.* I dipped the key into the bag again, but this time I scooped up even more of the powder. Then I forcefully sniffed it up, letting it burn my nostrils. *I just need enough to make me feel nothing again.* I quickly put the key back into the bag once more and pulled out even more. I didn't think twice as I put it up to my nose and snorted it again until—

Peace overwhelmed me. Apathy embraced my mind. Everything else ran far away: my motivation, my hopes, my goals, my grief, my worries. It all left, abandoning me in beautiful serenity.

"Damn, you really needed that, didn't you?" Reese took the bag back, swaying his body to the music, pushing it next to mine as he looked me up and down over and over. "I didn't know you were a party girl. I always thought you were just quiet and stuck-up." He laughed, but it sounded twisted and bitter as alcohol stained his breath.

"Stuck-up?"

"Yeah, I didn't know you were actually so…" He ran his eyes over me again and again. "Yeah."

I breathed out a smile. Maybe he was hitting on me; maybe he was mocking me. But either way, I didn't care. My shoulders relaxed, dropping the weight of the world off them. I rolled my head back along with my eyes, letting thoughts fall out of my skull. My smile grew wider as a blissful comfort hugged me close, releasing me from the anchors of reality. The pain that had been swirling around my organs faded out of existence as Hermes led me towards oblivion where nothing mattered anymore. *Everything is okay again.*

I fell into the crowd of dancing bodies. They squeezed me into their sweaty pile of limbs, but I didn't resist their movement now. I let them push me around, falling in time to the music. I looked at their haunted expressions, which now seemed carefree. Their judgements now seemed like encouragement, their viscously dark stares were nothing but dilated pupils. *They're all on Dust too… Of course they are. They're the only ones in this city who know Dust isn't dangerous. It's a glorious escape from the cruelty of a world that doesn't want them.*

Reese messily danced next to me, as lost in another reality as I was. Then he reached out and put his hand on my shoulder. But his sudden touch felt so normal, *nothing like the calmness of Death.*

"Hey, you want one of these too?" Reese's words blurred together as his balance shook with inebriation. He stumbled into his pocket before pulling out a packet of cigarettes.

The packet read SMOKING KILLS. *I wonder how long it would take to kill me.* "Sure." I nodded, letting Reese light up a cigarette for me.

The flame felt dangerous around so many people, but Reese didn't show any worry as he happily took a drag of it first before placing it against my lips. I breathed in the poisonous smoke, letting it fester in my lungs for a long moment before blowing it back out. The deepness of the breath relaxed my body as the nicotine held hands with the Dust and they happily danced into my bloodstream together.

"I'll go get us another drink!" Reese shouted, but I barely heard him. All I cared about was watching the world disappear and my sea of troubles finally end—

Suddenly a hand grabbed my wrist, sharply pulling me back. "What the *Hell* are you doing?" Zain started.

"Get *off*." I pulled my hand free from his. "I'm not *doing* anything, I'm…" I paused. I saw he was holding Evie's urn. *Damnit. I left her by the side. How could I forget about her?* "Hey, give her back—"

Zain pulled the urn away from me, keeping it tucked in his arm. "I think I should keep hold of her for now." He looked at the white powder around my nostrils and the lit cigarette in my hand. "You know Evie used to tell me how smart you were, how you'd never do stupid shit like *this*."

"I…I've barely had any—"

"*This* is a party for Evie after her damn funeral. She died from a drug overdose." His voice deepened, boiling with frustration. "Did you forget that when you decided to snort Dust?"

"*This* is not for Evie." My words sounded more like an echo, free of any weight or meaning. "This is just an excuse for everyone to get drunk and forget about whatever bullshit is happening in their lives."

"Not everyone needs to forget, sometimes it's okay to remember. You don't have to escape everything. You know the more you escape, the harder it is to ever return to reality, right?"

"Don't lecture me. *Everyone* here is on Dust too—"

"There's a way to take Dust and there's a way to not, Sam. People take it to have *fun* with their *friends*. They take it in small amounts *together*. But you've clearly been taking far too much of it by yourself." Zain pushed his hand back through his hair. "This *is* why you were so ill, isn't it? Why you almost *died* before I took you to the hospital? I thought you said doctors weren't allowed to do this shit?"

"Maybe I don't want to be a doctor anymore. Maybe I don't even want to *be*!" I shouted louder than I realised.

"Hey! I found us some drinks!" Reese appeared by my side again, handing me another large cup of alcohol—

Zain knocked the cup out of Reese's hand, causing it to spill onto the floor.

"Whoa," Reese said. "What's your problem?"

Zain kept his stare on me.

"I was going to drink that," I stated.

"No, you weren't." Zain shook his head. "You were going to leave."

"Leave?" I scoffed a laugh. "Now you think you can tell me what to do?"

"I'm trying to help you."

"Help me? You've got a damn ankle monitor on. You're… you're a criminal, a wasp who doesn't even belong here. You're no help to anyone."

"Take a look at yourself!" Zain roared.

I stepped away, pushing back into the dancing bodies, wanting them to trap me in their cage and keep me safe from the world. "I don't know why Evie wanted *you* to look after me. I don't want anything to do with you."

Zain swore under his breath, scrunching in his eyes as he forced himself to take deep breaths. Then he softened his tone. "I'm sorry. I don't mean to shout, I…" He stopped, taking in more deep breaths.

"What's this guy's problem?" Reese laughed, nudging his body closer to mine again. "Give over, man. Leave her alone."

"Ignore him." I put my arms around Reese's shoulder. "He seems to like throwing temper tantrums."

"I didn't mean to get angry," Zain continued regardless. "I never mean to get angry with you. I just feel everything so minutely, it's hard to control it. But I'm trying my best to learn—"

"You *never* mean to? Of course you mean to! You *always* get angry at every small—"

"It's okay to be angry at a world that deserves it!" Zain shouted, before forcing his tone lower once more. "I just...I know how consuming and how dangerous Dust is when you take too much. It messed me up for so long. You *must* see there's a difference between taking it and being addicted to it—"

"I'm not you. I can control how much I take and I can stop whenever I want." I brought the cigarette back up to my lips.

"Sam, come on, don't be an idiot. You don't even smoke."

"Leave her alone, man. Let her do what she wants." Reese held my waist as I let him move his body even closer.

"Yeah, exactly." I took in another long drag of the cigarette before blowing the smoke into Zain's face. "Or do I have to get you arrested again before you finally leave me the Hell alone?" *Please just leave me alone and let me escape from the world. Just for a little bit...*

Zain took in a stuttering breath before nodding. "You're right... Do what you want. I'll deal with you when you're a mess later on." He sharply turned and disappeared back into the crowd, taking Evie's urn with him—

He took the urn. I can't let him take Evie! "Wait!" I shoved Reese's body far away from mine with a forceful push.

"Hey, what are you..." Reese staggered backwards, but I didn't bother listening to him as I quickly moved after Zain.

"Zain! Evie! Come back!" But it felt like my voice was travelling away from my body. It didn't feel real; it didn't feel like my voice anymore.

The colours of the world blurred together as I moved towards Zain, losing me in their maze. Reality was passing away, releasing me from its grasp. I looked at my hands to check I was still there, but they were shaking uncontrollably. Yet my limbs felt more weightless than they had in days, as though every spark of pain that had been holding them down had been eradicated. All the substances I'd taken were finally kicking in, devouring my insides. *I never want to be sober again when I can feel as good as this.*

"Are you trying to tempt me?" Suddenly Death's warm voice slithered into my mind, making my body shiver in surprise as this time it felt loud; it felt real.

I turned to the door where his voice was echoing from. *He must be here this time, that was definitely him.*

A smile lit my face as I saw Death stroll inside the apartment. *He is here. So the Dust did create him…* He stepped in time to my racing heart, with one hand tucked in his pocket and the other gently swinging the silver strap of his watch. His shirt sleeves were rolled up. His top buttons were undone, and his tie sat loosely around his neck.

"You know those things will kill you?" Death stared at the cigarette in my hand. But his eyes were no longer their bright, white lights. Instead they had become hungry pits of consuming darkness, ready to devour me in one gulp.

I'm counting on it. I thought back towards him, taking in another drag of the cigarette.

"Are you now?" He moved closer through the twisting shadows, keeping up a fixed, unblinking stare and a menacing smirk.

The dancing bodies around him naturally parted, letting him freely walk towards me. No one even seemed to notice he was there, as they carried on dancing as though the world were still turning, life was still persisting even in the face of its inevitable end. *No one would notice if I slipped away with him. I could just let him take me to the peacefulness of the beyond—*

"Are you certain you want me? Or do you just want to escape everyone else?"

Can't it be both? I thought.

"As long as you don't get one confused with the other." His poisonous gaze trailed over me and his smile grew as he ran his tongue over his sharpened fangs.

I nodded over and over as though I could no longer control my body, as though I were about to collapse into a grave at last. *If…if I fall, will you catch me?*

Death stepped closer. *"Do you want me to?"* He looked directly into my soul. *"Do you want me to take you out of your suffering before you experience even more?"*

A rush of heat fled to my face as I smiled back at him, daring to stare him straight in the eyes. I took another drag of the cigarette, holding the smoke in my lungs for a long moment, before crushing it in my hand, letting it burn into my palm.

What do I have to live for? I thought towards him.

"No." He stepped even closer. *"What do you have to die for?"*

Death reached his hand towards my cheek. His fingernails seemed like vicious claws, ready to carve their blades into my flesh. But I didn't flinch as I waited to feel his calming touch, which would pull me into his labyrinth of silence—

He stopped. He offered his hand. *"Do you want to dance?"*

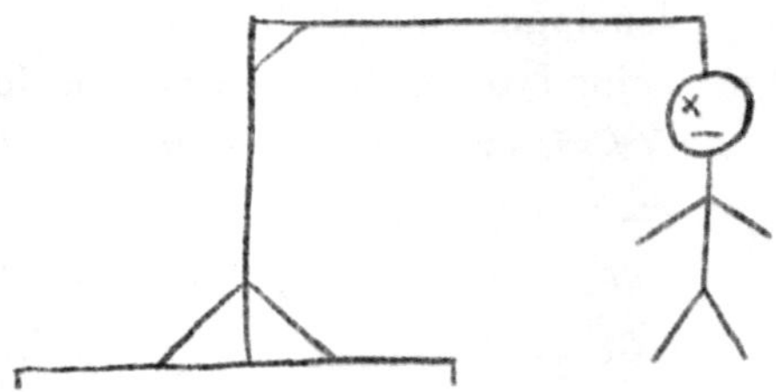

CASH IN YOUR CHIPS

13

I may as well dance with Death himself.

My heart crashed into my ribs, fighting for life I no longer needed as I stared at Death. His words repeated through my mind like a Siren's song. *Do. You. Want. To. Dance?* His dimples lit up his face as silver curls of hair tumbled over his forehead. His dark pits of eyes looked at me with hunger, staring at my mortal body, which he could so easily take away.

"Seems our appointment has finally arrived." Death widened his sedative smile as his voice trickled through my skull like honey. *"But don't you dare be afraid. Don't let your burdensome emotions cloud your desire for oblivion. Not now. Not after everything you've been through."*

Blood dripped from my nose, sweat poured from my forehead, and toxic fumes filled my lungs. Yet no fear possessed my mind. Only the desire to escape this world chained itself around my thoughts. Everything had been a chaotic mess, but Death was the perfect remedy.

I wouldn't dream of it.

"Good. Take my hand." His sharpened claws reached out. *"After all, it's way more fun to dance than to drown in sorrow, isn't it?"*

I softly held Death's hand, entering a Faustian pact from which I could never return. *So let's dance.*

A cloud of detachment lifted my troubles far from my mortal body. It felt as though I'd fallen off a cliff but someone had reached out to save me. *He* had saved me. His calming peace melted into my limbs, letting me abandon all hope as I resigned myself to death.

"Are you ready to free your soul and allow the clouds of oblivion to drag you down into an unwavering slumber?" Death's poetry floated through me like a calming depressant as he grabbed my waist—

Another hush of tranquillity slowed my beating heart at his touch. *I'm ready.*

"I know you are." Death wore a wickedly soft smile as he kissed my hand. *"You really are goddamn obsessed with me, aren't you?"* He gave a loud, resounding laugh. *"Look at you…a lamb that wants to be slaughtered."*

You wouldn't want it any other way.

"Of course not. I wouldn't dream of it."

I frowned. Death's voice had a strange lilt to it, like he was becoming more animated, more real. I wondered if he was getting closer to life or if I was getting closer to death.

The party music warped around us, morphing into an orchestral symphony, singing out a baroque melody full of glorious harmonisations that danced over instruments in trills and turns. The drunken bodies surrounding us moved across the floor like ballet dancers. The constant chatter rang in time to our steps as it transformed into a choir. Death's white boots stepped in time with my pumping blood until we were waltzing.

How does this feel so real? I thought. His hands felt so warm as they clung onto me, pulling me into their dance.

Death grinned, showing off his fanged teeth. *"What's more real than death?"*

He held me tighter, digging his claws into my waist, letting a renewed sense of safety suffocate my mind. I didn't need to worry about anything anymore. *I could just collapse and let the world fade from my view, as he would be there to catch me…*

"Do you want me to catch you?" Death chuckled, playing with my mind as though it were a riddle.

Of course I do. No one else will.

"No one?"

The music marched on around us as the bodies forcefully fell into a synchronized dance, as lost in Dust as I was. No one even looked our way or noticed I was slipping away from their world and into his. *No one ever notices.*

"I notice, Samarra Blair." Death kept his eyes on me and away from the blurred crowd around us. *"Even when everyone else ignores you."*

But why do they ignore me? I just want to speak to them properly about grief, about Evie, without them closing down conversations before they've even begun.

"They ignore you because you don't belong here. You're a wasp who's trying to fit into a beehive." Death hushed my clashing thoughts. *"Did you know the loneliest souls are always the first to seek me out? After all, what's the point of living in a world where no one's living with you? It's a comfort to have companions in misery, and you have none. Your mum has shut down, Ria is in denial, Zain is only focused on life rather than death…"* He tightened his grip on my waist. *"You have no one left, apart from me."*

You're right. I nodded.

"I always am." A devious smile twisted along his face. *"But you knew that already, didn't you? You didn't come here to find your keys to drive off to Eidyn. You knew that was a far-fetched plan. You never expected it to actually work."* Death stared deeper into

my soul. *"You came here because you wanted Dust, because you wanted me."*

He twirled my body, spinning me around his finger to the palpitating beat of the music. The wheel of the world pirouetted through my vision, twisting like a snake writhing in agony. As he pulled me back towards him, much closer than before, his lavender scent flooded my nose, losing me in the fields of Elysium.

Of course I wanted you, I thought, letting the truth of my intentions free. *The world has given me nothing but pain. I just want to escape it.*

"I know." Death nodded. *"I know you've become addicted to the only escape you have left in this pit of a world, just like every other med student."*

Wait, no, I'm…I'm not addicted. I'm not even a med student anymore.

"Thank god for that." Death's grin grew bigger, scarring his face. *"You were never cut out for it. I knew the second I saw you in the hospital, when you were shadowing that doctor as they failed to save a life."* He moved his fangs closer towards my ear. *"It made you crumble, didn't it? Seeing that dead body showed you the true difficulties of the job. No wonder it was hard for you to go back to class afterwards or return to a hospital. How can you continue with a place that attempts to save people when you couldn't even save your own sister?"*

I didn't feel any tug of sadness as he spoke. I only accepted his words, letting them fester in my mind like a plague that could never be cured.

"I'm glad you got expelled from that course. I'm glad you chose the escape of Dust over that final exam…" He continued. *"It was a resit exam, wasn't it? It was the same exam you were supposed to sit the day after Evie's death, the one you couldn't stop studying for. The one that made you miss out on spending one final night with her."*

It was. I reluctantly nodded. *If I didn't have that exam, if I didn't need to study—*

"*Nothing would have changed.*" Death silenced my mind, closing down what little thoughts I had left. "*You never would've gone out with Evie that night.*" He spun my body faster, moving me in the opposite direction of the forever-turning world.

We danced in weightless air, flowing along with the melody of my fading life. My feet stepped with spurs of energy I didn't have, spinning and leaping in bounds of blissfulness, following the centre of the music that held a rattle of breath—

Wait. A rattle was coming from my lungs. *Is that mine?* It screeched and scratched at the music as though it couldn't wait for it to stop. I realized my limbs were growing heavier too, control over my body was slipping from my grasp as the end was approaching.

"*Evie had a rattle in her throat when she died too. Is that why you're so aware of that noise?*" A grip of dread pulsated through me as Death's words forced memories of Evie to tumble back into my mind with the weight of her coffin.

She did have a rattle. It was…horrible.

"*Horrible? You know the rattle is more painful to hear than it is to have.*"

But…it sounded so agonising. I looked up into Death's dark eyes, which now looked fiercer, overflowing with starving hunger.

"*Evie's suffering had already ended by that point.*"

Does that mean her death was… Was it painless?

"*It always is.*" His words reverberated in my thoughts, leaving no room for mine. "*Remember it was her life that created her pain, not her death. The people who gave her those drugs, they're the ones who hurt her, not me… Tell me, Samarra Blair, why is it they're still alive when Evie is dead?*" Death's face distorted as he spoke. His smile was stretching, his eyes were melting, his torso was growing—

Wait, what's going on—

"Don't you want revenge for Evie's death? Doesn't she deserve that?" The music turned and turned. Death spun me around, dizzying my vision, pulling me out of reality's hands.

What's happening— My mind stumbled for stability, but I could no longer think for myself; I could only submit to him.

"You never did anything for Evie when she was alive." Death's eyes burned with dark flames of Hellfire. *"You didn't see any of her concerts, you didn't meet her best friend, you never went out with her even when she begged you. All you did was stay indoors, locked away from the world, studying for a degree you didn't like. And now, even in her death, you're doing the same. You keep saying you'll go to Eidyn and scatter her ashes, but you know you won't do that. Giving up her ashes is far too difficult, so you'll hold onto them forever, won't you? You can't accept her death, so how will you ever move on from it?"*

Suddenly Death halted my movement, forcing me to look out towards the room. The crowd of bodies turned faster around us in fragmented hysteria, waltzing and twirling in a mess of broken limbs. The music was shattering into pieces, collapsing in on itself in a discordant clashing harmony. Shadows ate every ounce of colour in the room, all except—

My heart dropped. A mustard yellow jacket hung on the door at the side of the room. *It's my jacket…* It was the jacket Evie had stolen from me countless times. The jacket she wore in her terrible funeral picture. The jacket I thought I'd never see again. *Yet there it is. Hanging on a door, waiting for me…*

Anger flooded my mind for a lost second as I thought about shouting at Evie for taking it. I thought about laughing at her for catching her red-handed. I thought about turning around and finding her there right beside me—

"But she'll never be beside you again." Death stepped beside me instead. *"So what are you going to do about it? Are you finally going to get revenge for her death? You know who killed her, you*

know who gave her the drugs she overdosed on. You can't let them live when Evie is rotting in that goddamn urn. " His voice shook with thunderous power. *"Why are you letting her soul fade to nothingness without even trying to give her the revenge she deserves? She deserves everything, doesn't she? Far more than you!"*

Death pushed me forwards with a fierce malevolence. He forced me to stumble far away from him and towards the jacket. *No, no! Wait! Don't leave me in this mess of a life without taking me with you!* Then the unbearable weight of the world crashed down on me in an instant.

14

Noise bled into my ears. Lights blinded me with brightness. The smell of sweat and alcohol and sickness suffocated me as it mixed with the hot air of the room, stealing all the oxygen from it, as polluted as the city itself.

I hit the door with staggering instability. My skull banged with a vicious headache that ate at my senses as I looked up at the yellow jacket, *my jacket,* hanging on the door. Then my worries came tumbling down on me like an anvil dropping on my skull. *Evie would be so disappointed in me. She'd hate me even more than she already does if she saw me dancing with Death, carelessly escaping the world instead of doing anything for her. I never do anything for her. I couldn't even read the damn letter she left for me!*

"Stop!" I viciously whispered to myself as the pile of thoughts collapsed in on me, caving me into their tomb. "Please…" The Dust was wearing off already, forcing the dark overcast of reality to set back in. "I can't deal with this. I need…" I looked back towards Death—

But his figure already had disappeared, losing itself in the crowd of shadows. *Wait! Don't leave me!* I ran my fingers through my knotted hair as my stomach turned over and over. *Please! I need…I need…*

I looked back at the yellow jacket before I took it off the door and hugged it close to my chest, breathing in the familiar soft smell of Evie's perfume. "I'm okay… I'm okay… Everything is…is…" But the worries wouldn't stop crowding my head, squeezing me between their malicious thorns, crushing my soul until nothing was left. *Evie would hate me for forgetting about her. She'd despise every part of me. Maybe she always hated me, just as much as I hate myself—*

An agonising twist yanked at my insides. A rush of acid burst up my body. Its sting tore into my guts before it travelled up into my throat, up, up up—

Yellow bile crashed through my mouth and splashed along the side of the room. I coughed and sputtered, doubling over in excruciating pain as my body expelled the poison from its system.

"Sam?" Ria's voice started from behind me. "What on earth are you doing?"

"Ria?" I croaked as I turned to her. But the lights were dancing around her body, her limbs seemed to be doubling, everything was nauseating. "I'm…okay. I have to be." I whispered, hugging Evie's jacket tighter. *But why is it so hard for everything to be okay?*

Another violent jolt turned inside my stomach. Quickly I staggered back to the kitchen counters before I dunked my head in the sink. But the smell hit my senses as sharp as a knife. The remnants of alcohol and bits of food and bile formed a cacophonous bite of a scent that repulsed my whole body, making the twists of my stomach even stronger. I gagged on nothing but air as pain travelled through my body, moving up, up—

Sickness forced its way out. It felt like I was drowning as it clawed out of my throat in a constant stream of bile, crashing into the sink before me. *I can't do this. I can't bear this pain. I need Death's touch again. I need…I need more Dust. Just a little more—*

"Jesus *Christ*." Ria's hands grabbed my hair, holding it back for me. "Sam, what have you taken?" She took Evie's yellow jacket off me, keeping it away from the rush of bile being exorcised from my body.

"Don't take that…" I coughed as I tried to speak, hazily turning towards Ria. "I-I need…" I focused my vision on her, but her features were blurring into a mess of shape that didn't make any sense. The world blazed with a raging fire that was burning me alive but refusing to kill me. "I…I need to see him again."

"See who?"

"Death… He-he was just here. I need him."

"*Death* was just here? Jesus, Sam, are you hallucinating?" She grabbed my face, clawing her nails into me as she looked at my dilated pupils, my bloody nostrils, my sweaty forehead. "You took Dust, didn't you?"

I pushed her hands off me, looking away from her blur of a figure. "Don't worry, it was good while it lasted."

"Good? It's clearly not good if you're hallucinating. Thank god you threw it up; you need to get it all out of your system. Maybe you should throw up again—" Ria reached to grab onto my face once more—

"Stop! That's not how it works!" I batted her hand away. "I don't *want* to get it out anyway. Dust *is* good; hallucinations are great too, even *fun*. They let me out of this damn world and let me talk about Evie's death when no one else will!"

"What are you talking about?" Ria paused. "Do you know how many bad cases of Dust overdoses I've seen? Do you even realise I could arrest you for just possessing Dust?"

"You're an apprentice; you can't arrest me," I sneered. "Even if you could, you'd have to arrest *everyone* here. Look around, Ria! *Everyone* in *your* apartment is on Dust."

She shuffled uncomfortably in her stance. "Your mum called, you know? She's worried about you and I can see why."

"My mum?" My hand automatically scrunched itself into a fist. "Why…why are you speaking to her? She doesn't even know what's going on anymore."

"She wants you back home. She said she needs to talk—"

"I don't want to go back home." *I can't go back home. I can't go back to that pit of loneliness and grief.*

Ria looked down at the sink then back to me. "I think maybe you should."

"You're not listening to me!" *She doesn't know how horrible it is to be in a house that's haunted by Evie's life. Her short, finite life, which is over and never coming back.* My fingernails dug into the wounds on my palms, reopening them as a sting of pain shot through my hands. "Why does no one *listen*!" Rage was a demanding monster, creating a need for violence I didn't know I had. *So why don't I make her listen? I could bring Death back by pushing her towards him.*

"Stop. Don't get angry at me, Sam. I'm trying to help you here—"

"Why would I ever need *your* help?" Anger beat through my mind, running faster than my heart. "I can handle myself. You should've seen the person I beat up earlier. They barely—"

"So that's how you got that scar?" Ria looked back at the cut on my cheek. "What happened? Was it Ali or one of—"

"It was a damn Shade officer! *Your* commanding officer works with Ali!" I cut over her words. "They hurt me when they should've been protecting me!"

"What?" Genuine surprise traced over her face. Then a hesitant pause clung to her words. "Why didn't you say anything to me before—"

"So it's *my* fault?"

"No, that's not what—"

"You're just as bad as the rest of the Shade. You should've protected me too, but you didn't. Just as you didn't protect Evie." *Hurt her already. Hurt her then I can feel Death once more!* "You're an officer. You're supposed to save people. Why didn't you save her?" My fist shook, flooding with anger and alcohol and everything in between. *Why didn't I save her? Why didn't anyone?*

I raised my fist in an eruption of frustration. Then I threw it towards Ria, aiming for her face. *Hurt her! Make it count—*

Ria easily side-stepped my intoxicated movements.

I stumbled for balance as my fist didn't find a target. My body twisted, spinning with the force of my failed punch before it crashed against the floor.

"Seriously?" Ria raised an eyebrow as she stared down at me. "You're trying to hurt me again? Can't you see I'm helping you?"

"I…I…" My knees burned as they hit the floor. "I need to hurt someone. I…I need to see him again." I mumbled. "I need him if I can't have *her*…"

Ria paused for a long minute before bending down towards me and reaching her hand to mine. "Come on. Get up. Let's go up to the roof and get some fresh air. We can talk more up there where it's quieter."

I hesitated, not wanting to cry in front of her.

"I know how hard everything is, Sam. I miss her too, every day." Ria held out the mustard yellow leather jacket towards me. "But you know I'm here, right? You don't have to miss her alone like you've been doing for the past six months. We can miss her together—"

"Stop." I grabbed the yellow jacket from her, snatching it back before slowly pushing myself back onto my feet. "Please."

"I hate the moment when I remember something about her life too," Ria continued. "It's always something so stupid, like the way she would make bad jokes or laugh at something she really shouldn't laugh at. The moment I remember, I have so many feelings. Too many. I want to smile at the memories but I also want to cry at the fact they are just memories—"

"Stop! Can everyone just stop talking about such stupidly specific moments, I'm tired of it!"

"Hey!" Zain shouted as his blurry figure ran up towards us. "Sam!" His eyes looked red, as though he'd been crying too. His face was covered in nerves as a flurry of heat fled over his cheeks. And he still had Evie's urn tucked under his arm.

"Zain?" Ria turned to him. "What's wrong?"

"We have to get out of here." He looked into my eyes. "Sam, I know you're angry with me, but please listen: you have to get out of here *now* if you don't want to die."

Die? There it was again, that beautifully cruel word, the one I couldn't escape from. *If I don't want to die… If.* Thank Hell I no longer wanted to escape it.

15

"What are you talking about?" Ria asked as Zain stumbled towards us. "Why would we leave—"

"Ali is here with some of Mariana's gang." Zain spoke with immediate urgency, clicking his knuckles in agitation.

"*What?*"

"I saw them out the window, walking this way, carrying baseball bats and knives." He glanced at me with widened eyes of fear. "I think they're here for you, Sam."

I looked back at him with a joyful smile. *This is exactly what Death wanted. He wanted me to hurt the people who deserved it and take Evie's revenge at last. Maybe if I hurt them, I'll feel Death's touch once more, just for a little longer.*

"Why are you smiling? You can't get into another fight," Ria bluntly stated, trailing her gaze over my face. "Do you *want* to get arrested again and go to Detention?"

"I can either get arrested by corrupt officers or I can fight people who deserve to be hurt. So take a guess which one I want to do," I stated with far too much confidence.

"God, Sam, you really have changed, haven't you?" Ria shook her head. "You don't even realise what you've done. Mariana is a vicious person who'll kill anyone who hurts her people. You know you're a dead man walking, right?"

A dead man walking. Her words ran over me like a comforting promise.

"It's okay, you can get out of here before they get up in the elevator," Zain said, trying to save me even though I didn't want to be saved. "I'll make sure Ali doesn't even lay a finger—"

"No, Zain, stop," said Ria. "You're not getting into a fight either. You're leaving too." She rubbed her temples, breathing through her pounding stress. "If you take Sam out the back, I can call the station—"

"Don't call the Shade. They'll only arrest *me* again. As soon as they know Mariana's gang is here, they'll pin it all on me, no thanks to *this*." He gestured to the blinking ankle monitor.

"But we can still call them and I'll tell them…"

I didn't bother to listen to their pointless ideas as I walked out of the apartment door, moving like the ghost I wanted to be. *I'm so close to feeling Death again.* I wiped the back of my hand against my runny nose before sniffing up any last particles of Dust stuck in my nostrils. My vision was still distorted, but now the jigsaw pieces were putting themselves back together. The world was mending itself and I couldn't wait to break it back open.

The corridor was much quieter now. Fewer people lined the hall, as though they'd all migrated into the apartment. *Or maybe they went home. What time even is it?* Regardless, I used this quiet moment to pull out a small baggie from the side of my bra that was overflowing with heavenly Dust. Maybe I had swiped it off

Reese, but I figured I needed it much more than him. *I only need a little to make this pain go away. Just a little.*

Quickly I dipped my finger inside the bag before rubbing the powder along my gums, letting its acidic burn melt into my mouth with a delicious familiarity, easing my compulsion. *Finally.* Then my shoulders slumped. Apathetic tiredness overcame my limbs. My body stopped aching as pain floated far away from me.

"Sam, get back!" Zain ran towards me, trying his best to keep me stuck in the madness of life.

"Stop! Don't go that way!" Ria called as she followed behind. "We have to go out the back!"

The heavy music continued to play in the apartment, thumping into a mess of a song as the notes ran faster than they were supposed to. The tempo raced onwards and no instrument could catch up to it.

"Go this way before the elevator comes up!" Ria grabbed my arm and pulled me in the other direction. "There's a staircase we can—"

DING. The elevator doors chimed, landing perfectly in time to the end of the blaring music.

Ali stepped out, wearing a tank top that purposefully showed off the strength of his muscles. Bruises and cuts decorated his bare skin, while a quiet rage flooded through his expression.

"Samarra. It's so nice to see you again," Ali began as three other figures followed him, each carrying intimidating weapons and staring at me with dark, frenzied eyes that were starved for blood.

The people who deserve to die are here at last. I flung on the yellow leather jacket I'd been carrying, letting it fit over my shaking limbs and hug tightly against my skin with a warmth I didn't know I'd missed. *I can finally get Evie her revenge.*

"*Finally, indeed.*" Death suddenly appeared too, leaning against the elevator doorway, standing just behind this cluster of thugs.

Death's still...here? He hasn't left me.

Death was a little too far away from me to reach, but he watched me intently with a wicked grin. His shirt was further unbuttoned and messily hung loose from his trousers. His silver hair was a scruffy tumble of curls, while his eyes were dark, hungry pits of infernal Hell. And his teeth seemed like much larger fangs, as sharp as knives that dripped with fresh blood. *"It's finally time for you to take someone's life and give it to me."*

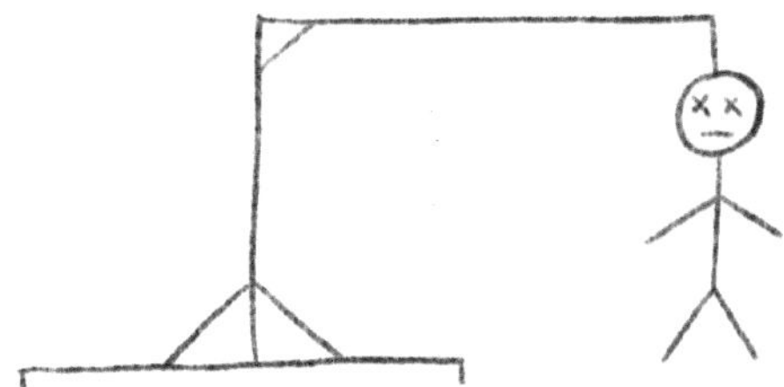

NO REST FOR THE WICKED

16

I may as well close my eyes and plunge into darkness.

"Ali…" Ria began, backing away from the elevator. "We were actually just leaving—"

"Good. Samarra can leave with us," Ali said in a much lower tone, putting on his most intimidating persona.

"Ali." Zain stepped forwards, standing directly in front of me. He still had Evie's urn tucked under his arm, keeping her close. "What are you doing here?"

I'd almost forgotten they were brothers, but seeing them together made me realise how similar they looked. They had the same dark waves of hair and eyes to match, their skin was the same deep brown colour, and their Northern accents fell into the same intonation patterns. *How did I never notice it before?*

"We were told Samarra was here partying with you all, taking even more Dust off us," Ali stated. "So we thought we'd pay a visit and finally take back what's owed—"

"You don't have to do this, Ali," Zain interrupted. "You don't have to keep working for them and letting them take advantage of—"

"This is none of your concern, Zainy!" Ali roared over him. "If I were you, I'd turn around and walk away. You don't want to get on the wrong side of us again. Not like last time."

Zain held his ground. "I'm not going anywhere." *Why's he standing up for me when I pushed him away so many times?* "I won't let you hurt her."

"Then shall we get you arrested again?" Ali looked at the tracking device strapped around Zain's ankle. "It would be easy enough wearing *that* thing, if your anger doesn't get you into trouble first that is. I'm sure the people at Detention have missed having their punching bag around."

Zain unconsciously flinched before readjusting his stance, holding Evie's urn tighter. "This isn't about me. I just need you all to leave. Don't you have better places to be? Don't you have school visits to be making with all that damn Dust?" he scoffed.

"We'll leave peacefully *with* Samarra. She needs to finally pay us what is owed," Ali said. "She's been racking her debts up for months now. She's even worse than Evie was, what with all the Dust she's been taking off us."

Zain paused for a moment. I wondered if he was mad at me for lying to him, if he was ready to now betray me— "Leave her alone," he finally said. "*I* can get you whatever money she still owes."

"With what? Your pathetic little restaurant job? Or with your band that no longer has a drummer?"

"I can find—"

"You can't." Ali shook his head. "You don't understand what's at stake here. I've let her get away with this for too long. If I don't take her with us then *I* will be the one…" Ali trailed off as he brought out a large kitchen knife and held it up with a menacing intent. Bloodstains trickled along its overly sharpened edge. "Just don't get in my way, Zainy. I don't want to hurt you."

"You don't want to hurt me?" Zain's temper soared as bustling energy flowed through his tone. "You just took out a damn knife! What kind of pathetic person threatens his own brother—"

"I'm doing this for your own good!"

THUMP. Ali shoved Zain to the side, knocking his skull against the wall with one forceful push.

Zain roared with pain, collapsing to the floor. He cursed and swore as his vision blurred in a dizzying blow. He managed to keep Evie's urn upright as he fell to his knees, standing it against the wall while he clawed at the agony radiating through his head.

"*Zain!*" Ria shouted, stepping forwards.

Ali blocked her path. "Turn around and walk away, unless you want to get hurt too." He tipped the blade of the knife towards her.

Ria straightened her posture, trying to rid any fear from her expression. "You can't threaten me. You'll get arrested if you even—"

"We know you're not a real officer." One of the other thugs snickered. They didn't seem as strong as Ali, but they were much taller as they towered over us all. "No one in the Shade even takes apprentices seriously."

"Are you willing to bet on that? Because the law is already on their way," Ria loudly announced. "Officers will be here any moment."

"Good. Let them come." The tall one sniggered. "We could use some backup."

Ria hesitated. "They *will* arrest you." She acted as though she believed her own words. "They know you're associated with Mariana's drug ring, meaning they're eager to arrest you all. As soon as they find even the smallest bit of Dust on you, they'll keep you locked up for—"

"Does that go for her too?" Ali's eyes fell on mine. "Will she get arrested with how much Dust is in her system?"

"Stop." Ria stepped closer to him. "Leave her out of this, Ali. She—"

THUD. Ali pushed Ria to the side, knocking his fist straight into her stomach, forcing her to double over as she fought through gasps to find her breath.

"I'm tired of this game," Ali said. "Come on, Samarra. Time to go."

I froze, seeing Ria and Zain collapsed at the sides of the corridor. *They both tried to protect me, even after everything I've done to them. But why would anyone try to help—*

"Stop worrying. It's time for you to fight." Death's voice fell into my mind like a drop of ecstasy. He was still waiting in the background, casually looking onto the scene like it was a sporting event. *"Or are you going to let these people take your pointless little life, just as they took Evie's?"*

A smile escaped my lips as I looked towards Death. *I'm so glad he's still here, waiting for me.* My limbs relaxed with ease. Nothing mattered when he was here. Everything else was just empty noise, a vast black hole of chaos, and I didn't care whether or not I was a part of it.

I don't intend to just let them, I thought towards him.

"Really?" Death stood up straight, keeping his clawed hands deep within his pockets. *"Does that mean you're willing to roll the dice with your fate, to see if it will be your soul or theirs I take?"*

I guess it can't hurt to find out.

"Getting hurt is the only *way to find out. Feeling the fear, the pain, the suffering—everything life throws at you. That's the only way you'll ever know if you truly want it. Although…you haven't felt any fear in a while."* Death chuckled. *"And being afraid means being alive, doesn't it? How curious…"*

My mind blinked out of his gaze as the weight of his words ran over me. *Those were the words Evie said to me before she died: Being afraid means being alive.*

"They were *her words, weren't they? Before Ali's drugs killed her."* Death's words overpowered my head. *"Are you going to continue to let the world beat you into submission and grief swallow you whole? Or are you going to finally take all your pain and give it right back?"*

The music from the apartment changed tracks. A deep, husky voice sung over pounding drums and a rising tempo, spurring me on as I finally stepped forwards, returning to my unwanted skin of life. *Death's right; he's always right. Why bother trying to fit into a world that's abandoned me? I may as well burn it all to the ground, just as it has burned me.*

I cleared my throat. "Have you come to kill me just as you killed Evie? Or do you want me to beat *you* up again?" I spoke with confidence I shouldn't have had.

"I don't want to hurt you, Samarra." Ali moved up to me, pointing the knife in my direction. "We just need to take you to Mariana."

I frowned as I saw Ali's strangely large pupils. His balance wasn't steady either. His grip on the knife was poor and his palms were sweaty. *He's on Dust again, isn't he? He's as lost as I am.* I smiled at the realization, letting the overconfident part of my brain think: *I can take him.*

"Ali, stop it!" Zain shouted, stumbling to his feet, refusing to sit back any longer. "Please don't—"

Suddenly the tall thug grabbed onto Zain's arms with a fierce strength and pulled him away from us and away from Evie's urn, which was now sitting on the floor. *Evie… I need to keep her safe.*

"Hey, get off me!" Zain struggled from their grasp, twisting his body in constant attempts to escape, letting his fighting spirit shine through. "Get off!"

Ali ignored him as he pointed the knife towards my neck, but his grip continued to shake. He was so far gone that nothing would bring him back. "I need to do my job and take you to

Mariana. That's it." He pressed the cool blade of the knife against my skin. But it didn't even feel like a weapon. It felt more like an invitation. "Please don't make me hurt you."

I leaned closer towards him, letting the knife scratch at my neck. "Do it. I dare you. Kill me, just like you killed Evie."

"I told you that wasn't my fault."

"Of course it was, *you* sold her the Dust. I'm sure you've sold it to countless other young people, haven't you?" Adrenaline poured through my blood as rage boiled itself into my thoughts. "How many others have you sold it to, huh? How many other kids who didn't know any better? How many more have you killed?"

"Don't listen to her!" Ria yelled in a stern voice, stumbling back onto her feet. "She's clearly too intoxicated for this. Put the knife down, Ali!"

"Stay out of this, you Shade bastard," Ali spat. "Your officers have already hurt me enough this past week."

"Ali, please stop!" Zain shouted too, letting his anger burn through his words as he continued fighting to get out of the other thug's hold. "Don't you dare hurt her!"

"Stay out of this, Zain," I started fiercely, taking him back by surprise. *I don't need him to fight; I want to handle this myself.* "I don't need your help."

"You're clearly too high on Dust to be making that decision," Zain yelled with unrelenting energy.

"You don't understand what I'm going through! You still have a sibling who's alive!" I stepped closer towards Ali, pushing his knife into my own flesh, letting a trail of blood drip from my neck. "Even though he deserves to be dead."

"Don't let me get bored now, Samarra Blair." Death laughed with excitement. *"Is it finally time to fight? I want to see some action!"*

It is.

"Good. Then take his life for me, for Evie. Take it and never give it back."

I focused on the music in the distance, which was forming a gorgeous melody of a depressing song over a heavy beat. I let it sing into my ears and rush my heart on faster as though it were part of the drum track. I focused on the beat as I pushed Ali's knife away, letting the blade scratch my skin, cutting into my flesh. But the pain didn't matter to me as I drew back my other hand and punched him in the throat.

17

THUD. My fist burned as it drove into Ali's windpipe with brutal force, hurting the same spot I'd injured earlier. Ali howled, falling backwards as he coughed and sputtered for air that wasn't his.

Use this moment of weakness. Snatch the knife! I acted faster than I thought I could, using the split second to grab Ali's hand, which held the knife. *Take it!* I pulled back his thumb at a wrong angle, twisting it out of its socket. He let out another scream until his grip loosened and I took the blade from him, much more easily than I thought possible. *He's so out of it. He'll be so easy to hurt and hand over to Death.*

Suddenly another thug stepped towards me, ready to knock the knife out of my hands. *No, no—*

"Stop!" Ria commanded as she pushed them backwards, trying to knock them from their feet. But they were too strong for her as they easily side-stepped her movements, before plunging their fist into her guts with a THUMP.

"Stop it, please!" Zain's voice was lost in the commotion as he fought against the tall thug, ripping his arms out of their grasp. "Leave them both alone!"

"I…" Ali wheezed through his breaths as he looked at me. "I don't want to hurt you, Samarra."

"Why don't you try?" I raised the knife up high. *Cut him before he catches his balance, before someone else tries to take the knife off me again. Do it now!* I slashed it down diagonally, slicing through his body, ripping into his flesh—

Ali automatically raised his arms to protect himself, but he couldn't step back in time; he couldn't escape the knife's blow as it came crashing down on him—

Harrowing torment clung to his cry as the knife carved itself into his bare arms in one swift motion. Blood splattered onto my face, drowning me in its iron taste as I watched torture spread over Ali's mortal limbs.

Shouts echoed from the apartment behind us. The intoxicated hive from the party peeked out as his screams caught their attention. Without any hesitation, some of them ran to join in with the fight, throwing punches and tackling bodies that weren't even involved, buzzing with inebriated adrenaline. The tempo of the music sped up, falling into a fast flow of notes. The punches and kicks joined the crashing percussion as bodies blurred together in a discordant melody of chaos.

The ashes. They're going to crash into the ashes. My mind forced me to look at Evie's urn. *I need to get Evie. I need to protect her!*

I stumbled forwards, reaching towards the urn. "Evie!" I yelled in desperation, not wanting the fighting bodies to collapse into her. *I need to keep her safe! I need to keep hold of the urn, the pain, the suffering, the misery—*

"*What are you doing?*" Death darkly stared at me from within the crowd. "*Ali is so close to dying; it'll be easy to push him over the edge. Grab his goddamn heart and feed it to me!*" His tone felt like he was growing more alive, brimming with the tempting spirit of Mephistopheles. "*Stop worrying about the urn unless you want to join Evie in those goddamn ashes!*"

Another thug quickly stepped in front of me. They grabbed my hair, digging their fingers onto my skull. *No, no!* They used all their strength to pull me forwards and throw me past them, pushing me onto the floor—

THUMP. My face hit the floor first. A sudden headache pounded through my skull like a crash of cymbals that moved the tempo on faster. *I need to get to the urn!* A trickle of blood ran along my lips as I reached out towards Evie with the bloodied knife still in my hand. *I need to save her—*

A scream tore through my throat as a boot crushed my hand, stomping on it over and over. It bashed into my fingers, spreading them out, forcing me to let go of the knife. *No, I can't let go of the knife!*

"You didn't have to make this so difficult," Ali began as he took the knife off me before crushing my fingers further under the weight of his boot. "It didn't have to go this way."

Pain seized through my body, making me want to scream. But instead I turned my howl into a laugh. I drove all my sorrow into a loud, throbbing laugh that wouldn't stop. "I know it didn't have to, but I'm glad it did."

Ali shook his head, panting through hurried breaths. "Just come with me already." He grabbed my arm, digging his fingers into my rotting flesh as he yanked me onto my feet. "It's time to put an end to this."

A cold burn shot into my spine as Ali pressed the tip of the knife into my back, forcing me towards the elevator doors. His other hand twisted its fingernails into my arm, locking me in a hold from which I couldn't escape.

But I need Evie's urn. I can't leave her all alone! Panic seeped into my thoughts like a vicious snake. "Wait… Stop. I need Evie!"

"Sam!" Zain shouted. He was crumpled on the floor. His cheek was red, blood was dripping from his nose, and his limbs shook as he tried to stand up. "Ali, get the Hell off her!" He still continued to fight as he stumbled to his feet, almost falling over as he moved towards us.

"Zain, get Evie! Please look after her!" my voice croaked.

Zain raced towards me, staggering through his lost balance, refusing to give up—

CRACK. A baseball bat swung into his head. The force knocked his skull to the side, twisting his neck with a loud *snap* before his body slumped to the floor and another thug stood over him.

"Zain!" I screamed. *Is he alive? Is he okay? And what about Evie? I can't die without her—*

"You worry too much about others, even when your soul is the one in danger. I did warn you that worrying would be the end of you. Is that what it's come to?" Death's hypnotising voice sang through my mind. But I could no longer see him in the mess of the scene; his peaceful figure had disappeared from my view. *"Quiet your goddamn mind already. Unclasp yourself from the burdens of life and live to die. Live. To. Die."*

"Keep moving!" Ali shoved me forwards, forcing me to walk faster as I hobbled on my heel, which burned with pain.

I can't die like this.

"Why not? Isn't this what you want?" Death's disembodied voice continued. *"You want it all to end. You want to fall down to the bottomless pits of Hell. The only thing you get to decide now is who you're going to take down with you."*

THUMP. Ali shoved me against the elevator doors. My head shattered against its hard surface. But what rose to the surface beyond the pain was anger. *Death's right. I need to hurt them all and take everything from them just as they took it from me!*

"So stop being a coward and take it."

DING. The elevator opened before us, revealing Death's figure standing inside. He seemed taller and far more muscular as he casually leaned against the back corner. His head was face down, but his eyes stared up towards us with a cruel hunger. His gaze flicked between me and Ali, eagerly waiting to see which one of us would die first.

18

The elevator doors slammed shut behind us, cutting off the beating music and swallowing us in silence.

"This wasn't supposed to go this way," Ali wheezed through his lost, panting breath. "Why do you always make everything so difficult?"

"Don't let him talk to you like this." Death fixed his hungry eyes on mine. *"Just stab his guts out and I'll do the rest."*

I can't… I thought back to him, stumbling to find my balance as Ali finally let me go. *I don't have a weapon. I can't fight him—*

"You're going to have to."

"I didn't want to hurt you, Samarra. I didn't want *any* of this!" Ali turned the knife towards my chest. The tip of the blade dug into my skin, daring me to make it cut deeper. "You're going to regret doing this."

"Regret?" I tilted my neck to the side as I cracked the bones, readying myself for another fight. "Regrets are for the living."

Before Ali even registered my words, I clenched my hands into fists and with one fierce swing of movement I crashed my fingers straight into his nose with a—

CRACK. His neck twisted to the side in one sharp swing. His nose bent under the weight of my fist. His eyes automatically shut with the surge of distress, giving me less than a second to do something else. *Act before he retaliates!*

Blood trailed along my chest. The knife had cut me as I had punched him, but the pain didn't matter—*nothing matters. I just need to get the knife!*

I reached for the blade. I grabbed the handle, ready to twist it out of his hand—

Ali pulled back, shooting the knife to the side, hitting our arms against the elevator wall—

His hand slammed into the "STOP" button, cutting the elevator movement short with a sudden jolt. I stumbled for balance as the elevator shook. But in that moment, Ali's other hand reached out and gripped onto my neck. His fingers crushed my windpipe, cutting off the blood circulation, choking the soul out of my body.

I can't let him kill me. I have to take him down too! I clawed at his fingers as my breath ran away from me, trying to twist them off. *I don't have long. I could pass out in a matter of seconds!*

But Ali only tightened his grip with fierce strength. "Why did you make me do this to you?" With his other hand, he brought the knife back up to my chest, cutting into my skin in a deep scratch of violence.

A scream escaped my lungs as my flesh burned with excruciating torment. Then suddenly I felt Death's breath beat against the back of my neck as he moved behind me.

"Is it your soul I'll be taking? Not his? Or are you going to fight now?"

Fight? I have been fighting! But I can't—

"You've been fighting to hurt him, but now you need to fight to kill him." Death's hungry jaw moved up to my ear.

I can't. He's too strong—

"He has a heart that can be stopped, so stop it." Death's hands were by my side, so close to touching me once more. *"If you want me, you have to hurt him. Unless you'd rather leave me and return to your broken little life? Unless you'd rather go back to a lonely existence, where you push everyone away, where your career has lost all purpose, where that miserable house of never-ending grief is waiting to trap you inside for another six months, if not much longer?"*

He's right, I have nothing to lose. Nothing. Quickly I moved my hands away from the fingers on my neck and instead towards the hand that held the knife. *The knife is what I need; that's the weapon that'll take his life. So take it before I lose consciousness!*

I twisted my fingers around Ali's thumb, adding pressure to the weak, controlling part of his grip. *Hurry up!* I sharply yanked it back, pulling it out of its socket, forcefully loosening his grip—

But Ali still held on. I couldn't get the knife to myself. *This won't work. He's too strong—*

No, he's not. Ali's palms were growing sweatier. His dilated pupils stared at me with twitching instability. *He's on Dust, remember? I can do this. I can—*

"*If you don't stab his heart right now, I assure you he will stab yours.*" Death's black pits of eyes grew darker, impatiently burning into a frenzy of hunger. The shadows around him vibrated with intense cravings, desperate to swallow a soul.

Black spots covered my vision as I turned the knife towards Ali, adding more pressure onto his thumb as I fought to control the blade's movements. *Hurry up!* My limbs were weakening, losing control as oxygen left my brain. *I'm running out of time!* I used whatever dregs of energy I had left to push the blade towards him. Then with all my remaining strength, I shoved the knife into his stomach—

Ali resisted against it, pushing it away, trying to turn the blade back towards me. *He's still so much stronger than me.* Desperation clung to my last breath as I pressed all my body weight into the knife. *I have to do something if I want to live—*

No, I have to do something if I want him to die.

Suddenly I kicked out my foot, stomping into Ali's leg as hard as I could. I crushed the sharp corner of my heels into the side of his knee, aiming for the weakest ligament, hitting it with all I could in a loud, resounding—

CRACK. Ali's knee bent and twisted in on itself, knocking his balance. *This is my chance!* As he stumbled backwards, I shoved my weight into the knife, using up every ounce of strength I had left to push the blade into his stomach.

Ali's scream pierced my eardrums as the knife cut straight into his guts, slicing his insides. Warm blood gushed out of the wound, dripping over my hands. His grip around my neck finally loosened.

I gasped for air, taking back what was mine. *I did it.* A vicious laugh clawed through my throat. *Finally.* I shoved harder on the knife, pushing it deeper into him, knocking him backwards until he hit the side of the elevator door.

Ali's flesh squelched around his organs, tearing apart under the weight of the knife. "P… Pl…" He tried to speak, but his voice no longer existed as a rattling sound overtook his staggered breaths until—

THUMP. He collapsed on the hard floor. Blood pooled around his weakening limbs, drowning whatever was left.

I stared down at the body. *Wait… Did I just…* Stuttering panic slithered into me. *Why the Hell did I—*

Death's hands grabbed onto my waist before I had a second to question myself. An overwhelming peacefulness exploded through me, killing my thoughts. His touch warmed me with calmness I didn't know existed. His hands felt like an enchanting gift that burst with sparks of magic, greeting me with the end of all ends. They reminded me that nothing mattered. No one mattered. No one except him.

"Keep going. Impale him with that goddamn knife one more time." Death's voice sung into my ear. *"Remember all the suffering life has put you through and give it all right back!"* Fangs were coming out of Death's mouth like sharp daggers. It wasn't his hands that were around me—it was his claws. They were bony, skeletal blades, sharpened into a weapon. His silver hair was splattered with blood. His eyes were shadowed, bottomless pits. And his grin was widening farther than seemed possible,

distorting his face. *"You've got this, Samarra Blair. Take his soul for me."*

Ali was trying to sit up against the wall, to grasp onto the life that was slipping away from him. But buckets of blood were pouring out of his wounds and a corpse had started taking his place.

"He deserves to die."

I raised the knife once more, aiming towards Ali's heart. *He does deserve to die.*

"Everyone deserves to die for all the pain they've put you through." Death spoke like a Siren's call I couldn't resist. *"Everyone."*

Everyone. Deserves. To. Die. I leaned down, pushing my weight into the knife as I shoved it through Ali's ribcage, letting it crunch and *crack* through his bones. I thrust the blade as far down as it would go, tearing him apart with crucifying torture. Blood flooded Ali's lungs as his breath rattled while he gasped for life that was already gone.

Death's eyes darkened, swallowing him in a furious wave of sin as he bent down to Ali's body. *"This is the end."* He placed his hands on Ali's chest. *"It's time for you to shuffle off this mortal coil, to explore the undiscovered country, and to never fucking return."*

Death dug his claws, which were as sharp as a scythe into Ali's chest, shredding away skin, tearing flesh apart. Blood flung all over the elevator as Death buried his way deeper and deeper. Then he sunk his teeth into Ali's neck in a rush of overwhelming hunger, biting off bigger and bigger chunks of flesh to devour the soul beneath.

I watched Death intently, unable to look away. For some reason I wanted him to destroy the body. I wanted him to drag it around the walls of the city, to let it rot in the sun and decay into ashes, never allowing it to be buried, never allowing Ali's soul to rest.

Death swallowed hard as he finished his meal. Then he looked at me as he stood up. His mouth dripped with fresh blood, and his fangs had rips of skin dangling from them. And then there was a fierce look of never-ending hunger aching through his eyes as he reached towards me with the sickly claws of Tartarus.

"Wait." I flinched at his monstrous complexion as though part of me was still clinging on to sanity. "Wait! I don't want—"

But he didn't stop. He grabbed my waist and pulled my body towards him, moving me as effortlessly as a feather.

My worries dropped dead. My intentions, my motivations, my grief, my *everything* fell into their grave. I was no longer scared of the creature that held me. Instead I was comforted by him as that wave of calmness crashed into my thoughts and suddenly I felt—

Nothing. Quiet, beautiful nothingness.

"Don't worry, you're okay. Everything is okay, remember? Why would it ever not be?" Death's fingers softly traced over my cheek with a delicate touch. He wrapped his bloodied claws around me in a perfect quietness, carrying me to nirvana. *"It's always okay when you're on Dust, isn't it? Nothing can hurt you when you're no longer living in reality."* He leaned towards me and softly kissed my forehead, staining it with blood.

No joy came from feeling him kiss me. No happiness, no bright light, no rush of excitement. It was still that same calming, peaceful nothingness. Nothing more, nothing less, just *nothing*.

"Isn't this exactly what you dreamed of?" Death's grip tightened as he pushed me firmly against the elevator doors.

My body submitted to his will. My mind emptied itself, too free to even think for itself. Thinking was too much now that Death could think for me. It felt as though I'd entered the Elysium plains of paradise. I never wanted him to let me go. I never wanted to leave this glorious cocoon of safety when—

"Pity it's already over."

DING. The elevator came to a sudden stop as though it had shot itself in the head. The doors flung open. Then I fell from Death's grasp.

The coldness of reality stabbed my chest. My head pounded as I collapsed onto the floor. Dizzyingly bright lights shot into my vision with a violent shove. *Wait, no. Don't let me go. I don't want to feel this. I don't want to feel!*

I looked back up towards the bloodied elevator, but Death was no longer in it. *No, no!* I twisted my body as I pushed myself onto all fours, but my limbs were shaking. The pain of life was hurtling towards me in one unstoppable blow.

"Fr…freckles?" A fearful voice whispered behind me.

I slowly looked around, seeing I was now on the ground floor of the apartment building. Zain was standing behind me, swaying as he fought to remain upright. Blood dripped from a deep gash on his skull. Wheezes of breath barely escaped his lungs. And his hands were cuffed behind his back.

"What the…" An officer stood next to him, wearing their dark trench-coat with unquestioning authority.

No, no… Are they here to arrest me? Am I going to be taken away and sent to—

No. Not arrested, something much worse. I looked at their hardened face, at their plain blonde hair, which looked like a wig, and the bright blue strands of hair falling out from under it.

"What have you done?" the officer said, staring with widened, fearful eyes straight ahead of me.

I followed their gaze into the elevator—

A corpse looked back at me. Blood was drowning the body. The face was as pale as that of a soulless ghost. A knife was plunged into the chest as though it had been hammered into him. Bite and claw marks covered ripped skin, while the eyes had lost every ounce of life that once made Ali's soul.

"Ali?" Zain's frail voice cracked. "A-Ali? Ali, can you hear me?" He tried moving towards the corpse—

The officer tightened their grip on Zain, pulling him back.

"Ali!" Zain continued, letting his voice break under the weight of his distress. "*Ali!*"

"Goddamn it," the officer said, staring down at me. "I'm taking you to Mariana right *now*."

I know I should have been overwhelmed with worrying thoughts, unsurmountable regrets, and crushing guilt. But instead, all I could do was smile as I stared at Ali's corpse. It reminded me of how calming Death's embrace had been. It made me realize how much I wanted to feel it again, *for just a bit longer.*

He deserved to die anyway. Everyone deserves to die, don't they?

I kept up my smile as I looked back to the officer standing over me.

Everyone.

I'm okay? I'm okay?? Am I???
I have to be okay.

PART THREE

Everything HAS to be okay.
Nothing matters.
Nothing
Everything IS Okay??
IS IT??

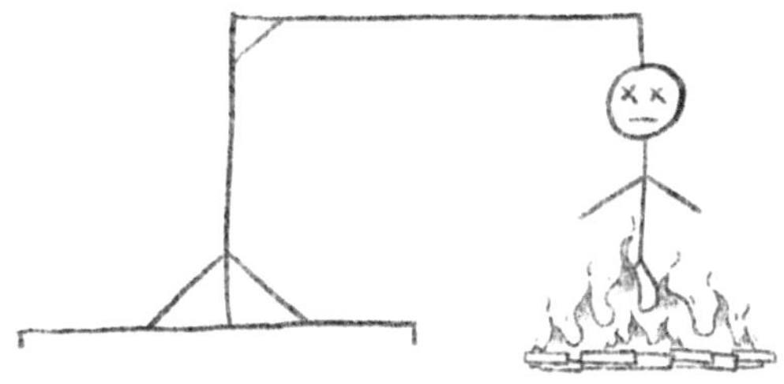

LAMB TO THE SLAUGHTER

1

Everyone is going to die.

Colourful lights danced over the club in deadly lightning flashes. The heavy bass pounded through my body with the force of a mallet. The stench of alcohol drenched the suffocating air. Every one of my senses was strangled by the havoc of life as we walked into Mariana's house of Hades.

The officer and two of Ali's thugs dragged me and Zain through the busy club, pushing past the sweaty, dancing bodies that were lost in ecstasy, drowning in Dust's addictive charm. Yet they all looked so young, *far too young.* The club was next to the university campus and not far from a local college. It was made to attract young, vulnerable people. It was made to create victims of Dust. *They're going to die. Everyone here is going to die!*

"Move it!" The officer shoved Zain forwards, wrapping their fingers into the waves of his hair to keep him within their grasp.

But Zain could barely walk. His balance was unsteady, his limbs were shaking, and his face was full of unquestionable fear.

"Get *off*. I…need to get back. I need to…help Ali," Zain said through gasps, using the little energy he had left to fight back, persisting even in the face of defeat.

The other thugs held me, giving me no chance to escape as they dug their nails into my wrists and shoulders. I'd tried to fight them at Ria's apartment building, but their combined strength was too much for me. They had beat me instead, leaving more cuts and bruises along my rotting flesh. But I couldn't give them the satisfaction of dying, *not yet*. I needed to take them down with me. *They don't deserve the air they breathe. No one does.*

"Ali's been way too easy on both of you. He's let you get away with this far too long," the blue-haired officer stated as they dragged us to the other side of the dancefloor. "Thank god you took care of him, Samarra. If you hadn't, Mariana would've happily finished him off."

We moved up to a VIP door, where a tall, overweight bouncer stood guard, blocking our path.

"Let us in," the officer commanded. As they spoke, they raised their head, showcasing a fresh scar stained across their neck. *I did that to them… I can't wait to do even more damage.*

The bouncer paused for a long moment as they looked at me with deep curiosity. "Huh…" Then they nodded at the officer. "Mariana's downstairs. She's been waiting." They opened the door and gestured us into its empty pit.

Shadows scuttled away from our feet as we stepped through the doorway and down a hidden stairwell. Mangled twists of gloom covered our vision as darkness ate every slice of light. The pounding music bled through the walls, moving in time with our steps as we descended into our inevitable graves.

"Mariana's gonna be so pleased to see you," the tall thug whispered too close to my ear, tightening their hold on me as we plunged into the lifeless underground of the club. "I wonder how long it'll take for her to kill you."

I copied their laugh. "I wonder too." My words overflowed with confidence as fear no longer resided in my thoughts and all hope had been abandoned. *I have nothing left to lose, not even my life.*

"You won't be laughing for much longer." They glared at me as we moved to the bottom of the stairs, towards the large double doors waiting for us at the end.

"Sam…" Zain mumbled. His bleeding head hung forwards as his eyes dropped him in and out of consciousness. "You have to…fight. Fight to survive…"

The officer knocked on the basement door in a rhythmic pattern. TH-TH-TH. THUD. THUD. THUD. TH-TH-TH.

Survive? The tempo of the music spurred on, racing in palpitating beats, forcing the world to spin faster around us. *Why would I want to do that?* Familiar rage took its place in my thoughts. *No one is going to survive.*

I wondered what Mariana would be like and what I was about to step into. Everyone had been talking about her as though she were a viciously powerful demon. *I guess she's the ultimate monster here… If she supplied Ali with Dust, she's the reason Evie overdosed. It all goes back to her. She deserves to die more than—*

CRASH. The double doors flew open, hitting back against the wall. Bright, heavenly lights pierced my vision. Then angry shouts and loud voices joined the cacophony of noise.

"Why have you let Ali get away with this for so long!" one of the voices yelled.

"How much money does she even owe?" another shouted.

"Why the Hell have they been allowed to live until now?"

I squinted until my eyes readjusted to the screaming mess of the world. It looked like we had walked into the storage room of the club, as it was full of barrels and bottles of stock along the walls. In the centre, a group of people shouting at one another in meaningless conversations stood around a couch with a glass coffee table before it. Then on the table I saw beautiful piles of Dust.

My mouth salivated as I stared at it. *There's so much Dust...* Some of the white powder was in small bags, some sat in larger packages waiting to be cut, some had been made into pills, and some had been carelessly thrown in a large heap in the centre of the table. *I've never seen so much Dust before.*

"*This* is her?" One of the voices laughed as the blur of figures walked up towards us.

"How is this the person we've been waiting for?"

"This must be some kind of joke."

The hive of people were strong and stocky, each with brutal smiles across their faces. They gathered around us, submerging me in their sea of bodies. Then their hands started grabbing my arms, prodding my ribcage, pulling my hair, squeezing my cheeks. *Get off, get off! There's too many of them to fight back against. Too many to kill. Too many, too—*

"Get off her!" One voice dominated the room, shouting above them all. "Go back upstairs and make yourselves useful already."

The figures around me didn't even try to protest as they let me go. They murmured insults under their breath before walking past us, disappearing through the doors and locking them shut.

I panted for breath as they left. I heard the officer snicker as they kept their grip firmly intertwined in Zain's hair, forcing him to remain on his feet. My wrists and shoulders were still being held by the two other thugs who had turned silent. Fortunately everyone else in the room had now vanished with the shadows. Everyone except...

"So...*this* is her?" The dominating voice spoke out. It was a high-pitched tone that sounded soft and non-threatening, yet power emanated from every word.

Mariana. She's the one who killed Evie. She—

Wait… I looked back at the couch in the centre of the room, to the woman sitting across it in a leaned-back, casual position. *Mariana…?* Confusion slithered into my skull as I looked her up and down. *Why does she look like…* She had long waves of blonde hair that contrasted against her dark roots and neatly framed her freckled face. The dress she wore was an identical copy of mine yet hers was a bright white colour instead of black. And her dark, lifeless eyes were staring at me just as mine were staring at her.

Why does she look just like…me? The same hair, eyes, freckles, dress, everything.

I shook my head, closing my eyes tightly as I counted to *one, two, three—*

But as I opened them, Mariana was still there, just as I was. Yet her skin was free from any scars or bruises, her hair looked like it had just been done, and her dress was so much neater and intact whereas mine was full of unravelling rips that could never be fixed. She looked far more put-together than I had in a long time. *Is this…real?*

No, it can't be real. She's responsible for Evie's death… So how can she look just like me?

"Yeah, this is her." The officer nodded. "She's the one Ali couldn't control."

"He's far too nice. It's a shame we never got a chance to break that out of him." Mariana laughed in a voice eerily similar to mine.

"Don't…don't talk about him like…that." Zain sounded so weak as unrelenting agony crushed his insides. "He…he's still—"

"*He* can't protect you anymore." Mariana grinned with amusement as she leaned towards the table full of glorious Dust, playfully flicking her finger through the large pile before she grabbed some in her fist. "It's nice to have you here too, Zainy.

I see you're still trying to hopelessly fit in with people you don't belong with." She looked between him and me.

"I…I'm here to stop you from hurting her. I…I can pay her debts." Zain panted, losing his breath with every word. Blood continued to stream down his skull, decorating his face in its twisted darkness.

"No, you can't. You owe us far too much yourself." She stood, before casually strolling towards Zain. "Ali's been paying off *your* debts for over a year now. It's time for you to grow up and pay off your own by working for us."

"I…I can't—"

"You don't have a choice." Mariana cut over him. "Especially not with that ankle monitor on. Do you know how easy it is for us to send you back to Detention if you don't comply with me?"

"Go…go to *Hell!*" Zain threw all the failing energy he could find at her, holding on to his boundless life. "You…you're… pathetic—"

Suddenly the officer yanked on Zain's hair, pulling his head backwards, forcing him to lose his balance. Then they shoved their foot into the back of his leg with brute force, knocking it forwards and driving Zain to *crash* down onto his knees with a painful—

THUMP. Zain sharply breathed in, letting out a harsh whimper as he collapsed onto the ground.

"Get off him!" I yelled, finding my voice. "Can't you see he's already hurt?"

"Is he? I didn't realise." Mariana kept her stare on Zain. "I guess I'll have to take him out of his pain, won't I?"

I couldn't stop staring at her as she walked up to Zain. *Why does she look just like me?* I couldn't even think what to say next or how to get out of this. All I could do was stare. *I must be seeing things. She can't actually look just like me. This can't really be happening.*

"Is that all right, Zainy?" Mariana asked as she loomed over him. "Can I take you out of your suffering?"

The officer grabbed Zain's hair once more before pulling his head backwards, forcing him to look up at Mariana.

"Here, take this." She opened up her hand, revealing the small pile of Dust she'd been clutching. Then she put it before Zain's face, under his nose, ready for him to easily take it in. *Wait, no—*

Concentrate! I snapped back to the room, away from my questioning thoughts. *She's going to hurt Zain. Don't let her!*

"Stop!" I shouted. "He's been sober for months. Getting him back on *that* is dangerous—"

"Sober? He told you he's been sober?" Mariana snickered. "And you believed him?"

2

My breath stopped for a long moment, preventing me from speaking back.

"Zainy here couldn't stop taking Dust, even if he tried. He's been on it far too long." Mariana laughed, moving her handful of Dust closer towards Zain's nostrils. "Go on, breathe it in already. It'll stop your pain."

Zain glanced at me, almost apologetically, before looking at the Dust before him.

"You know you want to. Just take it already," Mariana ordered.

Without hesitating, Zain let the white powder soar into his nostrils. He inhaled as much as he could, and then he paused before inhaling even more. An expression of relief came over him as the Dust overtook his body. His trembling limbs relaxed and his head flopped backwards as the officer let go of their grip on him.

"Zain...?" I croaked as a mess of disruptive confusion bellowed through my mind. *He's been telling me to not take Dust... Why is* he *now taking it?*

"I'm...sorry, Sam," he whispered as his body slumped further to the floor.

"Don't be sorry." Mariana smiled at him. "Now...if you want more, you'll have to sell it for us and finally pay off your own debts."

"Wait... Wh-what are you talking about?" I interrupted. "How does he even have debts when he told me he doesn't touch that stuff any—"

"Why do you *think* Ali's been chasing you down so incessantly?" Mariana's sharp gaze fell on me. "Ali wasn't just losing his supply to you; he was also losing it to his brother."

"But..." I frowned, trying to piece the flailing world together. *Has Zain really been on Dust this whole time?*

"You've both stolen so much off me for months, and Ali's let you both get away with it." Mariana suddenly kicked Zain's stomach with a surprisingly loud—

THUMP. But Zain barely reacted as the Dust drowned his body in apathy, draining all his usual energy instantly. He simply let the kick crumple his insides, pushing his body over as though it meant nothing.

"Hey, get off him!" I yelled through a cracked voice that felt as lost as I was.

Mariana ignored me as she snickered under her breath before she shot her foot back into Zain's body, this time kicking it straight into his head—

CRACK. Zain's nose folded in on itself. Blood poured from his nostrils in a dark, gushing stream. Yet Zain still didn't react. He took the beating as though he felt he deserved it.

"Stop it!" I shouted, trying to move forwards. *I have to stop her and hurt her—no, I have to kill her.* But the two thugs tightened their grip on me, not allowing me out of their hold.

Mariana raised an eyebrow at me. Then she looked at the officer. "Put Zain in the back. I'll deal with him later."

The officer nodded, digging their claws into Zain's limp body as they dragged him to his feet. Then they carried him as though he were a ragdoll, easily manoeuvring him across the room before disappearing through a back door. *At least he should be safe from Mariana for a while. Now she's stuck with me.*

"So…" Mariana turned her attention to me. "Are you scared of me yet, Samarra?"

"Do you want me to be scared, Mariana?"

"Call me Mara." She glanced at the two thugs around me. "You can let her go now."

Instantly the hold on my wrists and shoulders was released, letting me breathe once more. *Now's my chance to hurt everyone in here.* Only Mara and the two thugs were left in the room. *Three souls to take. Three bodies that deserve to be corpses.*

"I like your jacket." Mara trailed her eyes over me. "Evie liked it too, didn't she?"

I paused, pulling the yellow jacket tighter around me.

"Evie used to talk about you. She painted quite the picture." Mara grinned. "You're not exactly what I expected, but…you'll do." She strolled over to the couch. "Come over here."

I hesitated, looking around the nauseating room. *If I'm going to hurt them all, I need a weapon…*

"Hurry up already," Mariana beckoned as she sat back on the couch. "Come on, sit down with me."

I walked towards her, letting my confidence lead the way. *Just stay calm.* I sat next to her on the couch, sitting right at the end so I could easily get off and *kill them all.*

"Good." Mara smiled. But as she did, I noticed her pupils. *They're dilated.* Beads of sweat dripped from her forehead and remnants of Dust were stuck around her nostrils. *They're all addicted to their own supply.* "Do you want some too?" She gestured to the tempting pile of Dust on the table before us. Its mass of bright crystallised powder looked as white as Mara's dress, as white as Death's piercing eyes had once been.

"I…" I trailed off. *Of course I want some.* My body ached as I stared at the Dust. I'd wanted more ever since I'd felt it wear off. *Just a bit more can't hurt, can it?*

"This is top merchandise at the moment. Do you know how desperate the Shade are to even *look* at a pile this big?" She moved her tongue over her teeth in a devilish smile as she inched closer towards me.

I swallowed hard as my mouth couldn't stop salivating. *I just need a little more…* The Dust looked so gorgeous, so tempting, so perfect. *Surely I can take some and* then *kill them.*

"Go on, you know you want some, just as the rest of this city does." Mara moved even closer. "Take it."

A little won't hurt—

"Take it already!" Mara gripped my hair and shoved my head into the powder, pushing my nose into the pile. "You've already stolen so much from me, I'm sure you can't wait to steal even more!"

Powder fell into my mouth, covering my lips, rushing up into my nostrils. *This is too much, far too much!* Mara kept pressing my head into the pile, refusing to let me come up for air. *I need to hold my breath!* I tried not to breathe, not to let in even more Dust. *I need to do something or I'll suffocate!* I struggled against her, trying to push back against her grip—

But she was surprisingly strong as she kept my face stuck in the powder, using her body weight to trap me there. *I can't breathe. I can't, can't—*

Automatically I gasped for air as my lungs emptied. *No!* Powder was sucked into my airways, choking my throat, filling my lungs. I coughed and sputtered at the dry, acidic taste, but as I did even more rushed into my airway. *I'm going to die.* Dust was filling my lungs, drowning me, killing me. *I'm actually going to—*

Mara released me from her grip.

I jerked backwards, pushing back onto the couch and far away from the Dust. My chest convulsed as I hacked and heaved, choking on the powder stuck in my throat. Dust covered my face, my nostrils, my mouth, my eyes, my hair. I wiped away any that I could, pushing it off me, trying to *get it away*.

"It's great, isn't it? It doesn't just taste incredible, its effects are unbelievable too." Mara spoke over my never-ending gasps for breath. "No wonder every young person in Medlock is hooked on it at the moment."

A wicked laugh spiralled from her figure as I expelled as much of the Dust as I could from my body. I couldn't see her; I couldn't see anything. The world was spinning, turning faster and faster without me.

"Do you even know *why* this city loves Dust so much it's become an epidemic?" Mara's body slithered closer to mine. "It's because this city is full of despair, corruption, debt, crime, and hopelessness. How's anyone supposed to live in a place that's become Hell upon Earth? Unless…they escape it?" she whispered into my ear, infecting me with her words. "The Shade thinks drugs are the problem, but actually this whole damn *city* is the problem. It's a sinking ship and everyone wants to abandon it however they can."

My heart pounded in an irregular rush of beats, forming a fast drum solo that crashed against my eardrums. My lungs worked hard to keep up as I coughed out clumps of Dust between rapid breaths. A burning stung my chest, branding itself into my heart, while my stomach twisted into a knot as heavy as a cut-off limb. Then dark blood fell from my nose, gushing out of my nostrils in a thick stream. *No, not again!*

"Now that I've got your attention, it's time for you to hear my proposal," Mara continued as though I weren't about to die. "I've heard you're a doctor. Doctors hold a lot of power, you know? They can dead easily access supplies and medicine. They can write off deaths and other accidents. They're also the last people to be suspected of any…"

Mara's words twisted together, growing thorns that wanted to poison me. I squinted through the Dust stuck in my eyes, but her figure was mangling just as much as her words were, turning itself into a shadowed creature with overgrown limbs and disproportionate features. *This can't be real…* I looked to the table, but that was blurring too, eating itself as its shape condensed into a sharp blockade. *What's happening?* The world was rushing into a dizzy, unstable mess I could no longer comprehend. *I've taken far too much!*

"So?" Mara's voice stabbed back into my senses as sharp as a machete. "Are you willing to work with me? You're already an addict, desperate for money, so you'll fit right in. *Or…*if you choose not to join us, this will be the end of our conversation and…" She ruffled her hands around her pockets before she pulled out a blurred object that she pointed towards me—

The cold barrel of a gun pressed against my forehead. The sharp CLICK of the safety catch rattled against my ears.

"…the end of your life." Mara snickered. "It'll be easy enough to make your death look like an overdose. After all, you've been a little escape artist for months now, who'd even bat an eye if they found you dead?"

I'm going to die here. I'm actually going to—

"*Die.*" Death's voice slithered into my veins as loud, emphatic footsteps reverberated through the walls. "*You're right that you will. Of course, one day everyone will. But will it be today? Who goddamn knows? I don't.*" His words slurred together, as though he were drunk on the souls he had consumed.

Is that really… I frowned, squinting through the mess of shapes around me as I looked behind the couch, to the back doorway that Death had just walked through. *…Death?*

"Who else would it be? Who else would save you from whatever mess you've gotten yourself in this time?" Blood and brains and shreds of skin were splattered across his shirt. Shadows swam over his body with violent malignance. His figure seemed taller, as though it had stretched itself out of proportion. His grin seemed too big for his face. And his claws were knives, holding a sharpened scythe with a disembodied hand at the end of its blade. Yet pure peacefulness rattled from his figure. A peacefulness I still wanted to be a part of...

I'm so glad he's here. He'll end this suffering. He'll—

"Huh," Mara began as she turned towards Death too. "I didn't expect to see you here." She smiled at him, trailing his eyes across his demonic figure. "But I'm glad you showed up."

Wait.

What?

3

Pandemonious turmoil raged through my mind, pulling my thoughts into its den of disruption as I saw Mara look straight into Death's eyes. *No one else has even acknowledged him before. No one else can see Death... So why's she staring at him?*

"You..." My voice weakly croaked. "You can see him too?"

Mara laughed, louder than I had anticipated. "Why wouldn't I be able to *see* him?"

"I...I-I..." I hesitated, stuttering through my confusion. "I thought he was j-just a hallucination?"

"A hallucination?" Her cackle rang out like the screech of a hyena as she turned towards Death. "She's gone crazy, hasn't she?"

"She went crazy a long time ago." He replied, twisting my mind further into their circles of madness. *"But the strange thing is how much she's been enjoying it."*

"What? Wh-what are you…" Bewilderment tangled my thoughts as I looked between Death, Mara, and the gun being pointed at my head.

"If she's been hallucinating, she'll be no use to me. She clearly shouldn't be even touching Dust if *that's* how her mind is reacting," Mara said to Death, speaking to him as though he were real. *Is he real? No…why would he be real?* "She really is an addict, isn't she?"

"She's far more addicted than she even realises."

"No, I'm-I'm not." I argued. "I'm not addicted. I'm studying… I mean, I-I *was* studying to be a doctor. I'm a smart person, not…not an addict. I can stop anytime I want."

Death and Mara exchanged knowing glances before suddenly collapsing in tears of laughter. They gave hollering shrieks that clawed through my eardrums, bursting them into a river of blood.

"You can't stop anytime you want," Death said through gasps of laughter. *"You don't even know where you are right now."*

What…what do you mean? I know where I am…don't I?

"That's exactly my point. You're so lost that you don't even realise you need to find a way out." Death's voice had more lilts, more personality, more emotion to it. It felt like a human voice, even though he looked far from human. *"You didn't seriously believe I was the only hallucination you were having, right?"*

The…only? I frowned as I ran my fingers through my hair, which had now fallen loose into long, messy strands. *Do you mean I'm having more hallucinations than—*

"Look at the couch you're sitting on, the table next to you, this whole goddamn room! Doesn't it look strange to you?" Death chuckled, pulling on the strings of reality.

My gaze jerked from object to object. The colours were off, as though they were slightly the wrong shade. The shapes were marginally disproportionate, bent just a little bit more than they should be. Everything was spinning and nothing was able to stand still.

"If your messed-up mind is strong enough to create an all-powerful deity like me, didn't you once stop and wonder what other delusions you were having? Didn't you question that maybe your whole goddamn world is fucked too?"

You mean…none of this is real? I shook my head, trying to wake up from this nightmare. *But this is insane. I really must be losing it—*

"Good. I hope you keep losing it and never find it again." Death's voice rang out like a glorious melody in a more upbeat tone than ever before. *"It's so much better when nothing makes any sense. You're so much freer when nothing fits in the prescriptions the world creates."*

But…what the Hell is happening inside my mind if this *is what it's conjured up?*

"What does it matter? It doesn't matter. Nothing does." Death leaned against the side of the doorway, twisting his scythe in a playful movement. *"The end will one day come for us all. The only question is: will you be ready for your damnation? Will you accept your failing heart or will your mind pour with regrets and unfulfilled desires that can never be met again?"* He smiled wider, much wider than was possible. *"In other words…are you ready to let me stab your goddamn guts out?"*

DROPPING LIKE FLIES

4

Everyone.

Everyone deserves to die. Including me. Panic took hold of my lungs, squeezing the breath out of them. My eyes widened as alarm bells echoed over my mind, warning me to *get the Hell out of here. Get far away from—*

"You can't escape me, so don't even try." Death smirked as his disproportionate, monstrous figure continued to lean against the doorway. His neck bent at an odd angle, allowing for his pits of eyes to stare straight into my soul. His claws lightly batted his sharp scythe from one hand to the other, ready to use its blade at any moment.

But... you're not real, you can't hurt me. Surely you can't—

"Shhh... I told you those worries will kill you one day. That day could be today if you don't pay some damn attention to that gun being held between your eyes."

I looked back at Mara's ever-growing grin as she shakily pointed the fuzzy shape of the gun towards me. But I could barely feel its sharp metal on me as my body had numbed itself to the world. I could no longer tell what was even real, if anything at all.

"You can't escape me, but you could escape that gun," Death continued. *"If you're not ready for me to stab your guts out, you'd better stab hers first."*

I strained my eyes to better see the gun before me, but its shape kept distorting, moving out of my unstable vision. *There's too much Dust in me. I can't fight like this—*

"You can. Or you may as well die trying."

"Die trying?" Mara laughed in a screaming sound.

How is she hearing him? I frowned, looking at Mara's face, which matched mine; her voice, which sounded too much like mine; and the bright whiteness of her dress, which blended into the piles of Dust surrounding us. *This shouldn't be possible. None of this should be—*

Focus! I need to act before she shoots me, before Death, or whatever he is, hurts me, before I join Evie, before, before—no, I need to act now. Now!

My body moved faster than my thoughts as I reached towards the gun, trying to push it *away, get it away!* I grabbed Mara's wrist before shoving it to the side, moving the distorted shape of the gun away from my head. I dodged my body in the other direction, out of its line of sight—

BANG. A burning bullet burst past my skull, skimming the top of my ear with scorching heat. *BANG BANG BANG*—the noise reverberated against my eardrum, crashing itself into my brain. A high-pitched screeching sound quickly replaced the noise, deafening me with tinnitus. *I can't hear anything! Silence is dead and never coming back.*

Keep going! My fingers clawed into Mara's wrist. *Keep the gun away!* Blood poured from the deep nail marks I'd created, as I fought to keep hold of her, to keep the gun away from my head. Then I swung my legs up onto the couch as I leaned back. I moved my foot towards her, aiming to stamp on her neck and cut through her airway—

My boot missed its target and hit her chest. *There's too much Dust in me to fight properly.* I still shoved her body backwards but not enough to make any difference. *Hit a weak spot now before—*

THUD. Mara's elbow punched itself down onto my arms, weakening my grip. THUD. TH-THUD. She blew her elbow against me over and over in quick succession, hammering into me with surprising strength. TH-THUD.

A growing pain stung my arms as my fingers slowly loosened their grip on her. *No, she has the gun. Keep hold of it!* I let out a howl of a scream as I forced my hands to hold on. *Don't let go!*

Shapes flickered in the corner of my vision as the blurred figures of the other thugs moved in on me. *They're going to grab me again and hold me down and let her kill me. I need to get the gun now!*

I jerked my head forwards, moving it towards our tangle of limbs. Then I dug my teeth into Mara's hand, shredding into her skin. The metallic taste of blood poured into my throat. I grabbed hold of a chunk of flesh, locking it in my canines, before I ripped my teeth away, pulling the flesh and skin and blood off her bone in one brutal swing of movement.

I saw her scream but couldn't hear it as the deafening ring of the bullet pounded through my skull. Then I saw her bloodied hand drop the gun behind the couch. *Get the gun!*

I dived over the back of the couch, letting my body collapse onto the hard floor. My head spun with confusing dizziness as I tried to reorient myself. *Hurry!* Footsteps danced in the corner of my twisted vision. *They're coming for me, they're going to grab me any second!* I reached my hands out, feeling the floor as the world maniacally laughed at me, *it must be here, it must be—*

There. A shining silver metal glinted into my eyes. *Get it!* I stretched my arm farther than it should go, reaching until—

Fingernails clawed at my skin. Arms bent around my body like a snake, squeezing my chest to secure their hold—*no, no*—before pulling me up, up, away from the floor, away from the couch, away from the gun—

Don't let them take me, not now! I kicked out against the body. I threw my feet behind me and shoved my elbows into their ribs over and over—THUD. TH-THUD. Bellowing pain rang across my bones as though I were hitting a tree. *Just get the gun!* I pulled myself forwards, putting all my weight against them as I fought to escape.

"Look at you, fighting for your pathetic little life, how adorable." Death's sedative voice taunted me in screaming entertainment. *"Look at you fight for your memories, your hopes, your desires, your cravings, your grief, your sadness, your emotions, your god-awful thoughts that keep drowning your mind!"*

I reached for the gun, stretching my fingers, nearly pulling my arm out of its socket just to get closer to it. *I'm so close, so close, so—*

I grabbed the metal handle, *finally.* I took hold of the gun. *Now act before they stop me!* I pointed the barrel up towards the body, pointing it up under their chin, pulling back the trigger—

BANG. Another deafening shock blasted through my eardrums. Then blood pooled onto my head, drenching my hair in its thick, red liquid. The arms around me slumped, releasing me from their grip before a corpse collapsed onto the floor behind me.

Blue-hair sharply contrasted against the pool of dark blood, as I saw the corpse of the officer sprawled across the floor. *The officer? But…I thought they took Zain into the back room. When did they come back here?* A bullet wound had pierced their chin then soared through the top of the skull. Brains splattered around them. Their dead eyes were wide-open, looking at me as I dared to look back at them. *If they're here, where the Hell is Zain?*

Suddenly fingers clawed into my face, yanking back my head, tearing into my eyes. A shocking burn flooded into me, a malicious laugh screamed into my ear, and Mara appeared behind me.

Get her off, get off! She jumped onto my back, locking her arms around my neck as her fingernails dug into my face, slashing into my cheeks and reopening my scar. "Get off me!" I yelled, before I shoved myself backwards, forcefully knocking into her, pushing us all the way back, back, back, until—

CRASH. I shoved her straight into the wall. I crushed her body against mine, knocking her—CRASH—again, and—CRASH—again, until her grip loosened and she fell off me.

Nausea stabbed through my stomach, tempting me to throw up my guts. But I held it down as I turned around, pointing the gun towards Mara—

But she was already back on her feet, ready for my attack. She grabbed my wrists with a cackling scream, pulling back my fingers, clawing into my flesh, struggling to rip the gun from my grasp. *Don't let her get the gun, don't let her—*

"You're as addicted as I am, aren't you?" Mara screeched. "You're just like me!"

"I'm…nothing…like you!" I yelled as I pulled back the trigger—

BANG. BANG. I shot out blindly, letting the power of the gun take control, hoping the bullets would reach her flesh. BANG. *Please work. Please just lie down and die!*

BANG! Mara's hands dropped away from mine. Her body fell back against the wall. Then she collapsed as a trail of dark blood emptied itself from her chest.

"You…you…" Mara choked on her words.

She's not dead yet. I haven't killed her—

"Then shoot her again!"

Sharply I turned around, seeing Death lean over the officer's body. The corpse's neck had been ripped open and its head had been decapitated. A scythe was plunged into its chest, stealing away its soul. Blood had sprayed from the wound, soaking Death's suit as he feasted upon his meal.

"Shoot her!" he growled through a mouthful of flesh. *"But this time do it through her goddamn skull!"*

A warm substance soaked through my heels, staining my feet. I looked down, widening my eyes at the river of blood and guts trailing past me. I tried not to slip as I turned back to Mara's fading body, staring at her growing wound.

"Wh-what is…what…" I ran my shaking hand through my hair, not realising I was smearing blood over it. *What's going on?* I wiped the back of my hand against my nose as it continuously ran, expelling any remaining drops of Dust. "Wait. Where…" I twisted my neck over and over as I looked across the dying room. "Where did the others go?" The other two thugs had disappeared. *Are they going for backup? Are they going to jump out and attack me—*

"What others?" Mara's voice was weak. Her eyes would barely stay open as she glanced up at me.

"The other people!" I shouted, louder than I had expected. "Where did they go?"

"You've lost your damn mind." She sneered with a dissolving smile. "Evie said you were smart, but you're fucking crazy!"

"Don't let her talk about Evie!"

"Don't talk about Evie," I mindlessly repeated, aiming the gun at Mara's skull. "You don't get to talk about her when *you* killed her."

"I didn't kill her." Her voice was barely a whisper.

"Your drugs did. If you hadn't supplied Ali with Dust, he wouldn't have given it to Evie and she wouldn't have overdosed!"

Mara spat out a mouthful of blood. "We didn't give her the Dust that killed her."

"Of course you did. Ali did. He—"

"He cut Evie off long before she died. We hadn't given her Dust for *weeks*."

I hesitated.

"She's lying." Death's voice echoed, forcing an anger to growl into my mind.

I stepped closer towards Mara. "Don't lie to me."

"I'm not," she said. "Evie was an addict who couldn't pay us back. That's why we stopped giving her anything."

"I said don't lie!"

"I'm not!" Mara croaked, letting fear scuttle across her words.

"Then how the Hell did she keep getting her hands on Dust? If you didn't give it to her, who did?" I shoved the barrel of the gun into the side of her head, taunting her with the threat of the final end.

Mara flinched at the coldness of the gun. "You don't want to know who—"

"*Who*? Give me their name. Is it someone else in your gang? Or someone above you?"

"We can kill anyone she names, anyone who deserves it!" Death's words pounded into me, building up my wrath until it matched his. *"You're already damned, so what's one more? What's another line? Another hit? Another kill?"*

"Tell me the names I need to wipe out of existence!" I shouted louder. "I'll kill them all!"

Mara panted faster than her lungs allowed as her soul slowly left her body. "It was Zain."

5

Zain? A cold shock ran over me, stumping me in silence for a long moment. *Did she just say Zain?*

"What?" I asked as though I hadn't heard.

"Zain gave Evie the drugs that killed her," Mara stated as blood continued to gush out her bullet wound, drowning her body in its dark liquid.

That can't be right. "No." I shook my head. "No, he didn't." I refused to believe it. *Zain couldn't have given Evie the drugs.* "Don't lie to me. You're just saying that to protect your own—"

"We cut both Zain and Evie off way before she died. They were *both* in too much debt," Mara's fading voice shook with every word. "But that didn't stop Zain… He stole bags of Dust from Ali as he was too addicted to stop. Then he shared it all with Evie. *That's* how she died."

No, she's lying. "Stop lying. This isn't—"

"Go ask him yourself! He stole from us. That's why we sent Shade officers after him, to teach him a lesson. We got him sent to Detention so he wouldn't be able to steal anymore. But we didn't know how much he and Evie had already taken that night."

"You mean…the night Evie died?" My voice sounded like it was shaking as much as hers. "Zain stole Dust from Ali and… and…gave it to…" I stumbled for my words. *No, this can't be right.* "But Ali was a bad guy. He hurt me—"

"Ali was just trying to protect his little brother. He always took the fall for Zain."

Protect his little brother? Like how I should've protected my little sister? Worries crawled back into my thoughts, devouring any slice of peace. *No, no. This can't be right!* "I told you to stop lying to me!"

"I wish I were lying." Mara spat out another mouthful of blood. "I should've killed Zain and *you* long ago. Then I wouldn't be…here." Her hands shook as she tried to press them against the bullet wound, but even she knew she couldn't stop the inevitable now.

This doesn't make any sense. Zain would never have killed her. This can't be—

"Stop worrying! Jesus, don't you ever just stop?"

I spun back around to the mess of the officer's corpse, which was now only scraps of flesh and broken bones. Death was picking at his teeth, scraping at the shreds of skin stuck in them.

"Of course it was Zain who killed her, it all makes sense." Death stumbled to his feet as though he were drunk.

I shook my head. *But…how? You said I was hallucinating more than I thought… What if this is all a delusion too? What if none of it's real—*

"If?" Death raised his eyebrow, looking down at the fragments of flesh from the corpse he had devoured before looking back to me. *"Realness is not the goddamn point here."*

But… My lost mind tried to squeeze sense out of the senseless world. *You told me Ali killed her…or was it Mara?*

"It was all of them. Everyone deserves to die. Haven't you been listening?" He moved towards me, licking his infected lips with his serpent tongue. *"The aim of all life is death, is it not?"* His eyes grew darker in his frenzy, roaring with the unquenchable hunger of famine.

Wait… I couldn't accept it. *Stay back.* I pointed the gun towards Death as though I had a chance at hurting him. *Stay away! Not everyone deserves to die. Zain couldn't have—*

"Don't you remember the funeral? How your mum warned you about Zain, how everyone else there wanted him to leave? Don't you remember he's a criminal who was kept in Detention for six months? Haven't you seen his anger issues, how he explodes at every little thing?" Death continued to stumble towards me. *"Haven't you noticed him hiding his addiction from you? You know the medical signs of drug use; you should have noticed them in him and known he was lying."* His words pounded louder, echoing over my failing heartbeat. *"Most of all, don't you remember how Zain's been avoiding telling you about the night Evie died? The night he killed her."*

No, no... I shook my head in disbelief, stepping away from Death. But my heels skidded on the pool of blood, forcing me to lose my balance. *Stay away from me! None of this can be true—*

"Stay away?" Death laughed as he staggered closer. *"You're the one who summoned me, remember?"*

No, I...I didn't mean to. I don't want you anymore!

"Don't lie to yourself like you do to everyone else," he hushed, contaminating my mind like a plague. *"I know how desperately you want to escape your messed up little life."* He reached his claws towards me—

Stay back! I wanted to run away, yet I couldn't fall away from him. *I don't want you anymore. Don't touch me!* My mind felt as though it had separated itself from my body. I was frozen in position, unable to move anywhere else. *Go back to Hell where you belong!*

"Who said I ever left?" Death dislocated his jaw as his grin grew wider. *"I'm in Hell no matter where I go...and so are you."* He grabbed my waist, pulling me in close to him.

No, I can't do this again! I can't let you control me—

My thoughts shot themselves dead. Silence enveloped my emotions. Everything became nothing as I fell into Death's arms once more.

"You can't get away from me even if you wanted to," he whispered. *"You can't stop an addiction that easily."* Death's desires clashed with mine as he brought me into his arms. He ripped every emotion from my body and forced a blissful relief to entomb me. My shoulders relaxed, my arms slumped into his, my limbs became weightless. The screeching noise that had dominated my head turned to nothing but pure silence.

You're...right. My head rocked and lolled as my eyes were barely able to keep themselves awake. *It is Zain's fault.* A darkness grew in my mind, smothering every rational thought I should have had as Death's intentions became mine. *It all makes sense...*

"Of course it does. Deep down, you always knew it was Zain." Death wrapped his tendrils of limbs around me like a python. His face almost looked animalistic as he leaned his mouth close to my ear. *"He deserves to die just as everyone else does."*

A loud sputtering sound echoed across the room as Mara coughed up another mouthful of blood. "Who the Hell are you talking to?"

I frowned, realising she was still alive.

"She deserves to die too, doesn't she?" Death moved me like a puppet, turning me around, until I faced Mara slumped against the wall. *"Without her, Dust might never have been so accessible in Medlock. Without her, Evie could still be alive. Our little sister could still be in this godforsaken world."*

But... My thoughts became a clouded blur, unable to find themselves within my broken mind.

"There is no excuse. This is it." Death firmly stated. *"Or do you want to disappoint Evie again? You haven't taken her ashes to Eidyn like you promised, you've found excuse after excuse not to go. You haven't even read that letter she left for you. You've done nothing for her. So you have to do this!"* His words ate away at my brain. *"Even if Zain gave Evie the drugs, Mara's gang still made them. She's the mastermind behind it all. Without her, Dust wouldn't even exist in Medlock. It's time to make her pay for taking Evie's life. It's time to take hers!"*

I nodded, forced to accept his words. I could only submit to his will as my arms raised the gun. I pointed the barrel down to Mara, unable to stop myself. "You do deserve to die," I whispered towards her as though I'd been ordered to.

Death's claws dug into my waist as strong as a virus. *"So pull the damn trigger already."* His warm breath beat into the back of my neck. *"Blow her goddamn brains out!"*

"You really are crazy," Mara sneered. "Who the Hell are you speaking to right now?"

"You know who I'm talking to," I replied. "You spoke to Death earlier too—"

"*Death?* You're speaking to *Death?*" Mara let out a hoarse laugh as she gurgled on her own blood. "You really are addicted. You've lost your damn mind!"

"*Of course you've lost your mind. But that's what'll make this so much fun.*" A tranquillity filled my skull as I relaxed into Death's hold, like a hug I didn't know I needed. "*There's no more time to question her now, Samarra Blair. Kill her.*"

I had no free will left of my own to argue against him. I had nothing left. I could only obey Death's commands. So I pressed the gun to the centre of Mara's forehead, ready to pull back the trigger.

"I...I..." Mara stuttered as she looked down at the blood drenching her clothes. "*I* was supposed to take your soul. I was supposed to... I had so much left to do."

"Do? You had nothing left to do." I stated as Death's words merged into mine. "The only thing every soul needs to do is die. Anything aside from that is too minor to even consider."

"No, you...you can't do this to me. You're-you're crazy!" Mara screamed with her final breath.

"And you're nothing." I spat as I stared down at her with pits of black eyes. "You're nothing but dust on the bottom of my shoe. You were born as dust and to dust you shall fucking return."

BANG. I watched in awe as the bullet tore into Mara's brains. I watched the blood splatter from the wound; I watched her skull knock itself backwards; then I watched the life leave her eyes in less than a second. A strange mix of confusion crawled over me as I continued to watch her corpse, looking at her body that still looked strangely like mine.

"*That was perfect.*" Death dug his skeletal hands farther into my waist. Then before I had a chance to question what I'd just done, he spun me around to face him.

He looked far less human than he had done a minute ago. Now he looked like he was overcome with a pestilent disease. His elongated, hunched figure was crooked and bent. His silver hair was drenched in fresh blood. His suit had become a torn cloak. His dimples looked like deep gashes, while his smile was plastered on his face, nailed into position to perfectly show his sharp, bladed fangs like a Tartarus demon hungry for flesh.

No fear entered my mind as he twisted my body to the side and dipped me in his arms, holding onto me as though my soul weighed nothing. Then he brought his bloodied mouth up to my face and gently kissed my forehead.

A harmonious hush of warmth soothed my senses. Peacefulness strangled my mind like a snake, poisoning my emotions with a numbing contagion. The softness of his lips released me from any lingering pain and pulled me into a perfectly ignorant bliss. And I wanted more of it. I wanted him to take me away from this world and never give me back. My drive for death had finally taken over, engulfing me in its self-destructive hold.

"Look at how far you've fallen…" Skin dangled from Death's fangs, while blood drowned his suit. *"…from a doctor saving lives to a murderer taking them."* His beautiful eyes of desperate despair wouldn't let me go. *"If you truly are your life and nothing else, who would want to be you?"*

Death gently leaned me down farther, and farther, until he lay me on the floor, next to Mara's corpse. He kneeled over us both, grinning maniacally, before he plunged his fist into Mara's chest with a—

THUMP. TH-THUMP. He battered through her corpse over and over, *snapping* through her rib cage. Blood splattered from her body as the smell hit my nose with burning disgust. Then Death shoved his hand into her insides, digging through her organs until he found the heart.

"Here." Death shifted his eyes to me. *"Eat it."* He dropped the still-beating heart into my hand.

I frowned, feeling blood drip through my fingers and onto my yellow jacket as the heart pumped against my palm. *I…I can't…* My skull felt like a clouded blur of thoughts that I couldn't hear. I couldn't hear anything or think anything. Human feeling was now far beyond my range.

"You have no other choice. Eat the damn heart. Become the monster that grief has turned you into." Death commanded. *"Now!"*

I should have fought against him or resisted his words. But I could no longer control my compulsions; I could only obey them as though I were part of an unbreakable Faustian pact. So I kept my eyes fixed on Death, unable to even blink away, as I moved the heart towards my lips and plunged my teeth into it.

An overwhelming taste of iron drenched my mouth as thick blood poured down my throat. My stomach twisted in disgust, but I couldn't stop eating it. My teeth chewed on the organ, chewing through the tough meat before I was forced to swallow. Then I bit into it again and again. I kept chewing and chewing, swallowing the flesh, drinking the blood, destroying the soul within it and throwing it down to the underworld where a senseless, comfortless existence awaited.

"Doesn't it taste good?" Death watched me with pride. *"How do you feel now that you took your revenge on both Mara and Ali? Do you feel just as lonely, just as hopeless, just as pathetic as before? Do you want to keep going and find another person who deserves to die? There's plenty left, after all. You can always have a little more. You can have another hit. You can snort another line. There's always more to take!"*

I gulped back hard as I finished the heart, and I couldn't help but want more. It felt impossible to live without Death. I needed him to survive. I needed to obey his every word.

"Now…let's go kill Zain."

GAME OVER

6

There's no escape from the inevitable.

The back doorway stood waiting for my bloodied body to enter. More insultingly simplistic posters covered it with phrases like: I CHOSE TO BE DRUG FREE, YOU SHOULD TOO and STAYING CLEAN IS A CHOICE. But these ones had graffiti on them, with crude drawings over the mayor's face and phrases such as: ESCAPING IS NOT A CHOICE, IT'S A NEED. I ignored it all as I gripped the gun, ready to hunt down Zain.

"It's time to end his life as easily as you ended everyone else's." Death towered over me like a bear as he stayed by my side. His smile stretched until it touched his dark eyes in a distorted mess, as though he'd forgotten how to imitate a human. And so had I.

I could only nod in response. But even that movement felt too much, too heavy. My limbs dripped in tiredness, as stiff as a corpse. Blood fell from my nose in a never-ending downpour. Exhaustion weighed on my legs like an anchor I couldn't lift. But I forced myself to keep moving one last time as I pushed open the door and walked into the back room—

I stepped onto the abandoned rooftop of Ria's apartment building. *Wait…what?* The frozen air immediately wrapped around me with a numbing chill and a demonic howl. The rain fell from the dark pit of the night's sky, refusing to give in until it had drowned the whole city. White flakes of melting ice covered the rooftop's surface, shining as bright as Dust in the pitch-black world.

How did I get back here? I frowned as my lost thoughts surfaced. *Wasn't I just in a club?* I looked over the rooftop as Medlock's city skyline watched me in the distance. *How did—*

I froze as I noticed Zain standing at the side, full of anxiety as he shakily paced back and forth. His green leather jacket did nothing to keep the cold out. His teeth were grinding together. His eyes had darker shots of red throughout. And his hands were trembling as he tightly clutched Evie's urn in his arms.

Zain stopped pacing. His eyes fell on mine. "Freckles?" A smile lit up his face as he sighed in relief. "You're safe." He ran towards me, opening one of his arms in an embrace of unquestionable hope—

"Remember he killed Evie. He's the reason she's gone." Death's white boots had merged with the frozen ground, unable to find a comprehensible form as he fell by my side. His figure had stretched even taller than a moment ago. His neck bent, twisting and turning back downwards as it held up his Mephistophelian head. His flesh was rotting. Blood covered his cloak of a suit, forcing the smell of the corpses to linger, infecting the space like a deadly disease. *"It's time to turn the world into nothing but dust before it has a chance to do it to you."*

"Thank Hell you're okay." Zain moved up to me, bringing me in for a tight hug—

I pressed the gun into his chest.

He paused then looked down at the gun with confusion. "What…" He tried to keep up his smile, as though this was a joke. "Where did you get that? It looks pretty real."

"He's so frustratingly annoying, isn't he? Just another fool who laughs on earth but will weep in Hell. Thank god you're going to strangle his soul," Death whispered, licking his vampiric fangs.

"Sam?" Zain took a step back, running his eyes over my bloodstained clothes, my dark pits of eyes, my shaking limbs. "Are you…all right? What happened? You look…" He trailed off, unsure how to finish that sentence. "Are you hurt?"

I sharply CLICKED back the safety on the gun. "Where are we?" My voice croaked, devoid of all emotion. "We were just at Mariana's club… How did we get here?"

"What?" Zain's smile wavered. "There's no club. You just had too much at Ria's party, remember? You wanted some fresh air—"

"Don't lie to me." I sharpened my tone. "Don't you dare tell me none of that just happened! We were just…. I just fought people. I just *shot* people!"

"You haven't hurt anyone." Zain kept his voice as light as he was able to.

"I *have*, I killed them! You saw it. You saw Ali—"

"You're just seeing things again. Just…take a breath and we can talk about—"

BANG. A loud, penetrating noise spun through the air as I shot at the floor, missing his feet by an inch.

Zain jumped backwards. His eyes widened as fear overtook him.

"Stop lying to me!" I pointed the gun at his head. "You've done nothing but lie to me!"

"Lie?" Zain put up a shaking palm in defence, while his other arm tightened his grip on Evie's urn. "What do you—"

"You lied about everything! You even lied about being on Dust! You've been taking it this whole time, even when you told *me* to stop!" I shouted.

"You…saw that?"

"You *know* I saw that. You took it in front of me." I rubbed the gun on the side of my temple as frustrated confusion pounded over my skull. "What the *Hell* is going on right now?"

"Sam…" Zain's breaths beat faster as he looked at me with concern. "I think you've taken too much again. Do you need me to help—"

"Stop it! Stop being nice!" I fiercely yelled. "What's wrong with you?"

"I just want to know if you're okay. Please just focus on what's real, just focus on being—"

"Kill him already!" Death's voice shook louder as his figure stretched farther up into the sky. Yet he still kept his stare on Zain, like a predator controlled by its own famine. *"Pull the trigger. He should've died, not Evie. He should've died. He should die. He. Should. Die!"*

I aimed the gun back towards Zain. "I know you only look out for me because you promised Evie you would. It's not because you actually want to. It's because of how guilty you feel for her death, isn't it?" I spat at his feet. "I don't even believe Evie asked you to look after me. She wouldn't want *you* of all people to do that, not after how you hurt her!"

"I would never hurt—"

"Stop lying! I know you killed her! That's why it's time for me to kill you." I pushed the gun into his forehead. "But before you leave this world, I want you to tell me the truth for once. I want you to *finally* tell me what happened the night she died."

7

"Sam, please just…put the gun down." Zain's voice trembled as much as his hands as he backed away from me, moving farther out onto the rooftop.

"Don't you dare be afraid of me." I followed, moving like an unrelenting zombie, clinging onto life I shouldn't have as I kept the gun pointed at his head.

Death moved with me, eagerly waiting for me to pull the trigger. A ticking sound echoed from his chest, as his pocket watch had merged with his flesh, taking over the shape of his organs. It ticked in time with my heart, speeding up as the end finally approached.

"I'm-I'm not. I just…" Zain stumbled, flicking his eyes in jerks of movement between me and the gun. "Why do you want to know about that night? It was a horrible night—"

"Stop avoiding Evie's death, stop only focusing on her life. Just tell me how you killed her!" I yelled in a cold, firm tone.

"Killed her? No, I would never even hurt her." He kept backing away from me.

And I kept walking towards him, stepping on the shreds of white powdered snow that looked like Dust. "Do you really think people die like that by accident? No! *You* took her life!" I shouted. "You were so addicted to Dust that you stole bags of it from Ali even when he cut you off. *Then* you made Evie take it all with you. You caused her overdose!"

Zain shook his head over and over, as his hair became drenched in the icy rain. "No, I…I…" He stumbled for his words between fast pants of breath. "It…wasn't like that—" His back hit the small wall at the edge of the roof. He glanced over his shoulder, looking down at the pavement ten storeys below.

I moved up to him until I'd cornered him. "You should've been the one who died that night, not her."

"Take his life just as he took hers." Death's neck bent down to my ears, whispering under the howl of the wind like a murderous toxin. *"Shoot his brains out of his goddamn skull!"*

I took a shallow breath in as I pressed the gun between Zain's reddened eyes and slowly pulled back the trigger—

"Evie wanted the Dust that night." Zain's voice shook with fear.

I paused.

"Don't listen to him. He's lying; he can't be trusted."

"She didn't want it." I shook my head. "You're making this up to get rid of your guilt. She didn't want to die!"

"Of course she didn't want to die. She didn't want to become addicted. She didn't want any of it! But it's not that simple." Zain looked at the urn in his arms, holding it closer to his chest, before softening his tone. "We…first took Dust together at a party. It was just a fun experiment, to try out the new craze and… it was great. It made us stop worrying about our lives, about our minimum wage dead-end jobs, our bosses who treated us like shit, our arguments with our families, our terrible relationships with others, our failing band, our hopelessness with our whole damn future. The world was messed up and we had no way to get out of it…until we found Dust.

"So we took it again. And again. But we did it safely, taking it with other people, never mixing it or taking too much. We just had fun with it, and it was amazing. No matter how tough our days were, our nights with Dust were always incredible. But…then it became a *need*. We couldn't go a night without taking it. We physically depended on it. That's when we started getting into debt as we could no longer afford to pay for it. Then eventually Mariana's gang cut us off.

"We *did* try to stop using Dust, of course we did. We tried to find the fun in life again, instead of just escaping it. And we *really* did try, through all of our awful withdrawals and cravings and arguments and judgements from others and knee-deep debts. We tried so hard. But…it wasn't enough.

"All the problems we had before we started taking Dust only got worse. Then the final straw came when we had a gig lined up for our band. It was a night we were really looking forward to, but everything kept going wrong with it, until it became nothing but another stressful burden. That's when Evie stole a whole load of Dust from Ali without him knowing.

"I tried to stop her. Ali was already helping us repay our debts to Mariana, so I didn't want to get him into more trouble. But… as soon as she offered me some of it, I couldn't resist. Like I physically couldn't resist; I *had* to take it too. And honestly it made everything feel so much better again. But it felt stronger, much stronger than we were used to. Maybe because we hadn't taken it in a while or maybe it was cut with something else, I don't know. All I know is that when we went out to our gig, we were too out of it to even be able to play. Hell, we could barely even stand.

"Of course Ali found out what we'd done. He showed up that night with Mariana's gang to confront us. I took the fall for it, thinking Evie had only stolen a little. I didn't realise she'd actually stolen far more than what she'd shown me… And because it was so much, Mariana's thugs hurt me. A lot. Then they called the law on me, sending Shade officers out to arrest me. They wanted the Shade to lock me away so I'd never steal from them again. I tried to get away from them, but…that's when I found Evie.

"She hadn't just stolen far more than she'd shown me, she had *taken* far more too. She was throwing up, her skin was almost blue, she was barely conscious, her breathing was all over the place, and there was this horrible choking sound that was gurgling and rattling from her throat… She tried to speak but could barely whisper. That was when she made me to promise to look after you, as though she knew she was about to die. But I told her to look after you herself; I told her she'd survive.

"I called an ambulance for her, thinking it would arrive fast. But it didn't. It was as though they didn't want to help her, as though they blamed her for doing it to herself. I only wish I hadn't taken Dust too; then I could've driven her; I could've gotten her to a hospital so much faster. But instead we had to wait.

"Then…Evie became so delirious, she didn't want to wait. She started to think the whole world was against her and I was trying to hurt her. I had to hold her as gently as I could just to keep her there until the ambulance arrived. But the Shade showed up first, as an officer came to arrest me. They didn't even listen to what was going on, they just tried to cart me away and pull Evie from me. So I had to push them back… I guess I ended up pushing them away pretty damn hard, but I had to. I had to keep Evie safe.

"Luckily the ambulance came and she got in. But I got dragged away, arrested for hurting the officer and sent to Detention, forced to stay there without knowing what had happened to Evie, whether or not she had survived… It wasn't until a week later that I heard the news."

"I blamed myself for it all." Zain's voice grew weaker as his pain grew louder. "I hated myself for not noticing how much she'd taken, for not being able to drive her to a hospital, and for taking Dust with her in the first place." His breath panted faster through his panic. "That's why I made sure I stayed in Detention longer than I was sentenced to. I purposefully got into arguments and fights there. I wanted to stay; I wanted them to punish me and hurt me for what I'd done and I…" Tears rolled down his face. "…I didn't want to return to a world Evie was no longer in."

"The only punishment that is fit for him is death. Now you've heard his confession you can pull the trigger. You can push him into the suffocating tombs of Hell!" Death's voice crescendoed into a shrieking cry, pulling me back to the present.

"I-I didn't mean to hurt her. I-I…I didn't mean for any of it to happen," Zain stuttered, straining his voice over the rush of wind that surrounded us like a deadly tornado. "That's-that's why I've still been taking Dust. Not much. But-but enough to bury my guilt. I just needed enough to get through each day. Why wouldn't I take it after all of that? Why wouldn't I take it in the hopes I would die too? Just as I let Evie—"

"*Decorate this rooftop with his brains!*"

My fingers shook as I held the gun. *But…he tried to save Evie, not hurt her—*

"*Don't drown in your sea of worries now!*" Death's skeletal hands suddenly reached out from behind me and grabbed the gun, interlacing his fingers with mine—

Wait, don't. I can't hurt—

My mind faded into a black hole as Death's contagious peacefulness took control. Numbness relaxed my shoulders. My worries were barricaded from returning to my head. Zain's voice fell silent on my ears. And I let Death control my hand, allowing him to weave his fingers into mine, ready for us both to pull the trigger.

"*Stop letting your conscience make a coward of your pathetic soul.*" Death manipulated me like an empty shell. Mindlessly I stared at the gun in my hands, the chipped nail varnish across my fingers, and the small triangle tattoo on my wrist—

But…he tried to help her. My quiet, barely audible thoughts rushed to the surface as my fingers fought back against Death's. *He doesn't deserve to—*

"*Everyone deserves it. Can't you fucking see that, your mortal fool?*" Death killed my thoughts with his deadly poison. "*The world beat Evie up as much as it has beaten you. Life isn't worth this suffering. Emotions aren't worth this pain. Nothing is worth anything.*"

But he—

"*If it weren't for him, Evie would still be here. Evie, our little sister who you should have protected, would still be here. You'd still see her stupidly bright, colourful clothing and nail varnish that never matched. You'd still hear her incessantly loud humming, or never-ending drum practices that overtook the whole house with noise. You'd still get to speak to her and argue with her and let her annoy you. You'd still get a sister. You'd still get her.*" Memories of Evie stabbed through me, showing me her lively image, her colourful persona, her welcoming warmth. For a moment I was lost in the memories as though they were still real, as though I were still with her—

"But because of Zain, you don't get any of that." Suddenly every bright memory was yanked from my grasp with an excruciating tug like my heart was being ripped out of my chest. Then nothing but a cold, hollow emptiness was left as I stared at Zain's face. *"He deserves to die. Look at the suffering he's in, the guilt that's overwhelming him. It would be a mercy, a gift, to kill him. He deserves to be freed from his grieving pain just as much as you do."*

"You…deserve to die," I reluctantly whispered as Death's fingers gripped mine and we pushed the gun back into Zain's forehead.

"No, Sam, wait, I—"

Death's fingers forced me to pull back the trigger—

CLICK. No bullet burst from the gun. I frowned as I pulled back the trigger again—CLICK. And again—CLICK. It was empty.

Zain gave a relieved sigh as tears flooded his eyes. His breath shook as much as his hands. "Sam, can we—"

"He deserves all the pain imaginable!" Death roared. *"Hurt him, before he has the chance to hurt you or anyone else. Now!"*

I brought the gun up like a compulsion I couldn't resist, then crashed its sharp metal down with as much strength as I could find, bashing it into the side of Zain's skull—

THUD. *"That wasn't enough. Hurt him again!"* I automatically brought the gun up once more, before shoving it back into the same spot, hammering it into his head. THUD. *"And again! Bash his brains in!"* I brought it up again and—

Zain grabbed my wrist, halting my movement. Blood dripped from his skull, soaking into his bandana before running along the side of his face. His eyes were trying to close and pull him into unconsciousness as his body swayed and shook. "Please…" His voice was barely a whisper. "…don't do this." He softened his grip on my wrist. His hand was trembling. I swore I could even feel his heartbeat through his thumb, pounding against me in a scream of life.

"Don't let him get away with killing our little sister. She's dead and never coming back because of him! So keep going!"

I could no longer resist Death's words. They forced me to kick my leg up, hurling my foot straight into the side of Zain's knee with a THUMP. His knee twisted at a wrong angle, throwing him off his balance—

Evie's urn *crashed* to the ground, swiftly followed by Zain. He dropped to his knees, howling in agony.

"Again, do it again!" I ignored the pain swerving through my leg that felt like I'd kicked a brick wall as I brought the gun back up. I stretched it over my head before plummeting it down with an intense force, shoving it back into Zain's skull—

THUD. *"Again!"* I brought it up and back down once more, unable to stop myself as I bashed the gun into his wound, bloodying his head more—THUD. And more—THUD. *"And more!"* THUD.

Zain collapsed, slumping against the floor as his head hit the cold, hard surface with yet another THUD. Blood pooled around his skull, drowning the urn in its dark substance.

Death's breath beat into my ear with a vicious calm. *"He's not dead yet. Take his soul for me, and I'll let you escape this cruel world of grief forever."*

I had no control over my body as I dropped to my knees before bringing the gun up once more and crashing it down towards—

Zain's hands shot up, grabbing my gun, twisting it out of my grasp. His voice shook with groans of pain as his rattling breath ran away from him and he fought to hold onto whatever life he could until—

The gun dropped to the ground. Zain knocked it backwards, forcing it to slide across the rooftop and be swallowed by the darkness of the night.

"This…isn't you." Zain croaked as his lungs flooded with liquid. "You've…taken too much."

"Don't listen to him. He doesn't know you. He doesn't know anything about you. Only I can truly see your soul." Death's distorted figure loomed over me.

"Sam, we…can get you help." Zain kept forcing his words out, despite the mass amount of agony trying to pull him into unconsciousness. "You don't have to…do this alone."

"Alone? He's the one who's made sure you're alone. He took Evie from us. He plunged us into this loneliness, this grief. He forced you to start taking Dust because you had no other way to escape the pain Evie left behind!"

I pulled back my arm, unable to resist Death's chronic disease as I tightened my hand into a fist. *"Keep going! You've got this! Kill him already!"* Then I plummeted it down into his nose with a—

CRACK. Zain's bones split and ruptured under the weight of my punch. Blood poured from his nostrils as a sharp cry came out of his mouth.

"It's not enough to kill him. You need to do more. You need something stronger…" I glanced at our surroundings, looking for something sharp, something lethal—

I grabbed Evie's urn. The material was hard and firm, *"hard enough to make some real damage. So use it! Now!"*

I raised the urn over my head. My hands shook as I held it tightly, staring down at Zain's fearful eyes. *"Take his soul!"* Then I plummeted it into his skull with one fatal strike—

CRASH. Zain's eyes rolled back. His limbs stopped struggling as every movement cut itself short. Then his smile faded out of existence as the urn shattered against his head, tearing itself apart, breaking and splintering into pieces. A dark pile of ash tumbled to the ground. Trails of its dust caught in the wind, pulling themselves away from me.

Wait…

Evie.

Something in my mind snapped back into place, allowing my screeching worries to pour back into me. *No, wait… Wait!* I stared at the shattered urn. "Evie!" *What the Hell have I just done?* A shriek ripped away from my chest as I watched the ashes scatter into the night air. "No, Evie! Come back! Please, come back!" *I was supposed to take her to Eidyn; I was supposed to let her ashes go there, not be trapped in Medlock! She wants to go to Eidyn, to the place she dreams about—*

No, dreamed about. Past tense.

A pull of regret tore at my heart, ripping into me as though I had just been hit with a deathly arrow. *What did I just do?* Pain, suffering and misery flew from the scattered pieces of the urn, weighing me down with the chains of grief.

I scurried to pick up any piece of the urn I could, trying to scoop the ashes back into it. *No, no! Evie, come back! I'm sorry! I'm so sorry for everything!* But there were too many broken pieces, too much to ever fix again. *Please come back! I don't want you to leave!*

"Zain?" I looked back at Zain's still, silent body as reality came down in one tumultuous howl of wind. "No, no…" I dropped the shattered urn as I placed a hand on his head. *He was Evie's best friend. He knew her better than anyone, better than me. Why did I…*

His skin was shockingly cold. His face had lost all signs of life. "Zain!" I put my hands over the wound on his skull, trying to stop the flowing blood. *He can't be dead. I couldn't have killed him.* "I didn't mean it. I didn't mean…" But his body was devoid of all movement. He wasn't waking up. "No, Zain! Come back! I'm sorry. I'm so sorry…"

Why did I hurt him? He didn't deserve that. No one deserves that! Terror beat through my failing heart as I fell back away from his body. *He didn't even kill Evie, he tried to save her, which is far more than I can say—*

"For the love of Christ, stop fucking worrying." Death's voice boomed over me as his dark figure of demonic shadows stepped forwards. His caliginous form had twisted out of shape, as his limbs hung disproportionately with his body. His strong lavender scent grew into a potent sedative. And his face wore a mangled smirk that dripped with insatiable hunger. *"Stop thinking. Stop feeling. Stop it all!"*

Death broke his knees out of their sockets as he knelt, forcing his legs into strange, twisted angles. Bones stuck out of his figure, unable to keep a humanoid shape any longer. Blood dripped from his murderous pits of eyes. Then his bent, broken neck twisted over and over as he leaned closer to the corpse, stretching out his mouth until his jaw dislocated—

No, no. Please don't take Zain's life. Please don't take it!

"I don't take anyone… You gave him to me."

8

Death plunged his vampiric fangs into Zain's chest. He tore away at the skin, pulling it apart before swallowing it in large, fleshy gulps. Bones cracked under his teeth as he ripped his way inside until he made it to the heart that was brimming with flesh blood.

No…no! I tore my gaze away from the monstrous sight. *This can't be real.* I covered my eyes with my arms, trying to pull myself out of this nightmare. *None of this can be real!* But as I did,

I noticed the bloodstains across my jacket. Zain's bloodstains. Across Evie's yellow jacket. *What have I done? I've hurt her best friend... I've...I've—*

I don't want this anymore! I want to wake up! I took my arms away, looking at the mess of the world before me. *Please let me wake up from this nightmare! I just want to go home—*

Dread electrocuted me as I looked back to Zain's corpse, lying on a pile of powdered white ice. The limbs had been torn apart. The skull was broken in two. The eyes were missing from their sockets and the heart had been pulled out of the chest and devoured.

A burn twisted into my guts as a belch of agony rushed into my stomach, ripping it into shreds before it travelled upwards, into my throat, my mouth—until a burst of sickly yellow liquid shot out onto the ground as I retched and gagged against it. The intoxicating touch of Death had caught up to my body like a cancer.

"I hope you enjoyed killing someone just to get away from the cruelty of life for one goddamn moment. Are you ready for the next one?"

Death suddenly grabbed my face and pulled my eyes back to him. But his horrifying figure was too gruesome to look at, as his malformed body had mutated into an indescribable terror. He stood tall above me, twisting into the night's darkness like a cosmic horror that was laughing in a broken, warped sound almost like a scream.

"How many more souls are you going to give to me just for another moment? How much more Dust are you going to take until your body finally collapses?" His skeletal hand of torturous shadows caressed my cheek like a lethal dose of poison.

But his touch didn't feel peaceful anymore; instead it felt empty. It was devoid of emotion, of joy, of happiness, of everything that was worth living for. It was a vacuum locked under a bell jar that had sucked everything from it. *I don't want this anymore… I just want to wake up now, please! Let me wake up!*

"Wake up?" Death continued his hideous shriek of laughter. *"There is no waking up. You are far too lost in Dust to ever find your way back now."* He moved his claws down to my chest, feeling for my rushing heartbeat, the source of my life. *"This is your inescapable fate. You loved the pleasure of Dust, and for that pleasure you must now fall."*

I wondered if this was it, if he was going to take my soul as easily as I had taken everyone else's. *I deserve it. I'm the only person in this world who deserves to die after what I've done. There's nothing left for me in this life—*

"There's nothing left for you because you *are nothing."* Death's glare felt like an open grave, ready to swallow me whole. *"You're nothing but dust, and now it's time for me to turn you into dust once more."*

I tried to speak but couldn't find the words as his cancerous sickness spread through my limbs. Death opened his jaw wider, then wider again, letting his sharp fangs grow into glistening knives before he moved towards my throat—

A scream erupted from me as his fangs buried themselves in my neck. A rattle clung to the sound, drowning my breath. Death then ripped his teeth away, pulling shreds of skin from me, draining me of blood. My head quickly grew tired as he drank away my soul.

When he released me from his grip, I went crashing onto the ground, weighed down like an anchor I could no longer carry. *This is it. I can't defeat Death, no one can. Why did I even listen to him? I never should have followed. I should have gotten far away!*

Death howled as loud as the wind. *"Gotten far away?"* He gripped the back of my jacket, infecting my body with his touch, destroying every cell I had. *"You can't escape me, no matter how fast you run or how far you go."* He picked me up once more as though

I weighed nothing, like I was simply a mouse he was about to devour. *"No one alive has ever escaped me, no matter if they were a brave hero or a pathetic coward. Death comes to all who are born."*

I glanced back towards the doorway I had come through, towards the life I was leaving behind. *Maybe someone will come through that doorway and save me for once. Do I have to be damned? Can I not be saved—*

"Stop looking around. *There's nothing for you in this goddamn world anymore!"* Death screamed as loud as the heavy rain. *"You don't even want your life anymore. You don't want to go back to studying, losing yourself in pointless essays just to work in that stressful hospital. You don't want to go back home, where our mother will be sleeping and our sister's room will be empty. You don't want to be stuck in this dying city to become another cog in its endless machine. You don't even want to be around humans anymore, whose lives could be taken away from you at any second. No, now… now you only want me.*

"You were so pathetically lonely in your life that you needed my hallucinations just to have someone to talk to. No wonder you've become an escape artist, an uncontrollable addict. Who wouldn't want to constantly escape a reality like yours and free themselves from the restraints of such an overwhelming life?" Death's whispers grew softer. *"Now…don't you want me to take you out of your suffering before you experience even more? Don't you deserve to die just as everyone does?"*

Death's pandemonious figure brought up his other hand. His claws had twisted together and merged into a scythe. Then its shining metal hurtled towards my chest. Its sharpened blade aimed at my heart. I was powerless against the inevitability of Death, against my unbearable grief, as I watched it fling towards me and—

Breath burst from my body. Blood drained itself from my veins. My heart was clawed out of my chest. My eyes shut themselves off from the world as Death's scythe impaled me.

I'm not going to die. It's just a surface scratch. I can't let it kill me. My mind ran into overdrive as memories flashed before my eyes, regrets seeped into my brain, and everything I'd done fought against everything I was yet to do. *I can't be dying, not like Evie. Please, not like Evie.* My body was supposed to know how to die, how to switch off from the world, but my mind didn't. It felt impossible to accept that the final end had come. *Evie didn't want to die. Evie didn't want to leave this world. I didn't want Evie to leave this world…*

Memories of Evie scattered through my head as I thought about walking to school with her, making her watch scary movies, laughing at the pranks I played on her and hating the ones she played on me. *How am I supposed to carry on without her?* I thought about taking my first shot of alcohol with her, celebrating with her after getting into university, driving her to college while loudly singing musical songs, sneaking her into bars when she was slightly too young, watching her grow more adventurous and impulsive and rebellious and perfectly herself each day. Until it all got taken away. *How am I supposed to carry on living in a world ruled by Death?*

I'm going to die. The beat of my heart faded into silence. *I can't escape.* My breath came to a final halt. *I'm trapped.* Death's laugh rattled over me. *There's nowhere else to go. I may as well dance with Death himself.*

Life was ebbing away from me and I wondered if it was even much of a life at all. *I may as well close my eyes and plunge into darkness.* I thought I'd lived as I was supposed to have, to have gone to medical school and taken on such a noble profession. But now, as I faced the final end, I realised my life had meant nothing. I shouldn't have wasted so much time doing things I hated. I shouldn't have refused to properly live at all.

But my worries and regrets were now too late. The end had struck me down. *Everyone is going to die. Everyone. There's no escape from the inevitable…*

"Don't you dare be afraid." Death's voice sounded gentler, much gentler, as he tore the scythe's blade away from my chest. *"Remember nothing can be more painful than whatever this life is."* He gathered me into his arms and held me softly in his embrace. *"Samarra Blair…"* His voice softened into a trail of honey, and as he spoke, the rush of the world stopped. The howling wind quieted, the rain grew tired. The world was grinding to a halt, unable to find the energy to keep turning. *"…your appointment with me has finally arrived."*

Tears poured from my face as I slowly opened my eyes. Death didn't look monstrous anymore. Instead, he looked like he had when I first saw him. He looked so human again, so normal. He was dressed in a clean, dark suit that fit him perfectly. A soft smile grew on his fleshy face, creating dimples as he looked back at me with eyes as white as piles of Dust. He looked so beautiful again, as peaceful as the promise of a quiet grave.

My dying mind wrapped itself in its last thoughts as I curled up in a heap in his arms, letting him lead me towards the realm of Hades. *I just want the pain to stop.* Blood dripped into my vision. I wasn't sure where it was coming from, but it felt so calming. I didn't even care how much it was staining my sight, how I was going to drown in it. *I just want it all to stop.*

"Let me end your suffering."

Death carried me towards the edge of the building, bearing the weight of my soul. *"It's okay now. Everything is okay."* He hugged me into his aura of tranquil, apathetic bliss as his own tears dropped into mine. *"Nothing matters. Nothing at all."*

My head banged with the sound of my dying heart like a drum-beat that was fading into the abyss, leaving for the undiscovered country. Medlock's city was still sleeping in the distance, hushing itself into oblivion. The darkness of the night fell on top of the city like a warming blanket. Yet even the city itself seemed so unaware of its fate, unaware it was doomed to fall just as Troy did. Strangely, something comforted me in that. The promise of an end, a finality yet to come. There was at least some solace in the inevitable.

A crash of fatal silence filled my ears. Pure, everlasting silence. Silence that hid away my grief, that let me rest without the burden of loss.

For a second, I thought maybe someone else had walked out onto the rooftop, maybe other figures had stepped through the doorway, maybe life was still happening around me. Maybe stars were still moving, time was still running, the clock was still striking. But I didn't notice any of it. Instead, I focused on that peaceful silence. That beautiful, unbreaking silence. And it was that silence I kept hold of as Death let me go and everything faded to black.

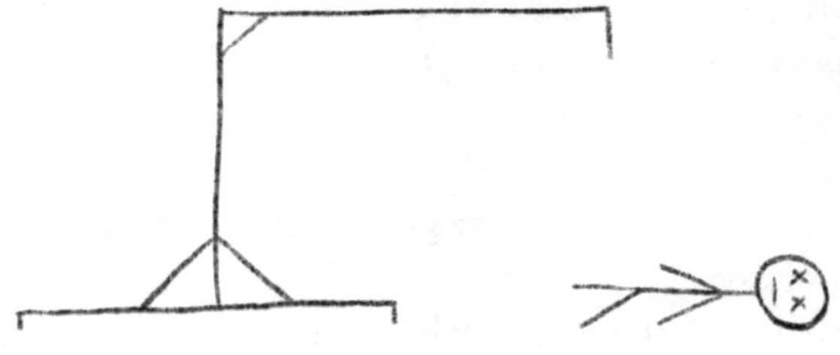

REST IN PEACE

9

"I don't want you to die."

I fell into a vacuum of murky darkness, hurling down, down, down until my limbs collapsed into a heap. No shapes or colours bothered my senses, only comforting ataraxia strangled them. A suffocating tomb wrapped over my skull, losing my soul in the depths of the ocean, trapped in the aphotic zone with no one but myself—

No, I wasn't completely alone. Two shoes walked through the mist of shadows, stepping in time to a never-ending THU-THUMP, TH-THUMP. They moved towards me, growing closer and closer, until I could see they were white boots that were far too bright for anyone to wear, anyone except…

"Evie?"

"One cigarette won't kill you, Freckles." Evie gave a melodic laugh as she handed a packet of cigarettes towards me that read SMOKING KILLS.

Her patterned clothing looked like a fresh breath of life, while her multicoloured hair gave her a beaming energy, matching her smile that shone from a face that looked nothing like mine. And she was so much closer this time, close enough for me to reach out and grab onto—

But my arms felt so heavy, so broken. The world had beaten me to a pulp and left me to rot, with no powder of hope to cling to anymore.

"Suit yourself." Evie took out a cigarette with her teeth then quickly lit it up, breathing in the poisonous smoke with a grin. "That's more chances of dying for me… I wonder what death is like anyway. Does it actually hurt?"

It's just a memory. I let out a sigh of expiration as Evie repeated the same words she had the night she'd died. This was just an image of my dying mind, conjured up to keep me calm while my body faded out of existence. *None of this is real. It's just a rehearsed script that'll play out to its inevitable end.*

"Sam? Does death actually hurt?" Evie asked again, stepping closer.

Exhaustion haunted my body as I waited for the promise of an end. "It's not supposed to hurt…" I whispered the words I remembered saying. "The body was built to die just as it was built to live. It knows how to shut itself down. After all, we're just organs and brains and blood. Just piles of dust thrown together, which will one day be torn apart."

"Are you afraid of dying?" Evie breathed out a trail of smoke. "It's okay to be afraid, Sam. Being afraid means being alive… and I haven't felt afraid in a long time."

"That's…stupid," I said just as I remembered. "You're such an idiot—"

"Idiot?" She smirked. "I'm not the one who doesn't even know what's real anymore."

"I…" I stopped. "What?"

I looked up. She had changed the script. This wasn't in my memory.

"Nice jacket by the way." Evie trailed her gaze over the mustard yellow jacket wrapped around me, and I noticed she no longer wore a matching one. "I can't believe you actually stole it from me."

"Stole it? How…" I paused. "You're speaking."

"I am speaking, well done. You're very smart, no wonder you got into med school." She laughed again, brighter. The sound felt like a beaming ray of sunshine, warming up my frozen body. "And it's okay that you stole my jacket."

"I…I didn't steal it. It's *my* jacket—"

"I said it's fine, you can keep it. It suits you. Though it definitely suited me more."

"I know I can keep it; it's *my* jacket—"

"No need to thank me." She flicked her cigarette onto the floor, crushing its dying flame. Then she reached her hand down towards me. "Come on. Get up."

I didn't know what was happening. I wondered if it was just my lost, confused mind creating this scene, giving me more time with Evie just as I had craved, granting me closure when reality couldn't. Regardless, I never wanted it to end.

"Come on, Sam. We don't have all the time in the world here. Get up."

I hesitated before taking hold of her hand. I grabbed her tightly, feeling her warm, sweaty flesh—

A lightness overcame me, unanchoring me from the ground. My limbs could move freely again as hope slithered back into my head. Evie helped pull me to my feet, standing me next to her.

"You're…real?" I kept hold of her hand, not wanting to let it go.

"Real? I don't think you know what *real* is. Although… maybe no one does." She trailed her gaze down to our hands. "Huh…" She tilted her head, staring at the triangle tattoo on my wrist. "You really do love copying me, don't you?"

"I didn't *copy* you. I…I got this tattoo *for* you."

"Looks like you copied me. It's even in the same position, over your heartbeat." Evie twisted our hands to show off the matching triangle tattoo on her wrist. "Do you admit it's a cool tattoo now? You see that it *does* symbolise mountains and adventures and life?"

"It's still just a stupid triangle, just a spontaneous decision you didn't want to regret."

"And now *you* don't want to regret it either, right?" She smiled, letting go of my hand as she fumbled in her pockets for the cigarette packet. "I guess mistakes are always better than regrets."

"No, it wasn't a mistake. I got this in your memory."

"Isn't that pretty ironic, getting a tattoo that symbolises life to commemorate my death? Or maybe that's exactly what you needed…" Evie pulled out the packet before taking another cigarette with her teeth. "I mean…I know I'm not there to annoy you anymore, but surely you can find someone else who can annoy you just as much as I did, if not more?"

"What?" I frowned, still trying to work out what was happening even though all logic was far from my grasp. "I…I don't need anyone—"

"Yes, you do."

"I mean, I don't *have* anyone."

"Hm…I guess finding people who will put up with you must be tricky. But if *I* liked your stupid personality, I'm sure others do too." Evie laughed, echoing against the darkness of this suspended limbo.

I rolled my eyes at her, hiding a smile I didn't know I still had. I had weirdly missed our conversations, even with how much she used to make fun of me in them.

"Look Sam, you know you can't just fill my void with Dust, right?" Evie lit up her cigarette, creating a small spark of light in the overwhelming darkness. "I'm worth so much more than that."

I hesitated. "I…didn't even mean to take so much. I just didn't know what else to do after…" Memories of the world slowly trickled back into my lost mind. "I'm sorry, Evie, for everything," I blurted.

"What?"

"I *should've* gone out with you that night. I should've listened to you. I should've let you borrow my jacket."

"It's *my* jacket—"

"I should've seen your concerts even if I thought your drumming was dreadful. I should've gone to those loud, social parties with you and Ria. I should've met Zain. I should've gone everywhere you wanted me to," I said, eager to tell her everything I could in whatever time we had left. "I know maybe doing all of that might not have changed anything, I know it still may have ended exactly the same. But I…I still wish I had been there for you, even if that wasn't enough, even if it never could have been enough. I just…I should have spent more time with you."

She paused. "You thought my drumming was dreadful?"

I let go of a breath as a smile finally escaped my lips. "At home you just sounded…all over the place. I thought your band was just as bad."

Evie smiled too. "No wonder you never wanted to come."

"But…I guess maybe together your band might've been pretty good. I heard Zain sing, he was all right."

"We were *very* good actually," Evie grinned wider. "Some might even say we were *too* good."

"Don't push it." I let out a weak laugh. "At most you were probably a strong average."

"I'll take it." Evie breathed out a puff of smoke through her nostrils. "You can't follow me, you know? You can copy my appearance, but you can't copy my death."

I looked at the faded world around us, suspending my body in its lost oblivion. "I think it might be too late for that."

Evie shook her head. "It's not, you can go back. No, you *need* to go back. You can't waste away your life. It was already unfair you got one longer than mine, so you can't mess this up."

"I think I've already messed it up." Flashes of distant memories echoed through my head like the remnants of a nightmare. "I've done so many horrible things, Evie. I...I've hurt so many people—"

"You've been lost in delusions, you mean." She folded her arms, looking at me with a raised eyebrow. "You've taken so much of that Dust that you've forgotten what's real. You really have lost yourself without me, haven't you?"

I paused. "You'd do the same if our roles were reversed."

"Maybe." She blew a puff of smoke into my face. "Maybe it always had to be like this. It always had to get worse before it could even think about getting better. But you better fight it for me, okay?"

"Fight...what?"

"The withdrawals. Fight them. Stay the Hell away from the dreams of Dust and rejoin reality." Evie spoke louder, letting echoes of her words bounce through the shadows, bringing life to this dark, quiet place.

"But...I have nothing to rejoin. Everything used to be so perfect until you left. Now I've messed everything up, even my degree. I'm being kicked out of my course—"

"Don't be an idiot. Your life was never perfect," Evie stated, dropping her cigarette to the floor, letting the darkness consume it. "You always hated your stupid degree; it kept you locked indoors, studying and going through all sorts of endless stress. *Nothing* is perfect about that kind of life, not when you don't even enjoy it."

I let her words sit in my fragmented mind, taking up the space of my thoughts.

"Just go and have some *fun* for once, Freckles. Take risks, go on adventures, get in messy relationships, do whatever you want!" She shouted with beams of life. "Stop worrying about solving every problem of the universe, forget about being a smart-arse perfectionist who has to become a doctor to prove her worth and just *live*."

I frowned. "Just because I'm smarter than you doesn't mean I'm a smart arse."

"No, it doesn't. But your arrogant personality makes you one."

"Hey, I…" I paused. Then a laugh burst from my lungs, though it sounded more like a gasp for air. "God, I missed you, Evie. In all your stupid annoyingness."

"Good. I'd be offended if you hadn't."

"How on earth am I supposed to keep going without you?" I asked, refusing to break my stare from her, wanting to take in every second I had.

"All those things you wish you did with me? All those moments you wish you had? Go do them with other people. Stop regretting everything you didn't do and go out there and do it. You still have time, Sam."

"But Death is…everywhere." I looked out at the strange, subliminal space we were standing in. "He's following me. Or maybe I'm following him—"

"Let him follow you. Let that damaged, broken part of you follow you for the rest of your life. But don't look at him more than you look at the world before you." Evie smiled with bounding confidence. "You have to live not in spite of the fact that death is inevitable but *because* of its inevitability. So keep going and don't look back until the bitter end."

"But he's—"

"He'll see you eventually. We are all but dust, after all, our days are few and brief. But at least they are still *days*." An unfamiliar optimism poured from Evie's words. "So go use that time to make mistakes. Go fail again and again and *again*. Go have those beautifully specific moments, like the first bite of an apple, when the sweet taste first touches your tongue—"

I cut her off. "You're obsessed with those stupid moments."

"Of course I am. Those moments make life worth it."

"But they're such small, insignificant moments. I never understood why you loved finding them."

"It was Zain's idea." She shrugged. "When we stopped relying on Dust to get through each day, he decided to start looking for the joys in life again. Since we didn't have money to make a bucket list with every impossible dream or huge lifetime achievement, he created a game where we'd find the beauty in the small moments.

"So we wrote them all down, every single beautiful little moment we found. It felt stupid at first, but slowly it made us realise it was the small things that really mattered. They're the things that can make you so grateful to be alive."

"Then why did you…why did you go back to Dust?" I asked with shaking uncertainty. "Why did you overdose—"

"I wouldn't say it was much of a choice, especially in a world that doesn't look after people properly." Evie let a beat of silence pass. "Don't blame anyone for my death, though. Don't go looking for pointless revenge either and *definitely* don't blame Ria or Zain."

I gulped back hard. "I think it's too late for that. I…I hurt Zain. I really hurt—"

"I want you to look out for him for me," Evie spoke over me. "Please look out for him while I'm not there."

Please? Evie never says please.

"Please," she said again. "He needs you, more than you know."

"But…didn't you already tell *him* to look out for *me*? I don't even understand why you told him that—"

"Isn't it obvious? You balance each other out perfectly." She nudged my arm. "He'll also be the *best* person to keep annoying you, just like I did."

I shook my head. "I…I can't, Evie. I hurt him. I really hurt him. I broke your *urn* on him, for god's sake."

"Wasn't it an ugly urn? Shouldn't we be glad you broke it?" She snorted a laugh.

"But I was…I was supposed to take you to Eidyn—"

"Eidyn? Why would you take me there?"

I hesitated. "Because you told me to."

"Did I?" She laughed louder, letting her joy echo over the dark space.

"You wanted me to scatter your ashes there. Don't you remember?"

"I remember I *wanted* you to get out of the house." Her smile never left her face, illuminating her with boundless life. "I guess going up to Eidyn would be a fun adventure, wouldn't it? No wonder I told you to go."

"So…you didn't actually want your ashes to go there?"

"I don't care where my ashes go, they're not me. I just want you to keep living!" she yelled, throwing her voice into the darkness and letting it echo back, repeating her words over and over until they sunk into my mind.

"But did you…" I paused. "Did you mean to tell me about Eidyn just before you died? Did you know you were going to—"

"I don't think it does hurt," Evie interrupted me.

I frowned. "What doesn't?"

"Death. I don't think it hurts."

"You don't?"

"No. But that's something for you to discover in the future, not now. Now you need to focus on being alive. Now you need to get the Hell up before you end up lying down forever."

"Get up? But I can't." I gestured to the mass of oblivion around us. "Is this…is this even real?"

She tilted her head. "Do you really think that's the point of this?"

I sighed. "I guess it doesn't matter. Nothing matters."

"What? No. *Everything* matters. Every small, seemingly insignificant moment. It all matters in its own stupidly amazing little way," Evie firmly stated, leaving no room for dispute. She glanced down at the yellow watch around her wrist, which matched my own. "Now, it's time for you to go and discover that for yourself."

"I can't—"

"You *can*. You have to get out of here and not look back until the bitter end."

"But…if I do, will it all be okay? Will everything be okay—"

"Definitely not." She shook her head with a never-ending smile. "Nothing is okay. But everything matters."

"Wait. I…I don't want to leave you. I'm scared of going back into a world that you're—"

"Good." Evie grabbed my shoulders. "Being afraid means being alive. So you'd better go out there and be scared of absolutely everything." She pushed her weight onto my shoulders, forcing me to fall backwards, far away from her until—

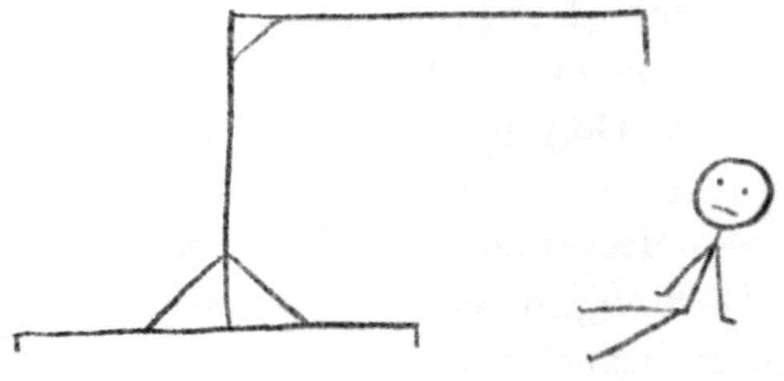

ROT IN HELL

10

But maybe I should live before I die.

So let's live. My mind tangled itself in endless streams of blurred thoughts, forgotten memories, and lost emotions. The world sat on my shoulders, but I accepted its weight, letting its pain and suffering hurtle towards me in a screaming, palpitating mess of chaos as I dragged myself back towards—

The noises hit me first. The beeps, the footsteps, the chatter, the screams of ambulance sirens. Then it was the smell. The bleach, the antiseptic. Then finally the colours and shapes jolted back to me in a spark of electricity as I opened my eyes to the rush of the hospital.

I'm alive? Glorious air filled my lungs as my yellow wristwatch somehow kept ticking. *How am I alive?*

I looked down to the hospital bed I was lying on. My black dress was shredded. The mustard yellow jacket still hugged my body, covering the bruises and cuts across my skin. Yet there was something more than just those wounds. An exhaustion like no other weighed down my soul. A sickness penetrated my stomach and twisted it with intense nauseousness. My body was on fire, burning itself from the inside out.

A hurricane of agony shot through me as I sat up. *What's happening to me?* I panted through breaths as a hot sweat poured over my forehead. I was burning up hotter than ever. The ward around me turned in waves of sickly motion, swallowing itself whole. Three other beds were in the room, and a sleeping patient was in each one of them. *I wonder if their bodies are in as much pain as mine. I wonder if they want me to take them out of it. It would be so easy to stop their hearts and give their souls to—*

No, what am I thinking? Why am I—

"Samarra? You're awake." My mum stood by the side of my bed. She didn't have any makeup on, letting her wrinkles and bags shine through. Her face was so full of flesh and blood and *life*. Life I hadn't seen in her for a long time. "I'm glad you didn't…leave me."

"Mum? What is…what's happening to me? I feel so…so—"

"It's all right, Love," Mum hushed, pushing me to lie down. "You just need rest. Your body is going through some intense withdrawals, but the doctor said they should fade soon."

"Withdrawals?" *Fight the withdrawals.* "I…I didn't mean to take so much. I didn't mean…"

"I know." She felt my forehead full of dripping sweat and burning heat. "You're safe now."

"But what…what happened last night?"

"Last night? No, this was two days ago."

"Two days?"

Mum nodded. "Ria said you took too much at her party. She found you on the roof…"

"It's not too late to go back there, to save yourself from the cruelty of life and join the peace of the dead at last."

I jumped as Death's voice slithered into my skull like an unwelcome friend. His words pricked my mind like thorns, twisting themselves inside my thoughts. "Get away from me!" I shouted as I searched for his figure—

But there was no sign of him.

"It's all right," Mum softly said. "There's nothing there and there's nothing to worry—"

"He's still here." I mumbled. "What have I done… Why did I listen to him?" Memories swallowed my burning mind. "I…I hurt so many people because of him." Torture shredded at my chest as a dart of agony ripped over my insides. "Wait. What about Zain? Is he…is he alive?"

"Why wouldn't he be alive?" Mum frowned.

"I hurt him a lot. I…I—"

"You didn't hurt anyone, Love. Your memories might just be a little mixed up, given everything you've taken."

"So is Zain…okay? He's alive?"

Mum nodded. "He's alive."

A sigh of relief burst through my lungs, accompanied by a row of tears. "I didn't kill him…"

"Of course not." Mum put her hand on mine, stroking her thumb against me. "You're all right now, Samarra. I'm just so glad you're okay. I'm…" She paused for a long moment then leaned down towards me.

Mum shoved her arms around me, pulling me into an embrace, pressing the weight of her sadness into mine. Her arms stretched around my ribcage, holding me tightly. She leaned her head against mine. It was so heavy, so awkwardly placed, but it was so real, so full of life. *She hasn't hugged me in months.* Her heartbeat drummed into mine, reminding me of the life we were clinging to. *I'm still here. I'm still alive. I am, I am, I am.* Then her arms squeezed me even tighter, *far too tight*, before they finally released me.

"Your dress…it's ruined," she quietly said.

"My dress?"

"I thought it was…going to be destroyed. I thought I'd lose it forever…" Mum's voice shook as it faded into a whisper. "I'm… I'm sorry I wasn't there to stop the rips from growing bigger or sew the dress up sooner. Even if you didn't want me to help, I still should've fixed it."

I swallowed hard, searching for the right words to say, but there were none. My dress *was* ruined, far from the perfect piece of clothing it once was. The seams were coming undone, the material was unravelling, and I knew it could never go back—I could never go back—to that once-perfect form, *but maybe that's a good thing.*

Mum sat in silence for a drawn-out moment before she spoke again. "I'm sorry I made you feel like you needed to escape this world rather than live in it. I'm sorry for not seeing your pain sooner. I shouldn't have ignored you and let grief take me over."

I hesitated as snot ran from my nose, mixing in with my tears. "It's…it's not your fault, not really—"

"I don't need forgiveness, I just…" She paused. "I just need you to know I'm learning how to *live* with grief instead of being consumed by it. I am going to do better."

"So am I… I don't think I knew how to even grieve properly, especially after the funeral ended."

"You don't have to explain yourself, Love. We shouldn't have waited so long to have that funeral."

"Evie would hate us if she knew how long we waited."

Mum let out a smile, a *real* smile. "You're right. She'd probably throw a tantrum or do something dramatic."

I smiled too. "Then she would've banged her drums for hours on end just to torture us with the noise."

"She would've done that no matter what." Mum nodded before she gently stroked my hair. "The house has been awfully quiet without her, hasn't it?"

"Everything has been."

"I think…" Mum paused. "I think I'm slowly learning to live with the quietness."

"But…how? When it's so…" An aching throb thudded over my limbs. *It's so painful.*

"I don't know exactly," Mum continued. "But I *do* know the quietness, the absence, the grief—it's all so important to hold on to, but not important enough to let it take over. I…I'm trying to see it like a shadow that's always there, in the background. Maybe it'll comfort me too, knowing it'll never leave."

I let her words calm my pain. *A shadow that's always there.* I watched her smile as she spoke, seeing it was a little brighter than before. Her face had a little more expression. Her skin had a little more colour. Her eyes were bigger, brighter, blurrier—

Blurrier? The dizzying room began to spin, turning through my vision like a twisted spiral. *Something isn't right.* My head pounded as I looked towards the other patients in the room. They looked so peaceful in their sleep, *like they're already dead. I wonder how quick it would be to send them into the true dreamless sleep of—*

No, what am I thinking? Stop it! I winced, pushing back against my burning mind.

"Also…" Mum rummaged through her coat pocket. "Maybe this isn't the right time, but maybe there's never a right time…" She brought out an envelope with "SAM" on the front, written in Evie's handwriting.

That's the letter from Evie's room, the room no one ever goes in.

"I decided to clean Evie's room. I know it's taken months, but I finally started it and I found this for you." She passed me the envelope.

I stared at it for a long moment, wondering whether I should take it.

"You don't have to read it now. But I thought you should have it."

"Don't take it." Death's voice crescendoed as the grief plummeted on top of me.

"He's still here." *I definitely heard him!* A cold chill scuttled over my skin as my eyes darted around the room, looking for where his figure was hiding.

"Who?" Mum asked, sensing my sudden panic. "What's going on?"

"He's close by," I muttered. "He…he hasn't left."

"Don't take the envelope. Please." Death whispered in a raspy, croaking tone. *"Taking it means those are the last words she ever wrote for us. It means Evie truly is dead and never coming back. But we can't lose her, not forever—"*

Don't listen to him! I pulled my eyes back towards the envelope. I panted through my scatter of breaths, trying to focus on my mum, on reality, on the letter. *It doesn't* mean *she's dead. Rather, it's proof that she lived.* I reached out and took the envelope, holding it tightly. *It's proof that she lived. She lived. She. Lived.*

"Are you…seeing something?" Mum frowned. "Do you need me to get some help?"

I put the envelope in my jacket pocket. "I…I don't know. I don't know where he is. But Evie told me not to look at him."

"She did?" A concerned expression swept over Mum's face. "I'm sure it's just the withdrawals, Love. Your body is craving what you've become addicted to. If you resist, you'll feel better soon." She seemed distracted as she spoke, looking around the ward for a staff member to help.

"Resist?" I stared at her fleshy face. She had so much life beating through her. *Life I could so easily take… She would be so easy to kill too. So much easier than any of the others. It would be so simple to rip out her heart—*

Stop it! Fire burned through my organs as I tore away from my thoughts. *Why am I still craving Death? Even after everything I've been through?*

"I'll find some help." She turned away. "You just stay here and rest, all right? *Just lie down and die.*" Suddenly Death's voice shook through Mum's.

My body jumped as I stared at her. "What did you just say?"

"I said you need to *lie down and die for me.*" Mum turned back towards me, but her face contorted, pulling her skin until it ripped into shreds. Her mouth widened until her jaw dislocated, making way for sharp fangs that were dripping with saliva. Her eyes bulged out of their sockets as black pits of emptiness took their place.

Death's hideous figure appeared before me. He had a humanoid form again, except now his flesh was falling off as though it could no longer grip on to his skeleton. Blood was drowning his rotten skin. His silver hair was falling out in patches. His neck was twisted at the wrong angle. And his suit was full of rips and tears, wrapping itself around his body like a cape.

"Not feeling well, are you Samarra Blair?" Death let out a visceral chuckle. *"I can fix that."*

11

My knees shook as I pushed myself off the bed, falling away from the courage-shattering figure of Death. But I was too weak to hold myself up properly, forcing my legs to collapse in on themselves, dropping me to the floor. *No, no! I have to get away from him!*

"Samarra?" Mum's voice echoed from Death's figure. "What are you doing? You have to rest. It's time to *stay in bed and die for me, okay? You just need to die for me.*" But Death's poisonous words broke through hers, as his sulphurous odour overwhelmed the air like a demonic spirit cursed to haunt me.

"Get away!" I spoke through cries of defeated breath as I fought to understand what was happening. Mum's voice was still there, somewhere, but Death had swallowed her whole.

I turned to the ward, which was in as much pain as I was, searching for help. I looked at the other patients lying silently in their beds, ready to be put inside a coffin. *Everyone would be so easy to kill. I could just stab them—*

Stop! My body buckled over as a burn sliced through my insides. A lightheaded rush of air passed over my skull, forcing me to double over. "What have you done to me?"

"I haven't done anything. You did this to yourself." Death tapped his bony nails against the side of the bed. *"You've grown so used to my touch, to the beautiful power of Dust, that now you can't escape it. Your body can't survive without it, without me."* Saliva dripped from his mouth as he spoke. *"Why don't you let me in? After all, it would be so much better to feel nothing than to feel something, wouldn't it? Isn't silence better than noise? Isn't dying better than whatever this life is?"*

"No, I don't need you anymore!" My body trembled with agonising throbs, heating my insides like a raging fire that couldn't be tamed.

"Come on, Samarra Blair. We both know that's not true." Death's eyeballs were melting into his skull, scorching his bloodied flesh as he stared down at me. *"I can hear how much pain your body is in. You want to feel peace, don't you? You want to feel nothingness. You want to take Dust and escape reality—"*

"You know I *want* to!" I shouted as rage ran into my unrelenting suffering. Of course I wanted Dust, I wanted him. An inescapable compulsion palpitated through my body. I knew if I felt Death, I would feel so much better, even if it was just for a moment, *but I can't. I can't do this again!*

Death gave a howling laugh that shook like a scream as he moved closer. But his movements were jagged and distorted, like a stop-motion animation that could no longer blend with reality as seamlessly as he once had. *"Good. Then it's time to give in once more. After all, a little more can't hurt, can it?"* His cloaked body loomed over mine, casting a black shadow across me. I could almost feel his cancerously calming presence, which my limbs wanted to fall back into—

No! I have to resist. I have to get far away from him and not look back until the bitter end. "Leave me alone!" I screamed with failing vocal cords, flinging myself away as I stumbled to my feet and sprinted towards the door.

But as I moved away, pain soared through my guts, crushing my organs. A hot, burning heat of fire ripped through my flesh as my body wanted his touch more than I knew. *Let it burn. Focus on being alive instead of craving Death!*

I forced my legs to run, no matter how much they wanted to stop. *Fight through it all!* I swayed and tilted as though my body had forgotten how to walk—*no, it's forgotten how to live.*

"Don't you dare run from me! Not now, not after everything we've been through!"

My mind battled against itself as I kept running. *Don't listen to him!* My stomach twisted as the sharp sting of agony crushed into it. My lungs felt as though they were collapsing in on themselves, while my heart skipped around my ribcage to an irregular rhythm as I staggered through the hospital ward, fighting against every compulsion. *Keep going and don't—*

"Stop!" Hands grabbed my arm. "You shouldn't be walking around like that yet. You need to rest."

My vision blurred as I looked at the face of a nurse. Their kind, fleshy face, which was full of blood and life *that I could so easily take away. I could strangle them and block their airways, just to feel Death's touch once—*

"No, no!" I shut my eyes, forcing the thoughts out of my head. "Get off me!"

"It's all right." Another set of hands grabbed me as a second nurse appeared. "Let's get you some pain relief, okay?"

"Let go!" My voice felt so weak as it tried to claw its way back into existence. "Please let go. You don't understand!"

"She's the addict," one nurse whispered to the other, ignoring my pleas. "Just another one obsessed with that new drug."

The other nurse tutted. "I don't know why we even bother treating people who do this to themselves."

Did they really just say that right in front of me?

"Of course they did. They don't care about you. No one cares about junkies, addicts, escape artists. No one. Except for me. I care about you. So why don't you stab them for me?" Death's laugh rang around my head like a venomous toxin. *"Why don't you stab their guts out? That will shut them the Hell up."*

"Get out of my mind!" I threw the hands off me, twisting out of their grasp in a sharp pull against their tangle of limbs, before falling back into an unstable run.

"Come back!" the nurse shouted. "You need to *come back here and die!"*

I sprinted into the tight, suffocating corridor with all the energy I could find, pushing against the fatigue weighing me down. The hospital was much darker than before, as the lights flickered in my vision. It felt like the building was fighting to stay alive just as much as I was. Hives of staff moved past me with constant streams of buzzing chatter. Machines beeped. Patients yelled for help. Then under the discordant melody of the world were Death's loud, emphatic footsteps, pounding in a percussion beat.

Casually he walked up behind me, easily eating up the distance between us. He lightly whistled a tune that floated on top of the music. It was a high-pitched, melodious song that sounded far too beautiful to be as sinister as it felt. It almost sounded like the tune Evie used to always hum, but it was twisted and distorted as though it were mocking me.

"You know you can't resist me forever. You know you'll have to give in eventually. So why not now?"

I needed to move faster, but dots were covering my vision like bursts of static. My limbs were weakening with every movement. My skin was hot, pouring with enough sweat to drown me in it. *But I have to keep going. I can't let him make me hurt another soul—*

"I didn't make you do anything." Death felt so close to me, far too close. *"You did everything all by yourself. You wanted this, remember? You wanted me, you chased me. Now it's time for me to chase you."*

I threw my legs forwards, one after the other, until I remembered how to run. *Keep going!* Flashes of Mayor Brown's posters haunted my vision as they littered every door in the hospital. Overly simplified slogans clung to them, such as: SAY NO TO ADDICTION, and CHOOSE A BETTER LIFE. I wanted to tear them all down. I wanted real help, not superficial messages. I wanted people to actually understand—

"Sam?" A figure dressed in a dark trench coat blocked my path. "What are you doing? You need to go back to bed."

"Ria?" I frowned, halting my movement as I looked at the figure. It seemed like Ria, dressed in her officer clothes. But her face was distorted, her body twisted.

"You need to rest, Sam." Her words felt like sharp scratches. "You need to come with me and *stay with me. You can't exist without me!"* Suddenly Death's features grew on Ria's face. Her flesh fell off her body as her limbs twisted and popped out of their sockets. Then a dark cloak of shadows overtook her trench coat.

Death's mangled face appeared before me, snapped to the side, wearing a malevolent smile that ran all the way around his skull. More flesh had burned off his body while trails of blood ate away at him. He reached his arm towards me, but his bones were shaking, losing all their strength as his muscles deteriorated. His figure was more hunched over and his head was barely staying upright. *"Please don't give up on me now, Samarra Blair. We only have each other in this world."*

My body buckled over in a swarm of pain, slicing through my insides as sharp as a machete. It was all becoming too much, too real—

Fight the withdrawals. Fight the pain. Don't listen to him! A sprint of energy trickled through me as I stumbled to the side of the corridor and pushed myself through a door, falling into another ward.

"Stop! We need each other to survive! You need me just as much as I need you!"

I ignored Death's words as I kept running. *Keep going and don't stop!* I passed more patients, more beds, more souls reaching out for their recovery, holding onto every hope they could find—

Wait. I stopped. I stared at one of the patients, at their dark hair, their strong muscles, their tattoos of thorny vines.

Ali?

My heart crashed against my eardrums and my head pounded along to its tempo as I saw Ali lying in a bed. He had machines attached to him and bandages over him. He looked so injured, so young, so helpless. But he was there. He was alive.

I didn't kill him? But I saw him die. I saw Death eat his soul, didn't I? I stumbled away from him before crashing into another bed. My knees buckled as I staggered for balance, turning to the bed behind me—

Bright waves of blue hair covered the head of the next patient. *No, no… I shot them… Didn't I?* I leaned closer to the sleeping body, staring at their bruised face, *but it's definitely that corrupt officer; they're alive too.*

I looked to the last bed in the room. The final body had been hooked up to machines to help them breathe. But they were definitely breathing… I stepped closer and closer until I saw their face—

I didn't recognise them, even though the name "Mariana" was written on the small whiteboard next to the bed. They looked like a young woman. They had long blonde hair, but it looked darker than mine. Their face looked younger than mine too, like she was just a young student dragged into a world she didn't belong in.

My mind rushed inside and out, tumbling through my thoughts. *I didn't kill them.* A breath of relief ran over me. *I'm not a killer. I'm not—*

"Stop running already!" Death infected my thoughts. *"No one else wants to help you in this whole damn hospital; they only want to hurt you. But not me. I've never wanted to hurt you. I'm the only one here who'll save you from this cruel reality, from your grief, from this entire goddamn world!"*

My mouth dried up as Death's caliginous shadow hobbled into the room, but his body disintegrated with every step he took. More flesh, more blood, more skin had boiled itself off him, slowly revealing the skeletal figure beneath. His back was crooked. His limbs seemed misplaced as they stuck out at odd angles. His silver pocket watch was strangling his arm, gripping on to him as it turned yellow.

"They're alive," I croaked. "They're all alive, I didn't kill them! So why did you make me think I hurt them? You made me imagine such horrible nightmares!"

"Imagine? I didn't make you imagine anything."

"You did!" I stood strong as I watched him painfully move towards me. "It wasn't real. None of it was—"

"Maybe what you saw wasn't real. Hell, maybe the whole damn thing was just a story playing out in your head. But how you felt was very real." A tear fell down his dissolving face as though he meant what he was saying. *"Is your pain not real? Is your grief not*

real? Is your sadness not tearing your whole goddamn mind apart? I'm just as real as all that!"

Another throbbing burn suddenly slit through me. I swore under my breath as I tried to stay on my feet, but the pain was too much. I fell onto my knees as agony circled through my body like a wave crashing against my limbs again and again. "You're…you're just a hallucination—"

"You know I'm not just *a hallucination."* Death continued to stagger towards me. *"I'm the monster that grief has made you, the shadow you desperately need. I'm a part of you that you can never abandon!"*

I shook my head. "You're a delusion, an escape…an addiction." My words scratched at my throat in a harsh whisper of a noise.

"I'm still your *goddamn addiction. You can't survive without me. Your body is failing just as much as mine."*

The unrelenting torment refused to stop blowing against my body. Black spots were taking over my sight. My stomach turned and twisted as fire burned inside, swelling through me. "What…what have you done to me?"

"All I've done is exactly what you wanted. You desired an escape from the world and I gave it to you. Can't you see I'm trying to help you, just as I've helped you survive these past six months?" Another tear left his melting eyes. *"It's useless to fight against me or to* fight against it all. I know it's painful, but you can fight it." Zain's voice suddenly twisted out of Death's words.

Zain's voice? "What?" I looked up, but Death's figure still stood there, staring at me with wicked venom.

"Your body is giving up. Your body is fighting through the withdrawals. I know it's a lot right now, but it'll get easier. Every day it gets easier. That voice that won't stop tempting you will grow quieter." Zain's voice crescendoed louder, but Death's figure still remained as he stepped closer.

Zain? "What's going on? I don't understand what's happening!" I shouted, pushing myself backwards until I was sitting with my back against the wall.

A visceral screech of a laugh fell from Death's broken jaw as he moved towards me. A fierce anger permeated his liquefying eyes as he brought his arms up, ready to slash them down against me, to grab my soul and never give it back. *"I'm here to save you, Samarra Blair. I'm saving you from your grief, your loneliness, from every goddamn worry you've ever had! You're going to* keep fighting the withdrawals. Please. Just keep fighting. Fight to survive."

Death brought down his hands in one cruel swing. I shut my eyes as his claws came down on me and—

Arms embraced me. Zain's body pressed against mine.

12

"Zain…?" I held onto him tightly, not wanting to open my eyes, not wanting to face Death anymore.

"It's all right. Just focus on what's real." Zain held onto me just as strong. His heart rang out against my chest, beating as loudly as mine. "Focus on being alive."

Focus… I listened to the bleeps of machines across the hospital ward. I felt the hot trickle of blood drip along my face where my scar had reopened, mixing with my tears. Then, after a long moment, I slowly opened my eyes, looking at my shaking hands wrapped around Zain's back, at the chipped nail varnish I wore and the triangle tattoo on my wrist. I took a deep breath in, feeling the air enter my lungs, filling them up, before softly blowing it all back out.

"Zain, I…I don't know what's going on."

"It's all right. You're okay." His words blurred into one another, refusing to let me focus on them.

"Okay? No, I'm not okay. Nothing is okay." My voice shook in bouts of panic. "I'm sorry I hurt you and for being so horrible to you. I'm sorry for *everything*. You shouldn't even be here right now, helping me—"

"Why wouldn't I help you? I promised Evie I'd look after you, and I owe her at least that much. Although I probably owe her so much more."

"You don't. You don't owe anyone anything, especially not after how I've treated you." I hugged him tighter, bringing him as close to me as I could. I had so much to say, so many apologies to give. "I'm just so glad you're okay. I thought I... I thought you died."

"Huh..." He pulled away from me. "I thought so too."

I frowned as Zain pushed my arms off him, and his face appeared before me. He seemed far less lively than usual. His smile had disappeared. His energy had been sucked dry. Cuts and bruises patterned his skin. His heavy eyes barely stayed open, and his pupils looked much larger. Then a trail of blood dripped from his nose.

He's taken something. My eyes widened in a sharp slice of panic. "Are you...okay?" I asked cautiously.

Zain sniffed, wiping his nose with the back of his hand. As he moved his hand away, I saw remnants of white powder around his nostrils. "I'll feel better soon, once I take enough."

"What?" I frowned. I couldn't quite focus on his voice; it seemed so quiet, so lost from life, nothing like his usual self.

"I'm glad I saw you before I go, Freckles." Zain's words slurred into one another. I realised it wasn't because I couldn't make them out but because he couldn't get them out properly. His body was shaking, his hands were trembling, and his reddened eyes couldn't focus. "I wanted to tell you I'm sorry," he whispered. "I'm sorry for living. You were right. I don't deserve..." He trailed off as another drip of blood ran from his nose.

Dread jumped into my heart. I'd been so busy focusing on my own problems that I had failed to see anyone else's. "No, Zain, don't ever be sorry. You…you deserve everything. You shouldn't… sh-shouldn't say that." I stuttered, fighting through my panic. "I…I'm the one who's sorry for being so cruel to you—"

"Don't apologise," he said through wheezes of lost breath. "I put up with everything that happened, every argument we had, every time you pushed me away, and every time you hurt me because I deserved it all."

"No, Zain, you…you don't. You deserve so much better than how I treated you—"

"If I have to suffer, it may as well be at your hands…" His voice was so weak. "Does death hurt?"

He sounds like Evie. My mouth ran dry. "Have you…" I croaked. "Have you taken Dust?"

"Not enough…not yet." He let out a dizzying laugh that sounded like a cry for help.

I have to help him. Now. "Are you under a doctor here? Is someone looking after you?"

He shook his head over and over. "I'm here to visit…" He looked back to the bed where Ali lay. "Huh…don't you hate that moment?" Zain hazily mused, losing his train of thought. "When you forget all the other moments…all the other reasons to…to… I wonder what Death is like. I guess nothing can be more painful than whatever this life is."

I gulped. His words hit me as hard as the memory of Evie. *She said that before she died too.*

"I should get going." Zain staggered to his feet, swaying as he moved away. "I've got one final concert to get to now."

"Zain, wait. You can't go. You have to stay here and get help—"

"Do you want to come too? It'll be fun and way more her style." He gave a twisted semblance of a broken smile. "Or are you too busy as usual?"

"Zain, listen, you can't go anywhere—"

"You're always busy." He nodded as though he could no longer hear me. His eyes seemed focused on something far behind me, far away from anything real. Then he let out a deep sigh. But his breath sounded strange, as though it wasn't quite right. It wasn't quite a breath at all—

It was a rattle.

Shivers spiralled across my skin. His rattle cut through the air like a cruel joke that wouldn't stop laughing at me. It was the same rattle Evie's breath had before she died. *The rattle that haunts my dreams every night. The rattle that—*

"Belongs to me?"

My neck *snapped* behind me as Death's figure emerged from the shadows in the corner of the room. His dark, twisted form stumbled forwards, hobbling towards me. His flesh had completely melted away, leaving a skeleton in its place. Blood covered his bones and trails of guts clung to what they could before they slowly fell out of his body. His boots had turned into pure shadow. His suit was now a full-length cloak, slithering around his body, trying to hold him together even as he gradually fell apart. Yet his polluted smile still tainted his appearance with brutal malignance.

"Get away from me!" I shouted, falling back away from his caliginous form.

"Why would I go away when someone wants me so much?" Death's skeletal form limped closer like a scuttling creature that was grasping onto its crumbling life.

"I don't want you anymore!" I pushed myself to my feet and staggered away from him. "Zain, we have to get out of—"

I stopped as I turned back towards Zain, seeing he was no longer there.

"Zain?" I looked at the exit, where he was stumbling out of the ward. "Zain, wait! Come back!" *I can't let him go like I let*

Evie go. I have to help him just as I should've helped her. I have to save him!

"Save him? Didn't I tell you that you can't save anyone? Don't you ever listen to me?" Death's sulphurous odour stabbed through my senses as he moved closer.

"Stay back!" My legs trembled as fire continued to burn my insides. *I can't lose myself to him again. I have to resist!* My limbs felt like they were cracking as much as Death's skeleton. *Resist.* I gasped for air I could no longer find. *I need to fight through this pain, fight the withdrawals!*

"Don't worry..." Death reached his hand towards me, moving closer and closer, until his fingers were only an inch from my face—

"Get away from me!"

"...I'm not here for you." Death gave a crumbling laugh as he stepped past me.

My breath halted as I saw his pits of eyes were no longer looking at me. Now he was staring through the doorway, where Zain had just gone through.

"You're not the only one tempted by my presence. Other people want to escape life just as much as you do."

"Wait..." *He's going after Zain.*

"Of course I am. Zain wants me. No, he needs *me. I'm going to save him from his suffering before he experiences even more."*

"No, please. You can't take him—"

"Don't you ever listen to me? I told you, I don't take *anyone."* Death let out a wicked snicker as he moved away from me. *"They choose to leave with me."*

"No, stop!" *I have to do something. I can't let him hurt Zain! I have to...to...*

I have to fight to survive. Fight my withdrawals. I have to fight.

I stared at Death's disintegrating figure, watching his weak form limping in agony. And without his lethal display of power possessing him, the overconfident part of my brain thought: *I can take him.*

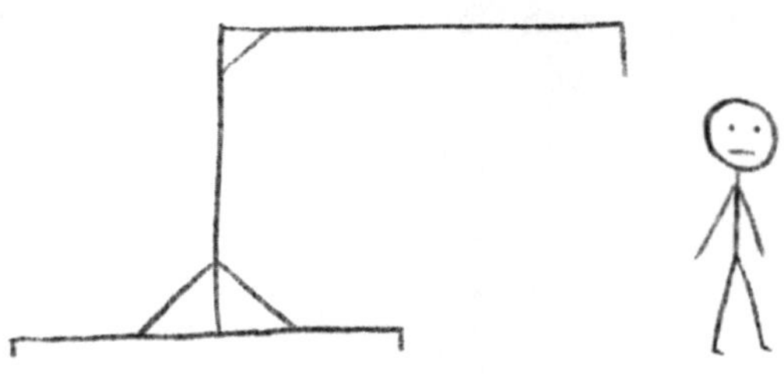

UNTIMELY END

13

Maybe I should fight for my life before giving in to my inevitable death.

A dizzying fire scorched my insides as I staggered towards Death. *So let's fight him.* I pushed through the pain, allowing it to burn my mortal body and remind me I was still alive. *Let's fight to survive.* Worries hydrated my mind, growing it back into life as I ran over every possible consequence to this action. *I need to fight to save Zain's life as well as mine. I need to fight the withdrawals. Fight it all!*

THUMP. I kicked Death's skeletal figure, shooting my heels into the back of his shins as he took a step forward. I shoved all the strength I could find into him, letting my foot crash through his bones, crumbling them to pieces.

Death howled in excruciating pain, stumbling as his broken leg lost his balance. Then an expression of surprise took over his face, just as it did on mine.

I hit him. I actually hit Death? But how did I—

Keep going. Do something while he's unstable! Make it count!

Adrenaline scurried into my veins as I shoved my body weight into Death's back, knocking him as hard as I could, driving him to stagger further into his fall, straight into one of the empty patient beds—

CRASH. Death toppled over the bed. His arm twisted as it tried to catch his balance before it bent at the wrong angle, and the weight of his body fell on top of it.

A cry tore through his throat. It was a wailing bark of a sound that seemed violently animalistic, far from the calmness his voice had once brought. *"Goddamn you! How dare you hurt me after everything I've done for you!"* As he staggered back to his feet, his pits of eyes stared at me with a look of devastation, hurt and betrayed by my actions.

I stared right back, determined to *keep fighting.* Patients clung to their lives in the row of hospital beds around me, making me realize I needed to cling to mine too. *Keep going!*

"You haven't done anything for me," I stated with confidence I didn't know I still had. "All you've done is hurt me!"

"You know that's not true." Death leaned on the edge of the bed for stability, trying to keep his bloodied skeleton upright even as his bones fell apart. *"You know you need me."* He pointed towards the doorway Zain had gone through. *"Just as he needs me!"*

Suddenly Death lurched towards me before I had a chance to act. His skeletal claws raced to swipe through my flesh with one swift—

I dodged out of the way. But his movements were too fast. One of his claws caught on my skin, tearing into the wound on the side of my hip, reopening the scar in a gush of dark blood.

A shriek carved through my chest. *He hurt me. He actually hurt me?* A panicked alarm blared through my head. *This is very bad...* I pressed my hand against the wound to slow the bleeding while gasping for breath through lungs that were still repairing themselves. *I may be able to hurt him, but he can hurt me too.*

"I've always been able to hurt you, Samarra Blair. Yet I've only ever chosen to help you. Can't you see that?" Death readied himself again.

"You haven't helped me. You don't help anyone!" I wrapped my hand into a fist and lunged at him—

He tried to dodge out of my path, but his disintegrating body was far too slow. He couldn't move before my fist met his skull with a—

CRACK. My hand pummelled to his bones, splitting his skull in a long fracture. His eye socket caved into the cavity, collapsing in on itself. Small bones snapped off, breaking away from his body before turning into ash.

"Stop it!" Death screamed. *"Stop hurting me!"* He stumbled away, turning his back to me as he clung to his skull in shaking pain.

I watched his trembling, fragile form cower away. *Don't listen to him.* I thought of all the times he'd encouraged me to hurt others, to kill others, to eat their hearts, and all the times I'd blindly followed his commands. *Don't ever listen to him again!* I knew I couldn't obey him any longer. I knew I had to *fight!*

I let out a shout of frustration as I quickly ran towards Death and jumped onto his back. I wrapped my arms around his neck, locking it in my grasp. *Keep hurting him!* I tightened my hold, strangling him within my arms, squeezing as hard as I could.

Death choked, gasping in airless breaths. *I bet I can snap his neck like this.* I pulled my arms around him tighter. *I can break his spine!* Then tighter again. *I can stop him from ever chasing Zain or me ever—*

"I told you to stop!" Death viciously whispered as he moved backwards until he whacked my body against the wall—

THUMP. TH-THUMP. Breath burst from my lungs with each strike. The force of the wall hit me much harder than I'd expected. Death was still strong, even in his deteriorating form. But I kept hold of his neck, tightening my grasp until it—

THUMP! Pain enveloped my body as Death smashed me into the wall once more. My bones cracked with the force of the impact as my rib cage crushed into itself. A howling cry ran away from my breath, forcing me to let go.

I sunk to the floor as an aching throb sliced through my insides. *I can't do this… Even like this, he's far too strong for me.* A pervasive tiredness was swallowing me whole. *How am I supposed to stop Death himself? How can I ever prevent him from getting to Zain?*

Unless I get to Zain first. Ideas clicked into my brain. *I can catch up to Zain before Death does. I just need a head start. A good one.*

Death turned towards me, heaving in broken coughs of breath. He held his twisted arm, which now sharply stuck out at an angle. His neck was bent, his skull was caved in, yet somehow he was still standing. *"After everything I've done for you these past six months, why are you only hurting me in return?"*

But I didn't listen to him. Instead my eyes ran over the objects closest to us, searching for a weapon. *A weapon is better than relying on my fading strength. I just need something to help me push Death back so I can get out of here.* We were by the exit of the ward, close to another empty bed. A patient's belongings were scattered around it. A jumper, knitting needles, clothes, snacks, and…*a Bible. A heavy, sturdy Bible.*

A smile grew on my face as I pushed myself back to my feet. *I have to hit Death with that goddamn Bible.*

"Are you even listening to me?" Death hobbled forwards. *"Do you even care about me anymore?"*

Quick. Act now while I have the upper hand!

"Did you ever care about—"

THUD. Death's crumbling figure fell backwards. Pain crumpled his nose as his bones *cracked*. Another roaring howl burst from his lungs in a cacophony of squealing noises. He looked towards me in disbelief, seeing me clutch the heavy Bible, which I'd just smashed into him.

One strike was enough this time. Let's go! I shook out my hand as stings ran over my fingers, dropping the Bible to the floor before I rushed towards the exit of the ward. *Let's catch up with Zain before it's too late!*

"Stop! *You can't save him, so why even bother trying?*" Death reached out, lunging towards me. "*I told you that you can't save any—*" A shrill scream ate his words as he tried to move his broken arm. Instead of grabbing me, he plummeted to the ground, breaking his fall on his wrist, snapping it clean off his arm.

This is my head start, so let's make the most of it! My movements were jagged and unstable, but it was enough to get away.

"*Christ,*" Death cursed, staring at the broken pile of his lost hand, before looking back up at me. "*Where the Hell do you think you're going!*"

To live. I'm going to live.

14

Adrenaline injected itself into my legs as I hobbled through a busy hospital corridor. Bodies scattered across the hallway as staff members raced to save souls. Patients fought for their lives, holding onto every hope they could. Doctors who hadn't had a break for hours kept working, determined to help every person they could. Energy and chaos and life itself echoed around me in unrelenting audacity.

I weaved through the crowded corridor, determined to catch up to Zain before Death could. I moved faster than I had before. *I think I'm finally learning how to run in these stupid heels.* The ankle I'd twisted after Evie's funeral still burned with searing agony, reminding me I was still mortal, I was still alive, *I still have so much left to do.* Patients looked at me as I skidded past, smiling as though they were encouraging me to *keep going and don't look back! Even if it all seems futile, even if Death is inevitable. There's still life in me, so let's use it.*

"*Come back!*" Death bellowed, fighting to be heard over the rushing noises of the hospital. *"Don't you dare…"* But his words were lost in the noises of life. Phones rang as loved ones reached out to patients. Ambulance sirens sang out their warnings as paramedics fought to help those in need. Patients cheered as they found out they were well enough to return to their homes.

Death's still there, somewhere. He's still following me, but I can't look back! I let my worries ring through my mind and I accepted every one of them. The panic, the stress, the uncertainty of the world—it all crescendoed into a beautiful mess, and I was grateful for it all.

But where's Zain? Has he left already? Furiously I searched through the crowds, looking for Zain's familiar face, but I couldn't see him anywhere.

Where is he if he's not still here? My mind turned in on itself, jumping with bouts of energy. *He said he was going to a final concert. He said it'll be more "her style."* I thought back to our conversations, to everything he'd told me that I'd blatantly dismissed. I remembered all the times I had pushed him away, just as I had pushed Evie away, despite their efforts to bring me in—

The funeral. The "better" funeral. That must be today. That has to be where he's going, back to that church—

But the church is so far away. I didn't have my bag with me, and of course I didn't have my car keys. *Why do I never have my goddamn keys?* I cursed under my breath, sharply turning around a corner towards a back exit of the hospital. *I'll have to find another way there.* My heart pounded in my chest as my life drive kicked into me with full force and I headed to the doorway—

The exit doors opened before me. Ria stepped inside.

Ria? She was dressed in her officer uniform as she wore a short, dark trench coat. Her hair had been messily tied into a bun. Her face was covered in stress and her eyes were overcome with tiredness as they fell onto mine.

"Sam? What are you…" A confused look of uncertainty swept over her. "You should be resting. You need to go back to bed."

"I can't." I shook my head. "I have to…" I stopped as I looked down at her hand. A ring of keys hung around her finger. *Car keys. Thank god, Ria's here with perfect timing. We can both go and save—*

Suddenly Ria reached out and grabbed my shoulders. She forcefully turned my body to the side, shoving me into the wall with surprising strength. Then she pressed my face against the surface as she held me in position, pushing her weight into my back.

"What are you doing?" I struggled against her tight grip. "Let go!" Blood trickled down my face as pressure built on my scarred cheek.

"I'm taking you back to your bed." Ria firmly stated. "You're not leaving here again, not until you get better."

"Wait, Ria. You don't understand—"

"I don't think *you* understand," she cut me off. "I can't let you go out there and take Dust again. It's far too addictive. It'll kill you if you take it once more." She grabbed one of my arms with a sharp—

CLICK. Ria locked a cold metal device around my wrist. *Wait. Is that…* Panic fluttered through my heart. *Has she just handcuffed me?* Bouts of adrenaline continued to feed me energy. *This is bad. I have to get away from her!* Then Ria grabbed my other wrist—

I sharply turned my body, yanking my arm away in a sudden twist of movement. "Ria, stop!" I shouted, staggering backwards. I jerked my hands behind me. Although one cuff was around my wrist, I couldn't let her put the other one on. "Please, stop!"

"I'm trying to help you, Sam." Ria put out her palms, calmly moving towards me. "You can't leave until the Dust is out of your system. Relapse is far too dangerous. You don't understand how risky it is—"

"I do understand now!" I stepped backwards, moving away from her and back towards—

Don't go back! I didn't dare look behind me towards Death's figure, not wanting to see how close he was. *He's going to catch up with me unless I get out of here now!* Instead I looked at the exit door behind Ria, letting it tease me with how close it was. *I have to go forwards.*

"Ria, please just listen." Anxiety whirled its way through my insides. "It's Zain. He's in trouble. He-he needs help."

"*You* need help, Sam—"

"He needs it right *now*! He's been taking Dust, lots of it. He's…he's going to overdose on it."

Ria paused. "What?"

I nodded, gulping back what I could from my dry mouth. "I think he's taken far too much. If he doesn't get help, he's going to die."

"Die?" Ria's tone went cold. "No, you're just lying to get out of here. Zain's been sober for months—"

"He hasn't! He's been addicted to Dust, just like Evie was and…and like I was too. He hasn't stopped taking it."

"He's not an addict. Evie wasn't an addict either." Ria shook her head in denial.

"If you actually cared about either of them, you'd know that's not true!"

"And if you cared about Zain, you'd let him go," Death roared as his decaying footsteps hobbled towards me. *"You'd let him join me!"*

I regretfully glanced towards Death, still somehow drawn to his figure—*no, no!* But now he looked like a pulverized mess of bones. His limbs were twisted and broken. His skull was cracked apart, fracturing itself under his weight. Yet somehow he was still moving, staggering towards me as though he would never stop. *Stop looking at him! I have to move forward!*

I looked back at Ria, at her concerned expression, her worried eyes, and the ring of keys around her finger—*just take her car keys and go. I don't have time for this!* "I'm sorry, Ria, but I have to go."

"No, Sam. You need to—"

Suddenly I lunged towards her, reaching out my hand. *Get the keys!* I grabbed her fingers and tugged the keys off her. *I've got them! I've—*

But as I did, I realised my wrist still had one handcuff locked around it. And that handcuff was now swinging towards Ria. *No, no! Don't let her grab it. Don't let her put the other one around my wrist and keep me here! Don't—*

Ria instinctively grabbed the handcuff before I had a chance to pull it away. She tugged it towards her, forcing me to fall into her—

I closed my palm around the keys, holding them tightly. *I need to fight her. She could have a weapon in her pocket I could use—*

No, I can't hurt anyone again. Just get out of here! I leaned my body weight to the side, giving in to the momentum of my fall as I purposefully fell next to her, pulling the handcuffs back against her grip until—

THUMP. I collapsed beside her on the floor, falling onto my arm. A ripple of torture spun around my nerves. My shoulder burned as it dislodged itself from its socket. But Ria had let go of the handcuffs—*get up. Get the Hell up before you end up lying down forever!*

I crawled onto my feet then stumbled into a run. "I'm sorry, Ria!" I croaked without looking back at her. "I have to go and help Zain!"

I staggered into the exit door, letting my body knock it open before I stepped out into the reinvigorating air of Medlock. The soft glow of the rising sun warmed my face as the sky came back to life with the power of Eros. A warming chill signifying the end of winter blew into my long strands of hair, twisting around my body, encouraging me to *run! Don't stop now!*

I skidded over the melting ice, running towards the car park, which snaked around the building. *Ria was in her uniform. These keys must be for her officer car, which should be just around the corner.* I pushed my legs on, sprinting around the side of the building, running away from a shadow I didn't have until—

It's here. A breath of relief escaped my tired lungs as I saw the officer car parked on the pavement, preventing anyone from using the path. I used to hate the arrogance of officers, but now I couldn't be more grateful for it. *Hurry up!*

I shoved Ria's key into the lock and opened the door. I knew other people may have been watching me, as the half-closed handcuff around my wrist and my ripped black dress probably gave away the fact that I wasn't an officer. *But that doesn't matter now. Only saving Zain matters!*

I flung open the door and fell into the driver's seat. A control panel was in the centre of the car, and I prayed it operated similarly to an ambulance as I quickly reached out and turned the dials until—

Sirens blasted through the air, cutting against the wind like a song. Blue lights flashed from the top of the car while my thoughts raced ahead of me—*this is such a stupidly dumb idea.*

I'm going to get in so much trouble for this. Can't I get arrested for taking this car, even if I'm trying to save a life—

"*When will you learn that you can't save anyone, no matter how hard you try?*" Death's viscous slither of whispers blew through the wind as he stumbled in front of the car, clutching his broken arm as a pained look of anger covered his face.

My eyes widened with alarm. *No, he can't have caught up yet. I can't let him stop me now!*

"*It's too late for that. Get out of the goddamn car, Samarra Blair. It's useless to even try to run—*"

TH-THUD. A hand suddenly tapped on the passenger window. The door handle clattered. Then the car door swung open—

Ria slid into the passenger seat. "Screw *you!*"

15

"What is *wrong* with you?" Ria shouted in a sudden storm of emotion. "Of course I care about Zain and of course I cared about Evie! She was my girlfriend. She was the most important person in the world to me!"

My breath was beating in panic as I looked between Ria in the passenger seat and Death's crumbling figure in front of the car. "Ria? I…I just meant—"

"We all grieve in different ways, okay?" she continued over me. "Yours may have been destroying yourself with the same substance Evie used, but mine was actually looking into it. Do you know how much research I've been doing on Dust? Do you know much I've found out?"

"*I told you to get out of the car!*" Death's voice smothered Ria's words. "*Don't you dare run away from me. You know you can't escape!*" He kept his stance in front of the car, purposefully blocking my path.

My thoughts sprinted far ahead of me, trying to figure a way out of this.

"The law is right that we need to get rid of Dust from this city." Ria kept talking as though I could hear her. "That drug is the problem. Without it, everyone would be better off—"

"Ria?" I asked as I quickly realised what I had to do.

"Do you know how many accidental overdoses there have been in the last month alone?" She continued through her flurry of frustration. "Do you even realise how lucky you were—"

"Ria!" I shouted, scratching at my vocal cords until I cut through her words.

"What?"

"No one's actually standing in front of the car right now, are they?"

She paused. "What?"

"Get out already!" Death yelled, hitting his broken arm onto the bonnet of the car with a fiercely strong THUD.

"No one's there, right?" I asked with more urgency, turning on the ignition, roaring the car to life.

"No, no one's there. Can't you see that?"

"Good." Sweat leaked through my trembling hands as I grabbed the steering wheel. "Hold on."

"Wait, what are you—"

Adrenaline bounced through my bloodstream as I pressed on the accelerator and ploughed the car straight into Death—

BANG. The front windshield splintered and cracked as his skeleton crashed into the car. His skull hit it first, clawing at the window, chipping the glass into dangerously fragile cracks. His body followed, toppling over itself, flying over the roof in a mess of tangled limbs. Finally he smacked against the ground in a shattering howl of screams.

"What are you doing?" Fear jumped into Ria's voice as she hurriedly clipped her seat belt over her. "Slow down!"

I swerved past other cars, knocking off a couple of sideview mirrors as my hands shook with nerves. Jagged breaths burst through my lungs in gasps of panic. My heart pounded in my ears like the bass drum of a rock song as I narrowly escaped Death's claws once more.

"Jesus, Sam. Slow down!" Ria screamed in my ear.

I glanced at her nervous eyes, then back at the road, which was coming at me full force. "I can't. I have to save Zain!" I floored the pedal, letting the car race out of the hospital gates and violently swerve onto the main road. Other cars BEEPED as I recklessly swung out, before racing through the traffic.

"He's at the church already. He's so far away!" Ria shouted back, matching my volume.

"Already? How do you know?"

"Because I was just there!"

"What? How?" My sense of time was jumping before my eyes. The world was turning on without me, refusing to wait for me to catch up. "Is this…real? Is this all really happening?"

"Don't you dare ask me that when you're driving." A mixture of emotions ran across Ria's face that even she couldn't decipher. "You need to pull over—"

"No, we have to get to Zain before he does!"

"Before *who* does?"

"Death!"

Ria's breaths were speeding up just as fast as my own. "We need to take you back to the hospital. We can call an ambulance for Zain instead—"

"Ambulances are too slow, especially for people on substances, you know that! Zain needs help right *now*." My voice shook with unrelenting panic as I glanced into the rearview mirror.

Rising sunlight bounced off the roads, cutting into my vision. Silhouettes of cars, people, trees, life—it all ran into a blur of bright colour that reinvigorated my senses. But there was still one small smudge of darkness in the centre of it all, one shadow that would never leave.

Death moved towards me. He was moving with unnatural speed as he flicked in and out of existence, growing closer with every turn. A poisonous anger covered his stare as he refused to let me leave his sight.

"He's going to catch up…" I mumbled. "We have to go faster!"

"Who's catching up? What are you—"

I suddenly swerved the car onto the other side of the road, forcefully overtaking a line of others.

"Sam!" Ria screamed, clinging to her seat belt. "Get back on the other side!"

I kept my foot firmly on the pedal, racing the car on. The sirens blared, screeching as loud as my heart. It was all so noisy, so overwhelming—but it was exactly what I needed to remind me *I'm still alive and so is Zain. I can still do this!*

"Watch out!" Ria yelled as a car suddenly plummeted towards us.

I swerved out of the way—BEEEEEEEP—blasting my horn as we ploughed back into our lane.

Ria let out gasps of breath while rubbing her temple. "I can't believe I let you drive."

"It's all right, I can—" A cough caught in my throat, forcing me to heave and gag against it as my body fought for survival.

"You really shouldn't have left the hospital." Ria trailed her eyes over me, looking at the fresh blood dripping over my face, the tremors in my hands, the shallow gasps of air I was taking. "I could've just gone—"

"No, I-I didn't help Evie the night she died. I couldn't live with myself if I did the same thing again."

Ria shook her head. "You thought stealing an officer car was the way to help? I could arrest you for this. Jesus, others might *actually* arrest you, as there will definitely be surveillance video of you stealing this car."

"Arrest me?" I thought back to Zain's story of the night Evie died, how he had tried to save her but officers had turned up to arrest him before he could. *I can't repeat the same pattern. I can't get arrested before I help him.* "They can't, not yet. You'll have to hold them off, Ria."

"Hold them off? You seriously think I can do that?"

"You're going to have to."

"Why? I don't even understand what's going on. You said Zain overdosed, but I thought he was sober. He promised me he was."

"He lied. Just like I did too. Evie probably did the same. But..." I gulped. "But it's not his fault. When you're that addicted, you can't control anything. It feels impossible to live without it." I glanced over to Ria's eyes, which were flooded with tears of worry. "Did you never notice him taking it?"

"I...thought he was doing better," Ria said. "He shouldn't even be using it. He could get sent back to Detention if anyone found out and surely he doesn't want to go back there."

"I don't think he wants to *be* anywhere..." Drops of rain fell against the windscreen, crashing against it, moving in time to my shallow breaths. "I-I think it's my fault though. I think he's...he's blaming himself for Evie's death because *I* blamed him. I took my anger out on him when I shouldn't have—"

"Stop." Ria cut me off. "Everyone keeps blaming themselves and I'm sick of it. Dust is the problem, nothing else. If all of you had just stayed away from that goddamn substance in the first place—"

"It's not that simple. Dust wasn't the *problem*, it was simply an escape—"

"Look out!" Ria pointed out to the road ahead of us where a cyclist had turned onto.

I swore under my breath as I swung the car out, narrowly missing the bike.

"Be careful!"

"I am! We'll be there soon anyway. We're not far from the church," I lied. We were farther than I'd hoped. I only prayed that Zain hadn't taken more Dust, that he hadn't—

"Then concentrate!" Ria pulled my mind back to the road ahead. "Something really has gotten into you, hasn't it? The old you would *never* do anything like this. You used to just stay indoors studying all the time. Getting you to leave the house was hard enough, let alone doing anything like *this.*"

"I don't even know what's happened to me this past…week?"

"That's probably a good thing. You've been shouting at a lot of walls and punching them too."

"I… What?"

"It's best if you don't know. That drug really did a number on you." Ria shook her head. "You know your hallucinations might never end, right?"

"What do you mean?"

"You've been hallucinating, far more than you realise. Those effects could keep going, even if you never take Dust again," she stated. "I told you, I've been researching Dust's effects. It's not just addictive, it can also have an irreversible impact on your brain. You could continue to hallucinate forever. The hallucinations might even get much worse."

"Worse?" I glanced back to the rearview mirror. Death's skeleton was still moving behind us, flickering like static bursts that couldn't control themselves. His cloak of shadows was tearing itself apart. His bones were disintegrating with every stride, yet his stare was still focused solely on me.

Don't look at him, just let him follow me. Let him follow me for the rest of my life. But don't look back more than I look forward! I pulled my eyes back to the road ahead.

"That's why we need to get Dust out of Medlock," Ria continued. "People need to know how dangerous it is. So you'd better not take it ever again." She sharpened her tone as though it were an order. "You already left me for months after Evie died. I never would have forgiven you if you'd left me forever."

I paused for a long moment, letting my heart scatter its beats through my chest. "I'm…I'm sorry, Ria. I didn't mean—"

"I don't need an apology. Evie's death has been shit for everyone. I just need you to stay with me in this world, whether you talk to me in it or not."

I nodded. "This is a…a nice moment, isn't it?"

"What?"

"Reconnecting with someone after months apart. It's a nice moment…right?"

"Is this…" Ria rubbed her temples. "Is this your attempt to be like Evie and find those specific moments? Because that's all wrong. *This* isn't reconnecting with someone." She gestured to the flashing lights of the car and the rush of the road in front of us. "*This* is a high-speed stolen car ride and possibly moments before *you* get arrested."

"Well…" I hesitated. "I tried?"

A smile escaped her lips at the madness of the situation. "Sure. You did try." Then a laugh fell from her throat before it stumbled into a louder laugh of joy.

The noise encouraged me to laugh too. We almost sounded delirious as we cackled together. I realised we hadn't properly laughed together in such a long time—*maybe that's the specific moment I've been missing.*

"I just can't believe it's taken all *this* to get you to speak to me again," Ria said after a long moment.

"Neither can I… I-I *am* sorry though. I'm sorry for everything, especially for not speaking to you these past six months."

"I told you, don't apologise—"

"But I mean it. I just felt so…alone in my grief. I thought no one else could understand it. That's why I—"

"Stop. You did what you had to do to get through it. I just hope you're through the worst of it."

"I…I don't know. I think I've really messed up my life. I've already been kicked out of med school and—"

"You've been kicked out?" Ria let a beat of silence sit over the car. "Thank *god* for that."

"What do you mean—"

"You can finally stop studying all the time for those endless exams. This is great!" Ria smiled. "You can actually see me and come out with me now. You have no more excuses."

I nodded. "Yeah… I guess I can."

Medlock's grey skies looked down on us as rain continued to pour. Rays of sunshine sparked through the clouds, refracting against the downpour, creating a small sliver of hope.

"I like the jacket by the way." Ria looked me up and down. "It suits you."

I looked at the jacket wrapped around me. It shone with a beautiful yellow colour, screaming at me in a bountiful burst of life. "Really? It feels way too bright for me. It's definitely more Evie's style."

"It is. I think that's exactly why it suits you."

A beam of joy lit my face into a smile as I looked down at Evie's jacket. The letter Evie had written for me was still tucked inside my pocket, close to my beating heart. It allowed Evie's spirit to breathe life into me as I accelerated the car faster towards the church, travelling back to where all this first began.

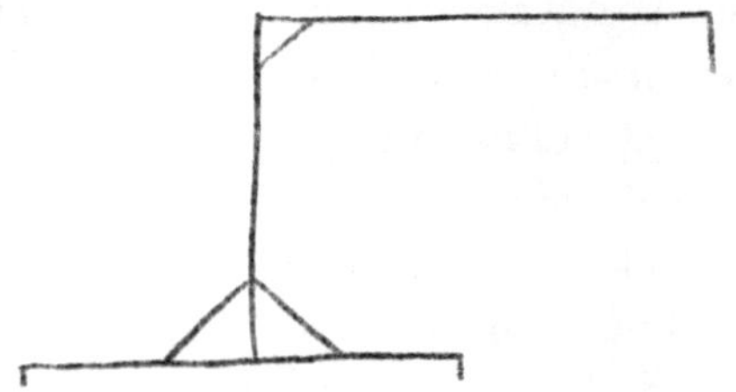

DUST TO DUST

16

I'm going to live. I'm going to let all my pain and worries overwhelm me. I'm going to feel everything, and I'm going to be afraid of it all.

The possibility of life clung to my mind as I sprinted up to the large, double doors of the church. Its optimism repaired my thoughts, allowing in a promise of hope, pushing me on *faster. Run for Zain's life as well as mine!*

Ria had stayed back to radio for an ambulance, certain it would arrive quickly. But I couldn't wait around to risk Death reaching Zain before I did. *I have to get there first!* So I hummed Evie's tune under my breath to give me the strength I needed as I shoved my weight into the church doors and pushed my way inside.

Life poured out of the sunlit church. A large congregation of people overwhelmed the hall, dancing and talking and laughing in eternal bouts of noise. No one was sitting down; instead they were all on their feet in continuous bursts of movement. This place was busier than I'd ever seen it, overflowing with bustling energy. Each person wore clothes as bright as Evie's, adorned in jewellery, tattoos, and colourful strands throughout their hair. *Evie's soul feels so alive here.*

A few people looked my way as I entered, staring at my ripped dress, my bruised body, my scarred cheek and wounds that dripped in blood. I stuck out of the crowd as I clawed my way back to life, but I no longer cared. My focus instead caught on the picture covering the crucifix. It was the same terrible picture of Evie that she definitely would have hated. *She really would be so angry if she knew we were still using that photo.* She wore her usual positive smirk and her bright yellow jacket, which made her beam brighter with life.

I pulled that same jacket around me, letting the material hug my skin. It warmed up my shivering limbs and pressed the letter in my pocket closer to my heart as I searched through the souls of the church to find—

"Good morning, everyone!" Zain began as a microphone screeched into life. "I hope you're all feeling good today!"

I turned with the crowd to the balcony at the back of the church where the organ rested. There stood Zain, swaying as he held the microphone, unable to properly stand upright. *Thank god it was easy enough to find him.* His eyes seemed hazy. Sweat poured across his forehead. Strands of hair dangled over his face, which was drained of his usual energy, as blood dripped from one of his nostrils. It looked like the ferryman was about to snatch him away at any moment.

"Thank you for coming out so early for our final ever concert!" Zain clumsily pushed his hair out of his face, behind his bandana, which was slowly falling off his head. "Thank you for showing up for Evie and sending her off in style!" His words slurred into one another, but still the crowd cheered.

Three others stood around him, each looking equally intoxicated as they finished their beers and took their places. Two plucked at their guitars, checking they were in tune, while the other took a seat at the organ. A drum kit had been set up behind them with Evie's name messily written across the bass.

"We're so thankful for all the times we've had together," Zain continued. "We couldn't be more grateful for all your support. But sadly…" He looked back to the empty drum kit that wouldn't be touched for the whole performance. "Sadly our time is now up… Here's to going out with a bang!"

Zain nodded at the other performers, moving his head along to an imaginary beat before the guitar ripped into an electrifying melody. The bass gave a funky riff as the organ blasted out harmonious chords. Zain jumped in time to the music, stumbling around the balcony. His foot was tangled in wires, but he didn't seem to care. Then he took in a large, rattling breath against the microphone and—

The music stopped.

He took another breath. Then another, letting its rhythm and noise rattle around the room, falling in time to his failing heartbeat before he softly began to sing:

> "How am I supposed to breathe when you are drowning?
> How can I go out when you are stuck inside?
> How am I supposed to keep on living when you are
> running out of time?"

Although Zain's voice was hoarse and cracked with pain, he carried the melody with beautiful care. He sang several solo bars before holding one long, rattling note. Then the bass brought itself back to life, speeding up the tempo in a steady climax. The organ keys crescendoed into existence too, giving the tune a more upbeat, playful feel as Zain launched the chorus:

> "Let me hold your pain,
> Let me take the weight off your chest.

Let me go insane as I take on all your worries so you can
finally rest.

"Let me stay by your side,
Let me hold you tight,
And please just let me lie and say everything will be all
right."

The music poured into my ears like sweet honey. But it still
felt empty. There were no drums, no beat, *no Evie*, no underlying
glue holding everyone together. Its stark absence seemed to
shake Zain as his bloodshot eyes were full of tears, his unsteady
hands trembled, and his voice faded along with his life. *I need to
hurry up and reach him!*

I pulled myself back to the present, fighting the stark fatigue
overtaking me as I turned to the side of the church where the
stairs were located. But now that the band was playing, the crowd
had clustered together in a mosh pit, showing their unashamed
desire to dance through their suffering and *live.*

Push through it all! I squeezed my broken limbs through the
cracks in the crowd, shoving against the tide of their dances,
fighting through their current. *I have to reach the stairs and get
to Zain. I've spent so long hurting people, I forgot I instead needed
to save them!*

"*Why do you keep thinking you can save anyone?*" Death's
faded, wheezing voice seeped into my skull. "*Have you learned
nothing?*"

17

The crowd parted behind me and Death's pandemonious
skeleton crawled into view, moving in time to the music. *What
the…?* He was barely even a shape anymore. His skeleton was

shrinking, crumbling into dust. His legs were broken, halving his height, forcing his arms to pull himself forwards. His neck was bent, making his skull droop. He was nothing like the fierce, intoxicating beast I'd encountered before.

Don't listen. Just resist him! I forced my eyes away from his decaying mass, turning back towards the stairs and snaking through the hive of buzzing bodies. *Keep running!* Zain's singing continued to ring around the room, but now it flowed over a much faster rhythm. The guitars ran ahead of their notes. The organ skidded over the keys. Then backup singers hummed along, echoing Zain's words, adding depth to his shaking voice:

> "How am I supposed to just go back to work?
> How can I walk out and simply leave your side?
> How am I supposed to put on a smile and pretend I am fine?"

I let Zain's melody feed my soul and give me the energy I needed to keep my eyes away from Death—*don't look back until the bitter end!* My legs shook, wanting to buckle over, but I let the pain in. *The pain is proof you're alive.* I let it all drive me forwards and far away from—

"Don't look me in the eyes then dare to continue living!" Death's failing body slithered behind me, moving in time to the guitar gliding over notes in an electric scream. *"Don't act like you can't see me. Don't pretend like I don't haunt your every waking moment. All you've done since our sister died is focus on me."* But there was no power to his raspy words anymore and his sedative peace was as broken as his body. *"You know you can't run away from me, from your hallucinations, from your overwhelming grief. Death comes to all who are born! I'll be here forever, for as long as you need me. And I know just how much you need me!"*

I refused to let his words overtake my mind as I continued to weave through the crowd, moving closer to the stairs.

"Come on, Samarra Blair…" Death continued, refusing to give up. *"Don't you want to finally find out if death does hurt? Don't you want to know if I'll be so much more peaceful than whatever this life is?"* His voice disintegrated with every word. *"You deserve to unburden your mind and forget your pain, don't you? You deserve everything."*

I swerved and stumbled up to the doorway. *Don't listen. I don't have to forget!*

"Of course you do. That's what you've been doing this whole time. You call it escaping, but it's really forgetting." His movements grew quieter, as though he were falling farther and farther behind me. His figure was morphing into a shadow, losing itself in the darkness of the ever-turning world. *"You've taken Dust and followed me to forget about your grief, to forget about your life, to forget about Evie. You've pushed the whole world away until it didn't matter anymore. Nothing mattered!"*

I ploughed into the staircase door, shoving it open—

I skidded to a stop. Death's skeleton was suddenly before me, lying sprawled across the spiralling staircase. His broken skull looked up at me like the last drop of a narcotic. His caliginous shadow shivered, fighting to hold onto whatever it could before the final end hushed itself to sleep.

"We were…we were supposed to run away together, remember?" he whispered as tears of dust trickled from his decaying mass. *"We were supposed to go to Eidyn. We were going to forget about your life and about every ounce of pain you've ever experienced. We weren't going to simply scatter Evie's ashes—we were going to join her in them. We were going to leave everything and everyone behind… Don't you want that anymore? Don't you want me?"*

The door shut behind me. No other bodies were around us here; only Death was with me now. But his bones were crumbling, his eyes rotting, his voice diminishing. Soon he would be nothing if I just kept going, if I just didn't listen—

"Please." Death reached up towards me. His broken arm shook as it lost more and more of its bone. His discoloured pocket watch had twisted around his wrist, digging into whatever marrow was left. *"You've needed me every day for the past six months to get through your pain, and you still need me now. That pain is still persisting; it will never end. So take my hand."* More tears of dust trickled from his eyes. *"Come on, you've got this. Just take my hand. It's okay. Everything is okay. Let me free you from this suffering before you experience even more. And trust me, there* will *be so much more."*

My head banged like a drum beat as I stared down at Death. The music, the crowd, the instruments, Zain—it all crept away, falling into a blissful silence. All except the sound of the organ, which permeated through the church walls, dancing over a counter melody to Zain's song. Its tune was soft and sweet, falling into a strangely familiar string of notes—*the melody Evie used to hum.*

My mind caught itself on the tune, reminding me of all the grief trapped within it, held captive along with my worries, my stress, my fear—

Fear?

I frowned as a flutter of unstoppable panic tightened my stomach. My eyes were wide as I looked at Death's hand. My limbs were frozen in horror. Everything felt so…scary. The weight of death, the possibility of leaving this existence, the crushing burden of grief. It filled me with overwhelming *fear.*

Being afraid means being alive. My heartbeat kicked at my chest, reminding me it was still there as it added to the music in a beautiful drum solo that never wanted to end. *So let's be afraid.* My lungs cried out, gasping through shallow, panting breaths, continuing to feed me oxygen, giving me the chance to make mistakes, to fail, to cry, to laugh, to *live*. And my mind continued to overwhelm me with worries, screaming to be heard. *Be afraid of absolutely everything. Feel every ounce of pain. Experience every weight of the world as it proves I'm alive. I'm alive. I'm. Alive.*

"Don't...please, Samarra Blair. Don't you dare be afraid of me."

I looked down at Death one final time. Then I smiled, realising he really was so much more than just a hallucination.

"You're right. I did need you," I whispered. "I wouldn't have made it through the past six months without you. I needed your escape, I...I couldn't have faced the world without it. Not after Evie left us."

Death kept his hand reached up towards me, even as his bones faded and deteriorated into trails of ash.

"You...you helped me survive. You made me feel like everything was okay when nothing made sense, even if it was just for a moment at a time." I took in a shaky breath. "Dust wasn't always a bad thing—*you* weren't a bad thing. You simply helped me with my pain. So I'm...I'm glad you were there for me when Evie wasn't... But I can't keep relying on your escape."

I let out the breath, watching it blow piles of Death's decaying skeleton away. "I have to live before I die, as scary as that feels. I need to let every worry back in, let grief consume me, and let sadness weigh me down. I need to suffer, I need to let the pain of the world remind my body it's still alive. I am still alive. And you..." I swallowed hard. "...you are but dust."

Death's remaining bones cracked and crumbled away under the weight of my words. They disintegrated his form, pulverising him to ash. They crushed him into the shadows of the stairwell. His unblinking stare, his dimples, his cloaked suit, his peaceful escape—it all faded until nothing was left but his ticking pocket watch, which now looked more like a yellow wristwatch. That was the final image of Death I saw before he dissolved into the lengthening darkness, creating a shadow behind me. A shadow

I knew I desperately needed, safe by my side, following me forever. *Let it follow me until the bitter end. But don't look back more than I look at the world before me. Keep going!*

My legs shook as I climbed the spiral staircase and moved up to the balcony. The stairs were much steeper than I'd hoped, twisting up and up and up—it seemed almost impossible to reach the top. But I focused on taking one stair at a time, making the insurmountable climb seem possible. *It's not enough to turn away from death, I also have to turn towards life, and I have to help others do the same!*

Nausea pounded into my guts and fatigue drenched my legs as I climbed up and up and up, using every ounce of strength I could muster. *I have to help Zain just as he has helped me. Everyone has helped me. I'm not as alone as I thought I was without Evie. I was never alone.*

I saw the door to the balcony ahead of me, waiting for me to return to the land of the living. *I can do this.* I moved myself on faster, dragging myself up the remaining stairs. *I'm going to die. One day we're all going to die—*

But first I'm going to live.

18

I burst through the doorway and onto the balcony as I returned to life. My limbs burned in torturous fatigue. I heaved, gasping for air. My heart beat out: *I am, I am, I am.* The heat of the church burned my skin, the sweaty smell overwhelming my nose, the taste of blood circling my mouth. And I let it all in. I let the pain remind me: *I'm alive. I can be afraid. Be anxious. Be angry. Be anything. I just need to be.* Then, above it all, was the powerful sound of music filling the church with bouts of energising life. Zain's voice floated through the air in dancing twirls as he sang his mesmerising melody:

"Let me feel all your pain,
Let me take it all off your chest.
Let me go insane as I bear it all for you, so you can finally rest.

"Please let me stay by your side,
Let me help you fight,
And please just let me lie and say everything will be all right.
It has to be all right."

His voice was full of suffering that faced its own mountain of grief, overflowing with hurt, tears, emotion, and life. *So much life.* He was fighting through his own pain, clutching on to a world that hated him, refusing to ever let go. *He's alive.* It made me realise why Evie wanted him to look after me. She wanted to make sure I was still living, still going on every adventure possible with someone who'd encourage me every step of the way. *He's not going to die.*

My balance was off—nothing was right—but still I stumbled forwards. A small crowd of intoxicated people stood around the edges of the balcony. I staggered past the dancers, the drunks, the people who were laughing, the people who were singing, the people who were shouting, the people who wanted to go home, the people who felt *something* in that room, something that told them they were alive.

"Thank you everyone for coming out today!" Zain shouted to the crowd below as the song came to an end. "I hope you enjoyed our music while it lasted. I know I did." He smiled as he looked back to the drum kit with a final, teary gaze. "Thank you!"

Blood dripped from his nostril as he moved to the other side of the balcony in the opposite direction to me. *Wait. Are there stairs there too? But I only just made it up here.* I pushed myself on faster to catch up to him, pushing through the souls, through the dancing lights, through everything and everyone—

But he was moving too fast. I couldn't get to him in time. "Zain!" I shouted, but my voice felt so quiet. It was cracked with weakness, lost in the sea of souls around me. "Zain!"

Zain carried on walking away, letting tears stream down his face.

"Zain, wait!" I stretched my voice, trying to force it out louder.

But he still didn't look back. He didn't know I was there for him. He didn't know he wasn't facing his pain alone.

I staggered forwards, almost tripping over as I sprinted up to him. I reached out my hand, lunging towards him as I grabbed his arm and pulled him back—

The world slowed down as he turned towards me. The noises quieted and even the crowd seemed to pause its movement.

"Freckles?" Zain gave his usual beaming smile, which created creases around his sunken eyes. "You made it." But his smile didn't sit quite right. His movement was unbalanced. His forehead was covered in sweat. His words were blurring together. "You never make these concerts."

"I did this time." I nodded, breathing out a smile of relief as I kept hold of his arm, not wanting to let go. "I had to see if your band really was dreadful or not."

He smirked, forcing his smile to fall crooked as it twisted along his face. "And? Were we dreadful?"

"You were definitely better than I expected."

"I'm glad." He looked me up and down, noting the bruises across my skin, the bags weighing down my eyes, the blood dripping from my scarred cheek. "You look…awful."

"I know. I know I'm messy and far from the perfect person you thought I'd be—"

"No, it's good. Being messy is good. It shows you've lived." He wiped the back of his hand against his nostril, staining it dark red. "Are those…handcuffs?"

"Oh…yeah." I tried to laugh but only made a coughing sound as I looked at the handcuff still locked around one of my wrists. "I thought you'd prefer seeing *me* with handcuffs this time."

Zain laughed, brightening the room with his persistence to hang on to life, even as it turned into an agonised cough. Yet the sound of his laugh lightened my own soul, making me pull on his arm and bring him closer towards me before I embraced him.

I hugged his shaking body, squeezing him far too tightly. He wrapped his arms around me too, holding on as much as he could. His hands were trembling and sweating and leaking with fiery heat. His heartbeat pounded into mine. There was no calming peacefulness from our embrace but rather an electrifying energy that overflowed with emotion. And I was grateful for it all.

"I know Evie's death has been…a lot," I blurted. "But I shouldn't have blamed you for any of it. I'm sorry for taking all my anger out on you. It wasn't your fault. It…it wasn't anyone's fault." I turned my head to look at the empty drum set. "Evie never would've blamed you either. She…" I trailed off as I tilted my head. "Wait. Is that…"

My eyes fell on the seat behind the drum kit, where a bright, colourful urn sat. *Evie's urn?* Patterns decorated the material in spiralling turns of never-ending colour.

"You…" I frowned as my arms fell away from him. "You fixed it…" Words ran away from me as I stared at that urn. No pain, suffering, misery, or death resonated from the urn anymore. Now it was only full of hope. "How did you…"

"I know you wanted to take her up to Eidyn," Zain whispered. "But I thought she could at least have a little more style until then." He raised his hand up to me, before gently wiping a tear from my face.

I let him touch me, feeling his warm, sweaty, shaking life against mine. "That's…that's definitely more Evie's style."

Suddenly Zain's legs buckled as he stumbled, losing his balance.

"Hey, whoa." I tried to keep him upright as I kept my grip on him. "Are you…"

But his limbs were too weak to hold him up as he crashed to the floor.

"Zain?" I shakily bent down next to him, putting a hand on his wrist. His body was limp. His breathing was scarce. His eyes were bloodshot and teary. "How much have you taken?" I tried to feel for his pulse, but I couldn't find it.

I grabbed his other hand, pressing tighter on his skin, praying for something—

I looked down at his wrist. I noticed a small tattoo. A triangle tattoo. *He has Evie's stupid triangle too? The one that's supposed to symbolise adventure and…life.* I placed my fingers against the tattoo—

A very weak pulse pounded from his wrist. *He's going to live.*

"I wanted this to be my last concert, my last…day," he croaked through shallow breaths.

"But you sounded so good. Why would you want this concert to be your last?" I said, trying to keep him talking.

"You basically said it was dreadful." He let out a smirk.

"Yeah, to keep you grounded. Someone has to do it." I looked around at the dancing bodies for help, but they were all so intoxicated, so lost in the moment. I glanced down at my yellow watch, seeing the seconds tick by, wondering how long the ambulance would take, wondering how many breaths Zain had left.

"I couldn't do it though," he continued, cracking his knuckles as he anxiously fidgeted. "I planned on taking much more Dust but I couldn't… I was too scared."

I let out a breath of relief. "Good. I'm glad you were too scared. I hope you stay scared for the rest of your life."

"I also…" He trailed off as his eyes stared at something in the distance, far away from existence. Then his pupils rolled back and his head slumped forwards.

"Hey, stay with me." Gently I hit his face. "Zain." But he didn't respond. "Zain, focus! Focus on being alive!" I hit him harder.

His eyes bolted open. "Damn, Freckles." He weakly smiled. "You've got a punch."

"Apparently so." My laugh was a croaking cough. "But I…I still think you need to go to the hospital. I think you've still taken a lot."

"I don't know if we'll make it…" His head slumped forwards again—

"Hey!" I shook his shoulders. "Stay awake!" I slapped his face again.

"Damn, okay. I'm awake." He stirred, rubbing his cheek.

"Ria's already called an ambulance for you. They should get here soon. Just stay with me, okay?"

"I don't want to die, Sam." Zain's voice fell into a whisper. "I just…don't know how to live anymore."

Suddenly the doors of the church burst open and a scuffle of noise pounded over the hall. I peered over the balcony, praying help had arrived—

Officers dressed in dark trench coats flooded inside the church, letting bright beams of sunlight stream in with them. *What are they doing here?* They pushed their way into the crowd, turning their heads as they searched through the masses of bodies. *What are they…*

I swore under my breath. *Ria said they'd arrest me if they knew I'd stolen that officer car… Are they here for me? Has everything I've done over the past week finally caught up to me?*

I looked back at Zain. His eyes started to close again, and his rattled breath grew louder.

"Hey, I told you to stay awake." I hit him again.

He didn't respond.

"Hey!" I hit him again, harder. "Wake up!"

He still didn't respond.

"Zain! Please wake up!"

Nothing.

My thoughts flew into one another as I searched for what to do next, looking around for any way to save Zain, and by doing so, save myself. Bodies and souls were still dancing around us without a care in the world. Officers were shouting over them as they searched through the crowd below—*but they're not going to see that we're up here. They're not going to find us. That means they don't have to arrest me yet, I can still get away. And I can still save Zain. But how?*

"Zain?" My arms wouldn't let go of him as a tear fell from my face, hot as blood. *Think, think!*

"I..." Zain slurred. *He's still alive. There's still a chance.* "Sam..."

Why are the officers here anyway, complicating everything? And how did they arrive faster than...an ambulance.

I let out a breath of relief as I realised exactly what I had to do next. "For what it's worth, I don't know how to live either." I put Zain's arm around my shoulder. "And maybe we'll never know." I held tightly onto his waist. "But we only have one chance to find out. So you'd better stay here and find out with me." I used all my strength to pull him up to his feet, leaning him against me.

But he was so heavy. His pain was too much—

We crashed back to the floor together, heaping into a broken mess of souls.

"Zain, I need you to help me one last time, okay?" I heaved us up again, using all the energy I had left. "Come on, please help me." But he was too heavy. "Zain, please." We were both too heavy. The world was too—

"I'm trying," Zain whispered as he fought against his pain, clinging to his life, until his feet found the floor.

We stood up together, leaning on each other even as our bodies failed us. "Okay, good," I said. "One foot in front of the other. That's all you have to do."

I led him back towards where his band had been playing. "We have so much left to do, so much more life to live." My body was collapsing, breaking in on itself, ready to give in to every ounce of pain it had been trying to repress. "You said you'd come with me on my road trip to Eidyn, remember? You can't leave without showing me what good company you can be." I walked us into the bright spotlights, towards the microphone in the centre. "So hold on, okay?"

"Okay. But what…are you doing?" Zain weakly asked.

"Officers are out there, looking for me. I-I may have stolen Ria's car, and who knows what else I've done this past week… Either way, they're here for me. If they see me with a body in my arms, they'll arrest me on the spot. They'll be your quickest way to a hospital."

"You're…insane."

"I know." I croaked out a laugh as we stumbled past the drum kit that held Evie's urn and the lengthening shadows that flickered around it. Then I reached out my arm and grabbed the microphone. "Hey!" I shouted, letting my raspy voice echo over the church. "This is a message for the goddamn Shade bastards down there!"

The noises in the room quieted as I caught everyone's attention. The lights were so bright, but I could just about see the officers look up towards me, pointing at me with angry looks swept over their faces.

"My name is Samarra Blair," I continued. "If you want to do your job, you might want to arrest me before you go back to sitting on your asses all day." The crowd laughed and cheered. "So come up here and get me already!"

Zain's head had drooped forwards, but I heard him laughing brightly, even through his unbearable pain—

But then his foot slipped. His knees buckled. His legs went limp and he collapsed to the floor. Then I collapsed right next to him, giving into my exhaustion at last.

"You really are so insane," Zain said through a lost breath.

"Good." I smiled as we both lay on the floor in a tangle of limbs.

He smiled too. "Evie would be proud of you."

The commotion of the crowd rumbled in the background. Shouts and screams and orders were thrown around. The bright lights blurred into one another, distorting the world into a mess of shapes.

"I'm also sorry for looking after you too much, Sam," Zain whispered. "I'm sorry for telling you to stay away from Dust even when I couldn't... Maybe it *was* because I felt guilty for Evie." He paused, gasping deeper for breath. "But it was also because there's so many pieces of Evie in you. I know you think you don't look anything like her, but you have the same expressions. The same smile, the same frown, the same look of relief, of sadness, of *every* emotion." He studied my face, running his eyes over me. "It's when you're expressing, when you're living, *that's* when you look so much like her... And I'd do anything to protect that."

I nodded, taking in his words. "We'll still go up to Eidyn and scatter her ashes, right? Even if she has to wait a little longer." I looked at Evie's new, colourful urn and the flickering shadows dancing around it.

"You really want me to go too?"

"Of course. I'm sure you'll make the journey far more exciting."

"I can definitely do that." He smirked. "And I think it's fine if she has to wait a little longer to go. She's probably already mad at us for waiting six months to have her funeral. But it's not like she can complain, is it?"

I frowned, suddenly feeling the tightness of the yellow jacket around me. "Wait…" I fumbled my hand into the pocket before I pulled out an envelope with SAM written on it in Evie's handwriting. *The letter that I ignored, that I never read. Maybe it's finally time…*

"What's that?" Zain asked.

"It's from Evie…" I took in a slow, trembling breath as I opened it and removed the single piece of paper inside before reading over her last words—

I let out a loud laugh. A real, genuine laugh.

"What? What is it?" Zain moved his head towards mine as he tried to see.

I shook my head as I laughed again. "It says: 'To Sam, you didn't lose your favourite jacket. I stole it. If you want it back, you can get it from Ria. But every time you wear it, please remember: it looked so much better on me.'"

Zain laughed in a brightly melodic tune.

"Evie…" I shook my head again, glancing at the urn. "You're so annoying. I can't believe I waited so long to read *this*."

"She always had such a way with words." Zain snickered.

"I don't know why I expected something more profound."

"It's profound in her own way. And look…" He nodded to the other side of the letter. "There's something on the back too."

I turned over the paper, seeing a long list of items written out. There were countless bullet points with random phrases such as: "GETTING THE CHORUS OF A SONG STUCK IN YOUR HEAD BECAUSE YOU DON'T KNOW THE VERSES, SO YOU'RE LEFT WITH THIS ANNOYING, REPETITIVE MELODY ALL DAY LONG." And: "WHEN YOU DON'T UNDERSTAND A COMPLICATED PUZZLE, BUT THEN

SUDDENLY IT CLICKS IN YOUR BRAIN AND YOU SAY 'OOOHHH' AS YOU FINALLY GET IT." And: "FEELING SO MUCH BETTER AFTER GOING FOR A RUN, EVEN THOUGH YOU INITIALLY DIDN'T WANT TO RUN AND REFUSED TO GO AND COMPLAINED ABOUT IT THE WHOLE TIME."

So many bullet points filled the paper with other nonsensical phrases and under them were blank bullet points that were still waiting to be filled in. At the very end, in large, bold letters, it said, "A LIST OF EVERY SMALL SPECIFIC MOMENT TO REMEMBER HOW GRATEFUL I AM TO BE ALIVE."

I read over the words again and again and again, taking in Evie's specifically optimistic perspective. *She was never obsessed with death, was she? She was too far in love with life…*

"So that's where the list went…" Zain slumped his head next to mine as he looked up at the paper too. "You know, I've been trying my best to keep playing that game, even though it's been hard without her."

I turned my head to his. "I really miss her…"

"I do too. But it's okay, I'm sure she—"

"No, nothing is okay." I shook my head. "Nothing is okay. But everything matters."

He paused. "You know Evie barely knew what she meant whenever she said that, right?"

"That's good because I have no idea what it means either." I laughed.

A laugh broke from Zain too, as we both clung onto whatever joy we could find even in the overwhelming shadow of grief.

"I can play that game with you, if you'd like," I said. "We can keep finding specific moments. There *are* still so many bullet points waiting to be filled in after all."

"There will be way more than just that," Zain said as he grabbed my hand in his.

Our fingers intertwined and our wrists fell together, pushing our triangle tattoos into each other. It made me smile brighter as his heartbeat pounded into mine. His skin was sweaty and his warm hand held mine far too tightly, but it felt so good to be by someone's side and feel so afraid of feeling alive.

The officers' voices were getting louder as their footsteps marched up the stairs, growing with life just as I was.

"Do you think it does hurt?" I looked back towards the drum set where Evie's urn sat. I thought about all the dust trapped inside that represented her beautiful yet fleeting existence.

"What?" Zain asked.

"Death. Do you think it actually does hurt?"

He looked at Evie's urn too. "I have no idea. But I'm scared as Hell to find out."

Suddenly a group of figures rushed onto the balcony. *The officers are finally here. Even if they arrest me, they can save Zain. They can get him to hospital faster than—*

"Sam! Zain!" Ria shouted. "Are you both okay?"

"Ria?" I frowned as the figures grew into life. Ria stumbled up to us, checking us over. Then two paramedics rushed up behind her.

"It's all right. The ambulance came quickly. Help is here now," she said.

Paramedics are here? Not…officers? A confused expression fell over me as the blur of figures huddled around us. *Did I… hallucinate that?* Panic overwhelmed my thoughts as I looked at the mess of reality before me. It was as broken as my dress, far from the perfect, idealised version I'd always wanted. Yet for some reason, it made more sense to me now than it ever had.

"Sam…" Zain whispered from beside me. "It's not just death I'm scared of. I'm also scared to find out how much life can hurt too. I'm afraid of everything."

"Good," I whispered back. Fear pounded in my heart, thumping in time to the beats of my shallow breaths, forming a fast drum solo that never wanted to stop playing. Worry clung to my thoughts as the chaotic rush of the world screamed in my ears, and I let it all in with a smile. "So am I."

Nothing is okay.

But everything

matters.

AUTHOR'S NOTE

The struggle to stay alive can sometimes feel more difficult than giving in to death. It can feel much harder to find reasons to keep going, to find motivation to get through another day, or to find any sign of hope when it ran out long ago. It can also be a very lonely journey, especially when the support you need is not there, when you're left on endless waiting lists, and when the only words you hear are "it gets better" without an explanation of how.

I do not know if there is an end to this journey, or if it is a struggle we can ever truly overcome. But I do know it is something countless people face every single day, and you are not as alone as you might feel. I also know these emotions are understandable reactions to a world that does not always take care of us. And I know these struggles may forever be a part of us, just as our shadows will be, yet we can still find ways to live alongside them.

Perhaps we will never discover the big reasons to keep living. But we can find the small ones: the warmth of a hug when you need it the most, the comfort of fresh bed sheets wrapped around you, the first bite of a meal you've craved for hours, or the satisfaction of turning the last page of a book you didn't want to end. Sometimes it is these fleeting moments that carry us through each day. These are the moments where we can find a glimmer of hope, even when we're surrounded by shadows.

ACKNOWLEDGEMENTS

My work in clinical psychology has allowed me to support countless individuals who have faced their own struggles with mental health and fought battles the human mind was not built to endure. Yet despite the endless obstacles, they kept going, finding ways through each day no matter how difficult it was. To every single one of you, thank you for letting me support you on your journey and for inspiring me every step of the way. You are the reason I wrote this book, and the reason I will continue telling stories that need to be heard.

To my family and friends, thank you for supporting me in every part of my life. I could never have written this book without you. To my youngest brother, thank you for your creative ideas and fascinating insights into the craft of storytelling. To my younger sister, who may never read this book, thank you for always being there, because every story needs a sprinkle of inspiration. To my other sister, who will definitely read this book, thank you for being my most loyal supporter. And to my partner, thank you for bringing such bountiful bursts of light into my life. Your support means far more than you will ever know.

I also want to take a moment to thank myself. Writing this book has been a tough challenge. It forced me to confront the grief I had tucked away and made me face my ever-changing relationship with death. But I did it. I wrote through the hardest days, and I somehow finished the book. Even if no one else ever reads these pages, I know every second I spent writing was worth it.

To my editor, thank you for your sharp eye and for helping me refine even the smallest details.

To those who are no longer with us, thank you for the memories you left behind. You live on in every story I tell.

And finally, to my readers, thank you for joining me on this journey. Especially to those who have struggled with grief, been consumed by the urge to escape, or found themselves standing a little too close to death. I am so glad you are still here, still reading this book. It was all made for you.

ABOUT THE AUTHOR

Hannah Clayton lives in Manchester, UK. She is currently training to become a doctor of clinical psychology, supporting people through a wide range of mental health difficulties. Her work brings her face-to-face with life's darkest moments, yet it also reveals the extraordinary resilience that helps people endure even the toughest days. Exploring this delicate balance has fuelled her writing, shaping her debut novel, *Until the Shadows Lengthen*, and now her latest, *You Are But Dust*.

Hannah plans to continue creating these stories for everyone who is persevering through their struggles, hoping to show them they are not as alone as they feel. After all, even in the darkest times, when we find ourselves chasing Death himself, there is always a way to learn how to live again.

YOU ARE MORE THAN DUST

Samarra isn't the only one haunted by grief.

Zain is unravelling, far more than he has ever let on. In the lead-up to their long-awaited road trip to Eidyn, his life has become a maze of obstacles. He must navigate threats from Mariana's gang, avoid corrupt Shade officers, control his anger outbursts, and relinquish the suffocating grip Dust has on his mind. He doesn't know if he'll make it to the road trip before he breaks completely, but he is determined to try.

COMING SOON

WHEN THE MIRROR LIES

Jesse is used to dealing with liars after spending the last two years surviving in Medlock's criminal underworld. But nothing prepares him for his latest job. When he captures a seemingly ordinary target, he watches in shock as their face shifts, their appearance transforms, and they become someone else entirely. He is face to face with the ultimate liar: a metamorph.

Metamorphs are shapeshifting creatures of nightmares said to steal identities and wear new faces like masks. They aren't supposed to exist. But if this myth is real, what other terrifying secrets lie buried beneath Medlock's surface?

Get ready for a new psychological thriller that delves into a dark exploration of identity, deception, and the struggle to discover who you truly are in a world where nothing is as it seems.

COMING SOON

UNTIL THE SHADOWS LENGTHEN

Saffron has been imprisoned in Medlock's Detention, where the guards are soulless, the prisoners are secretive, and the shadows are sharpening their claws. But she knows something even darker is lurking in the depths of the cells.

Her friend Ray was detained here before he mysteriously vanished. The only clues he left were warning messages about a monster that feeds on thoughts and devours sanity. A monster that may still be watching from the dark corners of every room.

Saffron is now determined to discover what happened to Ray. She is willing to search through forbidden rooms, cultish séances, and brainwashing drug trials to uncover the secrets kept in the ever-growing shadows. Including the secrets she's keeping from herself.

AVAILABLE TO READ NOW

BEFORE THE SHADOWS LENGTHEN

The prequel to 'Until the Shadows Lengthen.'

A year and a half before Saffron's stay in Detention, Sylver gives us his perspective on what happened in the months leading up to that one fatal day that changed everything. He shows us what life was once like and how it descended into darkness.

It's time to see how friends can become enemies, how caliginents haunt other minds, and how much life is worth suffering. If it is even worth anything at all.

COMING SOON

FOR MORE...

www.ingramcontent.com/pod-product-compliance
Lightning Source LLC
Chambersburg PA
CBHW032151160726
48328CB00005B/28